Books in the NEVER SAY SPY SERIES:

More books coming! For a current list, please visit
www.dianehenders.com

THE SPY IS CAST

Book 2 of the NEVER SAY SPY series

Diane Henders

THE SPY IS CAST
ISBN 978-0-9878188-6-7

PEBKAC Publishing
P.O. Box 75046 Westhills R.P.O.
Calgary, AB   T3H 3M1
www.pebkacpublishing.com

This book is a work of fiction. Names, characters, places and incidents are either the product of the author's imagination or are used fictitiously, and any resemblance to actual persons, living or dead, business establishments, events or locales is entirely coincidental.

First printed in paperback October 2011 by PEBKAC Publishing
v.4

Since You Asked...

People frequently ask if my protagonist, Aydan Kelly, is really me.

Yeah, you got me. These novels are an autobiography of my secret life as a government agent, working with highly-classified computer technology... Oh, wait, what's that? You want the *truth*? Um, you do realize fiction writers get paid to lie, don't you?

...well, shit, that's not nearly as much fun. It's also a long story.

I swore I'd never write fiction. "Too personal," I said. "People read novels and automatically assume the author is talking about him/herself."

Well, apparently I lied about the fiction-writing part. One day, a story sprang into my head and wouldn't leave. The only way to get it out was to write it down. So I did.

But when I wrote that first book, I never intended to show it to anyone, so I created a character that looked like me just to thumb my nose at the stereotype. I've always had a defective sense of humour, and this time it turned around and bit me in the ass.

Because after I'd written the third novel, I realized I actually wanted other people to read them. And when I went back to change my main character to *not* look like me, my beta readers wouldn't let me. They rose up against me and said, "No! Aydan is a tall woman with long red hair and brown eyes. End of discussion!"

Jeez, no wonder readers get the idea that authors write about themselves. So no, I'm not Aydan Kelly. I just look like her.

Oh, and the town of Silverside and all secret technologies

are products of my imagination. If I'm abducted by grim-faced men wearing dark glasses, or if I die in an unexplained fiery car crash, you'll know I accidentally came a little too close to the truth.

Thank you for respecting my hard work. If you're borrowing this book, I'd very much appreciate it if you would buy your own copy, or, if you wish, you can make a donation on my website at http://www.dianehenders.com/donate.

Thanks - I hope you enjoy the book!

For Phill

Thank you for being my technical advisor and the most tolerant husband ever. Much love!

To my beta readers/editors, especially Carol H., Judy B., and Phill B., with gratitude: Many thanks for all your time and effort in catching my spelling and grammar errors, telling me when I screwed up the plot or the characters' motivations, and generally keeping me honest.

To everyone else, respectfully:
If you find any typographical errors in this book, please send an email to errors@dianehenders.com. Mistakes drive me nuts, and I'm sorry if any slipped through. Please let me know what the error is, and on which page. I'll make sure it gets fixed in the next printing. Thanks!

CHAPTER 1

The ring of the phone made me swear. Extricating one arm and half my face from the toilet tank, I stumbled over the tools strewn on the floor. On the fourth ring, I snatched up the receiver with a dripping hand just as my answering machine kicked in.

"Hang on," I advised the caller, waiting for the message to finish playing. I held the phone to my ear with my shoulder and dried my hands on my baggy jeans while I waited.

"Hello?" I inquired when the line was clear.

"Is this Aydan Kelly?"

"Speaking."

"Aydan, it's Clyde Webb calling..."

"Spider!" I interrupted, smiling. "How the hell are you?"

He sounded pleased. "You remembered!"

"Of course I remembered. You never forget your first."

"Your first what?" he asked warily.

"The first guy you hit 'til he pukes. I still feel bad about that."

He laughed. "It's okay, it wasn't your fault... but, uh... about that..." His voice took on a wheedling note. "Aydan, how would you like to go to a gala affair? Dining and dancing, fabulous food and drink, rubbing shoulders with the cream of society?"

I looked down at my sweaty T-shirt and grubby jeans. "Um, Spider, I think you've got the wrong number."

"No, I haven't," he insisted. "It would be a thank-you for all you did for us back in March. You deserve a luxurious evening out!"

"Spider..." I paused, trying to be tactful. "I hate dressing up. I hate crowds. I hate making small talk with strangers. And I hate to remind you, but I'm the same age as your mother." I thumped my forehead with my free hand. I don't really do tact well.

"Oh, I wasn't asking you to go with me. Although I'd be proud to go with you," he added gallantly.

I laughed. He was such a nice kid. Well, twenty-something. Not really a kid.

"Okay, what's this about, then?" I asked.

"I'm asking you to go with Kane."

"What, you're Kane's social secretary now? Tell him he can ask me himself. He's a big boy."

I grinned, remembering tall, muscular John Kane with salacious appreciation. He was definitely a big boy. Too bad I'd never gotten the opportunity to find out exactly how big.

"Oh, he doesn't know I'm asking you," Spider replied.

"Whoa, hold on, Spider. What's really going on?" I asked, instantly suspicious.

"I can't tell you over the phone," he confessed. "I was hoping you'd be able to meet me. It's important."

I churned my free hand through my tangled hair, pulling the elastic out of my ponytail and yanking the knots out of the curly bits at the nape of my neck. "Important, as in 'national security' important?"

"I really can't talk about it over the phone," he repeated.

I sighed. "Okay. Where and when do you want to meet?"

"Can you meet now?"

"Why, are you standing on my front step?"

"No," he replied sheepishly. "I meant, how soon can you get here?"

"I presume 'here' means your office in Silverside?"

"Yes. Sorry, I'm just... Can you come? I hate to bother you, but it's..."

"Important. Yeah, I got that. Okay," I agreed reluctantly. "It'll take me about half an hour to get there, though. Unless you really want me to show up in the same clothes that I wore to fix the toilet."

"Um, no." He sounded uncomfortable. "Business attire would be better."

"What the hell, Spider?" I demanded. "Business attire? Since when?"

"Just... can you? Please?"

"Okay, for you. I'm on my way."

I hung up the phone, frowning. The disorganized and stilted conversation was so unlike Spider that a tingle of apprehension made me hurry to my closet.

I scowled at my business clothes, hanging clean and pressed, neatly organized by colour.

I really hate dressing up.

I swallowed a growl and stripped off my dirty clothes, yanking on a pair of slim cream-coloured pants and a short-sleeved green blouse.

Doing a quick mirror check, I flapped my hair up and down in an attempt to dry some of the sweat, and reassured myself the blouse adequately camouflaged the extra ten pounds around my waist. Someday I'd lose that.

Right.

I dragged a brush through my hair and decided to leave it loose. If Spider thought I needed to dress up, it probably meant I'd be meeting somebody important. My long red hair was my best feature. Well, mostly red. The grey wasn't too noticeable yet.

I put on a pair of flat shoes and stuffed my waist pouch inside one of my enormous handbags. Normally, I wear the waist pouch everywhere, but even I don't have enough chutzpah to defy the fashion police and wear it with business clothes.

On my way across the yard, I slicked on a bit of tinted lip gloss, managing to keep it in the general vicinity of my lips.

Despite my growing sense of urgency, I let my steps slow while I enjoyed the view. I'd moved onto my farm in March when everything was winter-brown, and the greens of July were still a delightful novelty. I let my eyes rest on the long vista of rolling farmland and took a deep breath of country-fresh air before hurrying into my beloved four-car garage, patting the hoods of my automotive friends as I passed.

My faithful '98 Saturn waited in the last bay, and I skimmed my fingertips over its front quarter panel as I made my way to the driver's door. The local body guy had done an excellent job. You'd never know there had been a bullet hole in it.

Turning off my gravel road onto the pavement, I headed for town, curiosity warring with nervousness. The last time I'd gotten involved with these guys, it had cost me in blood. Spider's agitated demeanour hadn't reassured me one bit.

In the tiny town of Silverside, I navigated through the two-block business district and turned into the semi-residential area that housed Spider's and Kane's shared office. Pulling up in front of the small house, I swallowed a faint queasy sensation.

In the summer, the yard was mowed and well-tended.

Perennial shrubs framed the house and accented the modest sign that read 'Kane Consulting' and 'Spider's Webb Design'. It looked welcoming and benign. I wasn't fooled.

I took a deep breath before walking up to the front door. Tapping the knocker, I stuck my head inside. The shared office space in the converted living/dining area was empty, but I went in anyway, calling out a hello.

Spider appeared from down the hallway, his tall, skinny body and lanky limbs clad in a dark suit, blue shirt, and tie. My mouth fell open.

"Who are you and what have you done with Spider?" I ribbed him.

He grinned and twitched his shoulders in a nervous shrug. "Aydan, it's great to see you. You look great. As usual." He gave me a quick, awkward hug. "How are you?"

"I'm fine," I replied. "You?"

"Great!"

I frowned. "I keep hearing the word 'great'. Why does that make me nervous?"

He shuffled his feet. "We need to go into our meeting now. Would you like something to drink?"

"Just a glass of water, please." My trepidation cranked up a notch while I waited for him to return from the kitchen. Something was definitely up.

He handed me the glass and ushered me down the hallway to the converted bedroom that served as a meeting room. I paused in the doorway, surveying its two occupants.

One dark suit, white shirt, quiet tie. One military uniform, loaded with braid.

Oh, shit.

When I stepped cautiously into the room, both men rose. Neither was as tall as Spider's beanpole six-foot-two, but they shared an almost-palpable air of authority. While Spider made the introductions, I assessed them, trying to figure out what this was all about.

"General Briggs, I'd like you to meet Ms. Aydan Kelly," Spider mumbled without making eye contact. The general stepped forward, stretching out his hand, and I received a firm, dry handshake.

He was a fit-looking man with piercing blue eyes, his short grey hair in a precise cut. His seamed face gave the impression of too much time outdoors rather than advancing age. I placed him in his late fifties at a guess. His ramrod-straight posture made him seem tall, but in fact he stood only about an inch taller than my five-foot-ten.

"And this is Mr. Charles Stemp," Spider introduced the other man. Stemp extended his hand, too, his movements as sinuous as a snake. He looked fit as well, and very tanned. His short-cropped sandy hair was almost the same colour as his skin, and his eyes were an odd shade of light brown, almost amber. His monochrome colouring and flat, expressionless eyes reminded me of a rattlesnake. Jeez. No wonder Spider was nervous.

"Mr. Stemp is the civilian director of our INSET team," Spider explained, referring to the counter-terrorism unit to which he and Kane ostensibly belonged. "General Briggs is Kane's commanding officer."

That was where things got a little more complicated. In lighter moments, I had nicknamed Kane 'James Bond'.

Spider drew me further into the room. "Have a seat," he invited. I perched warily, wondering why the big guns were here. The others resumed their seats as well.

"Ms. Kelly," the general began. "So nice to meet you at last."

I wasn't quite sure how to respond to that, so I put on my best pleasant smile. "It's nice to meet you, too, General Briggs."

"Thank you for meeting with us on such short notice," he continued. "This meeting is rather overdue, and I apologize for the long delay. Our country owes you a debt of gratitude, and we would both like to offer you a sincere thank you for your assistance in March. Your bravery and self-sacrifice did not go unnoticed."

I squirmed. "I appreciate the kind words, but I didn't really do anything. I was a dumb civilian in the wrong place at the wrong time. I'm just glad everything worked out all right."

The general's eyes bored into me. "I read the reports. I beg to differ. You uncovered a potentially disastrous security breach. You withstood torture to protect our national security. You saved the life of one of our top agents."

I shook my head. "It sounds good when you say it like that, but really, it was your team who pulled it all out of the fire. I was just along for the ride."

He smiled. "That may be true, but the entire operation would have failed without your unique talents."

"The whole thing was pure dumb luck on my part," I muttered. "Your team did all the work."

"I'm glad you're loyal to the team," Stemp said, his voice betraying no emotion whatsoever. "How would you like to help them again?"

Warning bells clamoured in my brain. "Help them how, exactly?" I asked slowly.

"We are chronically understaffed," the general explained. "We have a situation in which a female agent is required, and we have none currently available. The mission would entail almost no risk. In fact, you would probably find it quite enjoyable. We thought of you because of your excellent performance this spring, and because you already have the sufficient security clearances."

I hid my surprise and suspicion in a casual tone. "When did that happen? I'm just a bookkeeper. A civilian. I don't recall doing any applications for security clearances."

"You were thoroughly investigated in March," Stemp replied. "And your knowledge of our secured facilities and clandestine activities in effect gives you a top-level clearance. You already know more than many of our agents."

"Oh." I attempted to rub the frown away from my forehead. "Exactly what do you want me to do?"

"John Kane will be attending a formal function in Calgary the day after tomorrow." General Briggs picked up the narrative. "While there, he will be researching the layout and security of the venue in which it is held. A man doing this alone would be too obvious. He needs a female companion to attend with him." The general gave me an encouraging smile. "I'm told the food and entertainment will be quite magnificent."

"I'm not sure Kane would want me tagging along," I objected. "I don't have the first clue about spy stuff. I'd probably put him in danger just through my own ignorance."

"You would be fully briefed, of course," Stemp said. "We would also compensate you for your time. And there would be an allowance for your wardrobe and accessories for the event." He added that last bit as though it was an irresistible inducement.

I did my best to control my face. He really thought I'd want to go if he bought me a new dress. Poor deluded man. Little did he know I'd happily pay him if he'd let me go in jeans and a sweatshirt.

I shrugged. "If Kane thinks it's a good idea, I'll go with him. I'll help if I can. But if he thinks he'd be better off without me, then I don't want to be foisted on him."

"Excellent." The general nodded with obvious satisfaction. "Please come here for your briefing tomorrow morning at ten o'clock. You should be prepared to leave for Calgary immediately afterward so that you have time to purchase whatever you need for the following evening." He rose. "It was a pleasure meeting you, Ms. Kelly."

I recognized a dismissal when I heard it. I got up and shook hands again with him and Stemp, and turned to leave the room.

"I'll see you out," Spider said, his first words since the introductions. We went down the hall together, and he followed me out onto the front step.

"What the hell, Spider?" I demanded. "Those two big brasses came here just to blow sunshine up my ass and ask me on a date? I don't think so. What's really going on?"

He shook his head. "Later."

"Will they be here for the briefing tomorrow?" I asked.

"Yes." He regarded me tensely, and I could see I wouldn't get anything more out of him.

"Okay." I sighed. "See you tomorrow at ten. Do I have to dress up again?"

"Yes."

CHAPTER 2

I had just slid behind the wheel of my car when my cellphone rang. I swore as I rummaged through the unaccustomed handbag, and managed to snatch out the phone to punch the talk button before the caller went to voicemail.

The female voice on the other end sounded vaguely familiar. "Hi, is this Aydan Kelly?"

"Speaking."

"Hi, Aydan, it's Linda Burton calling."

I shuffled rapidly through my mental files and came up empty. She continued quickly, "You probably don't remember me. I'm a nurse at the hospital. We met back in March..."

"Oh!" I interrupted. "Sorry, of course I remember you, Linda. How are you?"

"I'm... actually a little desperate."

"Oh...?"

"I saw your card tacked up on the bulletin board in the post office. You're a bookkeeper, aren't you?"

I felt my shoulders relax. "Yes."

"Are you taking on new clients?"

I sat up a little straighter. "Yes! Do you need help?"

I heard a whoosh of breath at the other end. "Yes!" she replied gratefully. "I own a business with my grandmother. We've been trying to do our own books for the last few months, and we just can't handle it anymore. When can you meet? The sooner the better!"

I shot a satisfied glance down at my clothes. For once in my life, I was appropriately dressed for a meeting on short notice. "Do you have time right now? I just happen to be in town."

"Oh, yes! Let's meet for coffee at the Melted Spoon. Granny and I can be there in ten minutes."

"Sounds good. See you there." I hung up, feeling smug.

When I strolled into the tiny café a few minutes later, the mouth-watering smell of fresh-ground coffee filled my senses. I perused the menu board, impressed at the number of espresso variations. While I waited, the counter clerk passed a steaming grilled panini sandwich to a customer, the sharp smell of roasted peppers mingling with the coffee scent.

I chose an herbal tea and sat down at a vacant table to wait for Linda and her grandmother. Minutes later, they arrived, Linda as perky and petite as I remembered. The woman who accompanied her was tiny and delicate, and I could see a family resemblance in the fine bone structure. Her spun-sugar white hair and pink ruffled blouse made her look like a porcelain old-lady doll.

Linda waved hello, and they went to the counter to order their beverages. When they returned, I got a whiff of caramel from Linda's latte. Her grandmother carried a demitasse of what looked like black tar. The almost-scorched smell of espresso overpowered my herbal tea completely.

Linda made the introductions. "Granny Ives, this is Aydan Kelly. Aydan, Granny Ives."

"Lola," her grandmother corrected, reaching over to shake hands. Her voice was throaty, sounding larger than I'd expected from such a tiny woman.

"It's nice to meet you," I greeted her. "Linda mentioned the two of you were in business together, but we didn't talk details. Why don't you give me an overview?"

"We've had the business for about four years now," Lola told me. "We sell online, and the phone service is profitable as well."

"We're also trying to get started with a POS program," Linda put in.

"By POS, I presume you mean 'Point of Sale'," I said.

Delicate little Granny Lola snorted. "No, when I say POS, I mean 'Piece of Shit'."

I laughed out loud. I had a feeling I was going to like Lola.

"It's been nothing but trouble, and it's still not working right," she continued. "We're trying to get it to talk to our accounting program to bring the sales totals in automatically, and it won't play nice."

"Well, it sounds like I need to take a look at it," I said. "I've persuaded a POS or two to cooperate in my time. Sometimes all you need is a bigger stick."

Lola and Linda exchanged glances and laughed. "Oh, we have no shortage of big sticks," Linda assured me impishly.

"What's the name of your business, and where are you located?" I asked.

"Our business is called Up & Coming. We're just around the corner in the mini-mall. Do you want to walk over and have a look at the system?"

"Sure," I agreed. "Let's go."

We chatted easily during the short walk. Linda and I had hit it off at the hospital when we'd first met, and I was already enjoying Lola's audacious attitude.

We strolled up to the mini-mall and inside the enclosed breezeway, visiting like old friends. Linda removed a 'Back in ½ hour' sign from the storefront and unlocked the door for us. I stepped inside, involved in conversation with Lola, before glancing around the store for the first time.

I burst out laughing. It was a sex shop.

"'Up & Coming', you've got to be kidding me!" I chortled. "In a small town like this? Where everybody knows what everybody else is doing?"

"Everybody knows who everybody else is doing, too," Lola said slyly. "Actually, we do a booming business in mail order. We route our deliveries through Toronto in plain brown wrappers. But you'd be surprised how many people just walk in."

I gazed around. "My God, please tell me somebody left their thermos on the shelf by accident," I said, pointing to a black monolith.

"That's 'Big John the Wonder Horse'. People usually buy him as a gag gift," Linda said. "I think," she added doubtfully.

"We've got a great selection of products," Lola said. "Lingerie over here, toys and electronics there, books and videos on that wall, flavoured products over here..." She pointed out each section. "And we're getting some excellent new things, too," she enthused. "We've just gotten a line of body pillows and furniture."

She reached up to a shelf and lifted down a body pillow, standing it up beside her. Sure enough, the label read

'Bawdy Pillow'. It was an enormous stuffed penis, almost as tall as she was.

I snickered. "Reminds me of my ex-husband."

"Why, was he well-endowed?" Lola asked, bouncing her eyebrows suggestively.

"No, he was a big prick," I deadpanned to their guffaws. I reached over and poked the pillow. "It's a little soft for my taste."

"Oh, I can fix that," Linda giggled. She reached over and activated a switch at the base of the pillow. The penis gradually stiffened and straightened up. "It's got an air bladder and a compressor in it," she explained over my howls of laughter.

I eyed the rest of the 'Bawdy Pillow' line, still giggling. "I bet the boob cushions are popular. Do you sell them in pairs?"

"Sometimes in triples." Lola bounced her eyebrows again.

I flung up my hands in surrender. "Too much information. So don't tell me, let me guess. Your bookkeeper moved away in December, and the remaining one doesn't want your business."

"How did you know?" Linda demanded.

"I took over doing the books for Blue Eddy's Saloon in March. Your strait-laced bookkeeper doesn't want his business either. Are there any other dens of iniquity where I should visit and drop off a business card?"

"You've gotta admit, we're more fun than a church picnic," Lola said with satisfaction. A phone rang in the back room. "Oh, that's my 1-900 line, I've gotta go." She hurried into the back and I heard her pick up the phone. "Hi, honey, this is Lola," she purred in her throaty voice. "Guess what

I'm wearing."

I turned to Linda. "It's a small town. Do people really not know that Granny Lola is the sex goddess on the other end of the 900 line?"

Linda laughed. "Some don't know. Some just pretend they don't know. Some know and don't care. Some get totally turned on by knowing. But we get mostly outside callers from our website and phone listing."

I shook my head, still chuckling inwardly, and followed her into the small office behind the counter.

The point of sale program turned out to be just as contrary as Lola had warned, and I spent the next two hours utterly absorbed in figuring out its quirks.

On the drive home, my mind returned to mulling over the meeting with Spider. There was definitely more to this situation than I'd been told. There was no way two of the top brass needed to be there in person when a phone call would have sufficed for our short meeting.

And Spider was really buffaloed, though I couldn't tell whether it was by the brass themselves or something else as well. Stemp and the general were a pretty intimidating pair, so maybe that's all it was.

I trailed thoughtfully back into the house and stripped off my business clothes, sighing with relief as I donned my grubbies again. My mind still churning, I went back to fishing in the toilet tank and absently retrieved and re-attached the broken valve chain.

Recalling my last spy-related experience, I spent the evening figuring out what to take with me and trying to pack as efficiently as possible.

I snorted. Planning for the unforeseen was impossible by definition.

I slept restlessly that night and rose early to pack the last of my things into my backpack and get on the road. When I arrived at the office, Kane's black Expedition was already parked in front. I glanced at my watch, realizing I was ten minutes early. Even at that time of the morning, the sun was warm, and I started to sweat as soon as I turned off the air conditioning.

Screw waiting. I plucked my already-damp blouse away from my back and headed up the walk.

I stepped into the office just in time to hear Kane's deep baritone voice raised in the back meeting room. "Absolutely not! That's completely unacceptable!"

Oops. I was starting to ease my way back out the door when Spider appeared from down the hallway, catching me red-handed. I gave a guilty start and a feeble smile.

"That doesn't sound good," I whispered.

He frowned and shook his head. "Aydan's here," he called down the hall. The rumble of male voices ceased.

"Bring her in," someone responded.

I followed Webb's suit-clad back down the hallway, wondering what on earth I was getting myself into. If they were discussing me, it sounded as though Kane was about to veto the whole thing. Good. Maybe I could avoid dressing up after all.

When we entered the meeting room, Stemp, Briggs, and John Kane were seated around the table. Briggs and Stemp were as formally dressed as the day before. Kane wore a snug black T-shirt and dark jeans.

Black always made him look delicious, with his clear grey eyes and short dark hair shading to silver at the temples. His muscular arms were crossed over his broad chest, and he was frowning. I was shocked at the tired lines etched in his face.

The men rose as I entered, Kane towering over the other two. His square face softened into a smile as he reached for my hand. "Nice to see you again," he rumbled, his eyes crinkling into the sexy laugh lines I remembered so well from four months earlier.

"You, too," I replied, returning his gentle hand squeeze. I nodded to Stemp and Briggs, and we all sat.

Stemp leaned forward, his reptilian gaze fixed on Kane. "This is the best possible solution," he said, obviously continuing the argument I'd overheard. "This provides you with a viable cover story, as well as a second set of eyes and ears and a built-in detector."

Kane shook his head, his massive shoulders flexing as he planted his hands on the table. "Aydan has given enough to this country. She's a civilian. It's not fair to ask her to get involved in this again."

Briggs spoke with finality. "Ms. Kelly's participation is not at issue here. She has already agreed to do this. You have your orders."

Kane's face hardened.

"Hold on," I interjected. "I only agreed to do this on the condition that Kane approved it. He clearly doesn't want me. If I'm a liability to him, the deal's off."

"Ms. Kelly," the general addressed me, his voice unyielding. "We need you. You agreed to help us. This mission will go ahead as planned."

"Aydan," Kane said quietly. "Are you sure you want to risk this?" His eyes searched my face, and I frowned.

"I don't know what you're talking about. I was told yesterday there was almost no risk associated with this. I was hoping to find out more today."

Kane's shoulders bunched as he loomed threateningly over the table in Webb's direction. "You didn't tell her?" he grated.

"I... had orders," Spider stammered. His eyes darted between Kane's glower and Stemp's smooth, deadly face. His trapped gaze skittered toward me. "I'm sorry."

Alarm shot through me as Kane lunged to his feet. "Sorry doesn't cut it!" he barked.

He took a deep breath, visibly calming himself. When he turned to me, his voice was even, but I could read the tension in his posture. "Aydan, these people have lied to you. There may not be risk to any other agent we might send, but there is substantial risk to you. The reason I'm going to this event is that we believe there's a connection to Fuzzy Bunny."

I didn't realize you could actually feel your own face going pale. A burst of adrenaline made my head feel light, and my lips were cold and stiff when I uttered the first words that came to mind.

"Oh, shit."

"Kane!" Briggs snapped. "You are dangerously close to insubordination!"

"Yes, sir," Kane growled. With the small part of my mind that wasn't racing with fear, I noted it sounded more like agreement than obedience.

I forced my breathing to steady, slowing my whirling thoughts. Fuzzy Bunny. The deadly international corporation that dealt in arms, drugs, espionage and laundered money. Their incongruous cover as an exporter and manufacturer of children's toys. They hadn't been kind to me in March. My body had healed, but the thought of attracting their attention again filled me with dread.

I took a deep breath and controlled my voice so that when I spoke, I sounded almost casual. "Don't they think I'm dead?"

"Yes," Spider reassured me. "We're positive of that. That was the last report Sandler sent them before you ki... before he died."

Stemp leaned forward, fixing me with his flat eyes. "There's no reason to believe you would be identified at tomorrow's event. And we need you, specifically. Even if we had another female agent available, she wouldn't be able to do what you can do."

I eyed him, heart thumping. "Which is what, exactly?"

"Access a brainwave-driven virtual reality network using a password-cracking key hidden inside an attractive necklace."

I recoiled against the back of my chair. "Oh, no. No, no, no. Been there. Done that. Got the T-shirt. Can't get rid of the fucking T-shirt."

I shuddered, pushing away from the table. Men around the table. Bad memories. Barely realizing what I was doing, I stumbled to my feet and backed away.

"Aydan, you're safe." Kane's voice was deep and forceful. "It's over. You don't have to do this."

I shook my head vigorously, snapping back to the present and shaking off the repugnant flashback. I straightened and took a deep breath, squaring my shoulders. Chin up.

Kane and Webb both regarded me with troubled eyes. Stemp watched impassively, his immobile posture reminding me of a coiled snake. I held down a shudder. That was one creepy guy.

General Briggs leaned forward in his chair, his piercing blue gaze scanning my face. "I understand that accessing the network comes with some difficult memories for you," he said quietly. "But if our suspicions are correct, and if there is another network at this venue, your ability to detect and access it could protect others from what you experienced. And it could safeguard many other innocent lives."

I stood for a couple of long moments while his words sank in before letting my breath out slowly and releasing the fists I hadn't realized I'd clenched.

"You're right, of course. Sorry. It was just a shock." I sat down in the chair again and interlaced my fingers to still their trembling. "Okay. So what's the plan?"

"Aydan." Kane's voice was hoarse, his face set in grim lines. The general raked him with a look, and I knew another word would land Kane in serious trouble. I met Kane's eyes and gave him a tiny headshake. A muscle jumped in his clenched jaw, but he said no more.

"The plan is quite simple," Stemp said smoothly. "You and Kane will dress up and attend a gala event. Enjoy the food, wine, and entertainment. And while you do so, you will scan for a network while he notes the layout of the venue. Elegant, unobtrusive, and easy."

"Except that as soon as Aydan enters the network, if there is one, she's instantly visible," Kane ground out. "She might as well send out a press release inviting all the sickos to come and find her. Again."

I spoke into the silence around the table. "Maybe not." I turned to Spider. "Hey, Spider, remember how you told me a person could alter their own appearance in the virtual reality network if they weren't trying to maintain another simulation at the same time?"

He nodded slowly.

"So what if I just pop in looking like somebody else? I wouldn't be there for long, and I wouldn't be trying to do anything complicated."

Hope rose in his face. "That might work."

"So then it would only be a minor risk that somebody might see me and recognize me at the party in person. Mixed in with a bunch of other people, that doesn't seem too likely. Right?" I looked around the table. Stemp and Briggs were nodding with obvious satisfaction. Kane was still frowning, but he said nothing.

"Good, then it's settled," Stemp smiled. The expression was almost as disturbing as his previous inscrutability. "You can leave for Calgary as soon as you're ready. Webb will give you the necklace, prepare your paperwork and set up your accommodations. I don't need to remind you to safeguard the necklace with your life."

Kane shot him a murderous look that Stemp fortunately chose to ignore.

"I'll need to practice a bit," I cautioned them. "Can I use the Sirius network for a while today before I leave?"

Briggs nodded. "Done." He turned to Spider. "Arrange it with Smith."

I jerked my head up. "John Smith?"

"Yes, he took over as head of security when James Sandler died," Briggs replied.

"Oh."

"Is there a problem?"

"No problem," I muttered.

Stemp and Briggs rose, nodded goodbyes, and left. Spider, Kane and I sat silently at the table until we heard the outer door close. As the sound faded, Spider sprang up from the table, tearing off his tie. He flung the tie down on the table and wrenched his suit jacket off, too.

"This just sucks!" he exclaimed. "This just totally sucks!"

He turned to me wretchedly, bunching his jacket in his fists. "I'm sorry. I'm so... sorry! I couldn't do anything. I hoped you'd just turn them down, but I should have known you wouldn't. This is all my fault."

"Whoa, calm down, Spider," I told him. "I don't see how this is your fault. And anyway, you know it needs to be done and I'm the only one that can do it. It'll be fine. We know so much more about how the network stuff works now. And Kane's good at getting me out of trouble." I smiled at Kane across the table.

He met my eyes unhappily. "Not good enough."

I shrugged. "I'm still here. And a bunch of Fuzzy Bunny's guys aren't." I could see he was about to argue, so I got up from the table. "Let's go over to Sirius. I don't know how long this will take."

Webb sighed. "I'll call Smith before we leave."

CHAPTER 3

We piled into Kane's SUV for the short drive across town. When we got out at the nondescript two-storey building, I eyed its bland facade and discreet 'Sirius Dynamics' sign with distaste. No good memories here, either. I strode straight into the lobby before the other two could read my face.

When I hung back, waiting for Kane and Webb to approach the bulletproof security wicket, Spider waved me forward. "You're in the system now, too. Your fob should be ready."

Oh, goody. I kept my face expressionless as I stepped up to the window.

"Ms. Kelly. Kane. Webb." The uniformed man placed three badges in the turntable on his side and pressed the lever. The turntable spun around, disgorging the badges and the sign-in sheet. I signed the sheet and recorded the time, then stepped back to attach my fob and make room for Kane and Webb to do the same.

When we stood ready, Kane nodded me toward the entry door. "Try your fob. Make sure it works."

I stepped up to the card reader, and the door obligingly unlatched. "Second floor meeting room again?" I asked, but

Webb shook his head.

"No, we're going into the secured facility this time," he said, turning toward a thick, featureless steel door.

I'd noticed the heavy door back in March, and I'd wondered about it then. Apparently I was about to have my curiosity satisfied. Suddenly I wasn't sure if that was a good thing. It seems to me that the less you know about secret government research facilities, the better.

Both men eyed me expectantly as I approached the door. There was no visible card reader, so I didn't quite know what to do. As I bent to examine the latch, I recoiled from a sudden light emanating from what looked like a deadbolt keyhole.

Webb chuckled. "You have to stand still for the retinal scan."

I backed away from the door. "Since when do you have my retinal scan on file?"

"Since you showed up at the hospital last March," Kane explained. "When they brought you in, they thought you were a Sirius employee, so they scanned you. The record was kept on file."

I vaguely remembered a bright light shining in my eyes. "Tricky bastards."

Kane shrugged, the corner of his mouth crooking up. "Occupational hazard."

I gave him a rueful twist of my lips and stepped up to the door again. This time I held still for the scan, and the latch clicked as the heavy door released. We all stepped through it into a silent enclosure only a few feet square. The door closed behind us with a muffled thump, and I heard the latch engage. I stepped up to the door on the other side of the room, and let it scan me, too.

Nothing happened.

My heart began to race as I whipped around to eye Kane and Spider for reassurance.

"Thirty-second time delay," Kane explained.

I took a deep breath. Then another. It was a very small room. All concrete. The top of Kane's head was only a few inches below the ceiling. I turned away from the other two, controlling my breath. In. Out. Slow like ocean waves. My palms started to sweat.

I stared at my watch, counting the seconds down.

"Aydan, I'm sorry," Kane's voice was strained. "I forgot you're claustrophobic. Don't worry, we're not trapped here."

"Is there a thirty-second time delay to get out, too?" I asked, my voice a little tighter than I'd intended.

"Yes, I'm sorry," Kane repeated.

The latch in front of me released and I snatched the door open to stare down into a featureless concrete stairwell. There was a closed steel door at the bottom. My knuckles whitened on the door handle.

"We can go back out right away," Kane told me, his voice calm and soothing. "Just turn around and we'll go back out."

"What if there's a fire?" I demanded, my hand still clenched around the handle. "How does everybody get out?"

"There's a state-of-the-art dry fire suppression system," Webb explained. "Any fire can be suppressed in ten seconds or less, regardless of how it starts."

"Don't those suck all the oxygen out of the air?"

"Not the new ones that we're using," Spider reassured me. "This is so safe that the gas is used as a propellant in asthma medications."

I breathed carefully. The air smelled clean and fresh. I gradually uncurled my fingers from the door lever. "Okay."

"Okay?" Kane searched my face.

I nodded. "I can do this."

"Are you sure?"

I did some more deep breathing. "Yeah. It was just the surprise that got me. I'm fine." I started down the stairs, hiding my quivering knees.

The door at the bottom released immediately, and I stepped into a brightly lit white corridor. Glassed-in rooms lined each side, and I recognized the raised flooring that accommodated computer cabling beneath it. There was a constant flow of fresh, cool air. I breathed deeply, forcing my shoulders to relax.

Spider stepped forward. "This way."

To keep myself distracted, I eyed the windows while we walked down the hallway. Some rooms contained computers and electronics, and others were full of test tubes, glass gizmos, and microscopes. In a couple of rooms, lumpy equipment defied my imagination. I hadn't a clue what it might be used for, and I didn't think I really wanted to know.

Near the end of the corridor, Spider held his fob up to a prox pad and stood still for the retinal scan. When he opened the door, we all trooped into a small room lined with computer screens. Webb dropped into a chair with casual familiarity and pulled out a desk drawer.

"Sit, get comfortable." He waved an airy hand, and Kane and I each pulled up a chair.

At the back of the drawer, Spider punched in a sequence of numbers on a keypad. When the compartment released, he lifted out a black velvet box and handed it to me. "Here you go, Cinderella," he joked. "Don't lose it, or you might turn into a pumpkin."

I opened the box, tentatively touching the emerald

necklace inside. The large jewel was square-cut, set in a simple, elegant collar of heavy gold links.

"Wow. That's a bit of a change from the old amethyst key ring."

Spider returned my smile. "We damaged the original amethyst when we extracted the circuitry the first time around. We've done a better job with this one, so we can actually remove the electronics without destroying the setting. That way we can place the circuitry anywhere we want. Since you're going to a black-tie gala, you get the fancy necklace. Try it."

I lifted it reluctantly out of the box and placed it around my neck, fumbling with the clasp under my hair. The cold weight of the gold against my skin made me control a shiver. It was a good match for the cold weight of fear on my heart.

I dragged my mind back to the job at hand. "I don't suppose you fixed the pain issue while you were tinkering?"

Webb shook his head regretfully. "We think you get pain because your brainwaves aren't a perfect frequency match with the network. Without a modulator, your frequency is close enough to get you in, but not close enough to let you get out comfortably."

"You couldn't put a modulator in here?"

Webb grimaced. "We could. But that would make it visible if somebody was monitoring. As it is, it's completely passive and undetectable. Without you to drive it, it's useless."

"And you still haven't found anybody else who can use it?"

"No. Our pool of candidates is pretty small, since this technology is so highly classified."

"It's so good to be special," I mumbled. "Okay. Is the

network accessible from here?"

"Yes," Kane replied. "I'll go in with you. Webb will monitor the sim externally. Nothing can go wrong." He said the last words with determination, and I nodded.

He gripped the Sirius fob that would grant him network access, and I laid mine aside, making sure I'd be using only the emerald's hidden circuitry to get in.

"Okay. Let's do it." I closed my eyes and concentrated on stepping into the white void of the virtual reality simulation. Kane popped into existence beside me almost simultaneously. Instead of his real-life T-shirt and jeans, he wore full combat gear with a sub-machine gun slung across his broad chest.

I gazed up at the mountain of camo-clad man as he scanned the void tensely. "I think you're going to scare the locals."

He directed a grim gaze down at me. "I don't care. I'm not taking any chances."

I gave him a faint smile. "Well, you're not going to get any argument from me. Let's get a room." I realized what I'd said as soon as the words left my mouth. "I mean, let's get out of the portal." Kane's face relaxed as I felt a flush climb my cheeks. "You know what I meant."

He nodded, one corner of his mouth crooked up. I turned away, flustered, to visualize the corridor. When it materialized in front of us, one of the doors popped open and John Smith himself stepped out. At the first movement of the door, Kane pushed me behind him, unslinging his weapon in a fast, smooth motion. Smith froze, goggling at the business end of the large gun.

I eyed him with distaste. Even in the simulation, his avatar's clothes were mismatched, rumpled, and food-stained. And he hadn't bothered to eliminate his disgusting body odour, either. I breathed through my mouth. This research facility was probably the only place in the world where a man like that could be promoted to department head.

Smith nodded slowly and carefully as Kane lowered the weapon. "Kane. Ms. Kelly. I see you're beginning your tests." He eyed the necklace around my neck. "It would be better if you concealed that."

"Right, sorry." I tucked it inside the neck of my blouse.

Smith gave us a wide berth as we continued down the hallway to a room with a 'Vacant' sign.

"God, that guy gives me the creeps," I muttered, closing the virtual door behind us. I gazed around the blank white room, thinking. "Okay, I'm going to try to be somebody else now. I guess it'll have to be somebody I'm familiar with, or I won't be able to hold the illusion."

I pondered for a few moments. "I think I'll be a man. If you're going to go for deception, might as well go whole hog. I'll see if I can be my husband."

"Your ex?" Kane inquired.

"No, I'll be Robert. The one I actually wanted to keep. That way even if they do figure out his identity, they can't hurt a dead man."

Kane frowned. "You were widowed young. The death record said heart attack?"

"Yeah." I clammed up and concentrated.

"Um," Kane said. "Aydan. Clothes?"

I glanced down at myself, seeing Robert's naked body. "Oops. Last memory. Sorry, too much information." I waved a hand and Robert's favourite plaid shirt and jeans wrapped around me, or, more accurately, around him. I looked up at Kane. "How's that?"

"Fine, I guess. You certainly don't look like yourself."

I conjured a mirror out of thin air. For a couple of seconds, my dead husband gazed back at me before dissolving to leave me staring at my own face in the mirror. I turned away from Kane. Two years after Robert's death, I was mostly okay.

"Yeah, that was close enough," I said when I could trust my voice.

Kane's voice was quiet behind me. "Want to take a break?"

"No, let me try that again." I forced a chuckle. "With clothes this time." I concentrated again, turning back to face Kane. "How's this?"

I gave a quick downward glance. Good, I was dressed this time.

He nodded. "You look the same as last time. But this is really a little disturbing," he added with a crooked grin.

I laughed, feeling my body change back as I did. "And it's really damn hard to maintain. The instant I stop concentrating, I go back to being myself."

"I think that's good news." He gave me the full grin this time, and I laughed and nodded agreement.

"Okay, but here's the tricky part," I said. "Now I need to go out of the network, and then come back through the portal again, being Robert. Can you stand in the portal and watch for me? I want to make sure I'm fully disguised right from the first instant I enter."

He nodded. "Let's go."

We left the room and retraced our steps down the hallway to the virtual exit door. "Back in a flash," I told him, and stepped out.

Expecting the pain didn't help. And I'd forgotten how much it really hurt. Some of my more creative obscenities leaked through my clenched teeth while I screwed my eyes shut and held my head.

"Welcome back," Spider said when I cracked my eyes open. "Thanks for the vocabulary update. There were a couple of those I hadn't heard for a while." He was smiling, but his eyes were concerned. "I wish this didn't hurt you so much," he added.

"But just think of all the new language you'd miss if it didn't," I groaned, straightening up. I glanced over at Kane's immobile body, staring into space from his chair. Still waiting for me in the network portal, obviously.

"Okay, let's see how this goes." I concentrated on stepping back into the network, wearing Robert's body.

Kane stood at parade rest, waiting for me. "Aydan?" he asked cautiously.

"Yeah. I'm getting better at this." I took a few experimental steps. "This feels so weird."

"Tell me about it," he said.

I laughed, and my simulation vanished. I stretched. "That feels so much better."

Kane nodded. "No offense to your late husband, but it looks a whole lot better, too."

"None taken on his behalf. Okay. I'm going to try it once more. Here goes."

I stepped out again, managing to restrict myself to some inarticulate groans this time. I breathed through the pain, straightening slowly.

Spider nodded approval. "That looked good on the monitors. You can quit now."

"Just once more." I rolled my neck and shoulders.

"Why put yourself through more pain?"

"Because if my simulation slips and I show up looking like me, there's a whole lot more pain where that came from. And I won't get to choose when and where it happens."

Webb's young face hardened. "I see your point."

I shrugged one more time to loosen my knotted muscles, and stepped back into the network again.

Kane nodded. "All right, that looks fine. Anything else while we're here?"

"Nothing I can think of." I sighed and stepped out again, curling down in my chair to wrap my arms over my pain-wracked head. My lips moved while air hissed through my clenched teeth, creating an unpleasantly sibilant string of curses. I straightened gradually, pushing myself up with my hands on my knees.

Two sets of eyes regarded me with disquiet. "That can't be good for you," Spider observed, frowning.

I massaged my temples tenderly. "Let me know if my brain starts to leak out my ears." I rolled my neck and shoulders some more.

"I'm done here if you are," I said to Kane. "What do we do next?"

"Next we drive to Calgary. I go home and get some sleep. You go..." He paused. "Did you ever sell your house?"

"Yes, finally, last month. Thank God."

"You'll need a place to stay, then. Webb can reserve a hotel room for you. And you'll need to buy whatever you need to get ready for the party."

He rubbed his hands over his face, knuckling his eyes. "Do you mind driving? I flew in from Frankfurt this morning and drove two hours to get here in time for nine o'clock. I don't think I'm safe to drive another two hours on the highway."

No wonder he looked so bone-weary. I stared at him in horror. "Don't these idiots ever let you sleep?"

He shrugged, a half-smile tugging at his lips.

"Did you get breakfast?" I demanded.

"I ate at the airport."

"Which airport?"

"Calgary."

I consulted my watch. "Okay. I need lunch, and you probably need to eat again, too. Then we can head out. I have some more questions about this party, so I'll ask you on the way. If you can stay awake."

He nodded. "I'm not in desperate straits yet. I napped on the plane."

We all stood. "Oh!" My hand flew to the weight of the necklace around my neck. "I'd better take this off." Spider opened the box, and I laid the heavy chain into it. Closing it, I handed it to Kane. "I'll feel better if you're carrying it," I told him. "That's more responsibility than I care to assume at the moment."

We filed out of the room, and I headed eagerly for the door at the end of the hallway. Now that I was no longer focused on my network tests, the thought of being trapped underground was an oppressive weight.

I took the stairs two at a time and opened the door to let us into the timed exit chamber. I went immediately to the exit door and let the scan do its thing, counting down the time in my mind. When the latch released after what seemed much longer than thirty seconds, I yanked the door open and stepped quickly into the lobby, taking a deep, thankful breath.

CHAPTER 4

Kane drove directly back to the small shared office. As we got out of the Expedition, I frowned up at him. "Will you be comfortable riding with me?"

He grinned. "Why, are you a bad driver?"

"Very funny. No, I meant, will you actually fit in my car?"

He regarded the small Saturn doubtfully. "Maybe."

I stuck my key in the passenger door lock. "Better try it and see." I opened the door and leaned in, making sure the seat was as far back as it would go.

He folded himself into the car with his usual athleticism and turned a surprised face up to me. "There's a lot more room in here than I expected. This will work fine. Are you ready to go?"

"Lunch first," I told him. "Spider, do you want to join us?" He nodded eagerly, and I reached in past Kane to unlock the rear passenger door for him.

He stooped and clambered into the back seat, his bony limbs awkwardly uncoordinated. "Sorry, it's not too roomy in the back," I apologized, but he smiled.

"It's fine. I wouldn't have thought I'd be able to fit in with the front seats all the way back, but I'm good."

I went around to the driver's side, keyed open the lock, and slid into the seat, realizing as I did that Webb was chuckling in the back.

"What?" I demanded.

"I think you're the only person left in the world who doesn't have power locks. How old is this car, anyway?"

"It's a '98," I replied primly. "I love this car. It's never let me down."

He nodded understanding, his eyes still dancing. "It's a great car," he soothed.

I grinned at him in the rearview mirror. "It's about to haul your ungrateful ass over to Blue Eddy's for lunch. You better believe it's a great car." He laughed as I pulled away from the curb.

The excellent blues music made me smile when we walked into Blue Eddy's. My usual table was available, and I made a beeline for it and sat down with my back to the wall so I could observe the rest of the bar. Kane slid in beside me, and Spider sat across from us with a mischievous grin.

"You guys never change," he said.

I shrugged, taking him in good fun. "So I'm a paranoid freak. So sue me. It beats having my back exposed."

Eddy glanced up from behind the bar, and I waved to him. His face split into a smile as he came over to the table. "Aydan, hi! I thought you weren't coming in until Tuesday. And John. Long time, no see."

Kane smiled and shook Eddy's outstretched hand. "It's been a while."

"I'll be back again on Tuesday," I assured Eddy. "Today I'm just looking for food."

"As usual, Hungry Aydan," he teased. "Do you want a beer, too?"

I shook my head. "Want, yes, but I can't have one. I'm driving. Just a glass of water, please."

He turned to Kane. "John?"

Kane nodded. "I'd kill for a beer right now. Do you still have that dark draft on tap?"

The turn of phrase was a little frightening coming from him, and I kept my face carefully neutral. I'd seen him kill. It wasn't for beer.

Eddy nodded, obviously unfazed.

Spider shook his head as Eddy turned a questioning gaze to him. "I still haven't learned to drink. Just a Coke. Thanks."

Eddy dropped menus on our table and went back to the bar to get our drinks. I turned to Kane with a smile. "I finally get to return the chauffeuring favour."

He leaned back in his chair, hands clasped behind his head, and I briefly regretted not sitting across from him. I was quite sure Spider couldn't appreciate those bulging biceps the way I could.

Kane shot me a devilish look. "Now you get to suffer while you watch me enjoy my beer, instead of the other way around."

I shrugged, returning his grin. "Payback's a bitch." I picked up my menu, giving it a cursory scan. I already knew it more or less by heart.

Eddy returned to deliver our drinks and take our food order. Kane took a grateful slug of his pint, and I sighed as he licked the foam off his lips.

"You're a cruel man," I said, eyeing him wistfully. Quite apart from envying his beer, I was also having secret thoughts of licking that foam off his lips myself. I turned to Spider for distraction. "So what movies have you seen lately?"

He immediately launched into an enthusiastic account of his latest viewings. I knew it would be a lengthy exposition, and true to form, he chattered blithely throughout the rest of the meal.

Kane finished off his pint with obvious enjoyment, letting the conversation roll over him. Spider showed no sign of running down while we finished our food and paid the bill. It was good to see him back to his usual convivial self, but I was glad he wouldn't be riding to Calgary with us. Two hours of constant conversation, however stimulating, was too much for me.

We dropped Spider off at the office, and I steered the car toward the outskirts of the small town. We drove in companionable silence until we neared the turnoff for my farm.

I turned to Kane. "Do you mind if I pop in and change my clothes? It'll only take a minute."

"No problem. I was waiting with bated breath to see what befell your dress-up clothes this time."

I snorted. "Usually it's just dirt. I'm trying to quit with the blood."

"Good choice."

CHAPTER 5

Back on the highway, I drove in silence for a few miles before I turned to Kane again. "So tell me more about this party. What's the story?"

"It's being held at the home of a local businessman, Lawrence Harchman. He owns a drilling company with interests locally and internationally. He came up on our radar because he has financial ties to Fuzzy Bunny."

I raised a cynical eyebrow. "Petroleum drilling and children's toys. Seems like a natural combination."

Kane shrugged. "It may be pure coincidence. Harchman has very diverse business investments. But I just spent the last four months tracing a complex web of connections through central Europe, and I think this is worth following up. Webb has been monitoring the chatter, and we don't like what we're hearing."

I drove in silence for a few minutes, watching the fields roll by outside the window. "What's the reason for the party?"

"Harchman's company, Osiris Drilling, has developed some new drilling control software. They've invited all the movers and shakers in the petroleum industry, along with various consultants, to a party to launch the new product."

I nodded understanding. "Gee, and you just happen to be an energy consultant. At least as far as they know. So you'll be going as yourself."

"Right," he agreed. "I don't think you should go as yourself, though."

"You said oil and gas industry." I considered for a few moments. "I did business in Calgary for quite a while, but I was never directly involved in oil and gas. I probably won't see anybody I know. But I do know a lot of people in the business community generally. It would be pretty embarrassing if I was pretending to be somebody else and got recognized."

Kane frowned. "I still think this is a bad idea. I got blindsided by this whole issue. If I'd been here, I would have steered it in a different direction entirely." He paused. "If you got sick tomorrow afternoon, you wouldn't be able to go at all," he said slowly.

I sighed. "You know I can't do that."

"Why not?"

"I just can't. You wouldn't bail out of an investigation just because you were afraid for your own skin, would you?"

"No. But I'm a trained agent. It's my job. You're a civilian. It's not your job." I felt his eyes bore into me. "Right?"

"Yes, I'm a civilian. But apparently nobody else can use the key to access the network. That leaves me. Whether I want to or not."

I gave him a cheerful grin. "Besides, I'm getting paid this time. The extra cash will be nice."

He let me change the subject. "How is your bookkeeping business going, anyway?" he inquired.

"Fine. I'm working for the seamy underbelly of

Silverside."

Kane raised an amused eyebrow. "How so?"

"I lucked into a perfect setup when I moved in March. There were originally two bookkeepers in town, and one had moved away in January. The remaining bookkeeper is quite religious, so she won't touch any business that has any overtones of booze, sex, or gambling. That leaves all the good stuff for me."

He laughed. "So that's what Blue Eddy meant about seeing you Tuesday."

I nodded. "I love having Eddy for a client. He's such a nice guy. And it's a great excuse to go to the bar and listen to blues once a week."

I returned to the point. "I still need to figure out how to introduce myself at the party. God, I hate small talk."

"Could you use your maiden name?" Kane asked.

"I never changed my name when I got married. I've always been Aydan Kelly."

We lapsed into silence again, thinking. He scrubbed his knuckles through his hair. "How about Aydan Kane?" he suggested hesitantly. "We could go as husband and wife. I hate to use that as a cover, but it's the only way you can introduce yourself using another name and still be plausible if somebody recognizes you."

I grimaced. "It's a lousy cover. It'd just never happen."

There was a short silence. "What are you trying to say?" Kane asked in mock indignation.

I laughed. "Nothing personal. Anybody who knows me would know I'd never change my name. And I wouldn't get married again, either. I had one shitty marriage and one good one, and I'm not looking for a tie-breaker."

"Really?" Something in Kane's voice made me glance

over, trying to read him.

I trod carefully. "Have you ever been married?"

"Once."

I eyed his expressionless profile. "I guess it'd be pretty hard to maintain any kind of relationship when you have a job that could take you away for months at a time without even telephone contact."

"No, I was still in the army then," he replied slowly. "I was away on training a lot, and then I saw combat in Yugoslavia and came back pretty messed up. Alicia was devastated when she found out she couldn't have children, and I wasn't there for her. In the end, we just fell apart."

"I'm sorry," I murmured.

"But you had a good marriage, and you still wouldn't do it again?"

"No."

"Why not?"

I drove in silence, thinking. "In a good marriage, you give away part of yourself. I'm not willing to do that again," I said finally.

"Mm."

I couldn't interpret that, so I didn't bother to try. "Anyway," I said, "I don't think it really matters. I likely won't meet anybody there who knows me well enough to know this stuff. So we might as well go with the marriage cover. I'd rather do that than give my real name."

"Okay," he agreed. "We'll need rings."

"Shit."

"I'll take care of it," Kane assured me. "What size do you wear?"

"Seven, but don't bother. I brought my diamonds with me since it's a black-tie. I'll just wear one on my left hand instead of my right."

He glanced over at my naked hands. "I didn't figure you for the diamond type."

"I'm not. But Robert loved to buy me jewellery. I kept trying to get him to buy me tools, but he only listened part of the time."

Kane laughed. "He got you some good tools. I'll never forget you swinging around on me with that air nailer. I thought I was going get a spike through my forehead."

I laughed, too. "That's what you get for charging into my bathroom with a sub-machine gun."

We drove for a few more minutes in silence, occupied with our own memories.

"But getting back to the party," I said. "How black-tie is this black-tie? What's the age range you expect to be there? Are we talking long gowns, or just your typical cocktail dress type of thing?"

"I'd guess most people there would be in the thirty to sixty age range. And I'd say probably cocktail dress. But wardrobe isn't exactly my area of expertise."

I sighed. "Mine either."

I glanced at his tired face and felt a tug of sympathy. "Why don't you see if you can grab a nap? That's all the questions I can think of at the moment."

"Just one more thing we need to talk about." He hesitated. "We need to clear the air between us."

I frowned puzzlement in his direction. "Okay. What's on your mind?"

"I owe you an apology."

"For..."

"For my inappropriate behaviour at your house before I left in March."

"Oh." I grinned at him. "I don't recall any inappropriate behaviour. I thought it was all very appropriate."

Kane shook his head. "I should never have kissed you."

"Yeah, you really forced yourself on me." I chuckled at his expression. "Come on, John. Don't tell me you thought I wasn't into it."

His lips crooked up, despite his obvious seriousness. "Well, I didn't exactly feel unwelcome."

I shot him a humorous look. "Good. Because if you thought I was shocked and horrified, we'd have to have a pretty serious talk about how to interpret body language."

He paused. "I'm sorry I didn't call."

"Huh?" I frowned confusion at him. "When?"

"After we... parted... that way. Most women would expect at least a phone call."

I laughed. "There you go with that 'most women' thing again. I'm not most women. And I know what you do for a living. Half the time you don't even get to eat or sleep, let alone call for a chat."

He blew out a breath, his shoulders easing. "I'm glad you're not upset. But it was still inappropriate, and it won't happen again."

"Damn."

"You see, that's what I'm talking about," he said gravely. "We need to set some boundaries. In March, I thought... Well, it doesn't matter. Now we're working together, and it can't happen again."

I sobered. "I guess I can see where you're coming from. You're a big guy. All it would take would be some female co-worker saying she felt too intimidated to tell you to back off, and you'd get crucified in court."

He nodded slowly, and I thought he was about to say

something else, but he remained silent.

"You don't have to worry about that," I assured him after a short pause. I took my gaze off the road momentarily to meet his eyes, making sure he was listening. "Look, you should know by now I'm hard to offend."

"True," he allowed with a quirk of his eyebrows. "If you liked Arnie Helmand, you've got be hard to offend."

I laughed. "Right. So don't worry. If we're going as husband and wife, some physical contact is pretty much inevitable. If I feel uncomfortable with anything you say or do, I'll tell you. Trust me to do that. And I'll trust you to do the same."

I saw him relax in my peripheral vision. "Okay. Deal. Thanks, Aydan."

CHAPTER 6

When we approached Calgary's city limits a couple of hours later, I spoke his name quietly and his eyes snapped open, instantly alert.

"We're just coming into town," I told him. "Where do you live?"

"I'm down in Sundance. Just take the Deerfoot south and come up from 22x."

I followed his directions, eventually pulling up in front of an apartment-style condo building. "Should I take you to a grocery store or anything?" I asked. "If you've been in Europe for the last four months, the pickings are probably pretty slim in your kitchen."

He shook his head. "I've got wheels here. Do you still have my cellphone number?" When I nodded, he added, "Call me as soon as you're checked into your hotel. I'll pick you up there tomorrow night around five-thirty. And call me if you need anything else in the mean time."

He unfolded himself from the car, stretching. I popped the trunk so he could retrieve his suitcase, and he gave me a wave and strode toward the building.

I let the car idle beside the curb while I dialled my cellphone. "Hey, Spider, where am I staying?"

He gave me the name and address of a hotel on Macleod Trail, and I drove directly there and checked in using the information he had given me. As soon as the room door closed behind me, I called Kane. I figured he had a hot date with a pillow as soon as humanly possible, and I didn't want to keep him up. Even after his nap in the car, he still looked exhausted.

That done, I reluctantly headed for the mall.

I hate shopping for dress-up clothes. Especially when I haven't a clue what will be appropriate. Throw in a deadline, and the whole experience ranks right up there with a root canal performed by an inebriated chimpanzee.

The budget I'd been given for clothing and accessories had stunned me. It was more than I spend on all my clothes in a year. Granted, I'm not exactly a clotheshorse. My boutique of choice is Mark's Work Wearhouse, but I had a feeling Mark's wasn't going to cut it this time.

I cruised the mall, circling through the stores without committing. It had been months since I'd set foot in a fashion mall, and to my chagrin, most of the dresses were pink, purple, or black, with fussy ruffles. I hate ruffles. And my pale skin and red hair demand green, gold, or brown.

Annoyed, I retreated to the food court to ease my sorrows with ice cream. Thus fortified, I attacked the mall with renewed vigour.

By six o'clock, I'd done the first mall. I drove to the next one, hope fading. At eight o'clock, I shuffled out to my car in defeat. Clearly I needed a different strategy.

Back at my hotel, I flopped onto the bed and punched a speed dial on my cellphone. When I heard the lively hello on the other end of the line, I smiled, feeling better already.

"Nichele! It's Aydan. Long time, no talk!" We chatted

for a few minutes, catching up, before I broached the subject. "I need some serious help."

I heard her smile over the line. "Ya think?"

"Smart-ass. No, I need some wardrobe-related help."

"Oooh, shopping! You have sooo called the right person."

"I need a cocktail dress for a black-tie gala," I explained. "For tomorrow evening. No pressure."

"Oho! You've got a date," she teased. "Give me the dirt, girl."

Shit. I should have thought this through before I called.

"Um, it's not really a date," I mumbled. "It's kind of more like a business thing."

"Are you going with somebody?" she prodded.

"Um, yeah."

"And...?"

"And, um, well, he's just a guy I met through my business. It's just going to be a boring presentation on software."

"Names! Details! Spill it!" she demanded.

I sighed. I really didn't want to have this conversation. Especially when I had to lie through my teeth.

"His name is John. I don't really see it going anywhere. It's just a business thing. Can you help me buy something tomorrow?"

"Girl, leave it to me. You're going to look so hot by the time I'm done with you, he'll be on his knees before you even get to the party."

Now that was an enticing image. I shook my head forcefully to banish it.

"Thanks, Nichele. I'll pick you up tomorrow morning. What time, nine-thirty?"

"Perfect. Get ready to kick some fashion butt."

CHAPTER 7

I ate an excellent breakfast in the morning, delighting in the knowledge that I wasn't paying for it. Buoyed by food and optimism, I faced Nichele's cheerfully prurient questioning with good humour and fabricated evasive answers until she gave up.

By eleven o'clock, she had marched me into several exclusive downtown boutiques, and I realized the wardrobe budget had been well within reason. Yikes. The sad thing was that I knew I'd end up wrecking the outfit. Nice clothes just don't stand a chance around me.

Finally, I came out of the dressing room, and she nodded decisively. "That's the one."

I looked down at myself. I loved the colour, green with an unusual bronzy shimmer that made my skin look creamy and brought out the hint of green in my brown eyes. The fine, soft fabric slipped over my body like water, and the halter style was definitely flattering, emphasizing my boobs while skimming over the extra weight around my middle.

"But, Nichele," I said tentatively, "It's pretty short, isn't it?"

She snorted. "It's barely above your knees, girl. You gotta show off those long legs of yours."

"It's not my legs I'm worried about showing off," I complained. "The skirt pulls up so high when I sit down, I'll be sitting on my bare ass. And you know I can't remember to keep my knees together."

"Suck it up, buttercup," she commanded. "Come on, buy it. And hurry up. We still have to get shoes and purse and makeup and jewellery." She grabbed my hand and recoiled at the sight of my nails. "And you need a manicure. We'll get you some acrylics."

I gulped and handed over my credit card.

I'd had little hope for the shoes, but to my amazement, Nichele actually managed to find me a pair that were reasonably comfortable, the right colour, and on sale.

As I walked back and forth in the store for Nichele's approval, she nodded. "Those shoes are hot, girl. And I don't know how you manage to walk like a supermodel in them when all you ever wear is running shoes."

"The only other alternative with heels this high is to stick my ass out and waddle like a duck. I'm thinking that's not a good look for me."

She shrugged, her eyes twinkling. "Your date probably wouldn't mind if you stuck your ass out." I gave her a mock glare, and she returned an unrepentant smirk. "Here, buy the purse, too."

I paid up, and we left the store. "Next stop, jewellery," Nichele said determinedly.

"No need. That's covered."

"Oh, yeah?" she challenged. "What have you got?"

"I've got a heavy gold necklace with a big honkin' emerald in it," I told her. "It should be fine with the dress colour, and it'll work with that deep halter V-neck."

She eyed me quizzically. "Where did that come from? I

don't remember ever seeing you wear anything like that."

I did my best nonchalant shrug. "When was the last time you saw me dress up? Robert bought me lots of beautiful things. I just don't wear them very often."

All true, though completely unrelated. I really hate lying.

"Okay," she agreed. "You're right, the emerald will probably be fine. What about earrings? You need some nice ones. You're going to wear your hair up."

"I am?"

"Yes."

I sighed. "Yes, ma'am. Take me, I'm yours. Find me the perfect earrings."

By three o'clock, I had everything I needed and I was getting jittery. "Nichele, you know, this is such a pain in the ass. I hate dressing up," I whined.

She stopped in her tracks. "You're nervous! You really like this guy, don't you?"

"No! I mean, yeah, I like him, but it's not, you know..."

I shut up. Better she should think I was nervous about my date. I could hardly explain I was nervous because I was going to spy on international criminals and lives could be at stake. Including my own.

She bounced her eyebrows, giving me a conspiratorial look. "Come on, take me back to your hotel and I'll help you get ready. You're going to knock him dead."

"I hope not," I muttered.

"What?"

"Nothing."

Back at the hotel room, she pushed me into the bathroom. "Shower."

"Yes, ma'am."

I came out wearing a towel. "Don't you have a robe or

something?" Nichele scolded. "You're going to freeze while I do your hair."

I shrugged. "I never wear night clothes at home. I didn't think to bring any."

"But what if your date goes well?" She nudged me, leering. "You should have some sexy little thing to slip into."

I showed her my teeth. "If my date goes well, I'll tear off his clothes and bang him up against the wall. No lingerie required."

"You're such a savage," she chided, grinning.

I wrapped up in a blanket while she fiddled with my hair. When she was done, I eyed the simple, elegant updo in the mirror. "You're sure about this?"

"I'm sure." She cracked open the makeup bottle.

I grabbed her hand. "Don't put that shit on my face. I hate it. It all goops up and falls into my wrinkles. I look like a half-melted topographical model of the Grand Canyon. And I'm afraid to move my face all night in case a piece cracks off."

She shook her head. "Trust me. Makeup has changed since you were a teenager. Which is probably the last time you wore any."

"And?"

"And you should try this. If you really hate it, there's still time to take it off."

"Okay." I let her work on me without comment for a while. "Nichele?"

"Yeah?"

"Thanks. I'm sorry I'm being such a bag. I just really hate this."

"It's okay," she assured me. "But why are you going if you hate it? Do you really like this guy that much? Do you think it's smart to pretend you want to do this?"

I made a face. "He knows I hate it. He probably hates it, too. We just have to go. It's a business thing."

"You live a very strange life."

"You have no idea," I agreed.

CHAPTER 8

"Scram." I pushed Nichele affectionately out the door. "He's going to be here in ten minutes, and I'm nervous enough without you hovering."

She patted my arm. "You'll be fine. Just be yourself. Have fun. You look super-hot."

"Thanks to you. See you."

I closed the door on her smile and wandered over to look in the mirror. Calling Nichele had been a smart decision. She had worked wonders with my hair and makeup. I actually looked like I might belong at a black tie gala.

Now if I could just restrain my normal temperament and vocabulary, everything would be fine. Being myself would definitely be a bad idea.

I had a sudden mental image of letting fly with a rip-roaring fart halfway through the elegant meal, and snickered.

"You behave," I said severely to my reflection, struggling to quell its wicked grin.

A soft knock made me jump. When I opened the door, my jaw dropped. Kane filled the doorway, clad in a charcoal suit expertly tailored to his broad shoulders and taut midsection. His silvered temples looked impossibly distinguished with that short, dark hair. His freshly shaven square face looked rested, and I caught the faintest whiff of citrus. Not even the scar through his eyebrow and the bump from his badly healed broken nose could detract from the whole package. The man was breathtaking.

"Wow," I said inadequately.

Kane looked like he was doing a bit of deep breathing, too, and his grey eyes darkened. "Wow, yourself," he said finally, his deep baritone a little husky. We exchanged an awkward smile.

He reached into his pocket. "Don't forget this," he said, opening the velvet box. He lifted the necklace out and placed it around my neck, brushing my skin. As he took his hands away, he let one of the tendrils of my hair slide through his fingers.

He took a step back.

"Oh," he said after a short pause. "Rings." He reached into his pocket, withdrew a heavy gold band, and slipped it on his left ring finger. He held out his closed hand. "For you."

I held out my hand, and he dropped two rings into my palm. One was a plain band, the other an enormous diamond. I gazed up at him wide-eyed. "Holy crap, does this thing come with a bodyguard?"

He grinned. "Me."

"I've already got a ring," I told him, showing him the one I wore. Robert had had it custom made for me, a top-quality half-carat in a simple, sophisticated setting. It looked tiny beside the one in my hand.

"That's a nice ring, but it's not quite the bling we need for tonight," he said. "Put that one on your other hand."

I slipped on the pair of rings and mimed dragging my hand. "I'm going to have one arm longer than the other after tonight."

He laughed. "Let's go."

I grabbed my new purse, already regretting that it wasn't big enough to carry my waist pouch, and sighed as the door closed behind me.

When the elevator doors opened on the lobby, Kane offered me his arm, and I took it, smiling up at him. Even in my high heels, I was still a good three inches shorter than he was. I relished the novelty. If I'd worn these heels when I was with Robert, I would have towered over him by six inches.

When we entered the lobby, I froze.

"*Shit!*" I swung Kane around and hid behind him. "Take off your ring, quick," I hissed as I put my hands on his chest, yanking the rings off my finger and dropping them into his breast pocket.

He slid his arms unhurriedly around me and leaned down. His lips brushed my ear. "Relax," he whispered, his breath sending a rush of heat through my body.

Behind my back, I felt him remove his ring. He straightened, smiling down at me, and took both my hands in his, palming the ring. Getting myself under control with an effort, I smiled back and slid my hands down his chest, dropping the ring into his pocket with the others.

He offered his arm again, and we turned and made our way into the lobby. Nichele bounced up from one of the wing chairs, grinning.

"Hi, Aydan!"

I cut my eyes at her, silently promising her a slow death. She smiled and extended her hand to Kane. "You must be John," she chirped. "It's so nice to meet you."

I sighed. "John, this is Nichele Brown. Nichele, John

Kane."

He took her hand graciously and bowed over it, very European. Nichele's expression melted, and I knew I was in for some serious grilling the next day. Assuming I let her live.

At that moment the valet appeared, oozing respect. "Your car is ready, sir."

Kane thanked him courteously and discreetly handed him a bill. A large bill, judging by the valet's reaction.

"Nichele, it was a pleasure to meet you," Kane's baritone voice was pure velvet, and I could see from Nichele's tiny shiver that it had the same effect on her as it had on me. "We need to get going now," he added. "Have a nice evening."

He drew me toward the door, and my jaw hit the floor all over again. "You've got to be kidding me. Your 'wheels' are an Audi R8?" I demanded. The sleek, low-slung car purred sensuously at the curb. "Pop the hood, I want to see," I urged him softly.

He shook his head, smiling as he leaned close. "No," he whispered. "In the first place, you have to keep that dress clean at least until we get to the party. And in the second place, elegant ladies don't look under the hood."

"Lucky there are no elegant ladies present, then," I whispered back. "C'mon, please?"

He shook his head again, those sexy laugh lines crinkling around his eyes.

"Tease," I accused him.

He opened the passenger door for me, grinning. I did my best to slide in without flashing the bystanders, but my skirt slithered up my thighs when I sank into the low seat. As soon as Kane closed the door, I buckled in and tugged the skirt down again, willing it to stay put.

He came around to the driver's side and got in, buckling his seatbelt, too. "Ready?" he asked.

"Ready as I'll ever be."

Delving into his pocket as we pulled away, he fished out the rings and handed them to me. "Let's try this again."

"Sorry about that," I apologized. "I brought her in as a wardrobe consultant, but I should have known she'd do something like that."

"It's all right. The end result was worth it."

I stroked my hand over the dashboard. "How about if we skip the party and go for a joyride instead? I can't believe I actually get to ride in an R8. Is it yours?"

Kane shook his head. "Are you kidding? No. Unfortunately. It's just on loan for the evening, same as the rings. But at least we'll get to take it out on the highway. Harchman's place is out by Bragg Creek."

I beamed at him. "Life is good."

While the fine automobile devoured the miles, we strategized. "What exactly do you need to scope out?" I asked. "Couldn't you just pull floor plans from the building permits?"

Kane shot me a piercing look. "Most people wouldn't think of that."

I shrugged. "You must have come across my stint as an architectural draftsman when you were investigating me in March. I did practically nothing but construction drawings and permit applications."

"We did. I just never fail to find your career path... interesting. Draftsperson, computer tech, bookkeeper. It's an unusual mix."

I lifted a shoulder. "The drafting certificate was quick and easy to get when I finished high school and wanted to get a job. And I never really intended to work with computers, I just took some courses so I could deal with the network at the architectural firm. Bookkeeping is what I really like to do."

"We already have all the floor plans and the site plan," he informed me after a short pause. "Webb also managed to quietly obtain the installation diagrams for the security system." He grinned. "Don't ever try to hide anything from Webb. That kid can sniff out information you don't even know you have."

I laughed. "He's pretty amazing. Lucky he works for the good guys."

Kane sobered. "You can say that again. But to answer your original question, I'm going to be looking at the position and distribution of security personnel. I'm also going to be watching for anything that looks like a structural change from the registered floor plans. And I'll check to see if there's any additional electronic or physical security besides what we already know about."

"Do you have a copy of the plans with you?" I asked. "I'd like to take a look, too."

"No, sorry. I should have shown them to you earlier. I didn't want to have anything with us that could arouse suspicion, so I left them at home."

I shrugged. "Oh well. So what's your strategy for wandering through somebody's private residence without arousing suspicion?"

"That's where it gets complicated," he admitted. "It's not just the private residence. There's a guest house and several other lavish buildings on the property. It's quite an ostentatious layout."

"Excellent. That helps."

"Why do you say that?" He eyed me with interest.

"Ostentatious means there's somebody who just can't wait to give the grand tour to somebody who's suitably impressed. Is Harchman married?"

Kane nodded. "Twenty years. His wife's name is Maria. Not a happy marriage, from what we can determine. Seems he's got a roving eye."

"Perfect. Either he or Maria will be looking for a bit of admiration for their property. If it's him, I'll suck up. If it's her, you can."

Kane chuckled. "I'm pretty sure you'll be the one doing the sucking up. Harchman likes to be known as a high roller. Classic attention-seeker. His wife keeps a low profile."

"It still might be smart for you to show some attention to Maria," I said slowly. "If he's that much of an asshole, she'd probably appreciate a little gallantry. That could get you in some doors. If Harchman's hiding something, she might not know about it. She might let you in where he wouldn't."

Kane looked thoughtful. "You're right. That's a good idea. We may not meet her at all, though. According to what we've been able to find out, she doesn't often attend this type of affair."

"Okay. So, next question, how the heck am I supposed to wander through all these buildings looking for a network? I thought we were just going to a dinner party. If I zone out for a few seconds while I'm sitting in a chair, nobody will notice. But you know I fall down if I access the network when I'm standing." I grimaced. "And now I have to balance on high heels at the same time."

We drove in silence for a few minutes while I racked my brain for an idea.

"We need to agree on some sort of signal that you're

going to try to access the network," Kane said. "You give me the signal, and I'll make sure I'm holding you up. If you get in at all, it'll only be for a second or two. You might not even have time to fall down."

"Well, it's not perfect, but that's probably about the best we can do," I agreed. "What's the signal?"

"Put your arm around me and lean your head on my shoulder. That way if you go limp for a second, I can hold you up without being too obvious."

I sighed. "Okay. It's a plan."

"I really don't like this," Kane grumbled. "I know it needs to be done, but I just hate to put you in the line of fire again."

"Well, I won't be in the line of fire." I tried to reassure us both. "A short, nondescript, dead man will be."

"You're sure you can do this."

"Hell, no," I said grimly.

CHAPTER 9

The Audi hugged the road on the way into the foothills. Kane and I exchanged the fervent smiles of a pair of car fanatics as we rounded the first curves.

"I suppose it would be unbecoming for an officer of the law to speed," I suggested innocently.

Kane gave me a predatory grin. "Lucky I'm an energy consultant tonight." The purr of the big V10 engine deepened to a velvet growl and the car effortlessly accelerated, pressing me back into the seat.

"Ooh, yeah," I crooned. "Come on, baby!"

Kane glanced over, the corner of his mouth crooked up. "Do you need a moment alone with the car?"

I smirked at him, unabashed. "Yes."

"Too bad. Looks like we're here."

I sighed, eyeing the discreet sign beside the overgrown laneway as he braked. "Are you sure we can't just keep driving? I know where there's a road that this car could really sink its teeth into..."

"I'd love to," he assured me. "But duty calls."

"Duty sucks," I muttered as we pulled up to elegant wrought-iron gates. The uniformed attendant examined the expensive-looking invitation Kane displayed, and nodded to the gatehouse guard. The gates swung open and we purred sedately up the driveway.

The narrow strip of asphalt wound through heavy spruce forest for several hundred yards. As we swung around the final bend, a dramatic vista opened before us where the land fell away into a rolling valley with a spectacular mountain panorama spread out behind it.

We drove up the final hill, passing a parking lot on our right just before we arrived at a cul-de-sac where other guests were disembarking from their luxury cars. I spotted a couple of Vipers and a brand-new Lamborghini in the mix.

I nudged Kane. "Jeez, talk about embarrassing for those guys. They must hate it when they show up at a party and somebody else is driving the same Viper as they are."

He snickered. "Oh, the humiliation. But I think I could take it."

"No shit."

We pulled up to the curb and Kane turned to me. "Ready to do this?"

I groaned. "Okay, I'm putting on my well-behaved lah-de-dah act now. See if you can stand in front of the car door to block the view. If I manage to get out of this car without exposing myself, it'll be a friggin' miracle."

He chuckled and got out of the car, pacing around to the passenger side to open the door for me. He stooped, offering me a courtly hand. With intense concentration, I remembered to keep my knees together, unfurling my legs out the door and coming to my feet as gracefully as possible.

The perfidious skirt slithered up my thighs again, but not far enough to expose anything but a tiny sliver of the lace at the top of my stockings. I kept my face pleasantly composed while Kane and I strolled away from the car.

"I'm going to kill Nichele," I grated through my teeth as I smiled genteelly up at Kane.

"I'm going to write her a thank-you note," he rumbled in my ear. "You're stunning in that dress."

I managed a more genuine smile, hiding the shiver of heat that raced through me. "Thanks."

Kane turned over the keys to the valet and we proceeded along a paved walkway, cresting a gentle slope. We both paused, taking in the layout. I resisted the urge to gawp open-mouthed.

To our right, an enormous fountain splashed lavishly over a well-endowed bronze mermaid. The walkway meandered in curves down the side of the slope, past two sprawling slate-clad buildings with copper roofs.

A small lake nestled at the bottom of the slope, surrounded by a boardwalk. Several fountains played in the lake, their spray modulated and choreographed to the music that emanated from speakers embedded every ten feet or so along the low wall that defined the walkway.

Beside the lake, an open two-storey structure seemed to be the focus of activity, with tables and chairs set up on both levels. Other buildings dotted the landscape, each expertly designed to complement the layout and landscaping.

Kane tucked my hand into the crook of his arm and moved forward, rousing me from my daze. I glanced up at him. He looked confident and relaxed, his face pleasant and open. There was no sign of the intense focus I knew existed behind his eyes.

Nervousness skittered down my spine. Kane was a highly trained secret agent, putting his life on the line to protect national security. I was an idiot civilian. What the hell was I doing here? My ineptness could kill him. Could kill both of us. And if we failed, a lot of other innocent people could get hurt, too. I sent out a mental plea to whatever gods might be listening.

Please, please, don't let me screw up.

I willed the tension out of my body and pulled on my 'polite company' personality like an objectionable second skin. I let the high heels and slithery dress take over, changing my usual stride into the smooth, undulating movement Nichele called my supermodel walk.

As Kane and I strolled down the walkway, I straightened my spine, and heads turned as we passed. I felt a moment of misgiving. Kane's breadth of shoulder and his six-foot-four height drew immediate attention, and I was over six feet tall in my heels, too. We weren't exactly unobtrusive.

Another uniformed staff member was stationed halfway down the path, guiding the flow of guests. "Welcome," he greeted us. "Please join us in the gazebo." He gestured toward the two-storey building by the lake, and Kane thanked him graciously as we followed the pathway down.

I struggled to control my face when we arrived at the so-called gazebo. It was an enormous structure. Each level sported a full bar, and it had tables and chairs enough for at least fifty people per floor. Waiters and waitresses circulated with trays of hors d'oeuvres and drinks. With difficulty, I suppressed my natural impulse to dive into an immediate feeding frenzy. As I nibbled noncommittally on an appetizer, a waiter appeared beside us, offering white wine from the tray of glasses that he carried.

I met his eyes, creating a personal connection. "What is the grape?" I murmured, pitching my voice so that it would only be audible to him.

"It's our house white," he responded. "It's a

Chardonnay."

I let the faintest breath of disappointment tinge my "Oh." I smiled politely at him. "Thank you."

As I reached for a glass, he said quickly, "If you'd prefer something else, I'd be happy to bring it for you."

I let my smile reach my eyes. "That's very kind, but I don't want to trouble you."

"It's no trouble at all, ma'am," he assured me. "What would you like?"

I let my voice go a little husky. "I'd love a Sauvignon Blanc."

He swallowed visibly and turned to look up at Kane. "And for you, sir?"

"Do you have any single-malt scotch?" Kane asked him politely.

"Yes, sir, I believe we have several."

Kane nodded satisfaction. "Don't bother bringing our drinks, then. We'll go up to the bar so I can see what you have, and we'll get the wine there, too."

The waiter hovered indecisively. "It's no bother. I'll check with the bartender about the scotch and be right back."

Kane shook his head. "It's quite all right. Thank you." He discreetly laid a twenty on the waiter's tray and put his hand on the small of my back to guide me through the crowd. As we made our way slowly toward the bar, I noticed our waiter weaving his way expertly through the crush. He caught the bartender's attention and indicated us with a nod.

I smiled up at Kane. "Nicely done."

When we arrived at the bar, the bartender greeted us cheerfully. "I hear you're looking for a Sauvignon Blanc," he addressed me.

"That would be lovely, thank you," I responded, giving

him full eye contact. He smiled warmly and reached for a bottle.

Beside me, a short man in a tux turned, his gaze locking onto my boobs before struggling upward to my face.

He held my eyes as he leaned toward the bartender. "Don't give her that plonk, Dave. Open a bottle of the good stuff."

"Yes, sir, Mr. Harchman," Dave responded, and vanished behind the bar.

I let an intimate smile spread over my face. "Mr. Harchman. Our host for this lovely event. How nice to meet you." I infused the word 'nice' with a warm, husky undertone as I surveyed him as though we were the only two people in the room.

He stretched to his full height, which I guessed to be about five-seven, his pot belly winking with diamond shirt studs. Enormous diamond rings glittered on his pudgy fingers, and the strength of his cologne turned my stomach. I wasn't sure, but I thought I could see the plugs in his thinning blond hair. His pale blue eyes slithered south to my cleavage again.

He seized my hand, planting a wet kiss on my knuckles. I detected a brush of tongue, and clamped down my reflexive shudder with every bit of control I owned.

"Please, call me Lawrence," he murmured, still clutching my hand in a moist grip. "And you are?"

"Aydan Kane," I introduced myself. "And this is my husband, John."

I turned to discover Kane had faded away. I spotted him some distance down the bar, apparently discussing scotch with the bartender. I tossed my head and turned back to Harchman.

"It seems I'm temporarily without a husband." I gave the comment a meaningful intonation and watched Harchman's avid response with carefully concealed distaste.

Dave the bartender arrived with a glass, and I used the opportunity to disengage my hand from Harchman's clingy grasp.

"Thank you, Dave," I said warmly, and he smiled and nodded. I swirled the wine around the glass, inhaling its aroma, and then sipped, savouring it.

"What do you think?" Harchman inquired eagerly.

"It's quite unusual," I told him, realizing as I spoke that Kane had reappeared behind me. "I've never had an oaked Sauvignon Blanc."

Harchman nodded enthusiastically. "Do you like it?"

I sipped again, slowly. As I lowered the glass again, I flicked the tip of my tongue against the rim of the glass, catching a tiny drop of wine. "The oak gives it just the right amount of... texture," I purred. "I always think a touch of roughness makes things so much more interesting, don't you?"

A flush rose above Harchman's collar as his eyes glazed over. Nice to know I could still do that. I leaned languidly back against Kane, glancing up at him over my shoulder. "John, this is Lawrence Harchman. Lawrence, I'd like you to meet my absent husband, John."

Kane's arm went around my waist in a proprietary gesture as he extended his hand to Harchman. "Mr. Harchman. Pleasure to meet you."

Harchman straightened. "Please call me Lawrence. And you're with...?"

"Kane Consulting," Kane informed him. "I'm looking forward to your presentation tonight."

Harchman nodded and his eyes drifted back to the circulating guests. I leaned toward him, dislodging Kane's arm, and reached for his pudgy hand again. "Lawrence," I murmured intimately. "It was lovely to meet you. And your home is magnificent."

His gaze darted between Kane and me, assessing us. Then he smiled and leaned closer to me. "This is just the gazebo," he said. "Wait 'til you see the house."

I did my best wide-eyed admiration. "I'd love to. I always wanted to be an interior decorator. I'd love to see everything you're willing to show me." I almost gagged as I said it, but apparently Harchman was full of himself to the point of being totally oblivious.

He gave me a slimy smile. "I'd be happy to give you a personal tour later."

"Thank you, I'll look forward to it," I lied. "And now I suppose we shouldn't keep you from your guests any longer."

Harchman nodded. "Come and find me after the presentation."

"I will," I murmured.

He wove his way out into the crowd, and I sipped the wine again, relaxing against the bar and letting my eyes roam casually across the gazebo. As soon as Harchman vanished in the crush, I stepped back beside Kane.

"I think I'm going to puke," I whispered.

He chuckled. "You did fine. You're full of surprises. I didn't know you were an oenophile."

"I'm not. I'm a dedicated beer drinker. I learned the lingo so I didn't look like a total idiot at Robert's business dinners."

"Well, you had me fooled." He put his arm around me and leaned down, hiding his lips in my hair. "Try the network."

I slipped my arm around him and leaned my head on his shoulder. Concentrating on being Robert, I stepped into the void, then immediately backed out, heart pounding. Pain slammed into my head and I controlled my face and reflexive profanity with a supreme effort. Kane's arm was tight around me, and I stood on my own feet again as quickly and unobtrusively as possible.

Kane smiled down at me. His facial expression and body language were casual, but his eyes were filled with concern. I smiled back, linking my arms around his neck as I stood on tiptoe to place my lips near his ear.

My mind went momentarily blank when his arms closed around me, pressing me against his hard-muscled body. I refocused with difficulty.

"It's here," I whispered. "Broadcasting right out here. What the hell are they doing?"

He shook his head as we drew apart. "Let's circulate."

Kane moved confidently through the crowd, greeting people he apparently knew as business associates and making small talk. I followed, thankful I hadn't seen anyone I recognized. I laughed and chatted with a couple of people, channelling my alien business persona with more ease than I'd expected. Funny how the skills you never wanted to learn are the ones that stay with you.

I was turning to snag a curried shrimp from a passing tray when a movement at the entrance caught my eye. Kane and I exchanged a glance at the sight of the two large black-clad men who moved purposefully through the crowd, their eyes in constant motion while they scanned faces. They both wore security earpieces, and when one of them turned sideways to avoid a guest, I glimpsed a holster under his suit jacket.

My heart kicked my ribs when the second man's intent gaze fell on me, and I tried to hold my face in a pleasant expression. I smothered a sigh of relief when his eyes roamed past without reaction. Kane's arm slipped around my waist, and I managed a plastic smile while he introduced me to yet another person I wouldn't remember in ten seconds.

The two men concluded their walk-through and vanished, and Kane leaned down. "Okay?" he whispered against my ear.

I gave him my best confident smile. "Fine," I said, and concentrated on slowing my pounding pulse.

Willing calm, I nibbled a few more of the delicious hors d'oeuvres and finished my wine. No sooner had I drained the glass than the waiter appeared with a fresh one. I thanked him, Kane tipped him again, and I raised my glass in thanks to Dave the bartender as well.

The evening dragged on. My feet hurt and my face was stiff from smiling by the time dinner was announced.

I sighed silently as we made our way arm in arm up the walkway toward the main house. Kane must have felt the rise and fall of my rib cage, because he leaned down to my ear. "Hang in there. The food's going to be excellent."

I gave him my first sincere smile of the evening, my spirits rising. He knew the way to my heart.

CHAPTER 10

When we entered the magnificent foyer of the house, I let go of Kane's arm. "I'm going to go and freshen up."

He nodded, and I moved across the marble-paved space in the direction I'd seen other women take. Sure enough, there was a powder room a short distance down the hallway. I chatted politely with several other women while I waited my turn.

Once inside, I sat on the toilet, balanced carefully, and tried the network, wearing Robert's skin. Again, I popped effortlessly into the void and quickly backed out. This time I couldn't suppress a grunt when agony knifed through my head, and I hastily flushed the toilet to cover the sound while I held my skull and hissed quiet but sincere invective.

When the worst of the pain subsided, I moved to the sink, washing my hands and checking my makeup. Nichele hadn't lied about its quality. It was actually staying put, and I looked the same as when she'd finished with me hours before. Amazing. And I hadn't even wrecked the dress yet.

Kane was waiting for me in the foyer. I glided over the slippery marble tiles, concentrating fiercely on looking lithe and relaxed while keeping my footing in the high heels. Apparently I succeeded, because he eyed me appreciatively as I joined him. Or maybe he was just a really good actor. I decided to call it a success regardless.

I took his proffered arm and we paused at the entrance of the enormous dining room. The two large men were in evidence again, but they had split up, hovering on opposite sides of the room. Their hard eyes searched the crowd. Kane's gaze drifted over them without a change of expression, and I knew he was noting every detail of the room and the crowd as well, but far less obtrusively than Harchman's minions.

"Nothing like a nice, intimate dinner for a hundred or so of your closest friends," I whispered. "I wonder if the Harchmans actually live here, or if they secretly go to their real house when the party's over."

Kane chuckled, looking and sounding completely at ease. "This is their real house." I shook my head in disbelief.

We took seats at a table near the edge of the room, our backs to the wall, and I resisted the urge to kick the shoes off my sore feet. I almost never wear high heels, but I'm smart enough to know that if you ever take them off, it's really damn hard to put them back on again for the rest of the night.

I focused on keeping my back straight and my knees together. The acrylic nails felt thick and foreign, and I folded my hands casually in my lap, trying to abstain from picking at them.

"Talk to me," I whispered to Kane. "I'm losing it. If I don't concentrate on conversation, I'm going to get sucked into the network. And I'll create a simulation of me in my coveralls drinking beer and tinkering with one of my cars." The image was so inviting that I smiled, relaxing unconsciously.

I nearly leaped out of my skin at the bite on my earlobe. "Aydan!" Kane's baritone growled in my ear. "Stay focused!"

I jerked up straight again, my heart pounding with the realization that I'd almost blown my cover.

Well, the heart rate might also be related to the fact that a very sexy man had just nibbled my ear. I met his eyes, looking deeply and letting him see some of my reaction.

"You've got my attention," I murmured.

His eyes dilated, but he gave his head a quick shake as he leaned back in his chair. "Are you still renovating your house?" he asked casually. "Did you ever finish that bathroom?"

I switched gears to polite conversation. "I finished the ensuite I was working on in March. Now my main one is starting to have little problems here and there. I'm not sure whether I'll tackle it this summer or not. I'm pretty busy with my garden and outdoor work."

We made innocuous small talk until three other couples joined us at our round table. I concentrated on the introductions and the impersonal conversation that followed until the first course was served.

As Kane had promised, the food was truly superb. A rich lobster bisque was followed by a light, crisp salad with hints of tropical fruit. A small portion of delicate roasted butternut squash ravioli followed in a sumptuous cream sauce. Our empty plates were whisked away, and a tomato and sage sorbet arrived, cleansing our palates for the next course.

I felt Kane's gaze on me, and glanced up to catch him observing me with amusement. I grinned back. "I'm beginning to feel compensated for my suffering," I joked softly.

I turned back to my plate to give the roast lamb and vegetable mousse the attention it deserved, and made a valiant effort to stay engaged in the conversation, privately wishing everybody would just shut up and let me enjoy the meal. A delectable cheese course came and went, and while the hazelnut crème brulée and coffee were being served, Harchman began the software presentation.

I listened with half an ear. Most of the technology and jargon went over my head, so I occupied myself instead by surreptitiously people-watching. Harchman was an uninspired speaker, but his presentation was mercifully short. After a question period, the tables were cleared off, and we were invited to the salon for after-dinner drinks.

The salon proved to be a slightly smaller version of the cavernous dining room, and guests circulated comfortably around yet another bar. After a while, I manoeuvred Kane into a corner and leaned close, slipping my arm around him. It seemed the network was being broadcast throughout the entire house, because once again I ducked in and then quickly out.

Grateful for the string quartet sawing away next to us, I didn't even try to suppress my involuntary cry of distress when I re-entered the real world. When the punishing pain receded, I realized Kane held me crushed against him with one arm. His other hand supported my head while he trailed hungry kisses over my throat. I regained my balance with difficulty, slipping my arms around his neck. His grip loosened and we gazed into each other's eyes from close range.

"You sure give a girl mixed messages," I joked.

I felt the strain leave his shoulders as he smiled down at me. "You went down like a ton of bricks that time," he muttered against my neck. "Took me by surprise. Are you all right?"

"Just the usual," I whispered back. "It hurts a little more each time, when I go in and out frequently like this."

He drew back to look into my eyes. "You need to stop, then. I won't be able to cover if it gets any worse."

"Okay, I'll give it a break."

He released me and I stepped back. As I did, the two black-clad men interposed themselves between us and greeted Kane pleasantly. Kane caught my eye and I turned to stroll away, responding to his almost imperceptible signal.

I jerked back when I came chest to face with Harchman. Judging by his fixed stare, he had no complaint.

"Lawrence," I gushed. "Your presentation was fascinating. You're such a masterful speaker." I suffered a momentary pang of apprehension that a bolt of lightning would strike me dead, but nothing happened. Maybe the gods thought it was all for a good cause.

His puny chest puffed up. God save me from man boobs.

He moistly clutched my hand. "Thank you, my dear. And now I'd like to give you that tour I promised."

I gave him my best dazzling smile. "That would be wonderful. I'll get John." I turned and beckoned to Kane, who was still involved in conversation. He made a move toward me, but one of the men grasped his arm. He frowned and the man let go, but as Kane stepped forward, both men blocked his path again.

Harchman watched the interchange with a smirk. "I took the liberty of making sure your husband would be occupied. I'm sure we'll enjoy our tour much more without him."

A cold, slow trickle of apprehension oozed down my

spine. "Oh, but he'll be so disappointed if he doesn't get to see your beautiful home," I argued lightly. "Architecture is one of his greatest hobbies."

Harchman shrugged. "Beautiful women are one of my greatest hobbies. And I find husbands hamper my enjoyment of that hobby." He took my elbow, sliding his hand intimately up my arm and grazing my breast. "Come, my dear."

Trying to hide my fear, I glanced over at Kane again. Both men were blocking his path, and it was clear that short of a physical altercation, he wouldn't be able to break free. I couldn't even make eye contact with him anymore.

Not knowing what else to do, I let Harchman draw me away. I didn't dare make a scene and blow our cover, if it wasn't already blown. I swallowed hard and concentrated on keeping my posture relaxed, drawing a deep breath in an attempt to slow my racing pulse.

Please let him be just a garden-variety pervert. God, please don't let him be like the soulless animals who'd captured me before...

I pasted on a smile and nodded with as much interest as I could fake while he talked, guiding me further away from the crowd, down an empty hallway and into the private area of the house. While we made our way deeper into the labyrinth, I did my best to pay attention to the details Kane had mentioned in our strategy session.

At least I was getting to see the house. If I managed to escape... no, dammit, calm down. I was fine. Everything was going to be fine. *When* I saw Kane again, I could pass on information about the layout.

Fortunately, Harchman didn't seem to require any actual conversational input from me. As long as I nodded and exclaimed and looked worshipful, he kept babbling and showing me through the house.

Kane's earlier mention of Harchman's roving eyes proved to be incomplete. He also had roving hands. Icky, sweaty, roving hands. I avoided them when I could and tolerated the rest, pretending fascination with his self-important monologue. I began to relax as time passed. So far, it seemed Harchman was just a harmless asshole.

He turned suddenly and I backed away a step, fetching up against the wall behind me. He leaned close, his moist hand sliding down from my waist to my thigh.

"Would you like to see something really exciting?" he asked fervently.

I clutched his wayward hand in both of my own, feigning eagerness. "Oh, yes, Lawrence!"

He gave me an oily smile as he placed his thumb on a scanner beside the door next to us. When the latch released, he swung the door open, gesturing me inside and copping a feel when I stepped in front of him.

"The nerve centre of the house," he exclaimed proudly.

I scanned the banks of servers and monitors, my heart pounding. Could the server for the brainwave-driven network be in here? I turned back to Harchman, fiddling with his bow tie and trailing my fingertips down his pathetic chest.

"Oh, Lawrence! This looks so complicated! What does it all do?" I breathed.

I was punished for my enthusiasm when he locked both hands on my ass and ground his crotch against me. He was so much shorter than I that my thigh was all he could reach, but the sensation was revolting nevertheless.

I pulled away, clutching his hand and dragging him

toward the nearest terminal. "What does this one do?"

"Everything in the house is controlled from here," he said with a grand flourish of his pudgy hand. "All the security cameras, networks, internet, climate control, everything."

I read between the lines. He didn't have a clue.

A large man rose from behind one of the banks of servers. "Mr. Harchman," he said deferentially.

"This is the security station," Harchman burbled, pulling me forward. I eagerly surveyed the screens, doing a quick count of displays and trying to identify the camera locations from their point of view. "Everything is monitored twenty-four hours a day," he continued, puffed up with his own importance.

I plastered on what I hoped was an ingenuous expression of wide-eyed awe. "This is so impressive. But how do you stay comfortable knowing that you're surrounded by forest, so far away from the city? What if you needed the police?"

Harchman patted my hand. "I employ my own security detail. The entire perimeter is patrolled by guards and dogs. I can afford whatever protection I need." He slid his hand over my ass again as he guided me back toward the door.

A dumpy, black-haired woman in a baggy grey sweatsuit popped into the doorway.

"Larry!" she barked, her black brows snapping together in an unflattering scowl. "What the hell are you doing?"

"Maria, darling," Harchman responded smoothly, mercifully removing his hand. "You know I prefer you to call me Lawrence."

"How about if I just call you a lying, cheating pig?" she snarled. "Get your disgusting floozy out of here!"

"Now, darling," Harchman replied, apparently unfazed.

"I was just offering one of our guests a tour. She's very interested in interior decorating."

"Well, she can go and be interested somewhere else. You have ten seconds to get her out of here, or I'll call one of your precious security guards and have them drag her out. Your choice."

Harchman took my arm. "I'm sorry, but we'll have to cut our tour short. My wife suffers from migraine headaches, and she's not at her best right now." He ushered me past the glowering woman.

"And keep your hands off her ass!" Maria screeched as we turned the corner. "You disgusting pig!"

For a woman with a migraine, she had remarkably good vocal projection.

CHAPTER 11

We took a direct route back through the immense house, and Harchman kept his hands more or less to himself. Soon I heard the murmur of conversation, and we arrived at the salon by another door. Stepping gratefully into the crowded room again, I turned to offer an insincere thank you to Harchman for the tour, but he had already lost interest. He vanished into the crowd without a backward glance, shaking hands and greeting people.

I let out a heartfelt sigh and scanned the crush of guests for Kane. Standing head and shoulders taller than most of the people there, he should have been easy to spot, but he was nowhere to be seen. My relief vanished and worry flooded in to take its place. What if the two men had taken him? What if he was being tortured, or if he was lying dead even now?

I took a deep breath to calm my racing heart and moved nonchalantly through the crowd, heading for the front door. As I walked, I scoured the room with my eyes, hoping against hope.

I controlled my panic with an effort as I stepped outside and strained my eyes in the twilight. The grounds were illuminated by a fairyland of tiny white lights, and the effect would have been enchanting if I hadn't been desperately searching for one tall, broad-shouldered figure. I could make out small knots and couples of party guests here and there on the grounds, but it was too dim to identify anyone.

Heading for the walkway, I peered into the dusk, trying to stay calm and formulate a plan. Logic. Okay. Two possibilities. One, Kane was captured. Or two, we'd simply gotten separated, and he was looking for me just as I was looking for him.

I dealt with the most horrifying possibility first. If he'd been captured, the best thing I could do would be to notify his team immediately. I wasn't about to attempt a daring rescue by myself. I shuddered, my mind shying away from all the dire possibilities. My own experiences earlier in the year had left me with no illusions about what Kane would be suffering. If he was still alive.

I yanked my mind away to the better of the two possibilities. Maybe he was looking for me. Think like Kane. What would he do if he saw me being ushered away helplessly? He didn't have any reason to believe we had been compromised. I doubted he would make a scene if he thought our cover was still intact.

I blew out a breath through my teeth, still scanning the grounds. A movement caught my eye from the vicinity of the guest house, the second-largest building. A tall figure strode hurriedly up the path toward the house, and my heart gave a painful contraction when I recognized Kane's broad shoulders and athletic gait. I trotted up the path and called his name softly.

At the sound of my voice, his head jerked around. In a few long strides, he closed the distance between us and swept me into his arms. "Aydan," he said urgently. "Are you all right?"

I held him tightly, trembling with relief. "I'm fine," I assured him. "Are you okay?"

"Fine," he echoed. He rested his forehead briefly against my hair, then released me and took my hand, turning toward the house.

"I got the house tour," I told him quietly. "I did the best I could to watch for the things you mentioned. And I think I know where the server room is."

He squeezed my hand. "Good work. I got the rest of the buildings. Lucky we found each other. I was just about to make a major scene. I didn't know what was happening to you, and I was afraid to wait any longer."

"Same here," I replied. "I thought you'd been captured." As we approached the buildings, I glanced up at him. "Do you want me to check the guest house for the network?"

Kane paused, surveying me in the dusk. "Are you up to it?"

"Can we get into it inconspicuously?"

He shrugged. "It's a guest house. We're guests." We walked arm in arm up to the entrance of the building and stepped into the foyer as if we belonged there. The opulent decor stunned me. Wood, glass, and stone made a warm background for blocky, sophisticated soft seating in earth tones.

Kane led me to one of the chairs. "Sit this time."

I sank into the chair and he perched on the arm, holding me close against his chest. Just a tired couple taking a break from the party. I summoned up Robert again, stepping in and then out of the network one last time. Red-hot pokers jabbed into my brain, and my body jerked as it strained to curl up. I ground my teeth to hold back the profanity that fought to escape, and tasted blood. I breathed deeply against Kane's shirt for a few moments, waiting for the pain to subside enough that I could trust my voice.

"Ow," I whimpered softly. "Fuck." I touched the painful spot in my mouth and surveyed the smear of blood on my fingertip.

Kane tilted my face up, scanning it anxiously. "Aydan? Are you all right?"

I grimaced. "Fine. I just bit myself."

He gazed down at me for a few seconds more. "That's the last time. You don't need to do this again. Can you stand up yet?"

I nodded, and he helped me to my feet, tucking my arm into his once again. We left the building, and he led me up the path toward the house. Music poured out as the door opened, and the two guards hurried past us in the direction of the guest house. I suppressed a twitch.

"Sounds like the dance has started," Kane commented in a tone that sounded exactly like pleasant anticipation. Damn, he was good. My heart was pounding so hard after the sudden appearance of the guards, I couldn't have trusted my voice.

He smiled down at me and drew me toward the house. "Let's go in and dance."

"Dance? As in ballroom dance? Houston, we have a problem," I whispered.

He stopped. "What?"

I shot a glance in the direction of the guest house, gratefully noting the guards had vanished. "The only ballroom dance I know is a waltz," I hissed. "A poor excuse for a waltz. I haven't done it in years. And I always try to lead."

"Wasn't that part of your briefing?"

"No!"

Kane must have seen my consternation, because his face softened. "Okay. Don't worry. We'll do a quick rehearsal out here. Then we'll go in, make an appearance, and find some pretext to leave quickly."

Right on cue, the music's rhythm changed, and he held out his arms. I stepped toward him uncertainly, and he placed my hand on his shoulder and began a smooth waltz. I could tell right away he was an expert dancer, and it made me even more self-conscious. Trying not to move my lips, I counted "one, two, three, one, two three," under my breath and stiffly followed as best I could.

Sure enough, I tried to go one way while he went the other, and he chuckled and leaned down to my ear. "Relax. You're not facing a firing squad."

"That would be easier. I wouldn't have to worry about being dressed up and making polite conversation."

"You don't really hate it that much, do you?"

I made a face. "No. I hate it much, much more than that."

"I find that hard to believe."

"Do you have any idea how contrary to my nature parties like this are? I hate crowds, I hate making small talk with strangers, and I hate dressing up. I have to remember to keep my knees together, keep my mind out of the gutter, and not swear. And I have to pretend to enjoy myself while I do it. All I want to do is go home, put on my jeans, and swill beer."

He searched my face. "But you make it look so easy. You laugh and chat and draw people out. I heard you converse about everything under the sun tonight. Everybody warmed up to you."

"Just because you're good at something doesn't mean you enjoy doing it."

"True. But it usually helps."

"I'm good at fixing toilets, too, but I wouldn't be sorry if I never had to fix another."

He laughed. "I see your point. What's the latest toilet-related problem? Last time I saw it, you had a gaping hole in your floor."

"Oh, that's all fixed now. My latest escapade has been trying to fish a broken valve chain out of the tank and reattach it without completely demolishing the counter that goes over top of it."

"You know how to have a good time."

"I'm just a party animal."

The music changed, and he released me. "See, you were fine once you relaxed."

I looked up at him sheepishly. "You tricked me."

"Yes." He grinned. "Let's go inside and make our appearance."

"Only if you let me whine and bitch the whole time. Otherwise I'll stiffen up again."

I cranked another pleasant smile onto my face, and we went arm-in-arm into the house. Back in the salon, ties were loosened and the general atmosphere was relaxed thanks to copious amounts of free booze.

I leaned close to Kane. "Keep me away from the bar. Otherwise I'm going to go over there and chug-a-lug a pint."

He laughed, expertly snagging a glass of white wine from a passing tray. He handed it to me with a small bow and a wicked look. "For the elegant lady."

I successfully resisted the urge to blow him a raspberry,

and accepted the glass. I sipped while we circulated, chatting with a few more people. When the music changed to a waltz again, Kane gently removed the glass from my hand and placed it on a nearby table, drawing me to the dance floor. As we stepped onto it, he leaned down to my ear. "What did you think of that sorbet at supper?"

I beamed up at him. "It was fabulous. Everything was so delicious. That lobster bisque was just like velvet. And that ravioli. The cream sauce was amazing. And the dessert..." He swung me smoothly around, the sexy laugh lines crinkling around his eyes. My mouth fell open. "You did it again."

He chuckled and pulled me closer. "Keep dancing. And talk to me."

By the time we'd danced a couple more times, I was relaxed enough to enjoy it. Kane was a superb dancer, his normally athletic movements translating to smooth grace on the dance floor. I was slowly learning to sense where and how he wanted me to move, paying attention to the subtle pressure of his hands. I began to understand why people took up ballroom dancing as a hobby. It was almost as much fun as basketball. And I got to snuggle up to a hot guy. Hello.

Unfortunately, waltzes were few and far between, and we spent the intervening time trying to make conversation with the increasingly inebriated guests. Finally, I widened my eyes at Kane, and he nodded subtly.

When the next waltz started, he led me onto the floor again. We swung into motion, but as the dance progressed, his body language changed. He held me closer, his hands more demanding as he gazed into my eyes. By the end of the dance, our bodies were so close that his thigh was nearly between my legs. He held my hand clasped against his chest as we left the dance floor and guided me toward the lobby, his arm wrapped tightly around my waist.

When we reached the doorway of the salon, he pulled me into his arms and kissed me passionately. I stiffened in shock, and he moved his lips to my ear. "Sorry. Just go with it. Please."

Hell, he was preaching to the choir. This evening was finally starting to improve. I slid my hands under his suit coat, exploring the hot, solid muscles of his back and shoulders, and pressed the length of my body against him to kiss him back with enthusiasm.

A couple of steamy kisses later, I was beginning to wonder if my knees would hold me when he pulled away slightly and towed me out of the house and toward the parking lot.

He stole kisses while we stumbled down the pathway, holding each other close all the way. Even though my brain knew this was just a cover, nobody had informed my body. By the time we got to the valet's station at the cul-de-sac, I was ready to combust.

Kane shoved the key tag and a fifty at the valet, clasping me tightly. "There's another fifty in it for you if you get that car up here in thirty seconds or less," he told the valet, his eyes never leaving my face.

The young man's face lit up. "Yes, sir!" he exclaimed, and rushed off into the darkness.

Kane pulled me into another long, hungry kiss, his hands hot against the bare skin of my back. When Harchman had ground into me earlier, I'd felt as though I'd throw up. Now I thought that if Kane did the same thing, I'd probably have an orgasm on the spot. That seemed like an excellent idea. I pressed my hips against him, making slow circles.

Either he was packing a long-barrelled pistol in his pocket, or he was enjoying this as much as I was. Since I happened to know he carried a Sig Sauer 226R, I was reasonably convinced it was the latter. It pays to know your weapons. And your firearms, too.

I gasped and clutched at him when his teeth closed gently on my earlobe, and then groaned in frustration when the Audi squealed to a halt beside us and the valet hopped out.

Kane handed the kid another fifty and turned to open the car door for me. I slid in, making no attempt to control my skirt. It slipped up almost to my crotch, and Kane froze at the sight of the lace tops of my stockings and the bare thigh above them.

"What have you got on under there?" he asked hoarsely.

I let my head loll back on the headrest as I glided my fingers up past the stockings and brushed the edge of the skirt back to reveal some more naked leg.

"Why don't you take me home and find out?" I purred, mindful of the valet's gawking. The kid's face changed to a knowing leer as Kane closed the door and strode hastily around to the driver's side.

He swung in, slammed the car into gear, and peeled out of the cul-de-sac. When we approached the gatehouse, his hand drifted over to my knee, gliding up to my thigh as the guard approached the car.

Ha. Two could play that game. I reached over and ran my fingernails slowly up the inner seam of his pants. I stopped just short of ground zero as the guard peered in, smirking. He nodded to his counterpart in the gatehouse, and the gates swung open.

Kane hammered on the gas and we laid rubber out the driveway, the car snarling with unleashed power. As we slid onto the highway in a four-wheel drift, I let out a whoop of sheer delight.

CHAPTER 12

I laughed out loud as the Audi accelerated hard on the dark highway, pressing me back in the luxurious leather seat. Kane had both hands on the wheel now, and I reluctantly removed my own from his thigh.

I sat silently for a few moments, trying to calm down. Then euphoria bubbled up in me again, and I gave an enthusiastic fist pump. "Yes!"

Kane's smile gleamed in the dashboard lights as he glanced over at me, slowing the car to the speed limit. "What?"

"What do you mean, what?" I crowed. "The night is over. I can take off these damn clothes. We found the network. We scoped the buildings. We're both unscathed. I don't think anybody recognized me. And I love this car! I win! Yes!"

He laughed. "Sounds like a win to me."

I sat beaming for a few more minutes, feeling the tension ebbing from my body. I didn't want to admit even to myself how frightened I'd been. I eased back in the seat, letting out a heartfelt sigh and sobering when I realized this had really only been the first step.

Next step: ignore my incredibly horny body and focus on

the mission.

"Do you have anything to write on?" I asked. "I've got a pile of information in my head, and I want to get it on paper before I start to lose it."

He jerked a thumb over his shoulder. "My briefcase is behind the seat."

I stretched over to reach behind his seat and came up with a handsome leather portfolio containing a pad of paper. "Can I use this?"

At his nod of assent, I took out my pen, peering at the page in the dim light from the dash. Kane reached over and turned on the interior dome light, and I squinted at him in the sudden brightness. "Can you still see to drive?"

He nodded, so I began to sketch what I could remember of the house plan, noting security camera positions and the places where I remembered seeing staff members. I roughly blocked in the position of the server room. Too bad I hadn't seen the complete floor plans before entering the house. An oversight like that was unlike Kane, and I reflected that he must have been even more tired than I'd realized.

As if to confirm my surmise, he yawned hugely, scrubbing his hand over his face. I glanced over at him in sudden concern. "Do you want me to drive?"

He drove for a few more seconds and then sighed and pulled over, rubbing his eyes. "I'm secure in my manhood. Go for it." He shot me a sly look. "I know you're dying to anyway."

I showed him my teeth. "Out."

We swapped sides, and I kicked off my shoes and pulled the driver's seat forward, tucking my skirt between my legs so I could operate the pedals with some degree of comfort and modesty. Out of the corner of my eye, I caught Kane grinning as I accelerated with a rapturous "Oh, yeah!"

A few minutes later, he laid his head back and his face relaxed into sleep. Touched by his trust, I got on with the enjoyable business of driving. Too bad we were only half an hour away from Calgary.

I spent the intervening time trying to explain to my body that there was a difference between cover stories and real life, and that we weren't going to be getting laid tonight. Or any time soon, for that matter.

Apparently I wasn't persuasive. By the time we reached the city limits, the score was logic, zero; lust about a zillion.

Pulling up at the curb near Kane's condo, I spoke his name. He sat up, immediately alert.

"Where should I park?" I asked.

His brows drew together, puzzled. "No need to park here. I'll drop you off at your hotel."

"Later," I agreed. "I'm sorry, I know you're tired, but I really need to see those floor plans tonight while everything is still fresh in my mind. If you want, I can just take them with me and work on them at the hotel."

"Right. You'll have to come up, then. I'm responsible for the plans, so I can't lend them out."

I considered a raunchy comment about an invitation to come up and see his floor plans, but he was back to his usual air of calm professionalism. I wondered how he could just turn it on and off like that. Maybe it came with his training. I could use some of that.

I followed his directions and parked the car in the slot he indicated. He got out and came around to the driver's side to open the door for me.

An unreadable expression crossed his face. Caught in the act, I finished peeling off one stocking, and hooked my thumbs under the top of the other. "I'm just taking my stockings off. I'm not putting these shoes back on, and I don't want to tear the nylons walking across the parking lot," I explained.

"All right." He straightened and waited, looking away. I shoved the balled-up stockings into my shoes and grabbed my purse. Pulling the slippery skirt down between my legs, I swung out of the car. Such a relief to not have to keep my knees together.

Kane maintained his silence while I padded barefoot across the pavement beside him. During the evening, I'd grown accustomed to the extra height of the heels, and he seemed very tall when I gazed up at him questioningly. "So what's the next step?"

"Next step," he repeated. "Brain dump. Sleep. After that, we'll figure out our strategy."

He keyed open the exterior door, and we climbed two flights of stairs to the third floor. Unlocking his door, he flipped the lights on and ushered me in. I eyeballed the place, trying to conceal my curiosity.

The colour scheme was taupe and dark wood, the walls a warm neutral hue. Recessed pot lights created pools and washes of light. The main area was sparsely furnished with a clean-lined black leather sofa and chair and an expensive-looking stereo system. There was a small TV in the corner, but it looked as though it had been placed as an afterthought. Instead, the furniture arrangement focused on a stone fireplace.

One picture in a folding frame was propped on the mantel, but the walls were otherwise completely barren. In the empty space that would normally accommodate a dining table, a large punching bag hung suspended by chains from the ceiling. A weight bench and weights occupied the rest of the living room.

The only softness in the room was a crocheted afghan folded casually over the back of the sofa. I walked over to examine the blanket, smiling at the artistry of its muted colours. The design and colour blocking were masculine and contemporary.

I looked up so he could see my smile. "Arnie?" I asked.

He nodded, grinning. "When I got shot a couple of years ago, I couldn't do much for the first while. He spent a lot of time over here babysitting me. When he wasn't playing his guitar, he was working on this. Said it kept his fingers nimble."

I laughed. "It must work. I've seen those fingers in action."

He considered that with a half-smile, but apparently decided not to pursue it. "I'll go and get the plans," he said, and vanished down the hallway.

I wandered over to examine the photo on the mantel. A jaunty young man smiled out of the picture, his longish dark hair mussed. He wore a grass-stained T-shirt, and a football was tucked under his arm. His square face and grey eyes at first made me think I was looking at a photo of Kane himself, minus twenty years or so, but the bones were a little finer, the features more regular. I considered Kane's strong face striking. The young man in the photo was unarguably handsome.

I turned as Kane returned with rolls of drawings under his arm. "Who's this in the picture?" I asked. "He looks a lot like you."

His face softened into a smile. "My younger brother, Daniel."

"This picture has been around for a while, then."

He nodded slowly. "That was taken in the '80's. He died a few weeks later."

A hollow opened in my chest. "Oh, no. I'm so sorry. What happened?"

Kane's shoulders straightened. "He saved a young woman who was being attacked by a mugger. He was stabbed."

I turned again to look at the youthful face in the picture, trying to control the burning behind my eyes. "How old was he?"

"Twenty-three."

"What a waste," I whispered.

Kane's voice was steady behind me. "No. Not a waste. That young woman lived to get married and have a family. The daughter just graduated from university with a degree in music. She's an incredibly talented pianist. The son is married with a baby on the way. Never believe that Daniel's life was wasted."

I took a deep breath, composing myself before I turned back to him. "You kept in touch with the woman?"

"No. I only met her once. She came to Daniel's funeral. But I... check up on them every now and then. I think of them as Daniel's family." He shrugged. "Mine, by extension, I guess. I just like to know that life goes on."

"Whether you want it to or not," I agreed quietly. "I guess I understand why you went into law enforcement after you left the army."

He shrugged again, nodding. "Let's have a look at these drawings."

He spread them out on the counter that separated the kitchen from the open living space. I picked up my sketches and carried them over to compare.

"Can I write on these?" I asked.

"Yes. They're copies."

We perched on stools and started to mark up the drawings. I worked on the main house, while Kane filled in details on the rest of the buildings, noting security cameras, lines of sight, and positions of security staff.

Finally, I looked up with a sigh, rubbing the back of my aching neck. "That's all I can remember. Now I need to sketch out the server room and security monitoring centre."

Kane looked over my annotations. "This is excellent. You've done this before, haven't you?"

I nodded absently, blocking in the layout of the server room on a separate piece of paper. Kane's quiet immobility made me glance up to meet his intent gaze. Realizing what he'd really been asking, I backtracked hurriedly. "I used to do tons of site measures when I was drafting. After a while, observing this kind of detail just becomes second nature."

He nodded slowly. "Just a civilian."

"Yup. Well, and it didn't hurt that Harchman apparently thinks with his dick. And he's sadly under-endowed. He walked me right into the server room."

Kane frowned. "Why would he do that? Fuzzy Bunny runs a tight ship. They're not known for working with stupid people. That's why they're so successful."

"No idea. Maybe it's not Fuzzy Bunny's network at all. But look at this." I showed him my sketches. "The server room is biometrically keyed to his thumbprint. Here's the entire security console layout. Oh, and he runs guards and dogs through that forested area that surrounds the grounds."

I grimaced. "Too bad you can't get fingerprints from fabric. You could march right through the security scanner into the server room if you could lift some of the many full sets of prints he left on my ass."

Kane's face darkened. "I'm sorry you had to go through that."

"No worries," I assured him. "A bit of groping doesn't upset me much anymore. In fact, it was a hell of a relief once I figured out that's all he was after."

His brows drew together in comprehension. "I guess it would be, under the circumstances."

I frowned down at the plans again. "Let me walk you through this so we can call it a night. I want to get these damn clothes and fake nails and makeup off. And you must still be seriously jet-lagged."

We went over the plans, and Kane asked detailed questions that helped jog my memory. By the time we were finished, he'd managed to get more information out of me than I even knew I'd observed. Finally, he straightened with a grunt, massaging his forehead. "Okay. I think I've got the full picture now. Time to quit."

I glanced at my watch. "Yikes, it's after two." I studied his exhausted face, the lines carved deep again by fatigue. "Where's the phone book? I'll just call a cab so you can go straight to bed."

He shook his head. "No, I'll take you back to the hotel. When you're doing undercover work, it's the details that count."

"I don't see that it makes much difference. So maybe the date didn't go well. We had a fight and I took a cab home."

"Remember how I said earlier I was secure in my manhood?" He gave me a tired grin. "I do have some pride. My ego would appreciate it if you would at least pretend the date went well."

I laughed. "Okay, Stud, take me home."

CHAPTER 13

As we got settled in the car again, Kane glanced over at me. "I'd appreciate it if you didn't mention that you know where I live."

"Okay," I agreed slowly. "Is that because you don't want anybody to know where you live, or because you don't want anybody to know that I know where you live?"

He paused, apparently unravelling my convoluted question. "Both, actually."

"Does this fall into the category of 'Don't mention it unless asked directly', or the category of 'Actively lie about it'?"

"Depends who's asking."

I frowned at him. "If you're going to rely on my judgement, I need more information."

He blew out a breath. "I don't give out my address on general principles. Even my team doesn't know where I live. Not that they couldn't find out, or that I'd object to them knowing, just that it hasn't come up. Need-to-know. There are a couple of reasons for that."

He stopped the car at a red light and eyed me seriously. "First, you can't tell what you don't know. For example, if I got captured, I don't know where my team members live, or much about their personal lives at all. No matter what inducements my captors might use, I wouldn't be able to give out that information."

The light changed and he accelerated smoothly again, his gaze focused straight ahead. "Second, I have enemies. Anybody who has close contact with me could be endangered if one of those enemies decides to get to me through somebody I care about. By association, if you know where I live, then that could make you a target."

"Oh." I thought that through to its logical conclusion and wasn't quite sure how to react.

He scowled, and the leather steering wheel creaked slightly under his grip. "That's why I was so reluctant to use this cover. We were seen being publicly affectionate. If the wrong people saw us, that could put you in danger."

"Oh well, every relationship comes with some baggage. Torture, death, you know. The usual," I joked.

"Not funny."

"Tough audience." When he didn't smile, I went on. "Anyway, it's a little late to worry about it at this stage. Getting back to the original question, then, I'm thinking the answer is, don't mention it to the good guys unless necessary, and lie to the bad guys. Does anybody else know where you live?"

He kept his eyes on the road. "You. Arnie. My dad."

Wow, short list. He and Arnie had been friends all their lives. His dad, well, duh. Me? I pondered that for a second before deciding I probably fell into the category of team member, need-to-know. I changed the subject. "Your dad's still living?"

He grinned. "Old drill sergeants never die."

"You're lucky."

"I know."

When we pulled up at the hotel, I sighed at the shoes and stockings. "I should never have taken these off." I squirmed around in the slippery leather seat, pulling the stockings back on. The skirt slithered lasciviously around my thighs.

In my peripheral vision, I caught Kane eyeing my legs. I figured the chances of getting any action with him tonight were slim to none, but that didn't seem to discourage my body any.

What the hell. Acting oblivious, I let the skirt slide up a little farther while I finished putting on my shoes. I picked up my purse and was reaching for the door handle when his hand closed around mine.

"Wait."

I took stock of his half-smile in the dimness, feeling hopeful. "What?"

He gently slipped the rings off my finger and dropped them into his pocket. "We weren't wearing these when we left the hotel."

I gave him a half-smile of my own. "Details."

He nodded. "I'll come around and get the door for you." He got out, and I yanked the skirt down one more time while I waited.

I managed a relatively graceful exit from the car. There wasn't much of an audience at two-thirty in the morning, but if Kane thought it was important to keep up appearances, I'd do my part.

We strolled into the hotel lobby, his arm lightly around my waist. I did my best to match his manner of warm interest. Coming home from a nice date, but nothing more. Shit.

We rode the elevator and walked down the hall to my

room in silence, and I fumbled the key card out of my purse and turned to wish him a good night. A shock of heat rolled through me when he smiled and gently tugged the card out of my grasp, sliding his arms around me to pull me into a slow kiss. Still kissing me, he slid the card into the slot and backed me into the room, letting the door swing shut behind us.

As soon as the latch clicked, he stepped away.

Goddammit!

Using all my control, I kept my expression neutral while I surveyed him, internally debating the idea of pulling him into a hot kiss. That's all it had taken in March. My comment about banging him up against the wall hadn't been idle fantasy. If we'd had just a bit more time back then...

Trouble was, we were working together. I knew how seriously he took duty. And I really wasn't in the mood to deal graciously with rejection tonight.

"The necklace," he said.

"Huh?" Oh, eloquent me.

"I need to take the necklace with me now, but you had to be seen wearing it up to your room because you were wearing it when we left."

I shook my head slowly. "How the hell do you manage to keep all that straight in your mind?"

He gave me a wry look. "Let's just say I'm highly motivated."

I undid the necklace and laid it into the box that he held out. "Me, too, but I would have missed that one."

"That's why we're a team."

"I guess."

He took my hand and squeezed it gently. "Aydan, you were amazing tonight. I couldn't have asked for a better partner."

I felt my face heat up. Among other things. "Thanks."

He released my hand and reached for the door handle. "Oh, and thanks for the dance lesson," I added.

He smiled. "You're welcome. Good night."

"Good night."

I stood there for a few seconds after the door closed behind him, and then stomped over and punched the hell out of my pillow.

CHAPTER 14

I spent far too long removing the makeup and fake nails, and went to bed exhausted. Then I slept poorly and woke in the morning feeling edgy and irritable. My foul mood was compounded when I got out of the shower and realized I'd missed a call from Kane.

His deep voice was still edged with fatigue in the voicemail recording, and I wondered if he'd slept any more or any better than I had. Probably. That wouldn't take much.

"Hi, Aydan. Thanks again for last night. I'm going to have to stay in town for a few days, so you might as well check out of the hotel this morning and head back on your own. Take care. Goodbye."

Miffed at the cryptic message, I scowled into the mirror. It wasn't a pretty sight, and I growled and tried to rub the frown lines out of my forehead.

Thanks for risking your life, getting mauled by a fucking pervert, having red-hot spikes hammered through your brain multiple times, and dressing up to make small talk with a bunch of strangers. And NOT getting laid. The most annoying part was I knew I had no reason to be ticked off. He'd said thank you. He couldn't say anything more detailed or informative on an unsecured line.

I swore savagely at my reflection, and then did my best to put on an innocuous expression while I dragged down to the restaurant for breakfast. I was beginning to feel human about half-way through my Eggs Benedict when my phone vibrated. I pulled it out quickly and scanned the display.

Shit.

I pressed the Talk button. "Hi, Nichele."

"Aydan...?" Her voice was full of avid anticipation.

"What?"

"Well...? How did it go?"

"It went. I told you, it was a business thing."

"I need details!"

I sighed. "Nichele, I'm in the middle of breakfast. Can I call you later?"

"No, but you can meet me for lunch at Kelly's."

There was no way I was going to get out of this. Might as well get it over with.

"Okay. Make it one o'clock, though. That'll give me time to work out this morning."

Silence on the line. "You're working out? Girl, you mean you didn't get lucky with that hot hunk of man last night?"

The reply that sprang immediately to my tongue would have offended even Nichele. I bit it back with an effort. "No."

"What happened?"

"I told you, it was just a business thing. We'll talk later, okay? My Eggs Benny is getting cold."

"Oh, so that's what you're calling it now," she teased.

"Shut up."

She laughed. "See you later. Bye-bye."

I disconnected and glowered at the phone for a few

seconds. It didn't help. I rubbed the wrinkles out of my forehead again and went back to my congealing breakfast.

When I returned to my room to pack up, I was slightly cheered by the sight of the elegant dress hanging undamaged in the closet. I couldn't believe I'd actually managed to wear it for an entire evening without wrecking it. Maybe my run of wardrobe misfortune had finally ended.

There was no room in my small backpack for my new purchases, so I carefully folded the dress and tucked it into a shopping bag along with the new shoes, purse, and makeup. I made sure that neither the purse nor the shoes had any rough edges that could snag it. Despite my notorious aversion to dressing up, I really did like that dress.

My mood improved further at the gym. I pushed hard, putting on some extra weight for my strength routines and turning up the resistance for my cardio. By the time I was finished, I was drenched in sweat and my muscles were warm and relaxed. It was no substitute for the activity I really had in mind, but at least it took the edge off.

I showered and changed before heading over to Kelly's to wait for Nichele. When I strolled in, the shabby decor and low-key atmosphere wrapped around me like a hug from an old friend. Sunday was classic rock day, and Bob Seger was singing 'Roll Me Away' in the background. I headed for the back of the bar, smiling.

The waitress stopped in her tracks. "Hey, it's not Saturday!"

"Hey, Alanna! You knew I'd moved, right? I'm just down for the weekend."

"Corona?"

I sighed. "No, just a glass of water. I'm driving."

She nodded understanding. "There was a guy sitting on

your usual couch, but he just left. Go ahead and grab it and I'll come and clear the table for you."

"Thanks!" I made my way to the back of the room and flopped into one of the broken-down couches, my back to the wall. I scanned the bar out of habit, but didn't see anyone I knew.

I glanced up at Alanna as she returned. "I'm going to have wings, so I'll just go and wash my hands. If Nichele shows up, tell her I'm here, okay?"

"Sure, no problem."

As I turned the corner of the hallway to the washrooms, I glimpsed the rear view of a burly man in jeans, boots, and black leather striding toward the back exit. 'Hellhound' was blazoned across the back of his jacket, surmounting a picture of a toothy black beast, drool dripping from its jaws, its red eyes glaring.

I stopped so suddenly my running shoe squeaked on the tile floor. The owner of the jacket immediately glanced behind him at the sound. He did an incredulous double-take and turned slowly. A wicked smile gleamed under his grizzled moustache.

"Well, hell-lo, pretty lady," he rasped, advancing on me as he shrugged off his jacket.

His faded Harley-Davidson T-shirt stretched tightly across his powerful chest. Its torn-out sleeves showed off the bulging muscles of his tattooed arms and shoulders. I took a deep, shaky breath and involuntarily stepped backward. "H-Hi."

My back bumped against one of the columns that lined the hallway, and he stepped closer to leer down at me from well inside my personal space.

He indicated the post behind me with a jerk of his

bearded chin. "Gonna do a little pole dance for me, darlin'?" He licked his lips slowly, his gaze stroking down my body.

I let out a breathless laugh. "Sorry, not my kind of pole."

He planted his hands on the wall on each side of my shoulders. Inches away, his body radiated heat. His voice dropped to a deep, intimate growl. "I got the perfect pole for ya to dance with, darlin'. An' I know just how good you're gonna look slidin' up an' down on it."

I swallowed hard and my knees threatened to give way. His hot eyes were locked on mine, his lips very close.

"Aydan?" Nichele stood uncertainly at the end of the hallway. "Is... everything okay?"

My intellectual processes gradually rebooted and I blinked wordlessly for a moment while I tried to remember the English language. Then I ducked out from under Hellhound's arm.

"Hi, Nichele. Everything's fine. I'd like to you meet Arnie Helmand. Arnie, this is Nichele Brown."

Hellhound straightened and gave Nichele a friendly nod. Nichele eyed his tattoos, ugly face, and lurid jacket doubtfully. "I'll just wait at the table." She retreated.

I turned slowly back to Arnie. "Long time no see."

"Yeah, how ya been, darlin'?"

I knew it wasn't just casual small talk, so I answered the real question. "I'm really good, now."

He relaxed into a teasing smile. "Ya were really good before." Then he sobered. "I didn't hear from ya." It was a question, not an accusation.

"No. I wanted some time. I was feeling needy. You know how I feel about getting attached. Needy is a bad place to start."

"Darlin', you're about as far from needy as anybody

could get."

"And that's the way I like it. Funny, though, I was just thinking of calling you this morning."

"Next time, do it. Don't just think about it."

"It was three-thirty in the morning."

He grinned and bounced his eyebrows at me. "Even better."

I patted his flat, hard stomach where the incipient beer gut used to be. "You look so hot, I nearly passed out! What happened to the Molson muscle? And you trimmed your beard, too!"

Instead of the wild tangle he'd sported in March, his salt-and-pepper beard and moustache were closely cropped, emphasizing a chiselled jaw I hadn't known he possessed. With that and the new bulk and definition in his arms and chest, he exuded raw masculinity.

Nobody would ever call him handsome. Hell, it'd be a long stretch to call him tolerably homely. But he was definitely sexy. Maybe it was the muscles and boots and black leather. Or maybe it was because I knew exactly how good a pole dance with him really was.

His face lit up. "Ya like?"

"Hell, yeah! What happened?"

"I always keep the facial fungus a little shorter in summer. An' I told ya I was gonna start a fitness program."

"Yeah, but, wow! I thought you were kidding."

He shook his head. "No joke. I used to work out a lot, but I got away from it. I didn't know how fuckin' fat an' lazy I'd got 'til ya wore me out this spring. And knowin' how your husband died, well, shit... That ain't a bad way to go, if ya gotta go, but I'd rather stick around an' enjoy it."

He stepped close again, stroking his strong fingers

through my hair. His raspy voice deepened. "I'm ready to rock your hot body all night long now, darlin'."

I ran a shaky hand over his chest. "I had no complaints before."

"Wait'll ya test-drive the new model."

His hand slipped behind my head, and he kissed me slowly. Goddamn, I'd almost forgotten how good his kisses were. By the time he pulled back a fraction, I was plastered against him, ardently exploring the hard new contours of his arms and torso.

A bar patron walked by us on her way to the washroom, disapproval written on her face. Hellhound chuckled.

"Ya want me." His voice slid into that deep growl that never failed to light a fire in a very wet place. "Ya want me bad."

I slid my arms around his neck, purring hungrily. "Oh, Hellhound, oh baby, you want to know what I'm going do to you?"

I whispered a detailed description, brushing my lips against his ear and moving sensuously against him. The heat of his next kiss left me breathless, the touch of his magic tongue sweeping me away in a wave of lust. I had very happy memories of that tongue.

I was reminding myself we were in a public place when Nichele's voice intruded again. "Aydan, your wings are here. Are you coming?"

"Not quite yet," I mumbled against Arnie's lips. "But I have high hopes." I pulled away far enough to see his grin. Nichele smirked and rolled her eyes before disappearing around the corner again.

"I'm supposed to be having lunch with Nichele," I whispered. "What are you doing later?"

He gave a start and glanced at his watch. "Shit!"

"Shit, what?"

"Darlin', I gotta go. I'm gonna be late for a job."

"P.I. stuff?"

"Yeah."

I let my fingers wander down his chest, heading south. "Skip it. I'll make it worth your while." His eyes dilated as I toyed with the button on his jeans. "Come on," I whispered. "You know you want to."

He groaned and caught my hand as he stepped away, his gaze locked on me. "Ya got no idea how much I want to," he assured me hoarsely. "But no can do. For you, I'd blow off just about anythin', but this one I can't."

"When will you be done?"

"Dunno, darlin'. I'm goin' outta town. Could be days."

Dismay and frustration splashed over me like cold water. "You're kidding me, right?"

He shook his head, his regret obvious. "If it was any other client, I'd say to hell with it, but this one I can't." He met my eyes meaningfully.

"Goddammit. Kane. Isn't it. He's got you doing surveillance out by Bragg Creek."

Hellhound's face went expressionless. "What d'ya know about that?"

I shrugged and shook my head. "Can't tell you. Son of a bitch. Kane owes me big for this. Dammit."

His forehead furrowed with concern. "Aydan, are ya... You're not in any danger this time, are ya?"

"Not that I know of at the moment."

He blew out a sigh. "Good. Shit, I gotta go. And I ain't gonna kiss ya again, 'cause I won't be able to stop if I do." He squeezed my hand. "Take care. I wanna see ya again. Soon.

I'll call ya when I can."

I took a deep breath and let it out slowly. "Be careful out there. And ride safe."

"Always do, darlin'."

He slung his jacket on and strode out the door, and the fat rumble of his Harley faded into the distance moments later.

I trailed disconsolately into the bathroom and washed my hands. When I got back to the table, I threw myself onto the sofa and glowered at my wings.

Nichele smirked at me. "Got your Eggs Benny heated up again?"

"All hot and juicy, and nobody to eat it," I growled.

"Eeeeuuuuwww!" She clapped her hands over her ears. "That metaphor went 'way too far!"

"If you don't want to know, don't ask."

"Oh, I want to know," she assured me eagerly. "What's with you and this Arnie guy? He calls you darling? You never mentioned him before, are you holding out on me? Or are you just coming onto him because you didn't get lucky with that big hot hunk o' man last night? And why didn't you just go ahead jump John? He is definitely into you, girl! Or... have you got a thing going with Arnie already? Are you doing both of them?"

I bit into a wing, waiting for the barrage to cease. When I could get a word in edgewise, I attempted to answer with as few details as possible.

"I'm not doing either of them at the moment. Unfortunately. I told you, John is off limits. Business. And I'm pretty sure Arnie calls all women 'darling'. Saves him the trouble of remembering their names in the morning. Not that I'd care by then." My eyes unfocused slightly at the memory.

"You did do him! When? What was he like? I want details!"

I had to throw her a bone. My preference would have been a chicken bone to the head, but that would only delay the inevitable. Besides, I knew Hellhound wouldn't object to having his reputation boosted.

"Arnie's a musician, among other things. He plays guitar and harmonica. Think hands, lips, tongue, and rhythm. He's got a mighty fine instrument, too." I gazed into middle distance for a few seconds of juicy reminiscence. "That man knows how to make music."

"Oooo, when you put it that way..."

I wiggled my eyebrows at her. "If you ever get the chance..."

"Eeuw," she interrupted. "In the first place, he's ugly. In the second place, he's yours."

"I was going to say, 'if you ever get the chance, try a musician'," I said with dignity. "And he's not mine. He's just a friend." I leered at her. "A friend with a great benefits package."

"And anyway," I added, feeling a little put out on Arnie's behalf, "Looks aren't everything. All you ever go for are pretty boys in suits. You don't know what you're missing."

"I'm missing waking up to a scary-looking guy."

"You're so shallow."

"You have no standards, girl."

We grinned at each other, our well-worn exchange as familiar as our own faces. I lounged back in the couch and nibbled some more wings, hoping question period was over. Seeing Nichele's avid face, I knew I wouldn't get off that easily.

She leaned forward. "So...?"

"So?"

Nichele blew out a short breath. "Jeez-Louise! It's like getting blood from a stone! Give, girl! You really like Arnie, I can tell. That 'looks aren't everything' sounds serious."

I shook my head. "Absolutely not serious. You know I'm permanently done with the whole relationship thing. I like him, yeah. He's a good guy."

I paused, remembering his gentleness with my battered body and spirit in the spring. So unlike his tough-guy appearance. I smiled.

"And the best thing about him is, he's only interested in one thing. Getting laid. No strings attached."

"So, are you going to hook up with Arnie later? You guys were scorching the paint in the hallway something serious, girl. Or are you going to see John again?" She leaned forward, her face alight with lecherous anticipation. "Or both?"

"Don't you have a life?"

"Yeah, but it's more fun to dig into yours."

With as much finality as I could muster, I responded, "Arnie just went out of town. He doesn't know when he'll be back. John is working, and I probably won't see him again in the foreseeable future. I have to be back in Silverside to see clients this week. If you're looking for cheap thrills, you'll have to look somewhere else. 'Cause there sure as hell aren't going to be any in my life for a while."

"Well, girl, that just sucks."

"Tell me about it. Now I need to go work out again."

The conversation finally turned to more general topics, and I finished my wings with relief.

Nichele and I lingered on the sidewalk in front of Kelly's,

laughing and bantering for a few more minutes before we parted. I headed for my car smiling, my earlier frustration diminished by good food and Nichele's upbeat conversation.

The sun hammered the parking lot, and I was sweating before I even reached the car. As I keyed open the car door and slid into the oven-like interior, my breath caught in my throat. I sprang out of the car and staggered a few steps away, gasping and choking on chemical fumes.

When I'd recovered sufficiently, I wiped my streaming eyes and opened the passenger door as well. The breeze gradually cleared the interior, and at last I leaned in to study the damage.

My heart sank when I pinpointed the source of the smell. I opened the shopping bag with reluctant hands.

"Shit!"

I'd been so careful, too. I'd wrapped the makeup and hairspray in a separate shopping bag before placing it in the bag containing the dress. But in the heat of the car, the hairspray had leaked. And dissolved part of the bag. Which was now permanently embedded in the gooey mess that used to be an expensive dress.

Son of a bitch.

CHAPTER 15

On the drive home, my brain chewed at what I knew of the situation at Harchman's while the highway unrolled in front of me.

Harchman must be broadcasting the network throughout his property. Or was it confined to only the building site? And what the heck could he be using it for?

I didn't think operating a network of that type was illegal in itself, although I couldn't imagine how Harchman could have obtained such highly classified technology by legal means. I guessed Spider and his fellow analysts would be digging to discover its origins.

I sighed, worrying about Kane and Arnie and the rest of the team. It would only take one wrong move. Fuzzy Bunny played for keeps. I thought wistfully back to before I knew any of this. I had been so happily ignorant.

Now, in a way, being disconnected from the action was worse than being the middle of it. Four months ago I'd been terrified, but at least I'd known what was happening. Would anybody even think to notify me if one of the team was injured or killed?

I wrenched my mind away to more reassuring thoughts. Hellhound was a civilian private investigator, as well as

Kane's lifelong friend. I knew Kane had hired him before for other situations that didn't warrant putting a trained agent on the job. Kane wouldn't knowingly put Arnie in the line of fire. Maybe it wasn't as dangerous as I was imagining.

Letting that thought ease the tension in my shoulders, I sighed again and tried to let it go. Worrying wouldn't help them anyway.

At home, I tried to ignore my nagging sensation of dread while I got on with my regular routine.

Tuesday morning, I arrived at Blue Eddy's promptly at ten o'clock and let myself in the back door with the key he'd given me. The merry sound of the piano made my face split into a grin. Ragtime today. The music skipped and danced down the hallway and so did I.

One of the many benefits of working for Eddy was that he came in early, ostensibly to get everything ready for opening at eleven o'clock. In fact, he usually spent the time playing the piano, and I was the happy beneficiary of his efforts.

He looked up with a smile as I came in. "Hi, Aydan!"

His fingers never missed a beat. I was willing to swear his hands were capable of making music without any input from his brain at all. I envied his gift hopelessly.

I grinned at him. "Hey, Eddy! Have I ever told you that you're my favourite client?"

Quite apart from his musical talent, Eddy's quick thinking back in March was the only reason I still had all my body parts. He didn't know exactly what he'd saved me from and he never would, but I was eternally grateful.

He finished the piece, walking the bass home while I

beamed at him. "No. But it's sure nice to hear."

He returned my grin and turned back to the keyboard, and I retired to his cramped office to do the week's entries. I had been working steadily at the desk for about forty-five minutes when my phone rang. I picked it up, abstracted.

"Hello, Aydan speaking."

"Hey, Aydan, it's Spider."

I shook myself free of the train of thought I'd been following. "Hi, Spider, what's up?"

"Can you come over to the office this afternoon?"

"Um." I glanced at my watch, figuring out times. "I'm at Eddy's right now, and then I need to grab lunch and head over to the sex shop. I'll be a couple of hours there..."

A strangled noise on the other end of the line made me pause. "Spider? You okay?"

I heard the phone hit something hard on the other end, and desperate choking sounds receded from the speaker. Cold fear ripped through me as I bolted to my feet.

"Spider! Spider! Are you okay? *Spider!*"

Choked gasps sounded faintly through my phone, and I dashed out of Eddy's office, fumbling one-handed for my keys while I flew down the hall.

Bellowing Spider's name into the phone, I burst out the door and ran for my car. Just as I reached it, a hoarse wheeze came from the phone.

"I'm okay."

I sagged against my car, gasping relief. "Jesus, Spider, what the fuck? You scared the shit out of me!"

Eddy rushed out the door, his face tense. I put the phone against my shoulder and spoke to him. "It's okay. False alarm." He halted and clutched his chest theatrically before turning back to the building with a relieved smile.

"Spider! What happened?" I demanded.

"I choked on my Coke," he replied sheepishly, his voice still croaky.

"Christ! I thought somebody was strangling you!"

"Sorry. That's what it felt like, too. Where did you say you were going? It sounded like you said 'sex shop'."

"I did."

"Um." Silence lengthened, and I imagined his crimson face. "Aydan, that's, um... a little too much information."

I chuckled. "They're one of my bookkeeping clients. I thought you knew. Sorry, I didn't mean to shock you."

He rallied quickly. "I'm not shocked. I mean... whatever. I just... it was just the way you said it."

With difficulty, I contained my laughter. I heaved myself off the car and headed back into Eddy's, continuing the conversation as casually as I could. "I'll be there until about three-thirty or so. I could be at your office around four. Will that work?"

"That'll be fine. See you then." He hung up quickly, and I flopped back into the chair in Eddy's office, giving in to a long belly laugh. Eddy poked his head in the door a few moments later as I sprawled there, gasping and giggling.

"What was that all about?"

I shook my head feebly. "Sorry, I'm just blowing off some adrenaline. That was Clyde Webb. We were talking and he choked on his Coke. I thought he was dying or something."

True, but incomplete. Eddy didn't need to know I'd been afraid Spider wasn't strangling of his own accord.

Eddy grinned. "Thank goodness. You scared me, rushing out of here like the place was on fire."

"Sorry," I repeated. "I'll smack him for both of us when I

see him."

He laughed and went back to the bar while I returned to the papers I'd scattered in my mad flight.

On the dot of one o'clock, I strolled into Up & Coming. The seductive smell of warm chocolate tickled my nose as soon as I walked in and I scanned the store, trying to pinpoint its source.

A curvy, diminutive woman stood with her back to me as she reached up to arrange lingerie on one of the shelves, wobbling slightly on high, booted heels. Her feet were so tiny that if the heels had been any higher, she'd have been en pointe. The display lighting gleamed off her tight brown leather pantsuit and lit her short, spiky platinum-blonde hair like a halo. When she turned, I gasped at the sight of the sweet, lined face surmounting bodacious if somewhat wrinkled cleavage.

"Lola?"

"Hi, Aydan," she greeted me in her throaty voice.

I stared. "Wow, you look amazing! What happened to the delicate little lady with the white hair and pink ruffled blouse?"

She laughed. "Been there, done that. It was fun while it lasted. Some of my 1-900 customers really got off on it. But it was time for a change."

"Some change! I love your hair, it's a great style and colour on you."

"Thanks. I was going to go red like yours, but you can't get that colour out of a bottle."

I laughed. "Yeah, I don't think they make hair dye with this much grey in it."

"You hardly have any grey, honey. Your hair still looks completely red in this light."

"Thanks." I sniffed again, pinpointing the chocolate smell. "Is that you?"

"Yes, I was at a trade show in Vegas last week, and I picked this up. Scented leather. It smells better the warmer it gets. Imagine some big, hot hunk wearing nothing but a chocolate-scented thong."

Kane came immediately to mind, and I could feel my jaw slackening.

Lola shot me a wicked grin. "I see you get the picture."

I shook myself. "Thanks for nothing. Now I have to go take a cold shower." Curiosity got the better of me. "Does it come in any other scents?"

"Black is licorice. There's another shade of brown that's coffee-scented. Cherry red. Blue raspberry. Oh, and look what else I brought back!" She reached behind the counter and brought out a pair of thigh-high black leather boots loaded with buckles, fringe, and vicious stiletto heels.

I laughed. "Lola, you could fit your whole body inside those things."

"I know, but I couldn't resist bringing a couple of pairs back. We're going to carry the line on our website, and I needed some samples. I got a pair in your size. There wasn't any point in getting them for myself. Or for Linda. Her legs are as short as mine. Here, try them on."

"I have a very limited need for thigh-high stilettos. I don't dress up for Halloween."

"Oh, go on, just put them on," she cajoled. "I want to see how they look. With your long legs, they'll be great."

I shrugged and took the boots. "You realize I charge by the hour. You're going to pay for this one way or the other," I teased as I squashed the legs of my snug jeans inside the boots and awkwardly zipped them up.

Lola gazed up at me. "Holy cats, how tall are you anyway?"

"How high are the heels?"

"About four and half inches, if you count the platform soles."

"Then I'm just over six foot two." I prowled and swaggered across the floor, tossing my hair and striking a sexpot pose while she laughed. As I glanced toward the window, I realized a man was standing outside, rooted to the spot while he stared in at me.

"Shit!" I dodged behind a display.

Lola followed my line of sight. "Hey, free advertising. Thanks, honey!"

I unzipped the boots and jerked them off my feet. "Easy for you to say. You owe me big-time for that."

"No, if you were wearing fishnets and a leather miniskirt with the boots, then I'd owe you. Hey, I don't suppose..."

"No."

"All right, all right. Grumpy. Go do the books." She grinned unrepentantly and picked up the discarded boots as I made a beeline for the back office.

A couple of hours later, I emerged warily. Lola smirked at me. "Hey, I just had a great idea!"

"No. Whatever it is, no. Not when you're smiling like that."

"Oh, go on. How would you like to make some extra money?"

"No, I will not dress up in boots, fishnets, and/or lingerie and parade around outside the store."

"I wouldn't ask you to do such a thing," she said loftily. "But I do need a model for our online catalogue."

I was already backing away, shaking my head.

"Absolutely not."

"We wouldn't show your face in any of the shots. And we'd hide the naughty bits."

"Lola! No! Jeez! Do it yourself if you need a model."

"Now, there's an idea..."

I fled the shop while she thought it over.

CHAPTER 16

When I stuck my head into his office, Spider was clicking computer keys, frowning intently. A stack of papers overflowed the tray on his desk, and the entire desk surface was covered.

He glanced up with a start. "Is it four o'clock already?"

"Yeah. Long day?"

"You can say that again." He rubbed wearily at his stubbly chin.

I looked more closely at the stubble. "Are you growing a beard?"

He blushed. "Trying. It's not going so well. This is a week's worth."

I couldn't think of anything encouraging to say, so I took another tack. "Going for a new image?"

"I thought it might make me look older. I'm tired of getting asked for ID. I'm twenty-six, for crying out loud."

Actually, its fledgling state made him look even younger. I nodded and changed the subject. "You rang?"

"Yes, we have to set up the paper trail so we can pay you for your undercover work." He rooted through several piles of paper, restacking them until he discovered the one he was looking for. "I meant to have this ready, but time got away from me this afternoon. I haven't decided yet whether you should invoice Kane Consulting or Spider's Webb Design."

"Which would then flow money through from my actual employer, I presume."

"Yes."

"Um, Spider, I don't feel comfortable invoicing for bookkeeping services if I haven't actually seen your books. In my mind, there's some responsibility associated with this."

"We can't let you see the books unless you go through a bunch more security clearances." He scratched his chin again. "Darn, this itches. Maybe I'll just shave it off."

"How do you and Kane deal with the income?"

He shrugged, still absently fingering his stubble. "It's easy for us. We're both officially part of the INSET team, so we draw normal salary. If there's anything that can't be covered by that, it flows through our personal companies."

"What if we skip the bookkeeping angle and you just subcontract some of your web design out to me?"

"We can't take a chance on lying about it. It's too easy to check. That'd be a good solution, though, if you could do web design."

I shrugged. "I can."

His eyes sharpened, and I could see the wheels turning. "You can? Do web design?"

"Yeah. I'd never win any prizes for graphic design, and I don't do any of the complicated stuff. But I can do pure HTML and search engine optimization. I did my own website."

Spider turned back to his computer. "What's your URL?"

I told him, and his fingers flew over the keyboard. He

clicked around for a few seconds. "This is good. It's nice and clean and fast." He gave me a calculating smile. "We could kill two birds with one stone. If you're willing."

"Willing to do what, exactly?" I leaned back in my chair, regarding him suspiciously.

"I keep some civilian clients for cover purposes. It seems like they always need something right when I'm buried with CSIS stuff. Like now. I'm working sixteen hour days, trying to stay on top of everything for this thing at Harchman's. My civvie clients get pushed to the bottom of the pile. If you could cover for me, that would be fabulous."

"It depends on what they need," I equivocated. "I told you, I'm no guru. I can do basic stuff, that's it."

"Trust me, it's all basic. Minor updates. Please," he begged. "You have no idea how much it would help me."

"Okay, I'll try."

"Aydan, you're a lifesaver! Invoice me for the actual time you spend plus the amount for your undercover work."

I left the office with a stack of files and spent the evening at my computer, wondering what I'd gotten myself into.

CHAPTER 17

When my phone rang at 4:45 A.M., I levitated several inches off the bed. I'd been deeply asleep, and my heart tried to bang its way out of my chest while I groped wildly for the receiver. Fear shot through me when I squinted at the illuminated call display and recognized Spider's number.

I jabbed at the Talk button. "Spider, what's wrong?" I snapped.

"Nothing's wrong," he said quickly.

I collapsed back onto the bed and hyperventilated quietly for a few seconds. "Thank God. What's up, then?"

"I just got a call from Kane. He needs you there."

I rolled out of bed, shivering when the chilly air from the open window hit my bare skin. "Okay. What's the plan?" As I spoke, I dragged out my backpack and started to dig in my underwear drawer.

"You need to come in to the office. We can talk there."

Right, of course he couldn't tell me anything over an unsecured line.

"When?"

"ASAP."

"See you in twenty minutes."

I hung up the phone and threw on some clothes,

abandoning the packing effort until I knew more about what I was getting into. On my way through the kitchen, I grabbed a cereal bar and hurried out the door.

I failed to appreciate the beauty of the sunrise on the way to town. My nerves jangled while I wolfed the bar down without tasting it. If Kane needed me, it meant only one thing. I'd be going back into the network. Nothing like the anticipation of pain and fear to get you going in the morning.

I pulled up in front of the little house precisely twenty minutes later. The lights were on, and I strode up the walk and barged into the office without knocking. Spider gave a violent start in his chair, and I offered him a penitent 'sorry' as the phone rang.

He picked up. "Yes, she's here... Yes, I ran a sweep just a few minutes ago. We're secure... Okay." He put the receiver against his shoulder and spoke to me. "I'm going to put him on speaker now."

He pressed a few buttons, and Kane's deep voice filled the room. "Aydan?"

"Hi, I'm here."

"Thanks for coming so quickly."

"No problem, what's up?"

"We've had some activity here overnight. People coming and going from the guest house. In the night vision scope, it looked like at least one of them was bound and blindfolded. We need to know if they're using the network. The sooner the better."

"Shit, I should have stayed in Calgary. I'm at least three hours away by the time I get loaded up and on the road."

He sighed. "I know. But I didn't know when, or if, we would need you again. It can't be helped. That gives me time to make some arrangements at this end, anyway."

"Okay, what do you need me to do?"

"You still hold a valid Class 6 driver's license." It wasn't a question. Spider's research skills had obviously been at work again.

"Yes."

"Hellhound says you still ride."

I shook my head incredulously. "His memory is phenomenal. I made a passing reference to it. Months ago."

"But you do?"

"Dirt biking. I haven't ridden a street bike in years."

"I guess that doesn't surprise me," he said slowly. "But could you get back on a street bike?"

"I guess. As long as I have a chance to ride it around for a while and get used to it again. But I don't have a helmet I'd trust for anything other than tooling around the back forty."

"We've got a base camp set up a few miles from Harchman's, and we're doing all our surveillance from motorcycles. They're small and manoeuvrable and easy to hide. I'll arrange for a bike and a helmet for you. Do you have riding clothes?"

"Yes. But get me a cruiser. 750 cc, max. I've never ridden one of those hyperbikes. I'd probably kill myself."

"All right. Plan to be here for a few days. Camping. Sorry, it's pretty primitive."

"No problem. I'm happier in the bush than dressed up at a party."

His laugh boomed over the speaker. "Somehow I thought you'd say that. I'll bring you up to speed when you get here. Webb will give you the network key and the address where you can pick up the bike and helmet. When you're kitted up and leaving Calgary, call Webb. He'll relay a call to me and I'll meet you on the highway about five miles east of Harchman's. Any questions?"

"Lots, but I think they can wait."

"One more thing. We need to be able to get you out of the network reliably. You and Webb need to work on that before you leave Silverside. We can't afford a repeat of what happened in March."

"Agreed. We'll figure something out. I think it was the... other stuff that was the problem, then."

"Let's hope so. See you soon. Ride safe."

"I will." The words came out of my mouth sounding more like a prayer than a statement.

Spider hung up the phone. He was the first to break the short silence. "I guess we'd better head over to Sirius and get the network key. I'll meet you there so you can leave right after." He scribbled an address and handed it to me. "Here's where you can pick up the bike. Tell them you're picking it up for Kane Consulting."

"Okay." I headed for my car while Spider locked up the office. My heart pounded as I sank into the driver's seat. I was so far outside my comfort zone. Despite my confident words, I was terrified of getting back on a street bike. And I was afraid to go back into the network, too.

I drove over to Sirius on autopilot, mindlessly following Spider's custom-painted lime-green Smart car. Throughout the short drive, I racked my brain for a safer, less obvious way to get into the network. God, why couldn't I just be invisible?

We parked and let ourselves into the prison-like security at Sirius, my already-racing pulse accelerating even more in the cramped time-delay chamber. When we arrived in Spider's lab, he unlocked the drawer again and retrieved the emerald necklace. I cocked an eyebrow at him, clenching my quivering hands behind my back to hide my nervousness.

"A little overdressed for camping, don't you think?" I asked.

"Definitely." He carried the necklace over to a workbench and prised the backing off the gem with tiny tools, peering through a powerful magnifying glass. "The question is what to do with it. If it gets lost, we're sunk. It's so tiny, all you have to do is sneeze and it's gone."

I frowned, pondering. "I hate to take it out in the bush. That's just asking to lose it."

Spider extracted the circuitry with tweezers and held it up. "Any ideas?"

"I shudder to think I carried that around on my keychain without a care in the world for nearly six months. Now I'm afraid to carry it across the room."

"I think you need to carry it on your person this time," he said seriously. "I don't think we should take a chance on putting it in your waist pouch or on your key ring."

"I hope you're not going to tell me where to stick it."

He blushed scarlet. "No! I didn't mean... I just meant... you should carry it with you. Somewhere. I mean, somehow."

I chuckled. "I know what you meant. I'm thinking." We sat in silence for a few moments. "Would it go under my watch strap?" I took off my large, battered watch and passed it over.

Spider examined it carefully. "Maybe. Or maybe..." He carried it over to the workbench and got out his little tools. A few seconds later, he looked up with a grin. "Perfect. Your watch is so big and old, the circuitry fits right inside the body of the watch. And nobody would ever think it's valuable." He stopped himself awkwardly. "I mean... it's a nice watch, but..."

"It's okay, Spider, I bought it over a decade ago for twenty bucks. I have no illusions that it's valuable. Or that anyone would ever think it was valuable."

He handed it back to me with an embarrassed shrug. "Sorry."

"No problem." I strapped it back on. "Okay, let's give it a test run. Have you got the monitors up?"

"Give me a minute." He turned to his computer, fingers flying. "Okay. Ready whenever you are."

"Let's kill two birds with one stone. I don't want to go in and out any more than I have to. How about if I go in and wait, and you see if you can wake me from here."

He nodded. "Go ahead."

I concentrated and stepped into the white void of the simulation network, wearing Robert's image. I walked around experimentally, focusing fiercely on holding the illusion for as long as possible.

After several minutes, my head started to throb from the effort. With a sigh, I let my body regain its normal appearance and wandered back and forth a little while longer. Then I conjured up an armchair from nothingness and sprawled into it, wondering what was taking Spider.

Finally, I got tired of waiting and stepped back through the portal. I clutched my head and swore violently when the expected pain hit me. Straightening slowly, I squinted at Spider.

"Why didn't you wake me?"

"I couldn't. I shook you and yelled your name. You didn't come out." He gazed at me in consternation. "This isn't going to work."

"Shit. I didn't feel a thing in the network. I thought you

said you could get people out of the network just as easily as waking them out of a sleep."

"Normally we can, but I guess it must be something weird about the way you access it with the key."

"We've got to find a way to make it work. Slap me or something. Or hey, how about this?" I dug into my waist pouch. "Here. Stick me with this pin."

He recoiled. "No! That's gross!"

"Spider, we have to make this work. Have you got a better idea?"

"I'm not sticking you with a pin."

"Do it, dammit! Would you rather I get captured or killed because I'm messing around in the network and I don't know I have to get out and run away in my real body?"

He took the pin from me, revulsion in every line of his body. "I think I might puke if I have to stick a pin in you. Or pass out."

"Then find somebody who can. Go get John Smith. I'm sure he'd love to stick a pin in me."

He squared his shoulders, pale but determined. "No. He's not sticking a pin in you. I'll do it."

"Okay. Here goes." I stepped back into the network void and waited. Nothing happened. I'd always liked Spider for his soft heart, but this time it was a serious handicap. He was probably still standing there trying to get up the nerve to poke me. I sighed and waved my armchair into existence again.

I flopped into it and kept falling into agony. White-hot whips lashed my brain and blindness swallowed me whole. Screams tore from my throat and my body flailed helplessly, beyond my control as it tried to escape the torture. Time folded into an eternity of torment.

The blindness resolved into a kaleidoscope of brilliant colours. Nausea overtook me as they swirled, and I curled into a tight, whimpering ball. Finally, the pain and sickness began to subside as the colours faded. My clenched muscles slowly eased and awareness returned.

I lay on the floor of the lab. Spider was kneeling beside me, his face chalk-white. "I'm sorry, I'm sorry," he babbled.

I roused myself from my misery and dragged myself onto my knees. "Hey, Spider, I'm okay."

He wrapped his arms around me and buried his face in my shoulder, trembling . "I'm sorry..."

"It's okay. It's not your fault. Hey." I gave him a little shake. "It's okay. My fault. I should have guessed this might happen."

He pulled away, swiping his hand across his face and taking a deep, shuddering breath. "I'm so sorry," he repeated. "Are... are you really okay?"

"I'm fine. It wasn't anything you did. Remember when something like this happened before? When I went through the portal too fast?"

He nodded wordlessly, visibly working to compose himself. His face was still ashen, and I let him take his time. Finally, he took another deep breath, steadier this time.

"I... I couldn't do it at first. I just poked you, a little bit, and nothing happened." He ran a shaking hand over his eyes. "And then I thought about what you said... if your life was at stake. And I poked you harder... And then you fell off the chair and started screaming and thrashing and I couldn't..." he stopped and covered his face.

"It wasn't your fault. I didn't even feel the pinprick. But I guess this is just what happens to me when I get dragged out of the network." I hauled myself shakily to my feet and reached down to give Spider a hand up from where he still knelt. "Well, we can consider that a failure. Lucky these labs are soundproof."

Spider dropped into his chair and we stared at each other. "Now what?" he quavered. "You can't go out there unless we figure something out. And I don't ever want to see you suffer like that, ever again." He shuddered, his eyes still dark with distress.

I grimaced. "Wouldn't be high on my list of things to do, either. Is there some way you can send a signal into the network?" Then I answered my own question. "No. Dammit, that won't work. Not if somebody else is using the network at the time."

We thought some more. I made fists in my hair and tugged irritably. There had to be a way. Pulling me out of the network obviously wouldn't work. That meant I somehow needed to receive a signal when I was inside the network so I could step out under my own power. But any signal would be audible or visible to anyone else who might happen to be inside the network. Think, think, dammit!

I looked up slowly. "Hey, Spider, how does this circuitry work to access the network?"

He launched into a complicated technical description. I caught about every third word.

I waved my hand to stem the tide. "Hold on. Is it transmitting a data signal? Is that what keeps me logged into the network as long as I choose to stay there?"

"Yes."

"What if we could weaken the signal? Not break it completely, just weaken it? Kind of like dimming the lights. That would signal me, but nobody else in the network."

His brows drew together in concentration. "It's digital,

not analog. You can't really 'dim' it. But... some EMI interference maybe." He swivelled in his chair and began to dig through the plastic bins mounted above the workbench.

"Transformer?" he muttered as he scrounged. "No, too bulky, too much power draw..." He continued to mumble to himself and excavate bins. "Hold on, how about this?" He extracted a small device from the heap. "Hand me your watch."

I handed it over and he bent over the bench, engrossed. He worked steadily for some time with his tiny tools and soldering pen, fiddling and testing with his multimeter probes.

Finally, he straightened. "Okay, I've rigged this up so it generates a variable-strength EMI pulse. The only problem is, I don't know how much of a pulse we'll need for it to be noticeable to you without kicking you out entirely."

I shrugged resignation. "I guess we'll just have to try it and see."

"No. There has to be another way." Horror reflected in his eyes.

"I'm open to suggestions."

After a short silence, he drew in a shaky breath. "You're right. Okay. This device will have to be held right against your watch to affect the key inside. I'll set it to the lowest possible strength. You go into the network, and I'll send a pulse. If you don't notice it in, let's say, fifteen seconds, I'll increase the strength and try it again. And so on."

I rolled my shoulders, trying to ease the ache. "Okay. Here goes." I stepped into the network and hovered tensely, counting the seconds. My nerves stretched tighter when nothing happened. I took a deep breath and let it out slowly. Then another.

Please let this work.

Minutes dragged past. How much of an incremental increase was Spider using, for shit's sake? I paced, tension mounting.

There was a sudden blip in the sim, a barely noticeable fading. A small, sharp pain darted behind my eyes and vanished as quickly as it had come. Knowing Spider was watching the monitor, I grinned and gave a thumbs-up before stepping out of the portal and back into my aching head.

I groaned and ground my teeth, holding my skull together with both hands. When I straightened at last, Spider was beaming.

"It worked!"

I cracked my neck, grimacing. "Fabulous. Let's do some more tests at that intensity. I'll go in again. Watch me on the monitors. Send a pulse at random intervals. I'll give you a thumbs-up whenever I notice anything. If it works predictably, we're all set." He nodded eagerly, and I stepped into the void again with a sigh.

Some time later, I squinted painfully up at Spider. "I counted a total of twelve signals. How did I do?"

He grinned, elation sparkling in his eyes. "Perfect. You were right on with each one. A hundred percent accuracy. I think we're there."

"Thank God." I slumped over, propping my head in my hands. "I don't want to do this anymore," I whined softly.

"You don't have to," he said, sounding bewildered. "That worked fine. We're done."

"No. I'm not done yet." I tenderly massaged my temples. "I need to go in and try something else."

"Why?"

I met his eyes. "Because I'm scared shitless of going back in and getting recognized." I dropped my face into my hands again. "I'm such a chickenshit."

"Aydan, you're not a chickenshit. You're the bravest person I know." I looked up as he turned pink. "I can't believe you keep doing this. After what you went through before. And when it hurts you so much."

"Thanks, Spider. I wish I felt brave." I cracked my neck again and sat up straight. "Okay. This might look weird on the monitors. Don't worry." I considered for a moment. "Or it might just look like me stepping into the network. I don't know. I'm going to mess around for a while. I'll come out in ten minutes. Or less. Watch the monitors for every detail."

His forehead creased in confusion. "Okay. What are you going to do?"

I gave him a half-smile. "Wait and see."

I stepped into the void again, concentrating on being invisible. What the hell, it was a simulation. Why couldn't it work? I stood still for a few moments, looking down at where my body should be. Nothing but white void.

I walked around cautiously and waved a hand in front of my face. Nothing. My heart beat a little faster. This might work.

I created a mirror in the sim and walked in front of it. Still nothing.

Grinning, I conjured up a sofa and chair and sat down in the chair, watching the mirror. The chair's cushion compressed, but there was no sign of me. I got up again and pushed the chair over a few feet. That worked fine. Next test.

What would happen if I also imagined myself insubstantial? I turned back to the chair and passed my hand through it. Then I walked through it. No sensation of contact at all. The chair remained stationary. I turned back to it and gave it an intentional push. It moved cooperatively over a few inches.

Ha! I could interact with my own constructs any way I wanted.

What if...? I hovered weightlessly about eight feet above the furniture and floated effortlessly around the perimeter. Better and better. And it was far easier to maintain. Being invisible was almost as easy as being myself.

"Okay," I spoke out loud. "Spider, this is an audio test. I'll be out in a minute."

I floated through the portal. Pain crashed through my head again, and I couldn't even summon up enough energy to swear. I wrapped my arms over my head and groaned until it eased. When I opened my eyes, Spider was squatting in front of my chair, gazing at me anxiously.

"Are you okay? What was that?"

"Let me look at the data record," I croaked, dragging my chair over.

He gave me another worried look before stepping over to run the record. A smile spread across my face as the video progressed. Furniture moved of its own accord. There was complete silence except for the scraping of the furniture until the very end when my voice spoke out of nothingness.

I pumped my fist. "Yes!" I turned to meet Spider's baffled gaze. "That was me, being invisible!"

His jaw dropped. "Get out of here. Really?" He ran the video again, scrutinizing the monitor. "You were in there the whole time? How cool is that?"

"That is cooler than cool, my friend," I said smugly. Then I sobered. "One last test. I need somebody to be in the network with me while I do that. I want to be really, really sure. Because this could backfire in a really bad way."

He nodded slowly. "Yeah. Okay, I'll come in with you."

"That would be good, because now you know what to expect. But I also need somebody in there who doesn't suspect anything is going on. Just to see if there's any difference in what you observe. Is Mike Connor working today?"

Spider hunched over the keyboard to check his records. "No."

"Shit. Who else could we use?"

"John Smith is the only other person with high enough security clearances."

"Shit!" I scowled, tried to think of an alternative, and came up empty. "Well, it can't be helped. I need this test. Can you call him?"

"Is that a good idea? Didn't he attack you the last time you were in the network together?"

"Yes, but now he knows which side I'm on. I don't think that'll happen again. And you'll be there."

I was also reasonably sure it wouldn't happen again because I'd laid a pretty good virtual beating on Smith after that last little episode. I really didn't think he'd take a chance on pissing me off again, inside or outside the network.

"Okay." Spider picked up the phone. After several minutes of coaxing, he didn't seem to be making much progress. Finally he straightened and used an authoritative tone I hadn't heard before. "No. Not acceptable. This is time-critical and mission-critical. Get down here. Now." He hung up the phone firmly. "He'll be here in a few minutes."

"Nicely done. Very assertive."

He raised a humorous eyebrow. "It's the beard."

Smith duly arrived about five minutes later. His unwashed stench preceded him as he came through the door. God, lucky thing this place was well-ventilated. I breathed shallowly.

Spider briefed him, using the same decisive tones as before. "We're conducting some specialized testing. We need you to step inside the portal and remain there. Observe and record every single thing. Sound, sight, smell, sensation, everything. I'll come in with you. Aydan will conduct the tests."

Smith shot me a look of barely concealed alarm. "I... don't know if I'm the right person for this..."

"You're the only person available," I growled. He didn't look reassured at my tone, and I relented and explained. "The session will be recorded. From your standpoint, very little will happen. That's why we need you to be very focused on your observation."

"All right," he agreed reluctantly. "How long will this take?"

"Not more than ten minutes." I looked from him to Spider. "Let's go."

I watched the monitors until the two men appeared in the portal. The fixed stares on their real-world bodies in the lab reassured me all was going according to plan thus far. Time to rock and roll.

I stepped invisibly into their network simulation, going for silent and insubstantial. Just to be on the safe side, I drifted above their heads while they stood scanning the void.

"What are we looking for?" Smith whispered.

Spider shushed him impatiently. "Just watch. And listen."

I drifted over to place my lips right next to Spider's ear. "Spider," I breathed as quietly as possible. He jerked in shock, his head snapping around to search for the source of the sound. The side of his face connected solidly with my invisible nose. He let out a yelp and jerked back while I did my best to muffle my involuntary grunt of pain.

Smith stared at him. "What?"

"Shhh," Spider shushed him again.

I floated up ten feet or so and spoke. "This is an audio test. If you can hear me, point toward the source of the sound." Both men's heads swivelled, and both of them pointed upward at me. Hmmm. I concentrated on putting my voice somewhere else. "Where is the sound source now?" They both wheeled around, pointing across the void at shoulder height.

Excellent. And safer than whispering in someone's ear.

I created two chairs. "Sit down."

Smith glanced over at Spider. "Did you do that?"

Spider shook his head, frowning, and motioned to Smith to sit.

One more test. I drifted reluctantly toward Smith's smelly avatar. Focusing on one of the lank strands of hair draped over his collar, I carefully reached out my invisible fingers. This was harder than I thought. I couldn't see how close I was.

Concentrating on being insubstantial, I inched my hand forward. The problem was, I wouldn't know whether it was working or not until my virtual hand was halfway through his virtual head. I nobly resisted the urge to just slap him upside the head and see if my hand went through. If it didn't, oh well.

I muffled a snicker and refocused. And touched the lock

of hair with my fingertips. It moved slightly and Smith absently scratched his head, still staring around the void.

Shit. I'd been afraid that might happen. Despite my efforts at being insubstantial, I was still physically interacting with other avatars.

I drew back. "Spider, could you please create a chair?" Both men jerked around in their chairs to look behind them, but they obviously couldn't see me. After a second, another chair appeared in the void. I drifted over to it and tentatively reached out my hand. It passed through the chair like vapour. Good. Then I gave it a push, and it slid over several inches. Perfect. I could control my interactions with all constructs, regardless of who created them.

I threw my voice over beside Spider's ear again. "Spider," I whispered. "I'm going to touch your shoulder. Try not to react." He stared tensely straight ahead. I tried one more time for insubstantial. I misjudged the distance, and my hand dropped heavily on his shoulder.

He jumped. "Sorry," he said immediately.

"What?" Smith regarded him with unease.

I moved quickly away. "Thank you, gentlemen," I projected from in front of them. "That's all I need. Please wait here for two minutes, and then exit the network." They both nodded understanding, and I stepped through the portal.

Knowing I wouldn't have an audience, I let it all hang out, groaning and swearing and pounding my fist on the table. As the pain subsided, I straightened slowly, trying to look nonchalant. A few seconds later, Spider and Smith blinked and sat up, too, as they left the network and came back to the real world.

"What was that about?" Smith demanded.

"Just some tests. Let's run the data record back, and you can tell me what you observed."

Spider brought up the record and we reviewed it in slow-motion. Smith had little to add to what was visible on the monitor. He apparently hadn't heard or seen me except when I spoke aloud. He hadn't even consciously noticed me touching his hair.

When the record ended, I turned to Smith. "Thank you. That's all I needed."

"Are you going to share your findings?"

"Not at the moment. I need to do some more analysis," I lied.

Smith looked frustrated, but he got up and left without further comment.

"Why didn't you tell him?" Spider demanded when we were alone again.

"Mostly sheer bloody-mindedness," I admitted. "But also partly because there's a chance I might need an uninformed test participant later." I looked at my watch. "Crap! We've spent far too long here. I've got to get going."

Spider handed me the small EMI generator. "Here's your warning system. If for some reason you need to increase the intensity, give this screw a quarter-turn." He indicated a tiny screw on the side.

"I hope this works."

"I hope so, too."

CHAPTER 18

It was eight-thirty A.M. by the time I dragged my aching head back into my car. Tension wound up in my shoulders. I was still at least three hours away from any productive action. If Harchman was torturing some poor soul in his network, help was a long way away.

Nightmare memories shrieked at the edges of my mind and I pushed them away, steering my car to the Melted Spoon with shaking hands. I grabbed a toasted bagel to go and bolted it down while I drove home.

Back at the farm, I hurriedly packed several days' changes of clothes into my backpack and excavated my riding leathers from the depths of my hall closet. The pants and jacket fit a lot more snugly than they had ten years earlier but I could still squeeze into them, and the high-quality leather would protect me from some road rash if worse came to worst.

Glancing at my watch, I threw some snacks, orange juice boxes, and my water bottle into the backpack as well. Then I locked up the house and hit the road worrying.

By the time I parked at the motorcycle dealership at the south end of Calgary over two hours later, I was exhausted. My head and shoulders ached with stress. Something large and anxious flapped spiky wings in my stomach.

I got stiffly out of the car and stretched, shaking out the kinks before I squared my shoulders and walked in.

I had no idea what arrangements Kane had made, but apparently everything was well in hand. A helpful man fitted me with a top-quality full-face helmet and ushered me to the parking lot where a Honda Shadow lounged beside the building. He handed over the key and showed me a space in their fenced compound where I could leave my car. Then he mercifully left me to my own devices.

I jittered beside the motorcycle for a few minutes, looking it over. I'd ridden my dirt bike quite a bit in the past couple of months, so I was confident in my riding skills. I was just frightened of everybody else's driving skills.

Finally, I sighed and took my backpack into the washroom, where I changed into my thinnest gym shorts and a tank top. I wriggled into my leathers and creaked my way back out to the bike.

The sun burned down on my black-clad body and sweat trickled between my shoulder blades. I sighed again. Dawdling wasn't going to help anything.

I buckled on my helmet and slung my pack on my back. With a quick prayer to the god of bikers, if there was one, I fired up the Honda and pulled out into traffic, my rigid body fighting the corners, my trembling hands clenched on the handgrips.

On the edge of town, I turned off into the vacant end of a mall parking lot and stopped, peeling my aching fingers loose and letting my head hang while I breathed slowly and deeply. Calm. Just do a few manoeuvrability tests. Get comfortable. Relax.

I took a deep breath and kicked the bike into gear again

to run up to a reasonable speed, braking and cornering hard to get a feel for the extra weight and bulk. I didn't want to waste any more time, so I called Spider to let him know I was on my way before pulling out onto the highway to head west.

I hadn't ridden at highway speed for years, and the ache in my hands and shoulders reminded me once more to breathe and relax. At first I stared at the oncoming traffic, hyper-alert, but after a while I began to remember how much I used to enjoy riding. By the time I spotted Kane at the side of the road a half-hour later, the hot sun had relaxed my tense shoulders and I was smiling with the sheer joy of the open road.

There was no mistaking the tall, broad-shouldered figure leaning against a mean-looking black BMW K1300R. When I pulled up beside him, I took a few seconds to appreciate the view.

Like me, Kane was clad in a black leather jacket, which he'd unzipped in the heat. He wore black leather riding chaps over faded blue jeans, and I swallowed hard at the sight. Riding chaps for men are like cut-out lingerie. They just beg you to look at the good stuff.

I looked. And was amply rewarded. Oh, yeah.

I pushed up my visor, carefully keeping my eyes above his neck. The clean-shaven, distinguished businessman of the weekend had morphed into a dangerously hot biker, several days worth of dark stubble accenting the planes of his face and emphasizing his grey eyes.

"I wasn't sure it was you," he said. "What did you do with your hair?"

"I stuffed it down my jacket collar. Otherwise it just turns into a rat's nest."

He pulled on his helmet and started his bike. "Let's go."

We rode west for a few more miles until he turned onto a side road that was paved for only the first hundred yards or so. I followed him as he took a quick right over a gravelled crossing, threading between a couple of fence posts. The ground dropped off into a valley, and we rode down the short, grassy hill.

A blocky, muscular man swung open a gate at the bottom of the hill. I waved to him as we rode through, taking a sharp turn behind a copse of trees. An RV and an enclosed cargo trailer were concealed in the forested area, with a red Yamaha YZF-R1 motorcycle parked alongside. As we rolled to a halt and dismounted, our gatekeeper closed the gate behind us and strolled over.

I pulled off my helmet and slipped out of the hot jacket, leaving them on the seat of my bike. I surveyed the broad-shouldered man with a grin. "Carl! How are you?"

"Hi, Aydan. Nice to see you again." His brown eyes crinkled in a smile.

I regarded his black ringlets with a raised eyebrow. "What's with the rock-star hair? Or no, wait a minute, I know, you look like one of those long-haired WWF wrestling guys."

Kane laughed. "Germain's getting in touch with his feminine side."

Germain rubbed a hand over luxuriant black whiskers almost long enough to qualify as a beard. "If this looks feminine to you, you've been out in the bush too long."

I laughed. "Spider would kill for stubble like that," I told him. "He's growing a beard. Or trying. So are you growing your hair long?"

"Not intentionally," he replied ruefully. "It's driving me nuts. I just haven't had time to get it cut lately."

"We can socialize later. We need to get Aydan up to speed and get into position at Harchman's," Kane said. "Let's go inside."

As we trooped toward the RV, Germain grinned. "It sure is nice to see a face without a beard."

"Lucky I shaved this morning, then," I said, to their laughter.

Inside the RV, there was little evidence of the male-type clutter I had expected from guys who'd been camping out for several days. The sofa bed was pulled out, its covers rumpled as though recently occupied. I glimpsed another unmade bed in the bedroom at the back of the RV. There were a couple of backpacks lying in the corner, but the rest was surprisingly tidy.

We skirted the sofa bed and I chuckled when the two big men squeezed onto the benches of the dinette.

"They make these things for hobbits," Kane groused as we settled in.

"Still, pretty nice accommodations," I teased. "I thought you said it was primitive. Is this how city boys rough it? Queen-sized beds, microwave..."

Germain grinned. "If you really want to sleep outside in the mosquitoes, we'll let you."

"Nah. I've got nothing to prove."

Kane got straight to the point. "So here's the situation. Hellhound, Germain and I have been watching Harchman's place from the woods since Sunday morning, taking shifts. Hellhound's in place now. We've got Wheeler undercover with the security company, working the midnight-to-eight shift. Wheeler has placed bugs in the security office, employee locker room, and Harchman's office, but we haven't heard anything relevant yet. Wheeler also gained the confidence of one of the women who works with the housekeeping staff..."

Germain winked at me. "It must be nice to be tall, blond and handsome. If it was me, they wouldn't give me the time of day."

I grinned back at him. "Oh, I don't know. I think that rock-star hair's working for you."

"Getting back to the point," Kane said firmly.

"Right, sorry."

"This woman says Harchman has started a new business venture within the past few months, a wellness spa for businessmen," Kane continued. "It seems Harchman usually has several guests staying at the guest house at any given time, so there are quite a few people around. But last night around 3:30 A.M., a panel van drove up to the guest house and offloaded at least two people from the cargo bay, plus a driver and a passenger. We couldn't get a clear view, but we're fairly certain one person was bound and blindfolded. There's been no other unusual activity since. We need to know what, if anything, is going on in the network."

He turned to me, frowning. "This is where it gets dangerous. We need to get you close enough to access the network. We don't know exactly how close that will be, or how long it might be safe to stay there. We may need to move you, fast. Can we wake you reliably from the network?"

"Not really..."

His shoulders tensed as he interrupted. "This can't work, then. We have to be able to get you out. The risk is too great otherwise."

"Let me finish. There's an alternative."

His eyes bored into mine. "I'm listening."

"Spider and I did some tests. Unfortunately, we confirmed that I don't wake to the normal methods like touch or sound. It takes a pain stimulus to wake me from the network. And when that happens, it's the same as if I exit the portal too fast. I'm completely incapacitated. And I'm loud. You remember what it was like at the warehouse this spring."

Kane and Germain both frowned, grim lines deepening in their weary faces. "So what's the alternative?" Kane demanded.

I showed him Spider's device. "This. Instead of actually yanking me out, this device generates enough electromagnetic interference to weaken the signal that keeps me logged into the network. I see a blip in the sim, and I get a little jolt of pain. It acts as a signal to me that I need to exit the network. Then I can step out of my own accord, with no worse consequences than usual. All you have to do is hold the device against my wristwatch and press the button."

"Why your wristwatch?"

"That's where the network key circuitry is currently hidden. And the device has to be touching the watch, or the signal will be too weak for me to detect."

"How do we know it will work consistently?"

"Spider and I had a hundred percent accuracy in our tests. But if for some reason you need a stronger pulse, you can turn this little screw a quarter turn clockwise." I showed them the adjustment. "But then you run the risk of actually breaking the signal. With the accompanying noise and drama on my part."

Kane rubbed at his frown. "Okay," he said reluctantly. "I guess that's the best we can do. But we'll have to be ready to move fast, because you'll be visible as soon as you step into the network. Can you still use your disguise?"

I grinned at him. "You're going to like this part."

Hope rose in his eyes. "I could really use some good news right now."

"I can be invisible."

"What?" Both men jerked forward, faces intent.

"Spider and Smith and I tested it thoroughly. I can be completely invisible in a sim. And insubstantial, for the most part. I can walk through any construct, if I choose to, without affecting it or myself. Avatars are different, unfortunately. If you and I were in a sim together, I couldn't walk through you. You'd feel me, even though you couldn't see me."

Kane relaxed back into the seat, his face clearing. "Well, that changes things. That's the first good news I've had in days. All right. Then all we have to do is get you within range of the network."

I frowned at him. "I hope there's some spillover of the broadcast from the building site into the surrounding area."

"We won't know until you try," he admitted. "Your access was so widespread when we were there Saturday night, I hope we won't have to approach the buildings at all. I find it hard to believe they're broadcasting over a range that large, but Spider says it's technically possible. It just seems too good to be true."

"Only one way to find out."

He nodded. "Germain, you stay here. We'll go and relieve Hellhound. Aydan will try to access the network. We'll make plans afterward, depending on what she finds. Expect her back within one hour, tops. If she doesn't make it back in that time, assume we've been captured and go to Plan B."

Germain nodded, his usually cheerful face serious.

"Aydan, we'll try to get access from as far away as possible," Kane continued. "If we have to get closer, we will. You are the most important part of this plan. Your primary objective is to stay safe."

"But." He sighed, his eyes reflecting old pain. "If you're captured, I'll have to ask you to make that wristwatch your top priority. If you can do it undetectably, drop the watch and leave it concealed somewhere. It can't fall into enemy hands."

"Understood."

He reached across the table and took my hand. "You know what will happen to you if you're captured."

I nodded wordlessly, not trusting my voice.

"I hate to put you in this position. But if that happens... try to hold on as long as you can. Know that we'll get you out as soon as possible."

"I know," I said quietly. "Let's go."

CHAPTER 19

I followed Kane's bike past Harchman's driveway to a crossing about a mile down the road. He turned off and rode slowly through a narrow gap between two fence posts, and I threaded through behind him, acutely conscious of the unaccustomed width of my ride.

We idled quietly in single-file while he followed a twisting trail through the woods for a couple of hundred yards. We dismounted beside Hellhound's Harley Fatboy in a small clearing, and I strapped my helmet onto my bike for safekeeping.

I eyed the Harley. "Not exactly a stealth vehicle, is it?"

"He doesn't start it up until he's at the highway."

I grinned. "Lucky he's been working out lately. It's a hell of a big bike to push."

Kane led the way down a twisting game trail, and I followed, sticking close. "How much does Hellhound know about the network?" I whispered.

"Nothing."

"Okay."

Kane took out his cellphone and punched a speed dial button. Seconds later, he disconnected. Catching my curious look, he explained, "I'm signalling him that we're incoming. We keep our phones on vibrate. Otherwise he wouldn't know who was sneaking up on him."

"Right, makes sense."

A few minutes' walking brought us to another small clearing. Hellhound looked up from his binoculars as we arrived. A slow smile spread across his face as he looked me up and down.

"Well, hello, darlin'," he rasped. "You're the best thing I've seen in days."

He was wearing leather riding chaps, too. Kane couldn't see my face, so I didn't even try to hide the way my gaze zeroed in on Hellhound's crotch. He winked at me and licked his lips. Despite my nervousness, I felt a slow fire start down low.

Kane ignored his antics, as usual. "You can head back to camp now," he said. "I'll relieve you. We need to get a little closer."

"We, meanin' you an' Aydan?"

At Kane's wordless nod, Hellhound bristled. "Ya puttin' her in danger again?"

Kane sighed. "Yes." He met Arnie's eyes squarely. "No choice."

Hellhound scowled but nodded. "Okay, Cap. Watch out for the patrols. They've been random today." He handed the binoculars to Kane. "Stay safe. Both a' ya." He disappeared down the path.

I looked up at Kane. "Might as well try from here for starters."

I sat cross-legged on the ground and concentrated. Nothing happened. I got up, sighing.

"That would have been too easy. Onward."

I followed Kane as he zigzagged along the trail, gradually

angling toward the buildings. He stopped on a small rise. "Try it from here."

I dropped to the ground again and bowed my head.

"Still nothing."

"Damn."

Several more minutes of stealthy travel brought us considerably closer to the building site. Kane held up a hand to signal a halt and turned to me, raising his eyebrows. I obediently sat again, concentrating. This time, I drifted insubstantially into a void.

Heart hammering, I peered down at myself, making certain I was truly invisible. I took a deep, calming breath when I saw nothing. I began to drift silently, creating a barely-there ghost of the corridors that formed the network. Doors lined each wall, and I swore to myself. This could take a hell of a long time. I needed to see inside each room.

I pondered, floating. What if I created a sim of a tiny piece of one-way glass in each door? Theoretically, if the room was occupied, nobody would notice me peeking in.

Theoretically.

I steeled myself and floated to the first door, taking a quick peek through. Vacant. I did the same for the next. And the next.

I quickly evolved a system to save time. Unhampered by a physical body, I could zap from door to door without a time lapse. Zap. Peek. Zap. Peek.

I finished the first corridor and hurtled down the next one, gaining speed and confidence. Everything seemed deserted.

Peek.

I froze, gawking into the room.

Harchman was inside. The party scene from the gazebo

had been carelessly recreated. Faceless people moved around, providing a backdrop for the detailed scenario at the bar. I stood facing Harchman, wearing my party dress. In his fantasy, the dress was a lot more revealing. Apparently he liked big boobs, too, because mine were inflated like volleyballs.

As I watched, paralyzed with shock, the construct that looked like me brushed her tongue across the rim of her wineglass. Harchman's avatar smiled and unzipped his pants, and the construct sank worshipfully to her knees, opening her mouth.

Eeeeeuuuuwwww! I did a rapid about-face, compulsively wiping my lips.

I hovered with my back to the room for a few seconds, recovering, and then shrugged it off.

Whatever. I really wished I hadn't seen that, but it was harmless fantasy on Harchman's part. I'd been known to have a fantasy or two myself on occasion. The enticing aroma of warm chocolate wafted to my nose, and I closed my eyes and banished it determinedly.

Besides, Harchman needed all the help he could get. Fantasy was the only way he'd ever manage to achieve a boner that size. I stifled a snicker. Maybe all guys imagined themselves well-endowed in the sim.

I turned back to the job at hand and quickly finished all the connections in the corridor. Then I turned to the brick firewall at the end of the hall. Drifting carefully through it, I surveyed the next set of doors. Letting out my breath silently, I started again.

I'd slipped into an unconscious rhythm when I suddenly came upon an occupied room about halfway down the hall. I bit back a cry and jerked away so violently my insubstantial body rocketed backward through the opposite wall of the corridor and into another, fortunately vacant, room.

Pulling myself together, I took several deep breaths and drifted back to reluctantly peek in again on the nightmare scene. My mind wrapped around it whole, storing it away in an instant to haunt me later. I forced myself to ignore blood and instruments of torture and concentrate instead on the faces of the people in the room.

Two men stood over a third man, tied to a chair. I memorized the faces. The first two were burned into my brain. I'd never forget them. The man in the chair didn't have enough face left for me to identify. I'd never be able to forget that, either.

I backed away, swallowing hard. Just a simulation. The man in the chair was physically unharmed. Somewhere.

The knowledge didn't help much. I knew he was suffering as much as if it was actually happening to him in real life.

I drew a couple of ragged breaths and squelched my initial impulse to rush out of the network and report to Kane immediately. He had said two people were brought in. I forced myself into research mode.

I was just turning away to continue down the corridor when a gunshot exploded from inside the room. Horror drowned me as I jerked back to see the captive's limp body hanging from its bonds. A glimpse of the head wound confirmed that his torment had ended. Permanently.

I hung paralyzed in the corridor, struggling to force my lungs to expand as the two men turned away from their victim and strode toward the door. Toward me.

A blip cut through my vision and the small accompanying stab of pain galvanized me into action. I folded virtual space to stand instantly in front of my exit portal. Adrenaline searing my veins, I stepped through into pain.

I ground my teeth, trying not to make noise. My throbbing head jerked violently. After a moment, I realized it was because I was holding it with both hands and Kane was shaking my shoulders at the same time.

"Aydan!" he hissed. "Aydan! Come on! Dogs!"

I forced my eyes open and staggered to my feet, still half-blind. Kane dragged me down the path until I regained a semblance of motor control. Frenzied barking rang through the forest, too close.

I shook my head, desperately focusing. When he saw I could move under my own volition again, Kane shoved me in front of him on the path.

"Run! Get back to camp. I'll draw them off." I opened my mouth to argue, and he shook my arm hard. "Do it! Remember your priorities!"

I met his eyes, closing my mouth on what was probably a sob. Then I turned and ran.

I charged through the woods, trying to shield my eyes from the twigs that lashed my face. Men shouted and the barking reached a crescendo behind me. Fear for myself and for Kane drove me to reckless speed.

I burst into the clearing and flung myself onto the Honda, skinning my knuckles as I frantically twisted the key. I rocketed along the winding path, my dirt-biking reflexes wrestling the unfamiliar weight and bulk of my ride. When I finally gained the pavement, I cracked the throttle wide open.

The front wheel lifted as the engine roared, and I threw my weight forward to settle it, barely in control. Then the highway was flying by, my frantic panting drowned out by the engine noise. The wind whipped my watering eyes and tore at my hair.

Please, absent gods, don't let me crash. No helmet. No chance in hell.

I kept my gaze locked on the road, afraid to even glance at the speedometer. The turnoff rushed up and I braked hard and downshifted rapidly.

And forgot how big and heavy the motorcycle was.

I took the turn too fast, laying the bike over in a hard lean to compensate. Asphalt dragged at the footpeg. It didn't catch, thank God. My turn swung too wide, and I pulled out of it in desperate terror of high-siding. Somehow I managed to hold it together.

Braking again and trying to yank the bike into another too-tight turn, I overshot the entrance we'd previously used. Instead, I hurtled over the crossing on the other side of the fence posts. Too late, I spotted another post lying half-concealed in the grass, directly in my path.

My heart couldn't beat any faster, so it stopped.

I stood hard on the footpegs, bouncing the suspension and cracking the throttle as I jerked upward to take the load off the front wheel. And in my panic, I underestimated the power of the bike again.

The engine surged, the front wheel reaching for the sky. The rear wheel bumped over the fencepost, but the ground sloped down into the valley.

The motorcycle took air. My pulse rate redoubled, my vision blackening at the edges. Clinging frantically to the handgrips, I shifted my weight slightly back of centre and tried to adjust the throttle to maintain the right speed. The back wheel hit heavily before the motorcycle slammed forward onto its front wheel. The bike bucked and twisted and I barely kept my seat, braking again as soon as I dared.

I jerked my eyes up in time to see Hellhound swing the gate open.

Too close, too fast.

Clutch-brake-throttle.

The rear end swung around, a barrage of stones rattling against the gate as the tire gouged an arc in the dirt. Then I was through. I dodged around the corner and skidded to a halt in the clearing.

Germain bolted to his feet from a log beside the RV as Hellhound ran up from behind. I gasped a couple of shallow, hysterical breaths, air wheezing through my constricted throat. My hands wouldn't let go of the handgrips.

A voice I didn't recognize pushed out from between my teeth. "I think they got Kane."

CHAPTER 20

My breathing wouldn't work right, and I still couldn't let go of the handgrips. I jerked my arms, trying to free myself. Somebody whimpered, and I belatedly recognized my own voice.

Germain snatched out his gun and ran for the gate, out of my line of sight while I struggled.

I felt the motorcycle's suspension compress as Hellhound swung onto the seat behind me. He reached around me to turn off the ignition and leaned into me, his warm bulk at my back as he placed his strong hands over mine.

"Slow down, darlin'. Just breathe."

He gently massaged my hands while I concentrated on steadying my breath. In. Out. Belly breathing. In. Out. Slow like ocean waves.

The ocean waves jerked and wobbled as tremors rolled through my body. Arnie's gravelly voice growled soothing nonsense in my ear. Gradually, his warmth eased my frozen paralysis, and my deathgrip relaxed.

As my hands fell away from the grips, I sucked in a ragged breath and collapsed against him. His arms wrapped around me to hold me close. I allowed myself a few seconds of comfort before pulling away to sit up.

"I'm okay. Thanks." I forced my tight voice to steady.

Hellhound got off and lowered the kickstand, steadying the bike. I dismounted after him. My legs buckled, and I fell flat on my ass.

A shrill giggle escaped me as I looked up at him from my seat in the dirt. He gazed down at me for a second, his face creased in concern. Then he sat down beside me and tucked his arm around my shoulders.

The giggle went on a little too long, and I clamped my trembling lips together and did some more deep breathing.

Germain returned, frowning down at us tensely. "No sign of pursuit. Aydan, what happened?"

"I got in the n..." I began, and then caught Germain's eye and stopped. "I... We... The dog patrol found us. Kane sent me back while he drew them off. I can't see how he could have escaped."

Hellhound jerked around to look in my face. "The patrols never came out that far before. How close to the buildings were ya?"

I sighed. "Close."

"But, darlin', why..."

"He's resourceful," Germain interrupted. "He could have gotten away. He might be working his way back on foot. That would take some time."

I surveyed his face and saw the grim reality. "How long do we wait? I could go back there right now and know right away if he was in..." I shut up again. Then the fear and frustration burst out of me. "Dammit! Arnie needs to know!"

Hellhound's arm tightened around me. "Then tell me."

"Not my call," I gritted. I gazed up at Germain. He

shook his head. "What's Plan B?" I demanded.

"Plan B is a full-on assault. It's only to be implemented if you're captured with the key," Germain said reluctantly. "We can't justify it for any other team member."

"But..." I began, and he interrupted.

"I'm sorry. I feel the same way as you do. But we can't. Kane knew the score when he went in."

The strength of anger poured into my legs, and I lunged to my feet. "We can't just leave him! You don't know what they'll do! You have no idea what I saw..." My throat closed up and I spun away, taking a few shaky steps to stand with my back to them.

"Aydan." Germain's voice was firm. "We'll get him back. We just have to do it a different way, that's all."

I stood trembling, trying to compose myself. Sweat poured off me while I gasped shallow, ineffectual breaths. My legs shook uncontrollably.

Hellhound came around to stand in front of me, eyeing me worriedly. "Aydan, when did ya eat last?"

Nausea washed over me. "Around eight-thirty," I whispered.

"Shit!" He caught me as my knees let go again and lowered me gently to the ground. He knelt beside me. "Germain! We got any orange juice?"

Germain's worried frown hovered over me. "No."

"In my backpack. In the RV," I panted. "Sorry. Stupid. Meant to have a snack when I got here. Forgot." I struggled to get up, shivering in the heat. Sweat soaked my tank top.

"Stay put," Hellhound rasped. His arms closed around me and he pulled me back to lean against him. Germain reappeared and handed me the small carton of orange juice. I took it with both hands, trying to still their trembling enough to get the straw in my mouth. Arnie took it away from me and held the straw to my lips. I sipped, waiting for the nausea to pass.

"I'm okay," I insisted. "Just need a bit of blood sugar. I'll be fine in a minute. We don't have time for this. Kane doesn't have time for this. What's the plan?"

Germain squatted beside me. "The plan is that you stay there and drink orange juice until you're ready to walk to the trailer and eat something. After that, we'll talk."

"Talk now! Let's not waste time!" I struggled to stand again, but Hellhound held me effortlessly.

"I told ya to stay put," he growled. "Ya can get up when that juice's done."

I briefly considered doing a quick chug-a-lug, but despite the urgency that hammered at me, I knew Arnie was right. I subsided against him and let him feed me more juice.

Germain relented and sat down on the ground opposite. "First we need recon. We need to know if they have Kane, and if so, where they're holding him. We can't just go blazing in there."

"I can do that," I said. "I can go into the..." I stopped and gazed imploringly at Germain. He shook his head. I blew out a frustrated breath and continued obliquely. "I can check the rooms. If necessary, I can probably peek out a portal and see what's on the other side."

"Did you get in earlier?" Germain asked.

"Yes. I found a prisoner."

I swallowed hard as the memory rose in front of me. Germain's face hardened as he read my expression, and Hellhound gave me another sip of orange juice.

I shook off the horror and continued. "There were two men torturing him. He... I don't know if he told them anything." I dealt silently with my memories again. "They killed him. While I was watching."

Arnie's arms tightened around me, and I resisted the urge to turn and hide my face in his chest. I pulled away to sit up a little straighter instead.

"Did you get a good look at their faces?" Germain asked.

"Yes. Well. The torturers." I took a deep breath and let it out slowly. "The prisoner... wasn't identifiable anymore. If I had any way of uploading those faces... You don't have a n... connection here, do you?"

"We have a satellite uplink."

"Then I need to talk to Spider and see if there's a way I can dump that data to him." I struggled determinedly away from Hellhound's restraining arm. "I'm ready to eat now." I dragged myself shakily to my feet and tottered toward the RV.

Inside, Germain handed me a phone. "This line's secured. The uplink is over there." He pointed to a laptop on the counter in the kitchenette.

I turned to Arnie. "I'm sorry, if I'm not allowed to tell you about this stuff, you'll have to wait outside while I talk to Spider. I can't say what I need to say otherwise."

He nodded. "Do what ya gotta do, darlin'." He clumped down the steps and strode away.

I dialled Spider's number. "Spider, it's Aydan."

"Aydan, hi! How's it going?"

My throat closed up again and I struggled for a few seconds. "It's... been better," I said hoarsely.

Alarm sprang into his voice. "What's wrong?"

I tried, but the words wouldn't come. "Germain will brief you later," I whispered. I cleared my throat and took a deep, calming breath. "Spider, I need to know if there's a way I can access the Sirius network remotely. I've memorized some faces. If I could go into a sim and recreate them, then you could download the data and do facial recognition. Is there any way to do that from this satellite uplink?"

There was silence on the other end of the line. "Aydan," Spider said finally. "I need to know what's wrong."

I handed the phone to Germain and sank onto the dinette bench to bury my face in my shaking hands.

I heard Germain step to the door of the RV. "Hellhound!"

The trailer rocked as Germain went out, and his voice receded while he spoke to Spider. The door opened and closed again, and soon I heard the sound of the microwave. A couple of minutes later, a paper bowl slid under my nose. I looked up at Hellhound's scowl.

"Ya gonna eat this, or am I gonna hafta force-feed ya?" His gruff words were belied by the gentleness of his hand stroking my hair.

I gave him a smile that didn't feel convincing even to me. "I'll eat. Thanks." I picked up the fork and started to shovel in the food. I recognized one of the mass-produced entrees, some sort of pasta with tomato sauce. It didn't really matter. I ate without tasting it and scraped the bowl clean.

By the time I'd finished, Germain was back in the RV. I looked a question at him, and he said, "He'll check into it and call you back."

"Thanks." I eyed my watch. Nearly an hour had passed. Kane could be running out of time. Or dead already.

I shook my head to suppress the thought and got to my feet, feeling a lot stronger after the meal. "I'm going over there. See if I can see anything."

Germain blocked the doorway, his muscular arms crossed over his broad chest. "No. You're not."

"You know I'm the only one who can do it."

"Yes. But you still have important intel. You need to wait until we hear back from Spider. If we lose you, we lose everything."

"Don't try to hold me here."

"I won't. I just want you to wait a little longer." He pointedly eyed the fists I hadn't realized I'd clenched. "You won't have to fight me for it."

I sheepishly relaxed my hands and rolled my bunched-up shoulders. "Sorry. I didn't mean it that way." I sank down on the bench again.

He gave me a smile that didn't quite reach his eyes, his own posture easing. "I stood in your way once. I'd rather not do it again."

"Smart man," I joked.

The phone rang, and Germain picked up immediately. "Any luck?" he asked without preamble. I read the answer in the slump of his shoulders. "Okay. Thanks anyway." He hung up.

"It won't work," I said flatly.

"No. He's sending a link that will connect you to his facial recognition database. We'll have to search it manually."

I clamped down hard, trying to stay in control. When I finally spoke, my voice sounded dangerous even to me. "You don't seriously expect me to sit here for hours looking through a database."

"No," he replied quickly. "I want you to give me as complete a description as possible of the men you saw. I have to stay here while you do the recon anyway. I'm the only one who can implement Plan B if necessary. While I'm waiting, I'll use your descriptions to narrow the field. When you're back, you can look at the shortlist while we strategize."

I blew out my relief in a long sigh. "Okay. I'll need to take Arnie with me. He'll have to operate the... um, signalling device if necessary."

"Hang on a minute," Hellhound broke in. "If that patrol chased ya an hour ago, they're gonna have fuckin' massive security out there now. How the hell d'ya think you're gonna get close enough to do what ya gotta do? Ya said ya were gonna check rooms? Shit. No chance."

Germain scowled. "I agree. That place will be crawling with guards now. It won't matter how stealthy you are, you won't be able to get close enough."

"I'm not planning to be stealthy," I said slowly. "I think a direct approach will be better. I'll hide in plain sight. More or less."

"Too dangerous," Germain objected. "If they've captured Kane, someone may remember the two of you attending the party on the weekend together. You'd be walking into a trap."

"I wasn't planning on walking in. Do you have the site map with you?"

Germain pulled the roll out of the closet and spread it on the table. I leaned over it, calculating distances. "I think we were about... here... when I made contact." I marked a dot on the map. "Look at the layout of the building site. See how the road swings around here. Wouldn't you say this distance is about the same?"

I marked another dot beside the road. "What if a couple was just biking down the road and decided to pull off for a rest? Get off the bikes for a while, stretch out at the side of the road?"

"That could work." Germain's expression lightened. "They'll be expecting somebody covertly trying to approach the buildings. The woods will be crawling with security, but if you're not trying to approach at all..."

"Good, then it's a plan. I better go check and make sure I didn't blow out the front fork seals on the Honda, and then I'm ready to go." I slid out of the bench.

"Not so fast," Hellhound growled. "What about this signallin' thing? I can't go in completely fuckin' blind here." We both looked to Germain.

He grimaced and rubbed his chin, his hand rasping over the stubble. "I'm sorry, I don't have the authority to make that decision."

"Then call somebody who has the authority." I did my best to sound reasonable, and it came out just slightly less than a snarl.

Germain apparently took no offense. "I already did. I put in a call to Stemp while I was outside. I shouldn't have. I should've just gone ahead and asked forgiveness later. Now I have a direct order not to disclose." His hand squeezed into a fist, the knuckles glowing white.

I slammed my own fist onto the table. The paper bowl jumped and the fork clattered to the floor. "Fuck! Fucking moron! Head up his fucking ass! Goddammit!"

Hellhound laid a hand over my clenched fist. "Never mind. Let it go, darlin'. Ya know I never wanna know more than I hafta. Just tell me what ya need me to do."

I ground my teeth for a few seconds before deciding he was right. No sense wasting time bitching about it. "Okay. I'm going to tell you as much as I can without going into specifics. Carl, stop me if you have to."

I organized my thoughts for a few moments. "I'm carrying a very valuable piece of technology. It's inside my wristwatch at the moment. I can use that technology in ways nobody else can. If it falls into the wrong hands, the results could be disastrous. Think national security disastrous. By myself, I'm no use to anybody. With the technology, I can..."

"Stop. That's enough," Germain interrupted. He turned to Hellhound. "Nobody can know that Aydan is carrying this technology, or even that it exists. And nobody can know she's the only one who can use it. If you breathe a word, you're signing her death warrant."

Arnie's face hardened, and he nodded once.

I really didn't want any reminders about how dangerous this was. I sighed and continued.

"In order to use this device, I need to go into a trance-like state. When I'm in that state, I don't know what's going on around me. When I come out, if I do it correctly, I have some pain and it takes me a minute or so before I can function again."

I rubbed my aching temples. "That's the best-case scenario. Worst-case, I'm pulled out of the trance-like state by an external stimulus of some sort. If that happens, I'm completely incapacitated, for several minutes. I can't see or hear. I scream and thrash around. I can't stop it, and I can't control it. If that happened, you'd have to take the watch off my wrist and escape. That technology is the top priority."

"An' leave ya there? That ain't gonna happen," Hellhound growled.

"It has to happen," Germain countered. "There's nothing you can do. You can't carry her. You can't even hold her, she fights so hard."

"And another thing," I added. "If the watch comes off

my wrist while I'm in the n... trance, that'll trigger the worst-case reaction, too."

Hellhound glowered. "So you're tellin' me ya go into this trance, an' there's no way to get ya out without half killin' ya."

"No, not exactly." I held up Spider's invention. "This is a signalling device. If I'm in the n... Jesus! Trance, if I'm in the trance, you can hold this device up against the wristwatch and push the button. That signals me that I have to get out, um, I mean, wake up. It still takes me a few seconds before I can do much, but at least it's manageable."

Hellhound turned his scowl to Spider's invention as he took it carefully from my hand. "So there's no other way? This signallin' thing's the only way to get ya out safely?"

"Yeah. So the plan is, we take a ride. We find a nice comfy patch of grass in the ditch. And we kick back for a while. You watch, I... do my thing. I come out, we hop on our bikes and head back here."

"Good plan," Germain said. "If you're not back in an hour, I'll go to Plan B unless I hear from you otherwise. I hope this works."

"Me, too."

CHAPTER 21

I scribbled out the descriptions for Germain before heading outside. There was no visible leakage when I examined the motorcycle's front forks. I shrugged as I straightened, trying to hide the way my heart thumped painfully at the thought of getting on the bike again.

Hellhound caught my eye. "Fuck it, it's a rental."

I forced a laugh, trying to relieve the tension while we donned our jackets and helmets.

Clutching the handgrips with aching fingers, I led the way past Harchman's place once, watching for any evidence of guards or dogs. All seemed quiet. We pulled a U-turn several miles down the road and idled back to a spot I thought would work.

We rode the bikes down into the shallow ditch and dismounted. As I pulled off my helmet, Hellhound stopped me.

"Maybe ya should keep that on."

"It's too damn hot. I'll suffocate if I'm not moving. Besides, who keeps their helmet on when they're relaxing by the side of the road?"

He gave me a twisted smile. "Darlin', ya looked like the best wet dream I ever had, ridin' over that hill with your hair flyin' in the wind. But I don't mind if I never see it again. I'd rather ya rode safe."

"Me, too," I assured him. "But I don't think we'll end up leaving here in a hurry. We're too exposed. By the time we know we have to move, there won't be time to get away. If we have to move that fast, I won't be going with you."

"I ain't gonna leave ya," he said seriously.

"Arnie, it's not a discussion. If the shit hits the fan, take the watch and run like hell. And if you can't escape, take it and throw it away where it can't be found."

His jaw set. "I can do that."

I had a feeling I hadn't won that argument, but I didn't see what else I could do. I sighed. "Okay. You know the drill, right? If you need me to wake up, put the signalling device against my watch and press the button. Anything else happens, take the watch and run."

"Got it."

I lowered myself to the ground. "Let's hope this works. Let's hope I'm close enough."

He sprawled on his back beside me, one elbow crooked behind his head. His other arm pulled me close. "Good luck, darlin'."

I laid my head on his chest, listening to the steady, reassuring beat of his heart. Insects hummed in the hot grass, and I wished we were nothing more than we appeared. Two people out for a pleasant day's biking, a rest and a cuddle by the side of the road, and then maybe a nice meal and a cold beer. And maybe a hot night.

I closed my eyes and drifted into the void.

I checked each room, finding all the first ones vacant. Thank goodness, Harchman had apparently concluded his fantasy and left. As I approached the firewall, I steeled myself for what I might find in the next branch.

Reluctantly, I peered into the room where I'd discovered the prisoner. It was clean and vacant. Nice thing about virtual torture, no messy cleanup afterward. I swallowed queasiness, trying to harden myself with the black humour.

I moved slowly to the next room. I already knew I didn't want to look inside. Raised male voices and the sounds of heavy impact seeped through the door. Each impact was accompanied by a hoarse grunt. I was afraid I knew that voice.

I had to look.

I peeked in. My meal tried to escape. I jerked back into the corridor, gulping air and swallowing sour bile.

These men seemed to enjoy destroying their victims' faces. The raw meat from the neck up could have been anybody, but I could easily identify Kane's short dark hair and massive upper body.

Unlike the others, he was suspended by his wrists from the ceiling. They had apparently finished with his face and gone on to other pursuits. I tried not to think about the wounds on the rest of his body, but my memory persisted in showing me the nightmare image whole.

Without conscious thought, I propelled my insubstantial self through the wall and into the room. Inside, the smell of burned human flesh made me gag helplessly. One of the men was yelling questions at Kane, so the sound was masked. The thud of the iron bar hitting Kane's ribs galvanized me into action.

Frantic to make them stop, I was halfway across the room before reason reasserted itself. It was a simulation. If I attacked them now, Harchman would know there was somebody else in the sim. They would redouble security.

We couldn't afford it.

Surely they would have to stop soon. They wouldn't kill him until they got the information they wanted, would they?

There was an alarming amount of blood. Kane's breath was stertorous, each inhalation a rattling groan. He couldn't last much longer. They'd have to stop.

Another wave of nausea clenched my gut. Even though it was a sim, I knew Kane was feeling every injury as if it was real. I couldn't let him suffer like this.

I floated above his head. Sending my voice right next to his ear, I whispered, barely breathing.

"John. It's Aydan. You're in a sim. If you understand, move your right hand."

He tensed and groaned again. The clenched fist of his right hand opened slowly before squeezing closed again.

"Who are you working for? Where have you hidden the fob?" Another savage blow landed. Kane's body jerked, an agonized grunt wrenching from him. The side of his battered chest was already caved in and misshapen. Shattered ribs for sure, and probably a collapsed lung...

I gulped down nausea and whispered again. "John, I'm going to take away your pain now. You'll feel me touch your head. Then you'll feel a sensation like cool water running through your body. You'll still look wounded, but the pain will be completely gone."

God forgive me the lie. It was a sim. If he believed, it should happen.

I reached slowly and carefully toward his head, trying to judge the distance. When my fingertips touched his hair, his entire body went suddenly limp, dangling lifelessly from his chained wrists.

Panic lanced through my heart. Had I killed him? I

fumbled down his neck, searching for a pulse. Thank God, I felt the rapid beat. I withdrew quickly, making his blood vanish from my invisible fingers.

One of the torturers grunted. "Shit. He passed out."

The other man shrugged. "Whatever. Time for a smoke anyway. Come back later." They turned and went through the portal.

Just another day at the office for them. I should have killed them where they stood.

I threw my whisper again. "John, I'm going to move in front of you so we can talk. Keep your head down. Try not to react if I touch you, because I can't see what I'm doing. If you understand, take a deep breath."

His crushed chest rose and fell with a bubbling sound, blood drooling from what was left of his lips. I floated around in front of him, trying not to look at the appalling damage. At close range, the burns were horrific, and the smell of them made my stomach roil. I manoeuvred carefully, instinctively trying to avoid touching him even though I knew he wouldn't feel the pain.

"I'm in front of you now," I breathed. "You can whisper to me, and I'll hear."

"'Hanks."

I glanced down as I puzzled over that. I clamped down hard on control when I realized the white bits scattered on the blood-covered floor were his teeth. His face was so destroyed he could barely form words.

"You're welcome."

"Aydan, ge' ou'. 'oo dangerous."

"I'm not staying. I just need to know where your physical body is. We're coming to get you."

"Gues' house. Gues' room. 'oo doors down on righ'.

Guards."

"How many?"

"'Oo. 'ha I saw. One ou'side room. One a' gues' house door."

"Plus the two that were here?"

"Ya."

"Have you seen Harchman?"

"No."

"Are you tied to the ceiling like this in the guest room?"

"No. 'ied 'oo a shair. 'Ha's how I knew i' was a sim. 'hey screwed up."

"Hold on. I'm going to go take a look. I'll be right back."

I floated through the wall again and found the nearest portal. I wasn't sure if this would work or not. I willed a transparent window and floated a safe distance away, peering through my viewport.

I was looking out at the highway. Hellhound lay comfortably stretched out at the side of the ditch, one knee drawn up, one arm behind his head. His other arm cradled my head on his chest. Despite his relaxed posture, his eyes scanned alertly.

Shit.

I drifted back. "When I look through a portal, I can only see where I came from. I can't see where you came from."

"S'okay. Shair's no' 'ha' s'rong. I 'hink I could ge' free. Bu' I couldn' leave 'he sim."

"I have an idea. You need to be invisible now. I'll create a construct that looks exactly like you. I need you to imagine that you're invisible and insubstantial. Just float up above your own head. If it works, come and float about three feet in front of your body. Remember I'm here in front of you, so leave me some space."

"'Kay. Gonna do i' now."

I watched, holding his image in my mind. Nothing happened.

Shit, shit, shit! Now what?

I jerked and bit off a shriek when something thudded into my back. I whirled and made contact with something I couldn't see. A large hand closed on my shoulder, and then I was wrapped in Kane's invisible arms.

I felt his breath on my cheek. "That's an ugly mess, isn't it?" he whispered, his speech no longer impaired by the maimed face.

I tightened trembling arms around him. "I'm sorry. I'm so sorry! I should have told you how to do the invisibility before we left. You didn't have to suffer like that."

"I had to anyway. I couldn't take a chance on letting them know I knew I was in a sim. Thanks for the pain relief. How did you do that?"

"I didn't. You did."

There was a moment of silence. "Damn. I didn't think of that." I felt him shrug. "You said you had a plan."

"Not really, yet. This was just supposed to be recon. But I just had a thought. Those two were in the guest room with you when you went into the sim, right?"

"Yes."

"So if you were able to get free with your physical body, you could take them out if they were busy in the network?"

"Yes, but as soon as I disappear from the sim, they'll know. I don't think the guest rooms are monitored, but the sim definitely is. The guard at the door would be on me in seconds."

"What if... shit!"

The two men stepped into the virtual room again. I

towed Kane with me up to the ceiling and into a back corner. His construct dangled from its chains, groaning and coughing weakly. As the torture began anew, Kane and I continued our whispered conversation. I blocked out the gruesome activity as best I could, knowing the captors' own expectations would maintain the construct as long as they suspected nothing.

"I'll go look through the portal and see where they're positioned."

I felt Kane move away. There was muffled thud from the vicinity of the wall, then silence. I kept my back to the action in the room, but I could still hear all too clearly.

Kane's construct was beginning to sob feebly, driven by the expectations of its torturers. The harrowing sound drove me to the limits of my control. Clinging desperately to composure, I imposed my will over the construct, and it subsided into groaning again.

Something grazed my arm and I jumped, my nerves stretched to breaking. Large, unseen hands closed on my shoulders, and Kane's invisible forehead thumped into my cheekbone. I felt him readjust, and his lips brushed my ear. "Dammit! This is harder to do than I thought. Did you hear me hit the wall?"

"I did, but they didn't."

"Good. They're still in the guest room with my body. You were saying..." Kane prompted.

"What if I stay here and maintain your construct while you go back into your body and kill them in real life? Do you think you could take the guard, too?"

"With the element of surprise, yes. But if they die in real life, they'll disappear from the sim."

"Not if I maintain constructs of them. You could be long

gone from the guest house before anybody ever knows anything has happened."

"That could work," he murmured. "There's something strange going on with security. I think I could probably get off the property on foot. But that leaves you here. That's completely unacceptable."

"No, that leaves me and Hellhound having a nap in the ditch outside the property. You could meet us there. Once you're there, I could pull out of the network. By the time the alarm was raised, we'd all be down the road."

"Risky. But it could work. I need to think it through."

"Fine. I need to go back and check in with Hellhound. We're running out of time before Germain fires up Plan B. We'll have to contact him. Meet you back here in a few minutes."

I gratefully fled back to my portal. I stepped through very slowly and carefully. Now would be a bad time to be incapacitated.

The usual red-hot knives sliced and diced my brain, and I cried out and jerked my arms protectively over my head. The residual shock and horror of the sim combined with the physical pain to turn my curses into half-sobs, and I fought the tears that burned the backs of my eyes as I writhed.

No time, no time. I forced myself to uncurl, opening blind eyes. When vision returned, I found myself clasped against Hellhound's warm chest. He muttered rough comfort while he held me and stroked my hair.

I pulled away, wiping my eyes, and drew in a ragged breath. "All clear?"

"Yeah, darlin', what..?" His face was filled with worry.

"No time," I interrupted. "I'm going to get Kane out. He should be here in twenty minutes, half an hour tops if all goes well. I need you to call Germain, tell him we're okay and to give us another half-hour. Kane should be coming through the trees here from the direction of the buildings. Signal me as soon as you see or hear him. He can take the Honda, you can double me back on the Harley. Got it?"

"Got it." He was reaching for his phone when I dove back into the void.

I folded virtual space and appeared directly outside the room. Trying to ignore the atrocities within, I floated slowly and carefully up to the corner of the ceiling. I muffled a grunt when I collided with Kane.

His arms closed around me, and I quested blindly for his ear. "We're all set," I whispered. "We're beside the road just where it swings around close to the building site. Head straight north from here. You'll have half an hour, give or take, to get there. I'll hold the constructs here until Arnie signals me. Then you can take the Honda, and I'll ride back with him on the Harley."

"All right. But if I don't make it in half an hour, go without me."

"This is Hellhound we're talking about. You know that won't happen."

He sighed. "I know. He never did follow orders. Let's hope he doesn't need to."

"Good luck."

"You, too."

His hands slid up my shoulders to touch my face, and I might have felt his lips brush my forehead before he released me to float alone in the void. I dragged my shrinking attention back to the room. I'd thought it couldn't get worse, but I'd been wrong. I breathed carefully through my mouth, trying not to throw up.

Suddenly, one of the men blinked out of existence. I quickly filled in a construct in his place. Then the other was gone, and Kane's construct flickered, too, while I desperately tried to maintain three separate entities at the same time. This was harder than I'd expected.

Then the full horror of the situation hit me. I was going to have to torture Kane.

Ghastly time crawled by. I'd seen enough already to let my expectations of the two men fulfill themselves. I tried to detach myself, like watching a sickening movie, knowing what would happen but powerless to stop observing it. Even though I knew the constructs could neither think nor feel, making the action play out was an abomination. Slow hell unfolded before me.

At last, I felt the blip I'd prayed for. With a gasp, I folded virtual reality and stepped out the portal.

I couldn't stop myself. Cries escaped me while I clawed at my head, trying to dislodge the memories and the pain. When a powerful grip pinned my hands, I battered my head desperately against the nearest firm surface. A few moments later I realized the firm surface was Arnie, calling my name while he tried to restrain me.

My stomach heaved, and I jerked away from him to vomit in the ditch. Two shivering sobs wrenched out before I clamped down with the last remnants of my self-control. I took a couple of deep, trembling breaths, then spat and wiped my face.

When I looked up, Kane and Hellhound were both kneeling beside me. The sight of Kane's undamaged face and body almost undid me again, and I sucked in an unsteady breath.

"Thank God," I croaked. "Let's go."

Arnie helped me up and buckled my helmet onto my head before mounting up, and Kane half-lifted me onto the Harley. I clung to Arnie's warm bulk as if I was drowning, my helmet pressed against the snarling dog on his broad back. Then we were flying down the road, and I let the warm, sweet breeze wash everything away.

CHAPTER 22

I held on blindly and mindlessly until the bike came to a stop. Detached, I took in Germain's grinning face as he pounded Kane's back. I wobbled off the back of the Harley and pulled off my helmet, standing stupidly for a few seconds before placing the helmet on the ground and staggering toward the trees.

I was a few yards into the forest when Hellhound appeared beside me, holding out a small carton of orange juice. "Think ya need this, darlin'."

"Thanks." I took it, not looking at him. "I need to be alone for a while."

"Where ya goin'?"

"West." I kept walking, staring straight ahead.

He walked with me a few more steps, but I couldn't turn to him. He stopped, and I stumbled away.

I blundered straight through the undergrowth, not even trying to follow game trails. At last, I came upon a dense stand of spruce, their heavy boughs sagging almost to the ground. I crept into the gloom beneath them and curled into a ball, letting the sobs begin.

Much later, I sat up slowly. Everything ached. I found a tissue in my pocket and cleaned my face as best I could.

Thankful for the orange juice, I sipped slowly and let the acidic sweetness wash away the bitter taste of bile. My trembling gradually subsided, and I drew my first steady breath in a long time.

I leaned back against the trunk of the spruce, arms wrapped around my drawn-up knees. My primal self took comfort from the dim concealment, and I sat in silent stillness. The pungent spruce scent filled my nose, and a squirrel chattered somewhere in the forest. The breeze sighed through the tops of the trees. I narrowed my vision, concentrating on the fine details of the spruce needles and twigs and moss, clearing my mind and letting time slip away.

Animal-like, I sensed the vibration of the ground before I heard the raspy voice call out my name. I wasn't ready to be found yet.

I stayed silent and motionless.

A few minutes later, Hellhound tramped into view, and I watched through the screen of boughs as he scanned the woods. The worry in his face made me sigh.

The next time he called, I answered.

His head snapped around, searching for the source of the sound. Then he spotted me and advanced slowly, squatting outside my hiding place. "Can I come in, darlin'?"

"Come on in and pull up some dirt."

He shoved the branches aside and took a seat on the carpet of spruce needles beside me, leaning his back against the tree trunk. "Ya okay?"

"I'll live." I spoke quickly to drown out the response in my head. No, I'm not okay. I'll never be okay again.

"Kane said ya saw some bad shit. D'ya wanna talk about it?"

"No. Not ever." My voice wavered, and I shut up.

He took my hand and stroked it gently, and we sat in silence for a while. Finally, Arnie turned to me. "They need ya back at the trailer. When you're ready."

"Okay." I crawled out from under the tree and stood, brushing off spruce needles.

He followed me out. "We'll get some food into ya. That'll help."

I hunched over as my gut clenched. "I don't think I can."

He folded me into his arms, and I closed my eyes and huddled against him. The nausea slowly faded as his warmth surrounded me.

"Come on, darlin'. Just take it slow." He shepherded me toward the RV, his comforting arm around my shoulders.

The walking helped. When we reached the edge of the forest, I turned to him. "Thanks. Again," I said awkwardly.

Arnie surveyed my face seriously for a moment before giving me a preposterous leer. "Your debt's mountin' up again, darlin'. Ya better start payin' me back in bed soon, or you're gonna hafta marry me."

I laughed out loud at our private joke, my knotted stomach easing. "God forbid!"

As we approached, Kane stepped out of the RV. I blinked rapidly and scrubbed my hands through my hair. Those memories weren't real. This was real.

I felt Arnie's eyes on me, but I threw my shoulders back and walked steadily toward the trailer. Everything in the real world was all right. The rest was only a nightmare. I knew how to deal with nightmares.

Kane met us at the door and gazed down at me with concern. "Are you all right?"

"Fine. Are you all right?"

"Fine. Thanks to you."

I gave him a smile through stiff lips. "You're welcome. Did you call it in? Did they arrest everybody over there?"

"No."

"But..." A look at his troubled eyes made my protest wither on my lips.

He sighed. "We need more information. Evidence."

"But they killed that prisoner! I saw them kill him! They tortured you! What are you waiting for?" I demanded.

His hand flew up, shushing me. "I called Stemp," he responded. His eyes flicked in Arnie's direction, and I knew he couldn't tell me anything more. "We can't take them down yet. I'm sorry," he added as I opened my mouth to argue again.

I shut my trap and stepped up into the RV.

Germain glanced up from the laptop as I came in, Kane and Hellhound behind me. "Aydan! Are you okay?"

"I'm fine. I just needed some time."

His normally smiling eyes were worried. "Okay," he said slowly. "Do you feel up to going through this database now?"

"Sure. What do I need to do?"

"First she's gotta eat," Hellhound said firmly.

"Right, of course," Germain said. "Sorry."

"I'm gonna work my gourmet cookin' magic again," Hellhound joked. "What d'ya wanna eat, darlin', Salisbury steak or beef stew?"

"I'll take the stew, if that's okay," I told him. "Are you using the water system in here?"

Kane nodded. "The plumbing is all working. And the tap water's drinkable. Go ahead."

"Thanks." I stepped into the tiny bathroom.

Embarrassment flooded me when I caught sight of myself in the mirror. My face was streaked with dirt and tear tracks, and my eyes were red and puffy. No wonder the guys were treating me so carefully. Damn. I'd really hoped to keep my meltdown private.

I splashed cool water on my face and patted it dry, taking my time. The sun shone through the pebbled glass in the small window, and I assessed the lines etched in my face by its unforgiving glare. I looked like I'd aged ten years.

Hell, I felt like I'd aged a hundred. Ten was a heck of a deal. I pulled my folding hairbrush out of my waist pouch and brushed the last of the spruce needles out of my hair before stepping back into the living area.

A steaming paper bowl of stew waited for me on the table, and the microwave dinged as I arrived. I took my place and Hellhound squeezed in opposite me with his meal, fresh from the microwave. Kane fired it up again, and both he and Germain wedged themselves onto the dinette benches as well while they waited.

I eyed the three big men and laughed, trying to reassure both them and myself I wasn't about to burst into tears again. "I'm pretty sure the designers of this vehicle didn't have you guys in mind."

Germain grinned ruefully across the table, his shoulder jammed against Hellhound's. "Usually we eat in shifts. This is a little too much togetherness."

Kane's shoulder was pressing against mine, too. I revelled in the sensation of his undamaged body next to me.

My stomach gradually settled while I picked at the stew. We all ate in silence for a while before Kane turned to me, leaning back slightly in the cramped quarters. "Do you feel up to debriefing now?"

"Sure."

Hellhound shrugged. "Guess it's time for me to go for a

walk." Germain got up so he could squeeze out of the dinette, and he left, closing the door behind him. Germain sat again. We regarded each other in silence.

Germain cleared his throat. "I already filled Kane in on what you told us about the prisoner you saw in the sim earlier," he said to me. He turned to Kane. "What happened after you and Aydan got separated?"

Kane frowned. "It was strange. I ran off in the opposite direction to Aydan and made as much noise as possible. But when they caught me... it was like they didn't know what to do. I expected to get kicked around a bit, but they called the dogs off right away, and asked me quite civilly what I was doing on private property."

He shovelled in the last of his meal and continued. "So I said I'd been taking a walk in the woods. Told them I didn't realize it was private property, said I was sorry and I'd leave. And I think the one guard was actually going to let me go." He rubbed at his chin, looking perplexed.

"But then the other one called it in, and their dispatcher told them to bring me up to the house. I pretended to be surprised it was Harchman's place, told them I'd been at his party Saturday night, and they were very polite. They certainly didn't seem to be on high alert."

Germain's brows drew together. "Maybe they hadn't been briefed yet? But the day was half over. And they should have had their instructions before they went out."

Kane shrugged. "When we got onto the building site, two men met us. They told the guards they'd take me up to see Harchman. The guards handed me over, and that's when everything went to hell."

He got up, collecting our empty dishes and tossing them in the garbage. "Aydan, did you get enough to eat?"

"Yes, thanks. But I could sure use a drink. I don't suppose you have any beer."

They both laughed. "If we'd known you were coming, we'd have stocked up," Germain teased.

I gave a dramatic sigh. "I guess I'll have to drink water, then."

Kane chuckled as he filled a glass and brought it over for me. "So anyway," he picked up the thread as he sat down. "As soon as the guards were out of sight, they hit me with a stun gun. Dragged me into the guest house, but again, it was weird. There was a guard at the door, but they made up some cock and bull story about heatstroke when they dragged me past. Like he didn't know what was going on. The one outside the room was one of theirs for sure, though. They tied me to the chair and took us all straight into the sim. I missed the transition entirely. I didn't figure it out until they hung me up. I'd scoped out the guest rooms on Saturday, and I was pretty sure none of them had chains hanging from the ceiling. That's where Aydan found me."

I shuddered involuntarily, my mouth going dry. I sipped slowly at the water, staring at the table.

"Aydan, what happened from your end?" Germain asked.

I swallowed hard and cleared my throat before answering. My voice emerged hoarsely, and I took another sip of water. "Arnie and I parked by the side of the road and I went in as planned. Found the right sim. Went in and got Kane invisible while we figured out what to do. Came back out and told Arnie to coordinate with you, then went back in again. I held Kane's construct while he went out. Created constructs of the other two when they disappeared from the sim. I..."

My throat closed up completely, and I stopped, sipping

some more water. I took a deep breath. "I maintained the sim until I got the signal. Then I got out," I said steadily to the table.

There was a short silence, and I didn't look up.

"How do you think they identified you?" Germain asked Kane.

"They'd noticed Aydan's disguise popping up in the network during the party," Kane replied. "So they knew they'd had a breach, and they were on the lookout for any party guests who had been acting suspiciously. I was noticeable because I showed up on their security cameras a few too many times when I was checking out the outbuildings."

He shrugged. "I knew I was on camera at the time, but I'd been hoping there were enough other guests milling around that it wouldn't matter. I probably would have gotten away with it if they hadn't caught me in the woods today."

"What did they want?"

"They knew I was working with an accomplice, because they couldn't find a person that matched Aydan's disguise in any of their security footage from the party. They wanted to know who my partner was, who I was working for, and how we'd gotten into the network. I just kept telling them I didn't know what they were talking about, and I was just a guest at the party."

I finally looked up, and he smiled at me. "The really good news in all this is that you're still in the clear. They obviously aren't looking for you. And now that I've escaped and taken out three of their men, they'll be looking for me very enthusiastically indeed."

"Good news for me, not for you," I told him.

"At this point, I'll take any good news I can get."

Germain broke in, frowning. "So how did you get away?"

"The two men who were working me over actually came into the physical guest room to enter the sim," Kane explained. "So all our bodies were there. When Aydan took over the sim, I dropped back out of the network. I got free and took them out while they were still in the sim. I popped the guard and dragged his body back into the room. Then I went out of the guest house, thanked the doorman and told him I was feeling much better, and walked up past the house like I owned the place. They didn't even have extra patrols on in the woods."

"That's the strangest thing I've ever heard," Germain said. "That doesn't sound like Fuzzy Bunny."

"I think Harchman's an idiot," I agreed. "He showed me right into the security control centre. He told me about the patrols in the woods. And he sure wasn't doing anything productive in the sim network earlier."

"What?" Kane swivelled to face me. "You saw Harchman in a sim? What was he doing?"

I felt my face heat up. "He was, um, having a moment. Reliving a moment. With certain modifications. Apparently I made an impression at the party."

"Oh." He thought about that for a moment, and then changed the subject. "Is there anything else you can tell us about the prisoner who was executed? Did you hear any of the questions they were asking? Was there any way to identify him? Any distinguishing marks?"

"No." I swallowed nausea again. "There wasn't much left by the time I got there."

"Damn. So we're no further ahead. We still don't know who those captives are -"

"Or were," I interrupted quietly, the sound of the gunshot echoing in mind.

Kane gave me a sympathetic glance. "Or what Harchman wants from them," he continued. "In retrospect, maybe I should have just stayed there. As long as I was telling them under torture that I didn't know what they were talking about, they weren't sure they had the right man. They still don't know that, but now they know I'm out here and I'm dangerous."

"If you'd been in there any longer, they would've killed you," I snapped. "They killed that prisoner without a second thought, and they weren't stopping with you. If you died in the sim, they'd just call the ambulance and pretend you'd had a heart attack. There'd be no evidence to the contrary on your physical body. You would have had to blow your cover anyway and leave the sim just to survive."

"Right," Germain agreed. "And taking on three assailants while tied to a chair is a bit of a stretch even for you. Your chances of escape on your own would have been slim. This was better all around."

Kane lifted a shoulder in assent. "Probably true."

"But why can't you just go in and arrest them all and question them?" I burst out. "Why..."

"Stemp wants to know the full extent of the network, and he wants to know who the captives are and what questions they're being asked," Kane said. "If we rush in now, we'll lose the chance to gather valuable intel."

"But they're killing people!"

Kane rubbed his knuckles over the strained lines in his face. "Yes. Untraceably. No evidence. That's why we have to make sure we do this right. They'll be able to kill a lot more people and get away with it if we rush this investigation. The first step is to try to identify the captives and the men we saw in the sim."

He reached for my hand and held it gently, searching my face. "Aydan, I know it's hard, but I really need you to think back to what you saw of the captive in the sim. Can you give us anything at all to go on? Hair colour? Eye colour? Unusual clothing, tattoos, scars, anything?"

I closed my eyes, forcing my shrinking courage to revisit the memory. "Brown hair. Thinning. His eyes were..." I gulped, trying to convince the beef stew to stay put. "...gone."

Kane's hand tightened on mine. "It's okay, don't think about that. What was he wearing?"

A couple of deep breaths later, my voice started to work again. "Brown deck shoes... with... with white gym socks. Casual pants. Beige casual pants."

"That's good, keep going," he encouraged.

I squeezed my eyes tighter. Remember, dammit. Ignore the blood. What else?

"A polo shirt. I mean, I don't know if it was Polo brand, but one of those collared T-shirts. White."

Red by the time I saw it, though.

"Take a breath. Nice and slow," Kane murmured, and I eased a few pounds of pressure off my grip on his hand and obeyed. "Was he wearing jewellery or a wristwatch?" Kane prompted.

My eyes flew open. "Yes, a watch! It was one of those great big clunky black things with all the dials and gauges on it. And now that I think of it, he had a tattoo on his left forearm just above the watch. It was red, so it didn't really show up in all the blood..."

This time I took a few deep breaths without being

reminded.

"Can you remember what the tattoo looked like?"

"It was really plain. I can draw it."

Kane passed me a pen and a piece of paper, and after a couple of tries, I managed to steady my shaking hand enough to sketch the simple rectangular tattoo.

Germain sat up, grinning. "That's a diving flag," he said. "And it sounds like he was wearing a diver's watch."

Kane's smile crinkled the sexy laugh lines around his eyes. "Good work, Aydan. That's going to narrow it down. Is there anything else you can remember? Was he wearing any other jewellery? Any other tattoos or scars or marks? Any guesses as to age or height or weight?"

"Um. Height, I wouldn't know, he was sitting. Weight, he had a bit of a belly, but he wasn't fat. Age, I don't know, maybe middle-aged. The skin on his arm looked kind of... weathered, I guess? I don't remember any other jewellery or scars or anything."

"That's all right. You've given us a good place to start. Now we know we're looking for a middle-aged diver with thinning brown hair, average build, who's either currently missing or else died of a heart attack. If you can start looking through the database, that would be great."

I sighed. "Okay. Shit! Wait a minute!"

"What?" Kane demanded.

"What will happen to the other prisoner now? If..." I swallowed the tightness in my throat. "If he's even still alive. You killed off three of Fuzzy Bunny's men. Who'll take over? Should I be going back into the sim to see what's going on?"

"No," he said firmly. "Not tonight. I think Fuzzy Bunny will be sufficiently distracted by the loss of me and their men that they won't expend a lot of energy on their remaining prisoner tonight. And you need a break."

"I'm okay," I said reflexively.

"Good. Then you can get started on the database whenever you're ready." He got up. "I'm going outside. It's too hot in here."

I realized I was sweating, too. The icy sensation that had frozen me all afternoon had finally gone away. As Germain followed him out, I got up and peeled off my boots, socks, jacket, and pants. I was padding barefoot over to the sink to refill my water glass when Hellhound stuck his head in the door.

He raised a lecherous eyebrow as he took in my tank top and clingy shorts. "Gettin' ready for me, darlin'?"

I laughed. "Depends on whether you like an audience or not."

"What if I say I do?" He grinned and bounced his eyebrows.

I put on a severe expression. "I'd be shocked." We both laughed.

"Ya wanna come out for a walk?" He leered suggestively. "We could go... commune with nature for a while."

I looked him up and down. "Tempting. Except for the mosquitoes. But I need to get started on this database. I have a feeling it'll take a while. Germain said he'd narrowed it down based on what I gave him, but there are a lot of pictures in the shortlist."

"Ya don't know what you're missin'."

I sighed. "Sadly, I do."

CHAPTER 23

I had just gotten started with the database when Kane stuck his head in the door of the RV. "I contacted Webb," he said. "I've asked him to see if he could get a copy of the guest list from the party, just in case the man they killed was one of the guests. Then we can cross-reference that with anything he can dig up from the dive club memberships."

"How long do you think it will take?"

"I haven't a clue. He'll call as soon as he has something." He withdrew, and I turned back to the database.

The sun was setting by the time the men stepped into the RV again. They had left me to my work, but I'd heard the rumble of their voices outside while they strategized.

"Any luck?" Kane inquired.

"No." I blew out a sigh. "Slow going."

"It's all right. These things take time."

"But we don't *have* time!" I protested. "We need to -"

I was interrupted by a buzzing from Kane's pocket, and he pulled out his phone, his frown clearing as he glanced at the call display and punched the talk button.

"Webb," he said in greeting. "What have you got?"

We all eyed him tensely as he nodded slowly, frowning again.

"Right. Okay, thanks." He hung up and blew out a tired breath, massaging his forehead. "There was no record of anybody with that tattoo in the law enforcement system, so he wasn't a criminal. Webb's sending a list of possibilities from the dive club memberships, filtered by age. He doesn't see much chance of getting a list of party guests. The only way would be to hack into Harchman's computer system in hopes of finding it. He already tried, but it's secure and encrypted. And if Webb can't get in, I'm willing to bet nobody can."

Kane looked at his watch. "It should be dusk in about half an hour. That'd be a good time to go back and get my bike. We need to get surveillance up again, too."

"Are you nuts?" I demanded. "If they catch you..." My stomach lurched, and I gulped it down. "If they catch you again, they'll torture you for real! You really want to live the rest of your life blind and burned and crippled and drinking all your meals through a straw..." I realized my voice was rising rapidly and shut up. I clenched my hands in my lap to hide their shaking.

There was a short silence while Germain and Hellhound regarded the two of us uneasily.

Kane sighed. "Aydan, this is my job."

I took a deep breath and spoke evenly. "I realize that. I'm not trying to convince you otherwise. But don't take pointless risks. The bike's not worth it."

Germain broke in. "Aydan's right. We need to set some priorities here."

"Keep in mind that if they did catch me, they likely wouldn't escalate the violence that quickly in real life," Kane said. "If they did, they'd have a dead captive on their hands in short order, and no information. And they're going to want information from me now more than ever."

"Assuming they read the Torturer's Handbook and they follow the industry best practices," I interrupted sourly.

"They'd also be hampered by the location," he continued. "They wouldn't be able to do anything in the guest house. Too many other guests wandering around. Too much noise and mess."

"Goody."

"I'm not trying to argue that I should go over there tonight," Kane said patiently. "I'm just saying you're probably overestimating the actual risk. Effective torture is mostly psychological."

Germain shook his head, frowning. "Hellhound and I will cover surveillance for tonight," he said. "And we can bring the bike back, if it's still there."

"If I was Fuzzy Bunny, it'd still be there, all right," I said. "It's called bait."

Kane nodded. "I thought of that, too. But we have night vision and infrared scopes. If they have it guarded, we'll be able to spot their people easily."

"True," I said slowly. "But if I was Fuzzy Bunny, I wouldn't put a guard on it at all. After your performance today, I'd assume you were both smart and well-equipped enough to detect that. I'd route my patrols far away from it so you could get in easily. And I'd put a transmission device somewhere on the bike so I could track you down at my leisure."

Kane gave me a piercing glance. "I'd also followed that train of thought," he assured me after a second. "We've got a handheld sweep device. I wouldn't move the bike without making sure it was clean."

"Here's another question, though," he added. "Do they

even know the bike is there? And if so, do they know it's mine? I told the guards I was on foot. The patrols haven't been going anywhere near that far out. And it didn't look like they were on high alert. I didn't even run into a patrol when I left this afternoon."

"Why do you want the bike back so badly?" I asked.

"I don't like being one ride short," Kane replied. "It compromises our mobility. Besides," he added reluctantly, "It's my own bike. That 750 cruiser of yours just doesn't have the power and handling that I'm used to."

"Now the truth comes out," I teased.

He gave an unrepentant shrug. "The truth, yes, but I wouldn't risk a mission for it. I stand by my reasoning. If we don't retrieve it, we'll need to get another bike."

"Okay," Germain agreed. "Hellhound and I will take the Yamaha over. We'll check out the area with the scopes. If there's no guard, we'll go in and sweep the bike, make sure it's clean. If it all checks out, we'll bring it back. Otherwise, we'll leave it there."

"I'll take the first watch," Hellhound volunteered. "Germain can spell me off around two, an' we can swap again in the mornin'."

"What do you think about keeping a watch here at night, too?" Germain asked. "It overextends us, but with the extra activity over at Harchman's, we might want to be cautious. Especially with Aydan here."

"Good point," Kane agreed. "All right. You two handle Harchman's. I'll watch here."

"We'll take shifts," I corrected. "You guys are tired already. I can pull my weight."

Kane assessed me, and I met his eyes steadily. He'd looked tired when I arrived earlier in the day. Now he looked like death warmed over. He wouldn't admit it, but I knew his experience in the sim had taken its toll.

"All right," he said finally. "Let's do it."

"Wait," I said. "One more thing." They all turned to look at me. "Arnie needs some more information."

"We've already been over this," Germain said. "I have a direct order not to disclose."

"Everyone please note Carl has followed orders to the letter," I said. I turned to Hellhound. "You need to know that -"

"Aydan, there are serious consequences if you breach your confidentiality agreement," Kane interrupted.

"And there are serious consequences if he goes in uninformed," I retorted. "Arnie, the people you're watching at Harchman's are using a form of mind control to torture people. If you get captured, you need to remember that what's happening to you isn't real. It will seem very real, but it's all being done in your mind. Your body won't actually be damaged. That probably won't help much, if it comes to that, but..."

"Believe me, it helps," Kane muttered.

Hellhound nodded slowly, and I could sense the wheels turning. I knew not to underestimate him. The dumb-biker image disguised a brilliant mind and a photographic memory.

"That explains a few things. Thanks, darlin'," he said.

I turned to Kane and Germain. "I don't think I'm in breach of my contract. But just in case, I beg forgiveness. As opposed to asking permission." I raised my chin and looked Germain square in the eye.

His tense face relaxed and he laughed. "If this is you begging, I'd hate to see demanding." He sobered. "Thanks for covering my butt."

"You're welcome."

Germain and Hellhound put on their riding leathers, and we all trooped out of the hot RV into the cooler outside air. Germain swung astride his Yamaha and Hellhound grimaced.

"Shit. Can't believe I'm gonna hafta ride on the back a' this fuckin' piece a' Jap crap. Lucky it's gettin' dark so nobody'll see me. Why don't ya get a real bike?"

"It's better than that bone-rattling piece of shit you call a Harley," Germain retorted good-naturedly. "They've been making bikes for how long, and they still can't make one with a decent muffler?"

Hellhound perched precariously on the back, struggling to hoist his boots up onto the passenger pegs. "Why the hell d'ya wanna ride one a' these goddam crotch rockets anyhow?" he groused as he groped behind him for handholds. "Ya like bustin' your fuckin' nuts on the tank? Maybe ya ain't usin' your junk anymore, but I still wanna use mine."

"Don't they make a cute couple?" I observed loudly to Kane.

"Hey, Germain," Kane called. "That's got to be the ugliest girlfriend I've ever seen!"

Hellhound flipped him a stiff middle finger, and we laughed as they rode out of sight.

I turned to Kane. "I'm going to go and poke at that data a bit more, until Carl gets back and wants to go to bed. Why don't you call it a night? I'll take the first watch."

"You don't have to do that. It's not your job."

"So, what, you're going to stay up all night? And all day tomorrow? No thanks. I'd rather you stayed alert. I might need you to save my butt." I grinned up at him.

He chuckled. "All right. Point taken. I'm going to wait for Germain to get back, too. But I can take the first shift."

"I'd rather take it, if you don't mind. I need some time to think."

He eyed me seriously. "If you're sure."

I nodded. "Very sure." I went back into the RV and got back to work, my nerves on edge. I flipped through the photos with less attention than before, wondering what Germain and Hellhound were getting into over at Harchman's. Memories of blood and scorched flesh kept intruding at the edges of my mind.

I'd narrowed the list down to a half-dozen possibilities by the time I heard the quiet idle of the returning Yamaha, and the headlight flashed through the trailer as Germain pulled up. A couple of minutes later, he and Kane stepped into the trailer.

"So the bike's in the clear?" I asked.

He nodded. "Nobody around, and the sweep came up clean. We moved it to the second observation point, and Hellhound's settled in for the duration. He'll bring it back. And there doesn't seem to be any extra guard activity. Everything's the same as before."

"Bizarre," I said.

He shrugged and nodded. "I'm going to call it a night."

Kane turned to me. "We can make up the dinette into a bed for you."

"I don't see why. Only two people are going to be sleeping at a time. Two beds, good enough."

"If you don't mind sleeping in somebody else's sheets."

"No biggie. A bed's a bed. And we need as much space in this RV as we can get."

I reached into my backpack and pulled my baggy jeans and a T-shirt over my shorts and tank top. I grabbed my fleece hoodie and jacket before delving into the backpack again to extract an apple, my water bottle, and a handful of cereal bars.

I looked up to see Germain's eyes crinkle in amusement. "How much food have you got in there, anyway?"

"It's mostly food," I admitted. "I don't carry a big wardrobe when I'm camping. So if you were thinking of asking me to the prom, forget it."

He laughed and headed for the bathroom while Kane briefed me. "Stay within arm's reach of the trailer at all times. Your only role is to watch. If you see anything suspicious, anything at all, thump on the outside of the trailer. Then run away and hide in the woods. Don't try to help us. Understood?"

"Got it."

"I'll spell you off when Hellhound and Germain switch shifts. But if you need to quit before then, just come and get me. You're sure you're okay with this?"

"I'm fine. I like being outside at night. Get some sleep."

I went out the door and settled into the folding chair beside the trailer. I heard the men moving around inside the trailer for a short time before the lights went out. I relaxed into the silent darkness, my eyes adjusting so that the trees showed as black silhouettes against the paler sky in the west.

I let my mind drift while the sky darkened over the mountains. Coyotes howled in the vicinity of the small creek about a mile away. Stars gradually appeared, and I heard an owl's hoot.

The air slowly chilled and I leaned my head back, watching the comforting blanket of stars wheel overhead.

The moon rose over the horizon, silvering the trees.

I huddled into my jacket and ate a cereal bar, listening to the quiet night noises. In that safe, silent place, I took out the day's memories and examined them again as dispassionately as possible, working to reduce their impact.

My watch was so old it had no illumination, so I marked time by the position of the moon. When it had advanced over about a quarter of the sky, I heard movement from inside the trailer. In a few minutes, Germain stepped out, leather-clad.

"How's it going?" he asked softly.

"Fine. Beautiful night. I love it out here."

"Why don't you spell off with Kane? You need some sleep, too."

"I'm going to let him sleep a little longer. I'll wait until Hellhound comes back."

"Okay. See you later." He got on his motorcycle, and I closed the gate behind him as he idled quietly into the night.

About twenty minutes later I heard another soft rumble, and the approaching headlight bounced over the uneven ground. I swung the gate open, then closed it again behind the tall black motorcycle.

Hellhound dismounted stiffly, stretching and rolling his shoulders.

"Halt, who goes there?" I quipped.

He turned, his smile gleaming in the moonlight. "Lemme see if I remember the password." He pulled me into his arms and kissed me thoroughly.

When he broke the kiss, I smiled up at him. "That was pretty close."

"Nah, I don't think so. I think it was more like this."

By the time he paused, I was clinging to him, breathless.

"That was definitely it."

"Hmmm." His growl vibrated through my body as his lips and whiskers teased my ear. "I know some other passwords."

The sensation sent tantalizing messages to sensitive places, making me shiver. I pulled away from him reluctantly. "And I really want to hear them. But I'm going to sit out for a while longer. Go get some sleep."

"Come in with me. Your shift's done, let Kane take over."

"No, I want to sit out a little longer. He went through hell this afternoon. Let him sleep."

"Darlin', he ain't the only one that went through hell this afternoon. Ya gotta get some rest."

I sat down in the chair again, hiding in shadow. "If I sleep, you won't be able to. You'd better go and get a head start."

He squatted beside me. "What d'ya mean?"

"I mean I'll probably have nightmares. I'm staying up as long as I can. Maybe if I tire myself out, I'll sleep better. You go ahead. I'll come in a bit later. And if I start making noise in my sleep, any noise, throw something at me to wake me up before I start screaming at the top of my lungs. You'll be doing everybody a favour."

"Okay," he said doubtfully as he rose. He stepped quietly into the RV, and I settled down to watch some more.

Some time later, I heard movement from inside, and Kane came out. "Why didn't you wake me?" he asked. "I slept right through the shift change."

"You needed it. And I'm fine out here."

"Well, you'd better go in now. You've been up for nearly twenty-four hours."

I sighed and rose, my chilled body unfolding grudgingly

from the chair. "Don't worry if I start screaming. It's just my usual crap. I told Arnie to wake me if I start up."

He engulfed my cold hand in his big, warm one. "I'm sorry you had to witness that today. Try to remember, it wasn't real."

"I know. I'll deal with it. It'll just take some time. It was just... when I had to take over the sim... that was..." I stopped and took a deep breath. "Anyway, I woke a few other ghosts today, too. It'll take at least one night to get it all out of my system."

I turned toward the trailer, but he didn't let go of my hand. "What ghosts?"

I shrugged in the dark. He already knew about this particular ghost. "You nearly had to pry me off a fencepost today."

I felt him stiffen. "What happened?"

"Riding an unfamiliar bike too fast. I nearly high-sided coming around the corner up top. Scraped the shit out of the footpeg, and I probably damaged the front fork seals when I took air coming down the hill. I hope you've got an understanding with the bike supplier."

"I don't care about the bike. As long as you're okay. I was surprised when Hellhound told me you still rode after that accident."

"Well, it's good for me to get back on a street bike. It's been nearly ten years. You have to get over it sometime."

"I guess." He squeezed my hand. "Go get some sleep."

CHAPTER 24

I crept into the trailer as silently as possible and took my backpack into the bathroom without turning on the light. I washed up quickly and stripped down to my shorts and tank top again, shivering in the cold moonlight.

As I slipped out of the bathroom, Hellhound stirred. "That you, darlin'?" he croaked.

"No, it's Kane," I whispered as I headed for the back bedroom.

He chuckled and I heard him get out of bed. Strong arms caught me from behind just outside the bedroom door. His skin felt scorching against mine, and he drew in a sharp breath.

"Darlin', you're frozen!" He stroked hot hands over my icy arms and legs, and I backed closer, soaking up his body heat.

Warm lips brushed my ear and his deep, sexy rasp tickled my eardrum. "I can warm ya up." His hands slid slowly under my top.

I'd spent the last several months trying to convince myself his hands couldn't have been as good as I remembered them. As he lightly caressed my breasts, I realized I'd been right. His hands weren't as good as I remembered them. They were much, much better. Adept fingers teased me into mindless desire.

I arched back against him and his lips found that sensitive spot just above my collarbone. He nibbled my neck, prickly whiskers heightening the sensation. One of his hands drifted down into my shorts to make small, delicious circles.

I sucked in my breath at the rush of heat while his skillful touch threatened to empty my brain of everything but pure dumb lust. Just before I lost all ability for sentient thought, I pulled away with a supreme effort of will and turned to face him.

"About that audience. I'm pretty sure Kane's going to notice if the trailer starts rocking."

He closed the distance between us, steering me backward into the bedroom. "I can put a smile on your face without ever rockin' the trailer, darlin'." He kissed me deeply, and the touch of his tongue reminded me he was telling the absolute truth.

My clothes went away and he lowered me onto the bed. A few more hot kisses while his hands worked their magic, and a small, breathless moan escaped me.

"Ya gotta be quiet, darlin'."

"You know I'm never quiet!" I gasped.

"Shhh." He trailed slow, whiskery kisses down my stomach.

I grabbed the pillow and jammed it over my face.

A short time later, he lifted the pillow from my nerveless hands to peer down at me. "Ya still with me, darlin'?" His grin flashed in the moonlight.

"Ohmigod," I panted, the last waves of ecstasy still rolling through me. "No. I've died and gone to heaven. And if you bring that magic stick of yours a little closer, I'll stay there." I reached for him hungrily.

He caught my hands. "Thought ya didn't wanna rock the trailer."

"Rock the trailer. Please! Rock the damn trailer right off its wheels!"

"Nah. That'd be indiscreet." He chuckled softly. "Besides, I gotta leave ya somethin' to look forward to." He kissed me lightly and rolled off the bed.

I made a grab for him, but missed. He left the bedroom, and I heard him lie down again in the other bed. I sprawled limply for a few minutes, catching my breath. As soon as my legs stopped trembling, I was going to go over there and jump him, discretion be damned. I could be very persuasive. He wouldn't say no to me for long.

Exhausted satisfaction pinned my leaden limbs to the bed.

Just a few more minutes of rest, and then I'd definitely go over there.

A small electronic beeping woke me. Arnie lifted his arm off my waist and rolled over to turn off his wristwatch alarm.

I turned to face him in the morning light. "Well, this is discreet."

He chuckled. "I knew Kane wouldn't come into the trailer while he was on watch. An' this easier than gettin' up every time ya had a nightmare."

I pushed up on my elbow, looking down at his sleepy face on the pillow. "I'm sorry! Why didn't you just wake me up? I could have gone out and sat with Kane and you could have slept."

"It's okay, darlin', I slept." He rummaged under the covers. "Ya might want these."

I took my shorts and tank top from him and shimmied into them. He grinned at me, his eyes hot. "If I didn't hafta go relieve Germain..."

He shook his head and gave me a wry look. "If ya wanna use the bathroom, ya better go first. Ya won't wanna go in there after I'm done."

I laughed and kissed him. "A true gentleman."

When I came out of the bathroom washed and dressed, Arnie was just finishing another helping of Salisbury steak, and I shuddered.

"Don't you get tired of that?"

"Nah. I can eat anythin'."

"So can I, but I can't eat it day after day like that."

He shrugged as I started to open cabinet doors to check out the food supply.

I stuck my head out the door of the RV and wished Kane a good morning. "Do you want some chili for breakfast? I won't be able to eat the whole can."

He smiled back at me, and I was glad to see his extra sleep had helped. He still looked tired, but the greyish cast was gone from his skin.

"That sounds good. I'll come in. We've got a clear sight line around us now that it's daylight."

He came into the RV as I stuck my bowl of chili in the microwave. "'Morning," he greeted Hellhound.

"Mornin'," Hellhound mumbled around a mouthful.

"You're heading out shortly?"

Hellhound nodded. "Soon's I'm done here. Gotta take a dump first."

"Thanks for sharing that," Kane told him. "Aydan, can

you be ready to go with Hellhound?"

"I presume you mean to Harchman's, not to the bathroom."

"Yes." He pinched the bridge of his nose, grimacing. "Jesus, you're as bad as he is." Hellhound snorted laughter, and Kane ignored him with forbearance.

"I'd like you to check to see if there's any activity," Kane told me. "Then you can come back here and finish digging through the database. The sooner we can identify the captives, the better."

"Okay." I started shovelling in chili.

"Hellhound, you'll stay with Aydan while she does this. Be ready to signal her, same as before. Aydan, be quick. Just check things out and leave. Don't interact, no matter what." He shot me a stern look, and I nodded.

"As soon as you're finished, go with Hellhound to relieve Germain. Come back with Germain. I don't want you unguarded," he finished.

"Got it," I confirmed. Hellhound rose to head for the bathroom and I picked up my bowl and spoon. "I'm just going to finish this outside."

I grabbed my leathers on the way out and left Kane waiting for his share of the chili to heat up.

It was a cool morning, and I'd worn my baggy jeans again. I tried to pull the tight leather pants over top, but there was no way. Kane and Hellhound were still inside, so I stepped into a blind spot between the windows and changed pants. Then I dragged the folding chair into the sun and sat down to finish my breakfast.

Seconds later, Kane stepped out the door and settled onto the fallen log by the trailer with his bowl and spoon. "Smart woman. Lucky you're not easily offended."

I grinned at him. "It's not my first time camping with a bunch of guys. Besides, he gave fair warning."

"True."

I scraped out the bowl and laid it down beside the chair, relaxing as the sun's early beams warmed my black leather. My eyes drifted shut. When I opened them again, Hellhound stood in front of me.

"Ready to roll?" he rasped.

I yawned. "Yep. Let's go." We climbed aboard our bikes, and Kane let us out the gate.

Once more, we gave Harchman's place a drive-by, but all seemed quiet. We parked again in the ditch, and I shivered. This close to the mountains, the temperature varied dramatically between daytime and night-time temperatures.

I lowered myself gingerly to the cold ground. "Too cold to lie down."

Hellhound nodded and sat down, wrapping an arm around me. I rested my head on his shoulder and was about to go into the network when his voice stopped me.

"Aydan? Can I ask ya somethin'?"

"Sure."

"Does that thing in your watch make ya... telepathic?"

I pulled away to look at him. He met my eyes steadily, but I could sense his discomfort. I understood. I knew exactly what it was like to wonder if somebody could look inside my head at my innermost thoughts. I hastened to reassure him.

"No. I'm definitely not telepathic."

"So ya don't know what I'm thinkin'. Ya can't get inside my head."

"No. Absolutely not. I can't get inside anybody's head. I don't know what anybody's thinking." I nudged my shoulder against his and shot him a wicked grin. "But I know what you're thinking about, a lot of the time."

He laughed and relaxed. "I'm a guy. Duh."

His grin dissolved. "But yesterday, ya lay down in this ditch not knowin' anythin' more than I did. Ya woke up an' said ya were gonna get Kane out. An' ya had a plan you'd worked out with him. Times. Places. He was inside Harchman's. Ya never left my side."

I sighed. "I know it looks like telepathy, but it's not. I wasn't inside Kane's head, either. I have no idea what he was thinking then. Or now. Or ever."

"Okay, darlin'." He scowled. "None a' this makes sense. I know ya can't tell me, and I don't really wanna know. But tell me this, if ya can without gettin' in trouble. If I get captured, can ya talk to me like ya talked to Kane?"

"Yes. Assuming I can get in the right place to do it."

"Ya hafta be close enough. Physically close enough."

"Yes."

"Okay. Thanks." He pulled me close again. "Guess ya better get started, then. Germain'll be wonderin' what's keepin' me."

I laid my head back on his shoulder, marvelling at his trust. I knew he and Kane went back a long way, and I guessed that trust extended to me by proxy.

Then again, I was putting my life in his hands, too. I trusted him, Kane, and Germain more than anybody else I could think of offhand. I put away that unaccustomed thought for future analysis, and stepped invisibly into the network.

Like the previous day, I peeked into each room in turn. The rooms were deserted, and I picked up speed as I went. When I discovered one that was occupied, I jerked to a halt.

Harchman again. This time he had me bent over one of the desks in the security control room. I averted my eyes from the revolting sight of his flabby white ass as it quivered with each thrust.

This guy was really getting his money's worth from the sim. In real life, he would have had to stand on a step stool to manage that.

I made an invisible face and was about to move on when a sudden thought occurred to me. Unlike the scenario Harchman had created in the gazebo, the security room sim was very realistic. I knew Harchman wouldn't have bothered with that much detail. He didn't need it for what he was doing. Could this be a stored sim of the actual security room?

I drifted through the wall and into the room, looking away from Harchman and trying not to listen to his porcine grunting. I floated around to look at the security monitors and check their time display. Sure enough, it was real-time. The sim must have been created so the security room could be monitored remotely. This could definitely be useful.

Harchman squealed like the pig he was. I whisked through the wall, catching an unwanted glimpse of his sweaty, contorted face as he came. Really didn't need to see that. In the virtual corridor outside, I shook myself like a dog, trying to shed the mind cooties.

Focus.

I zipped invisibly down the corridor, checking the rest of the rooms. I slowed as I drifted through the firewall. Swallowing queasiness, I peeked into the room that had held the prisoner the previous day. It was clean and unoccupied.

I checked the next several rooms, beginning to regain my confidence. When I discovered a captive, the shock hit me almost like a physical blow. I wrapped my invisible arms around myself while I memorized him, holding my emotions in check. I wouldn't let Kane down this time.

Thankfully, they hadn't gotten to this prisoner yet. He was young, and his smooth face and hazel eyes reminded me disturbingly of Spider. Like the first man, his wrists and ankles were secured to a chair with nylon ties. He strained at his bonds, blood leaking from the gashes on his wrists where the ties cut into his flesh. I knew exactly how that felt. I shuddered and drew a few calming breaths, pushing away my own memories to concentrate on every detail of his face.

As I watched, he stared around the room, still struggling. His wild-eyed gaze met mine, and even though I knew he couldn't see me, the sensation of contact was so unnerving I ducked and scooted away.

I rapidly checked the rest of the rooms, finding them clean and vacant, and I let out a shaky breath as I zoomed back to the portal. I stepped carefully through, trying to prepare myself for the pain.

It slammed through my head right on cue. My resistance was low after only a few hours of sleep, and I jerked into fetal position and held my head together with both hands. I didn't bother to restrain my varied and extensive vocabulary of obscenities. I went on at length, trailing off gradually as the pain subsided.

When I finished and uncurled, Hellhound was holding me tightly. He gazed down anxiously at me. "Darlin', are ya okay?"

"Fine," I mumbled, massaging my temples.

"Really? Cryin' and throwin' up and swearin' is the best-case scenario?"

"Usually I don't cry and throw up. But the worst-case

scenario is much worse."

"I never wanna see it. It's hard to imagine it gettin' much worse."

I gave him a wan smile. "Let me put it in context for you. Lacking the necessary equipment, I can't swear to the accuracy of this, but imagine the best-case scenario is like getting a solid kick in the balls."

"That'd prob'ly make me cry an' puke an' swear."

"Then imagine the worst-case scenario is like being held spread-eagled while one of the CFL's star punters takes his best shot at your nuts. Wearing cleats. And then an enraged wolverine comes along and chews off anything that's left. Slowly."

He flinched and cupped his crotch protectively. "Stop it, darlin', you're scarin' the boys. If ya keep doin' that, I'm gonna end up with indoor plumbin'."

"Now, that would be a tragedy. The boys have my heartfelt apologies."

He grinned. "Ya can make it up to 'em later."

We got on the bikes again, and Hellhound led the way to a different access point. "Go on ahead," he advised me. "I'm gonna shut the beast down an' push it in." He pulled out his phone and pressed a speed dial button before disconnecting. "You're good to go now."

I idled the Honda slowly down the winding trail, hoping I wouldn't have to leave quite as quickly this time. I'd only ridden a hundred yards or so when I spotted a flash of red paint through the trees. Shortly afterward, I pulled into the clearing beside Germain's Yamaha.

He turned from his binoculars, looking alarmed. "Aydan? What's going on?"

"Nothing to worry about. Kane wanted me to check the

network again this morning, and he wanted me to have an escort both ways. Hellhound's behind me, pushing his bike in."

"Now, that's love," Germain chuckled. "I still can't figure out why anybody would want to ride a Harley. Especially after pushing it around for days."

Hellhound laboured up the slope into the clearing. "Liked the other viewpoint better," he panted as he leaned the big motorcycle on its kickstand.

"Get some modern technology," Germain needled him. "I can ride in and out."

"Yeah, but look what ya gotta ride," Hellhound retorted.

Germain grinned and handed him the binoculars. "See you later." He started his bike and led the way down the trail.

CHAPTER 25

There was no sign of Kane when we reached the gate, and Germain got off to open it and close it again behind us. Nerves twitched in my stomach as we wheeled the bikes up beside the RV.

I'd just pulled my helmet off when Kane stuck his head out the door of the trailer, the phone glued to his ear. He raised a hand in greeting before ducking back inside. I blew out a relieved breath and went inside, too.

He was obviously just finishing his conversation, so I slipped into the bathroom and changed back into my jeans. By the time I emerged, Kane was sitting on the edge of the pull-out bed while Germain heated some food in the microwave. I ran a glass of water and slid into the bench of the dinette.

"Anything new in the network this morning?" Kane asked.

"Yes. There's a new prisoner, and they haven't started working on him yet. I got a good look this time."

Kane straightened. "Excellent! That's the first break we've had. Can you get started looking through the database right away?"

"I can, but aren't you going to go in and rescue the new prisoner?"

Kane's face was composed, but I read his disquiet in the iron grey of his eyes. "We can't. We have to get more information."

"But we know what's going to happen to him! You can't just let him suffer like that!"

Kane made a calming gesture, frowning, and I realized I was half-way out of my seat, fists clenched.

"Aydan, I'm sorry, I feel the same way you do, but these are our orders."

"That's bullshit," I snapped. "Call Stemp again. That poor kid's going to die a horrible death. We can't just sit here."

Kane sighed. "I just got off the phone with Stemp. We need identities before we can move. Our orders stand, whether we like it or not." He turned to Germain, and I realized the subject was closed no matter how much I might rant. "Any sign of physical activity last night?" Kane asked.

Germain shook his head. "Everything exactly as before. No sign of body transfers. The usual guard patrols, on the usual routes. The only difference is they're using random timing now."

"Damn. So we have no way of knowing whether they pulled the bodies out yesterday afternoon while our surveillance was down, or whether they're still there. Aydan narrowed the list of divers down to a shortlist last night, but we can't go any further down that road until Webb gets back to us with more information."

Germain nodded glumly. "Or until we get a report of a middle-aged diver who died of a heart attack yesterday."

"So now what?" I asked, keeping my voice calm and level, emotions under control. "Do we just keep watching?"

Kane grimaced. "Yes."

I sighed and straightened out of my slouch. "I did find something else interesting in the network."

"What?" Kane leaned forward intently.

"I found a complete, real-time sim of the security room. All the monitors clearly visible, all up to date. Somebody's set it up so they can monitor remotely. I bet that explains why the network is so widespread. They'd be able to access it from anywhere on the building site."

"Isn't that interesting," Kane muttered. "I wonder why they need that." His eyes bored into me. "How did you find this? I told you not to interact. You shouldn't have been opening any sim files."

"I didn't. Harchman was in the sim."

"Monitoring the security?"

"No. Getting his rocks off. Again," I said moodily. "I swear I'm ready to buy that asshole a hooker just so I don't have to watch him do me every day." There was a longish silence. "That was probably too much information," I added.

"A little," Germain agreed.

"Sorry."

"I can see where that would be upsetting," Kane said diplomatically.

I shrugged. "I don't really care if he thinks it. It's a free country. They're his own private thoughts. I just don't want to have to watch it."

"Understandable. Anyway," Kane brought us back to the point. "That sim could have some potential for surveillance for us."

"Definitely," I agreed. "But I don't know what would

happen if I went in and opened it. I know anybody can walk into a sim while it's in use. But I don't know if another user would notice if it was already open when they accessed it. I'll have to talk to Spider."

I frowned, thinking. "And I'd need to know how the date and timestamp record on the sim file would work. If it's real-time, maybe it's always up and they'd never notice. Or not."

Kane stood. "Give it some thought, and then call Webb and talk it over with him. In the mean time, the sooner you get started on the database search, the better."

I nodded. "I'll do that right away." I eyed Germain's tired face. "I'll take the laptop outside so you can get some rest in here."

"Thanks." He got up and threw his paper plate in the garbage as I picked up the laptop.

"I'm going to wash up before you get to sleep," Kane told him, and headed for the tiny bathroom.

I went outside and settled into the folding chair. I'd only been working for a few minutes when Kane shouted my name from inside. I heard a slam, and the RV rocked furiously to the sound of pounding feet.

Adrenaline spiked through my system as I sprang up, unsure whether to rush to the trailer or run for the forest. I compromised by standing dumbly rooted to the spot. The RV's door crashed open, rebounding almost into Kane's face as he leaped out. Germain hit the ground immediately behind him.

My jaw dropped at the sight. Both were nattily attired in underwear, firearms, and nothing else. Kane showcased his considerable assets in hip-hugging black briefs, nicely colour-coordinated with his Sig Sauer .40 calibre. Germain was slightly more discreet though just as impressive in a pair of snug black boxer briefs, accessorized with a matching Glock.

Overloaded by all the luscious naked muscle and bountiful endowment, my mind spun its wheels wildly. Kane had been washing up, Germain was going to bed, right, that explained the underwear.

My brain slipped a few more gears as Kane jerked his head at Germain and they quickly secured the perimeter, offering me two magnificent rear views as well. Old, jagged scars marred Kane's powerful back. The bullet must have gone right through his chest. I knew it had been a near-fatal wound.

I heroically dragged my eyes up to their faces as they turned. Germain placed his back to the RV, scanning the woods and access points, his gun at the ready. Kane reached into the trailer and threw my boots, leathers, and backpack at me.

"Vanish," he barked. "Don't tell me where. Contact Webb for a rendezvous point. Leave your cellphone here."

My body was already scrambling to obey while my brain caught up. I kicked off my runners and skinned out of my jeans. A small, silly part of my mind congratulated me for wearing black panties today. We all matched. Fashion tips for the well-dressed spy...

"What are you *doing*?"

I bent to pick up my leather pants, trying to keep the thong back of my underwear out of direct view. I jerked the pants up my legs as I looked up to meet two frozen stares. "They don't fit over my jeans. What the hell's going on?"

Kane gave his head a quick, forceful shake. "We may have been compromised. Get out as fast as you can. Don't stop for anything. Good luck," he added as I wrestled my backpack over my jacket and jammed my helmet on. Germain ran to swing the gate open, and I jumped on the Honda and accelerated hard up the hill.

CHAPTER 26

I cracked the throttle open on the highway and glared frantically around me as I hit the speed limit. There was no sign of pursuit. My heart pounded furiously for several miles, but the light morning traffic looked utterly normal and nobody gave me a second glance.

I took the first available turn toward Millarville and started to relax as I headed south on the quiet highway. Barring an attack from the air, it would be pretty hard for anybody to sneak up on me here.

Forty minutes later, I pulled into the small town, shaking with fatigue and surplus adrenaline. I found a tiny coffee shop and gratefully downed a cup of herbal tea and a muffin, still watching vigilantly just in case. All was quiet. I got directions to a public phone and dialled Spider's number.

He answered on the first ring. "Spider's Webb Design." I could hear the overtone of tension in his voice.

"Spider, it's Aydan."

"Thank God. Are you okay?"

"Fine. What the hell's going on?"

"Germain will fill you in when you meet him." I thumped my forehead as I realized that he couldn't tell me anything on this line.

"When and where?"

"Calgary. Not before one o'clock. Call me later and I'll update you." I looked at my watch. Nine AM. At least four hours to kill.

"Okay. I'll call you later."

"Be careful."

I hung up the phone. What the hell was I going to do for four hours?

I shrugged. Might as well take the scenic route. It would use up the time, and I'd be hard to find as long as I kept moving.

Back on the bike, I headed south. It was a beautiful morning for a ride, and the highway wasn't too busy. I relaxed as much as I could and tried to enjoy the cruise.

At Turner Valley, I finally turned east, beginning to angle my way back up toward Calgary. Just before Okotoks, I pulled off beside the road for a rest. My sleepless night had caught up with me, and I was struggling to stay alert. Now was a bad time to start getting tired and careless, right before tackling Calgary traffic.

I jogged around a bit, trying to get my blood circulating. The air was getting warm again, and it didn't help. Right now, cold would be better. I shook the tension out of my hands and wrists and tried to formulate a plan.

I really needed sleep. I couldn't check into a hotel at ten o'clock in the morning just for the sake of a couple of hours of sleep. Anyway, I didn't have enough cash on me, and I didn't want to use a credit card. Shit.

My tired brain ran in tight circles. Must stay alert. Must have sleep. Finally, I hit on the best compromise I could manage. I climbed wearily back aboard the bike and rode up through Okotoks to connect with Highway 2. A few miles north, I turned off and pulled into Sikome Lake, a manmade recreational lake at the south end of Calgary.

By that time of the morning, families were already staking out their spots on the warm sand and the concession stands were in full swing. I parked the bike and staggered a few steps away to collapse on the grass. I leaned my back against a tree and rested my elbows and head on my drawn-up knees.

A dog barked sharply close by. I jerked upright, swiping my hand across my chin where I'd been drooling. How attractive.

I checked my watch. Out like a light for nearly thirty-five minutes, right in the middle of a public place. Dangerous. Real spies probably didn't do things like that.

I hauled myself to my feet and massaged my butt. The parts of it that weren't asleep hurt like hell. I walked back and forth and did a few stretches. Nobody paid any attention to me, which pleased me immensely.

I found a pay phone and called Spider again. "Hi, Spider. Any news?"

"Yes. Meet at one o'clock. Where you first met Hellhound."

"Okay, got it. Does that mean we're all in the clear?"

"So far, yes, but Kane says to stay alert."

I hung up the phone, smiling at the memory of my first encounter with Hellhound. He'd nearly punched my head in, and I'd returned the favour by slamming his face into the side of a building and slugging him in the throat. Funny how things work out.

Arriving at the strip mall a few minutes early, I cruised

past the parking lot once as a precaution. The RV was easy to spot with the cargo trailer hitched on behind it, and I pulled into the lot and parked a few slots away. The sun had turned the asphalt into a shimmering griddle, and I pulled off my helmet and jacket gratefully. As I did, the RV's door swung open, and Germain beckoned me over.

I was heading in that direction when Kane rode up and swung off the BMW. Riding chaps again. Jesus.

As we sat down in the RV, I concentrated hard on their faces. All I could think of was black underwear.

Wrestling my dirty mind into submission, I made an attempt to focus. On something besides firmly-packed black underwear.

Shit.

"What happened?" I demanded. "Is Hellhound okay?"

"He's fine. We left him on surveillance," Kane said. "I wasn't concerned about that part of the operation. I was afraid I'd compromised our base camp."

"*You'd* compromised it? How?"

"Through my own carelessness," he said through his teeth. "Stupid. We ran a sweep on my bike, but we didn't run one on me. When I went to wash up, I discovered an electronic device attached to the back of my neck. They must have slapped it on me while I was recovering from the stun gun."

"They were tracking you? Why the hell wouldn't they have just come and picked you up last night, then?"

"I don't know," he growled. "That's why I didn't want you to waste any time getting out."

"What did you do? I presume you're not harbouring any electronics now."

"No. I saw you turn east on the highway, so I gave you

twenty minutes' head start. We swept everything while we waited. There was only one device. I got on the road carrying the device and headed west to circle around as a decoy while Germain broke camp and pulled out. Webb set up a rendezvous for me with Richardson here in Calgary, and I dropped it to him. He'll take it up to Silverside so Webb can analyze it at the Sirius lab."

"Yikes." I leaned back in my seat and blew out a long breath. "So now what?"

Kane shrugged irritably. "Nothing about this situation makes sense. I'd feel better about it if there was some logic somewhere, but if there is, I can't find it. Now we go back and watch some more. Try to figure this out."

His fist clenched. "I can't believe I was that stupid. We'll have to find another location for the base camp, too."

"Minor detail," Germain said. "No harm done."

"This time. A mistake like that could have blown the whole operation," Kane said grimly. "And put Aydan and the network key into enemy hands."

"You know you can't play the what-if game," I told him. "You're always on top of every little detail, but you can't be perfect. Let it go. Nothing bad happened."

He shrugged again, obviously still kicking himself. "I'll go and scout out a new location for us. Aydan, we'll load up your bike in the cargo trailer, and you can ride out to the new camp in the RV."

He looked from me to Germain. "Both of you look beat. Get some sleep before you get on the road. There's no hurry until I find another place for us to set up. I'll call Webb when I've got a new location." He rose. "Come on, let's get Aydan's bike loaded, and then I'll head out."

They tethered the Honda securely in the cargo trailer

beside Germain's Yamaha, and Kane rode away. Germain glanced over at me and yawned. "Are you okay with sleeping in the RV here in the parking lot?"

"I'm okay with sleeping on my feet while I'm standing here."

His eyes crinkled with amusement. "Okay, whatever floats your boat. But I'm going to go in and lie down on a bed."

"That sounds like a better plan."

We climbed back into the trailer, and he waved me toward the back. "You can have the bedroom."

"Thanks." I sleepwalked into the room and dropped onto the bed, my eyes already closed.

A shock of alarm drove through me. My body instinctively rolled off the bed and onto my feet even as my eyes were opening.

Germain took a quick step back from my clenched fists, his own hands rising defensively. "Aydan! It's okay!"

I blinked and focused slowly as my brain woke up. "Wha...?"

"It's okay," he repeated. "Kane's got a new location for us. We need to get on the road."

"Oh. Sorry." I straightened out of my crouch and rubbed my face groggily. "God, I hate sleeping in a hot place in the middle of the day. My brain doesn't want to start working when I wake up."

"There's nothing wrong with your reflexes, though. Do you always wake up combat-ready?"

"No. I was dreaming," I said sheepishly. "Sorry, the only time you ever see me is when I'm totally messed up. I'm usually quite sane and normal."

He laughed as we made our way to the front of the RV. "Define normal."

"Good point."

We buckled in, and I turned to him as we pulled out of the lot. "So what's the plan?"

"Kane's booked us into a campground for the night. It's not an ideal solution, but we need to get set up so we can relieve Hellhound and regroup."

"Campground? As in, a camping spot with a firepit?"

"I assume so."

"Then we need to stop at a grocery store. We're eating steak tonight."

He returned my grin. "I like the way you think. It was time to restock the cupboards anyway."

After a short side trip for provisions, we hit the highway. The air conditioning helped, but the sun burned in on my black-clad legs, and my eyes tried to close again of their own volition. I fought sleep for several miles before I finally reached into my backpack for a cereal bar to keep me awake.

As I munched, a thought hit me. "Hey, Carl, which campground are we in?"

"Beaver Flats."

"So we'll be going right by Harchman's."

"Yes."

"We can do some quick recon on the way by, then."

He shot me a cautious look. "Maybe. What did you have in mind?"

"I want to check the network. Having the RV is perfect. You can just pull over by the side of the road where I showed you on the map. I can access the network in cushy comfort. And if we have to leave fast, you can just drive away and let me scream my head off. Nobody will ever know."

He thought it over. "That's a good idea. Tell me where you want to stop."

As we approached Harchman's, I pointed out a spot at the side of the road. "Right there."

Germain pulled over and activated the flashers, and I closed my eyes to concentrate. I started violently at his touch on my arm.

"Maybe you'd better lie on the bed. Just in case."

"Oh. Good idea." I stepped back into the RV and flopped down on the pull-out bed. "Except I might fall asleep."

He grinned. "If you start snoring, I'll throw a pillow at you. I'm not coming within punching range, though."

I grimaced embarrassment. "That might be smart." I closed my eyes and drifted into the network void.

I immediately began my usual routine, rapidly checking each room. At the security room sim, I jerked to a halt.

It was occupied once more, but not by Harchman. This time, his wife Maria sat at the desk of the security console. I drifted silently into the room behind her and floated. Watching over her shoulder, I scanned the security camera feeds. Why would she be monitoring these?

Her fists clenched when Harchman appeared in one of the displays. Apparently he'd discovered another female guest who wanted a house tour. Maria and I observed the action while he guided his latest conquest through the house. She was short, blonde, and cute, and she responded enthusiastically to his groping.

Maria toggled the cameras' views to track his progress. Harchman ushered the blonde into the real security room and, as he had done with me, grabbed her ass and ground against her. She reacted with apparent delight, and they went into a prolonged clinch.

Maria lunged to her feet and left the sim at a run.

Afraid my presence would keep the sim alive and betray me, I shot out of the sim immediately behind her. She dashed through the portal without a backward glance, and I heaved a silent sigh of relief before peeking back into the room.

The sim was still running. Excellent. I seeped back through the wall and hovered, watching the monitors again. I was afraid to interact with the controls, but Maria had left the view of the security room up, and I wanted to see what would happen.

Within seconds, Maria appeared in the doorway of the real security room. Harchman and his blonde gave a guilty start as she apparently yelled at them. Words were exchanged, and then they left. Too bad there was no audio feed. Then again, I had a pretty good idea what she was saying.

Maria glowered down the corridor at their receding backs. Then she turned and sat down at the real security console, again manipulating the cameras. The camera views in the simulation updated along with her changes, so I lost sight of her while she panned through other views.

Apparently she was only spying on her husband, and I quickly lost interest. Germain would wonder what was taking me, and I still had the rest of the network to check.

I slipped out of the sim and worked my way up and down the virtual corridors, peeking in each room in turn. Faint sounds drifted to my ears from up ahead, and my stomach clenched in sick anticipation. I dragged myself toward the room in question and took a moment to gather my composure before I peeked in.

I froze in pure shock at the scene in the room.

Then I clapped my hand over my gaping mouth, not sure if I was going to be able to hold back my shout of inappropriate laughter.

A tubby, balding man sprawled naked on a sumptuously made-up bed, smiling beatifically while a soundtrack of meditative flutes played in the background. His body hair had obviously decided to compensate for the follicular failure on his head. From the neck down, the resemblance to a silverback gorilla was striking, although he'd apparently shaved the backs of his hands. The thick black hair ended in a sharp line at his wrists, like a fur suit.

All of which would have been startling enough without the three beautiful naked women who were actively and enthusiastically engaged in keeping the smile on his face. Their Barbie-doll-like proportions were straight out of a porn animation. The two blondes kissed and fondled the man and each other while the brunette rode him as if she was going for the gold buckle at the rodeo, her ridiculously huge breasts bouncing and jiggling like inflatable Jello.

I backed away, gnawing on my knuckles in an attempt to maintain control. After a few moments, I sobered and peeked in again to memorize the man's face. I didn't bother with his companions. There was no way they existed in real life. They wouldn't even be capable of standing upright.

Down the hallway, I continued reluctantly with my room checks. Porn was better than violence, but I really didn't want to see either one. Particularly if the porn featured fat men in gorilla suits.

All was clean and quiet, and I heaved a silent sigh of relief and stepped out of the portal.

CHAPTER 27

I jerked into a ball, holding my head and groaning through clenched teeth as the pain hit. I breathed deeply and tried to relax through it. After a couple of hissing breaths, I uncurled and massaged my temples as I squinted my eyes open to see Germain's concerned face.

"Are you okay?"

"Yeah, fine." I rolled stiffly off the bed and crept into the passenger seat again. "Grossed out, but fine. There's no sign of any prisoners, but some fat little hairy guy is doing porn, and Maria is using the security sim to spy on Harchman. He has a new blonde toy, so maybe he'll give me a rest for a while."

Germain let that pass without comment as he pulled back onto the highway. A short time later, we arrived at the Beaver Flats turnoff, and we drove up the narrow, twisting campground laneways, looking for the number Kane had provided.

Near the end of the campground, Kane stood up from his seat at the picnic table as we came around a curve. It was a long, narrow site, and it offered a screen of trees on one side. On the other side, visible through low shrubbery, a couple of men lounged beside the neighbouring campfire among an impressive array of empty beer cans.

Germain drove past the entrance, and expertly backed the large RV and cargo trailer into the site.

"Wow, you've done this a time or two before," I congratulated him.

"I have a Class 1 license," he said off-handedly. "This is a pretty small rig by comparison."

"I guess," I agreed. "I'm still impressed, though."

He shot me a grin, and we got out of the RV. The men in the next site fixed us with vacant stares. Kane came over and spoke in a low voice.

"Too bad about the neighbours, but this is the best site I could get today. We'll move on tomorrow. Let's go inside."

Once we were seated inside, Kane blew out an irritable breath. "No word from Webb yet about the electronic device. At least if it's a tracker, they'll think I'm far away. I stopped in to see Hellhound on the way by. He's still set up, no movement so far, but that was a couple of hours ago. You'll need to relieve him soon, Germain."

Germain nodded. "I can head out right now."

"Take Aydan with you," Kane said. "I want to know if there's anything going on in the network."

"Already done," I told him. "We checked it on the way here. No prisoners, and Maria is using the security room sim to spy on her husband." I didn't bother to mention the Barbie-doll-and-gorilla porn. The less said about that, the better.

"The monitoring works really well," I continued. "There must be some kind of two-way link between the sim and the control system, because she could alter the camera views from within the sim."

"That could turn out to be very useful," Kane mused.

"Yeah. And the sim stayed active even after she'd left. So I should be able to pop in any time I want."

"I don't think you should take a chance on manipulating the camera controls from there, though," Kane cautioned.

"That's what I thought, too," I agreed. "If there's a two-way link, that kind of activity would be really easy to spot. I wonder who wins, if there's somebody trying to work the controls both in the sim and in reality."

"Good question. You should talk this over with Webb," Kane said. "In the mean time, though, we really need you to tackle that database again. We've lost nearly the whole day."

"Right," I agreed.

I was sliding out of the bench to collect the laptop when Germain reached out a restraining hand. "First, you have to eat. We don't want to have to pick you up off the ground again."

I ignored the involuntary growl of my stomach. "I'll look at the database for a while and then get supper."

"No," Kane said firmly. "Eat first."

I gave in. "Okay. I'll get the fire going."

Kane frowned. "What for?"

"We've got a firepit, and we've got steaks."

Kane's face lit up, and Germain's fell.

"Damn," Germain said with feeling. "I wish I didn't have to leave right away." He sighed and pulled a can of beans out of the cupboard.

"I'll cook yours anyway, and you can just heat it up when you get back," I comforted him. "How do you like it cooked?"

"Medium-rare," he said, brightening. "I'll look forward to that." He stuck his bowl into the microwave, and I went out to light the fire.

Kane followed me out. "Do you have enough wood?"

"Probably," I told him, surveying the small stack. "But I hope you have an axe."

He reached into one of the external cargo holds and handed me one.

"Thanks." I split some kindling and stacked it into the firepit. "Matches?"

"In the RV," he said. "If you're going to be occupied here for a while, I'm going to go in and have a shower. Hopefully without incident this time."

"Go ahead. I'm going to do some potatoes, too, so it'll be about forty-five minutes before supper's ready."

"You don't have to cook for us," he said seriously.

I shrugged. "I don't mind. I'm going to cook for myself anyway. It's no trouble to throw on a bit more food while I'm at it."

"All right, if you're sure you don't mind." He turned, and I followed him into the RV. He and Germain hashed out the details of the night's watches while I collected matches and cooking utensils.

I had the fire going by the time Germain emerged. He unloaded his bike from the cargo trailer and waved as he rode away.

I laid the foil-wrapped potatoes on the grill and sat back to watch them. Unfortunately, the firepit was on the same side as the neighbours. I needed to turn the potatoes every few minutes, so I kept my back to the men and ignored their drunken scrutiny as best I could.

About ten minutes later, I was turning the potatoes over again when the shorter man hailed me from across the clearing. "Hey! Wanna come over and have a beer?"

"No, thanks," I replied, trying to sound pleasant but

dismissive.

"Stuck-up bitch."

I didn't bother to respond to that. Instead, I went into the RV to get the steaks. I took my time going back out, but the potatoes needed to be turned again.

I carried the steaks out with me and tended to the potatoes, then opened the packages of steak and laid them out on a plate.

"Hey!"

I ignored him.

"Hey! How do you like this meat?"

I made the mistake of glancing up. He was exposing himself.

I snickered before I could stop myself and looked away quickly, hoping he hadn't seen my smirk. I've never understood why guys do that. It just seems like begging for ridicule.

"Hey! What're you laughing at?"

Now there was an opening line, if I'd ever heard one. I bit my tongue furiously to avoid making the obvious insulting rejoinder. I kept my eyes on the potatoes and tried not to snicker again.

I heard footsteps crashing through the undergrowth toward me. Shit. This is why I hate public campgrounds.

Without looking up, I stepped casually closer to the RV and the axe. These two likely didn't pose much of a threat, particularly since Kane was probably just about finished his shower by now. He'd make short work of them. But I hoped a bit of assertiveness would convince them to give it up without a confrontation.

I looked up and met their eyes as the two men approached. "I didn't ask you to join me. Go back to your own campsite."

"Come on, George," the taller man said. "Let's go have another beer."

George eyed me blearily. His dick was still hanging out of his pants, apparently forgotten. Nice.

"I wan' you to come an' have a beer with me," he repeated.

"No. I'm busy cooking. Go away." I reached over and turned the potatoes again.

His friend took him by the arm. "Come on, George, buddy, let's go," he said, trying to steer the smaller man back the way they'd come.

George jerked his arm free and took an aggressive step toward me. "I gotta teach this cunt some manners," he slurred. "Hey, cunt, suck this." He waved his flaccid penis at me.

My temper flared instantly. I don't like being threatened. And being called a cunt just spoils my day.

"The only way I could suck something that small would be if I had a pair of tweezers and a magnifying glass," I snarled. I picked up the axe and swung the handle into my palm with a smack as I took a step toward him. "Now fuck off. Or lose what little you've got."

At the edge of my hearing, I'd registered the rumble of an approaching engine, but I'd been too focused on my unwelcome visitors to pay attention. At that moment, Hellhound rode into the campsite on his Harley.

He took in the scene and came off his bike fast as the two men half-turned toward the source of the noise. George's buddy blanched.

I'd always assumed Hellhound's nickname was just wordplay on his last name. I'd grown accustomed to his gentleness toward me, and the more or less constant twinkle of humour in his eyes. I'd forgotten exactly how scary he'd looked the first time I'd met him.

I was suddenly reminded. He was a fearsome sight, striding toward us in his leathers. His ugly, scowling face was hard as granite as he shoved his solid bulk between the two men and me. George blinked owlishly, and a fine sheen of sweat appeared on the other man's face as he backed away slowly.

"What the fuck?" Hellhound ground out, glowering dangerously at the two men.

"We were just leaving," the second man stammered. "My buddy was just joking around, weren't you, George?" George staggered uncertainly, obviously trying to decide whether to back down or keep being a moron.

Hellhound took a step toward them, his shoulders swelling. "My ol' lady ain't laughin'."

George's fists clenched, and I could see he was about to do something truly stupid. If this came to a fight, I was certain Hellhound would win. And he'd likely end up getting arrested and convicted for assault as a result. I doubted the courts would be kind to a large, ugly biker who'd beaten the crap out of some little drunk idiot. No matter how richly the little drunk idiot deserved it.

I stepped quickly to Hellhound's side and clung to his arm. "Baby, don't forget what your parole officer said. If you kill two more guys, they'll declare you a dangerous offender. I don't want you to go to jail again."

The taller man's face contorted with fear. He grabbed George by the arm and began to drag him bodily away. George mouthed off a bit more, and Hellhound took another step closer, apparently oblivious to my grip.

He fixed the two men in a basilisk glare. "Ya were just leavin', weren't ya. Leavin' the entire fuckin' campground. For good. Weren't ya."

The taller man nodded vigorously, his prominent Adam's apple bobbing as he gulped. "Yeah, we've gotta go. We're going right now." He finally managed to dislodge George and haul him back to their campsite. They packed their gear under Hellhound's deadly gaze and gravel sprayed from their tires as they sped away. I pulled out my phone and dialled.

"Who ya callin'?" Hellhound asked, still watching the receding half-ton.

"Drunk driving hotline. Those two shouldn't be on the road." I gave the license number and vehicle description to the officer on the other end of the line, and then hung up. "I hope they catch them before they hurt anybody." I shuddered at the bad memories.

Hellhound's face softened and he smoothed the hair away from my face with a gentle hand. "Ya okay, darlin'?"

I looked up into his kind eyes. "I'm fine. You scared me, though. I was afraid you were going to kick the shit out of them and end up in jail."

"Nah." He chuckled. "I liked that bit about my parole officer, though."

Kane came out of the RV, freshly shaven and smelling of shampoo. "What's this about a parole officer?"

I leaned the axe up against the trailer again and turned back to tend the potatoes. "We had a small altercation with our neighbours. They decided to leave when they discovered that Hellhound's parole officer warned him not to kill anybody else." I laid the steaks on the grill. "How do you like your steak?"

"Medium-rare," Kane said slowly. He frowned at the

axe, and then at Hellhound and me. "What kind of an altercation?"

"Arnie, what about you?" I asked.

"Medium-rare for me, too."

"You guys are easy to cook for." I turned back to the fire.

"Helmand!" Kane rapped out. "What happened!"

Hellhound straightened to attention. "Just words, Cap. I rode in an' I see these two shitheads got Aydan backed up against the trailer. One's got his dick out, an' she's gettin' ready to swing the axe. So I told 'em to move on."

"He didn't even say anything threatening," I added. "It was all legal."

"All legal," Kane repeated incredulously. "Except for the part where two men sexually assaulted you. Are you all right?"

"I'm fine. And it wasn't sexual assault. It was just words. He was just drunk and stupid, and it was probably partly my fault..."

"It ain't your fault," Hellhound grated. I glanced up at him and took a shocked step back at the look on his face. "If a man can't keep himself under control, that's his fault, not yours," he growled. "Ya didn't do anythin' wrong."

"No, I didn't mean that," I agreed quickly. "What I meant was, I aggravated the situation because I lost my temper and insulted him." I turned away to flip the steaks and potatoes.

"Aydan, tell me exactly what happened."

Unlike Hellhound, I hadn't spent twenty or so years in the army, but the commanding tone of Kane's voice was almost enough to make me snap to attention, too.

"I was over here cooking and he called over and asked me to join him for a beer. I said no thanks, and he called me a stuck-up bitch. I ignored him, but he kept yelling over, and the next time I looked up, he was waving his dick. I made my first mistake then, because I laughed."

"You laughed."

"Well, yeah. He was just this stupid little drunk shit. And it was such a dumb thing to do. I mean, really, what did he think I was going to do?"

"He thought he'd intimidate you," Kane said grimly.

I snorted. "Not. Anyway, he got mad because I'd laughed, and that's when he came over."

"Why didn't you call me?" Kane admonished.

"I would have, if I thought there was any real danger," I assured him. "But his buddy was trying to get him to back off, and he was so wasted I could have knocked him down with a good slap."

"Go on," Kane said expressionlessly.

"Well, that's when things got a little out of hand," I admitted reluctantly. "He said some things, and I got mad."

"What things, exactly?"

"He called me a cunt. Said he was going to teach me a lesson. And told me to suck his cock." I looked up at their frowns. "Just for the record, if you ever want to really piss me off, now you know what to say."

"So you got mad. Then what?"

"I made a crack about his tiny dick and told him to fuck off." I studied the ground intently. "And I kind of threatened him with the axe, a little bit," I mumbled. "That's when Arnie showed up."

Kane sighed. I chanced a glance up at him as he massaged his forehead. "Sorry," I added. "I wouldn't have really hit him with the axe. Well, maybe with the blunt end..." I shut up before I could dig myself in any deeper.

"You should report this," Kane said.

"Under the circumstances, I'm inclined to just let it go. I threatened him with a weapon. Arnie as much as forced them to drive drunk. And I called them in to the impaired driver hotline. And if I have to go in and report the whole thing, we'll lose even more time that I could be using to look through the database."

Kane's fist clenched as he thought it over. "All right," he agreed finally. "I hate to say it, but you're right, we have bigger fish to fry."

"And steaks." I snagged the sizzling steaks and potatoes off the grill. "Let's eat."

CHAPTER 28

After we cleared away the dishes, I glanced at Hellhound's exhausted face. "I'll take the laptop outside so you can sleep."

I set up the laptop on the picnic table and settled in with a sigh, concentrating my efforts on the captive I'd seen in the morning. Spider's database was far superior to anything I'd used before, and I quickly finished entering all the parameters, feeling optimistic.

My high hopes were gratified only about ten minutes later when the database disgorged a shortlist of seven men. I sprang up and trotted to the RV carrying the laptop. When I stuck my head in the door, Kane and Hellhound looked up from the site plan they were discussing, and Kane broke into a smile at the sight of my face.

"You found something," he prompted.

"Yes, the man I saw this morning in the sim. His name is Richard Willis. He was easy to find because he has the funny little scar up by his hairline." I passed Kane the laptop.

"Excellent." He pulled out his phone and punched a speed dial button. "Listen, Webb, Aydan got a hit from the database. We'll send it to you via the uplink. Can you run it? All known associates, the usual. Thanks." He carried the laptop over to the counter and hooked it up, punched a few keys, and waited. A few seconds later, he disconnected it and handed it back.

"Good work," he said. "Now if we can find the others, we'll be making some progress."

Feeling slightly deflated, I returned to my seat at the picnic table and started scrolling data again. A few minutes later, I was so engrossed that the slam of the RV door made me jump.

Kane ambled over and sat backward on the bench beside me, stretching his legs out and leaning his elbows on the table behind him.

"How's it going?" he asked.

"Fine. Slow."

He paused and frowned before speaking as if carefully choosing his words. "Aydan, about what happened here tonight. I know you're used to taking care of yourself, and everything worked out all right this time. But as long as you're on this mission, I need you to be more careful."

He met my eyes seriously. "You should have called me right away. You're a key component of this operation. If anything happens to you, we're dead in the water."

I made a face. "He was just a stupid little drunk flasher."

"And if that stupid little drunk had pulled a weapon, then what? Last night, you got on my case for taking unnecessary risks. Now it's my turn to tell you the same thing."

I scowled at the laptop. "Okay. Fine. I'll try to be as helpless as possible."

"You know that's not what I meant."

I sighed. "I know. Sorry. I'm just tired. And I get edgy when I miss my workouts."

"It's all right. Thanks for putting your life on hold for this." He rose. "I want to take the first watch tonight, so I'm going to go and get a nap, too. Sit in the chair next to the RV. And thump on the trailer if even a squirrel gives you attitude."

"Roger that." I obediently carried the laptop over to the chair beside the trailer as he went inside, and returned to the tedious task of looking through the database manually.

A couple of hours later, my numbed brain belatedly reacted. I stopped my search and flipped back a couple of records to the one that had caught my eye. I was looking at one of the dead torturers.

I had my fist raised to knock on the RV and wake Kane when I thought better of it. No need to jerk both Kane and Hellhound out of a sound sleep just to tell them I'd identified a dead man. He wasn't going to get any deader.

I made a note of the name, and then, on impulse, ran a cross-reference check for any known associates. Sure enough, the second torturer's face appeared in one of the records.

Elated, I wrote down his name, too, and turned back to the database with renewed zeal. Maybe I could find the first man, too. Only one to go.

By the time I heard movement inside the RV, my enthusiasm had waned. Kane stuck his head out the door as I yawned and rubbed my eyes.

"How's it going?" he inquired sympathetically.

"Great! I got two more hits," I told him.

"Why didn't you wake me?" He swung out of the RV and frowned down at me.

"They're not the captives. They're the two guys you killed," I told him. "I didn't think it was worth waking you up for two dead guys."

"Next time, wake me," he said firmly.

"Okay. Sorry."

"It's all right. Let's get these up to Webb and see what he can find."

"Poor Spider," I said. "Is he getting any sleep at all?"

Kane shrugged. "Probably about the same as us. Speaking of." He looked down at me. "I'd like you to go over with Hellhound and check the network, and then come back with Germain, same as before. And then it's time you got some rest, too."

"Okay." I followed him into the trailer and grabbed a glass of water while he spoke with Spider on the phone.

He was grinning when he hung up. "Webb cracked that electronic device that was planted on me."

Arnie and I both leaned forward in anticipation. "What was it?"

Kane's laugh lines crinkled. "I absconded with a state-of-the-art re-engineered fob. That's why I didn't notice the transition. I wondered how they'd done it. So it wasn't a tracking device at all."

Arnie's shrewd eyes darted between Kane and me. "I'm missin' somethin'."

"Sorry, need-to-know," Kane told him.

Hellhound shrugged. "As long as it wasn't trackin' ya, that's good news."

"That little piece of technology ought to make Spider very happy," I observed.

"Yes, indeed," Kane agreed cheerfully. "And it makes me very happy, too. We can move back to our original base camp tomorrow."

Hellhound's face fell. "Shit. No more steaks." He

turned to me. "That was the best meal I've had in a helluva long time. Thanks, darlin'."

"Yes, thank you," Kane echoed.

"You're welcome." I got up. "I guess I'll get ready to go."

I slipped into the bathroom to don my leather pants with a little more modesty than the morning. By the time I emerged from the RV, Kane and Hellhound had rolled the Honda out of the cargo trailer, and Arnie and I mounted up.

We rode back to our usual spot beside Harchman's. In the long beams of the setting sun, we pulled off the road again. Hellhound cast a wary gaze around us.

"I don't like bein' in the same place over an' over," he growled. "We been here too often. We stick out like turds on a sidewalk."

I snickered. "Speak for yourself. But I hear you. I need to look at that site plan again and see if there's another place we can try."

"Well, might as well get at it," he grumbled. He lay down in the warm grass, and I took my place beside him.

"Sure like those tight leather pants on ya, darlin'," he murmured, his rough-edged voice teasing my eardrum.

"Sure like those chaps on you." I ran my hand up his leather-clad thigh and dragged my fingernails lightly across the denim at the top.

He let out a growl as he rolled over on top of me and pinned me to the ground. We were both breathless by the time he broke the kiss.

"Have we got time for a little walk in the woods?" I panted. I ran my hands down his back to grope his ass and pressed myself up against the hard ridge I could feel through his jeans.

He groaned. "Darlin', ya ain't makin' this easy. I gotta

go relieve Germain." He kissed me again, moving slowly against me in spite of his words. Hot hunger flared through me.

"Just a quickie," I breathed against his lips. "Come on. I'll find a nice fallen tree to bend over."

"Jesus, darlin', have mercy," he rasped. We both started as an eighteen-wheeler thundered by and laid on the air horn. "I think we're attractin' a little too much attention," he said wryly as he rolled off me and sat up.

I sighed. "Shit. Nothing like a clandestine operation. All right. Here goes." I closed my eyes and drifted invisibly into the network.

I fell into my usual routine, my heart beating rapidly. My stress level ratcheted up as I peered into each room, riding a roller-coaster of emotions. First afraid to look, then limp with relief at the sight of an empty room.

When my ear caught faint noises emanating from up ahead, I tried to smother my burst of adrenaline while I listened. Some of the tension leaked out of my shoulders when I identified a male rumble embellished with the grace notes of female giggles. The flute soundtrack provided a melodic backdrop. Thank God. Some porn would be a relief. Anything but more torture.

I peeked in but quickly drew away, embarrassed. It was definitely sex, but it wasn't porn. A middle-aged man and woman occupied the bed, laughing and kissing, their love for each other glowing in their smiles. Their tenderness opened a hollow ache in my chest, and I turned away hurriedly to continue down the corridor.

I drifted through the firewall and began on the next set of rooms. When I discovered the handsome naked man, I froze, staring. I wasn't quite sure what I was seeing. Well, scratch that, I knew what I was seeing, and it was definitely worth looking at. But...

His longish blond hair was in an artful disarray that would take an hour with the hairdresser to achieve. Steady bright-blue eyes watched the door intently. Anticipation or dread? I couldn't tell.

He was tied to the bed, wrists and ankles secured with heavy leather straps. I could read the tension in his smoothly-muscled body, and a faint sheen of sweat glistened on his chiselled chest and abs. A little too young for me, maybe late twenties or early thirties, but what a picture.

I dropped my eyes, feeling like a cheap voyeur but unsure whether I was seeing a bondage fantasy or a prisoner restrained against his will. When he called out, I started guiltily.

"Come on, honey." His words were light, but his voice was edged. "Don't keep me waiting like this."

I took another quick look, still wondering. He was smiling, his gaze never leaving the door, and I backed away, trying to shake off my discomfort.

I waited as long as I dared, but no one came down the corridor. Urgency hammered at me until I finally gave in and shot back to the portal, nerves twitching.

This time, I made an attempt to control my reaction when I stepped through, and I managed some quiet, sibilant obscenities while the air hissed through my clenched teeth. I opened my eyes against Hellhound's chest as he held me. I straightened up, massaging my temples.

Hellhound caressed the hair away from my forehead, frowning. "Why does this hurt ya so much? Why can't they fix that thing in your watch so ya don't hafta go through this every time?"

"They can fix the pain issue, but then I'd be a sitting duck," I told him. "As long as it's hurting me, the bad guys don't know I'm doing this."

"Well, that fuckin' sucks."

"Tell me about it." I dragged myself to my feet and shuffled over to the Honda. The more stressed and tired I got, the more the pain seemed to take over my entire body when I came out of the network. Everything ached, and I rolled my head and shoulders without much effect. I sat heavily on the bike. "Ready to roll," I mumbled.

Arnie searched my face. "Ya sure you're okay, darlin'?"

"Yeah, I'm fine. Just tired. Headache. This really takes it out of me."

"Okay. Don't forget this." He handed me my helmet and kissed me lightly. "Stay alert. Ya don't wanna get careless when you're ridin'."

"Thanks." I smiled up at him. "I'll be okay."

By the time he and Germain switched places and we arrived back at the campsite, I was fighting to stay focused.

I slumped at the table across from Kane and rubbed my still-aching head. "Just more porn tonight. I think."

He frowned. "What exactly does that mean?"

I eyed him dully, trying to force my brain to function. "Oh, right, I didn't tell you earlier. I'm beginning to wonder about Harchman's so-called wellness spa."

"In what way?"

"Earlier, there was some guy having a porn fantasy with three Barbie-doll clones. Tonight there was..." I hesitated. It just seemed wrong to say something crude about that couple. "...There were a few more people using the network for recreational purposes. But one bothered me. The way he was tied, I don't know whether he was a prisoner or not."

Germain raised an eyebrow. "If he was tied, I'd say definitely a prisoner, wouldn't you?"

I felt a flush climbing my cheeks. "Not... necessarily."

"Oh." Germain became suddenly absorbed in rummaging through the cupboard.

Kane sighed. "You look beat. Get some sleep, and then hit the database again. The more we can find out about who's in the network, the sooner we can satisfy Stemp and end this."

I told Germain his steak was in the fridge and staggered into the back bedroom. I didn't even hear the sound of the microwave.

I jerked awake, eyes wide. The faint illumination from the moon outlined a large, dark figure in the doorway of the bedroom.

"Aydan." Kane spoke softly again, and I resumed breathing with a gasp of relief.

"What?"

"Sorry to wake you. Germain's going out to relieve Hellhound. Do you feel up to going with him to check the network again?"

I rolled stiffly off the bed. At least I wouldn't have to get dressed. I hadn't even taken off my boots before I fell asleep.

"Okay. I just need to pee, and then I'm ready to go."

I stumbled into the bathroom without turning on the light. When I came out of the RV, the cool night air woke me like a slap. I shivered over to the Honda, and Germain and I rode quietly out of the campground.

CHAPTER 29

Back at Harchman's, we pulled over beside the road and crossed the ditch to fade into the shadows of the trees. The rush of cold air on the ride over had chilled me to the bone. I left my helmet on for warmth and shivered miserably as I sank down and propped my back against a fence post.

Inside the network, I found the security room sim active. A man sat at the virtual security console, and I studied his face, memorizing him before continuing down the virtual hallway to recheck the rooms.

The flutes still played in the room occupied by the couple. Unwilling to invade their privacy a second time, I pressed my ear to the virtual door instead, and was rewarded with the sound of the man chuckling, followed by whispers and giggles. I let the sound ease my strained nerves, and floated away to finish my reconnaissance.

I held my breath when I peeked into the room that held the blond man. Air leaked out between my teeth when I discovered him uninjured but still bound. His face was turned toward the door, his eyes closed. His chest rose and fell with his unhurried breathing, but still I sensed the tension in his body. Waiting. Not asleep.

I watched his splendid nakedness a few seconds longer,

fear for him warring with faintly queasy arousal. Then I turned away and floated uneasily back down the corridor.

Back at the security sim, I drifted silently inside and hovered behind the operator to see the monitors. He flipped briskly through views of the deserted interior of the house and exterior views of the main house, guest house, and outbuildings. I noted a sentry still posted at the door of the guest house.

Then the displays shifted to show another view I hadn't seen before. We examined the gatehouse briefly as the single guard slouched in his chair. While we watched, he sat up, stretched, and luxuriously picked his nose. I invisibly mirrored the watcher's grimace as he toggled the display to another unfamiliar view.

I tried to puzzle out what I was seeing. As the views flipped by, I realized extra cameras had been added to the system. We were now looking at a much larger perimeter, mostly in the forested area surrounding the building site. In one view, the patrol guard and his dog walked past directly below the camera.

I suppressed a gasp when the next view came up. I thought I recognized that clearing. Thank God, Hellhound was using the other one for surveillance tonight. Fear slammed into my veins. What if they'd discovered both surveillance points? Had they captured Hellhound?

When the next view appeared, my heart kicked my ribs once before rattling frantically in the vicinity of my throat.

The monitor showed two shadowy figures leaning against fence posts by the highway.

Smothering my yelp of dismay, I shot through the wall and halted abruptly in front of the portal. If I went through too fast now, all would be lost.

I stepped carefully through, jerking in silent pain. As soon as I could speak, I croaked, "Run! Busted! We're busted!"

Germain grabbed my arm and heaved me to my feet. I clutched my head with my free hand and tried to squint one eye open while he dragged me to our motorcycles. I managed to sling a leg over the bike before slumping on the seat, trying to force my eyes to focus. Germain stood alongside to balance me and I gritted, "Gotta get Hellhound," through clenched teeth.

"I'll get him," he promised.

A few too-long seconds later, I finally regained enough vision and equilibrium to sit up straight, and Germain dashed for his bike while I fired up the Honda and pulled a hard U-turn. I rolled on the power with a trembling hand, and a few seconds later the throaty whine of the Yamaha rushed up behind me. Germain pulled abreast and gestured decisively to me, then forward. I nodded.

He'd get Hellhound. I'd run for the campground. He cut the throttle and peeled off into the ditch while I rode on as fast as I dared in the dark, adrenaline surging.

Glancing fearfully behind me, I spied no sign of pursuit. When I arrived at Beaver Flats, I idled quietly through the sleeping campground, clamping down on the urge to ride the twisting path at top speed. Kane stood up from the chair beside the RV as I pulled up. He strode quickly over as I cut the engine.

"Where's Hellhound?" he demanded. "You weren't supposed to travel without an escort."

"We got busted," I told him tremulously. "They've got a camera on the highway." His head jerked up, scanning the quiet campground.

"I don't think I was followed," I added. I tried to make my voice steady, but it quavered with my uncontrollable shivering. "I don't know if Arnie got out. Germain went to get him. They should be behind me. I hope."

"Goddammit!" Kane swore softly but with great feeling.

"What do we do now?"

"We wait." I could see the tension in his shadowy figure.

"How long?" I demanded.

"Twenty minutes. If they're not back by then, we move. Keeping you and that key safe is still our top priority." He held up a hand as I opened my mouth to argue. "They'll make it," he said firmly. "Tell me what happened."

"I went into the network from our spot by the side of the road. There was a man in the security sim, watching. They've expanded the perimeter of the security system. They've got cameras at the gatehouse, on our spot on the road, distributed through the trees, and I'm pretty sure there's one on the first surveillance point you were using. I don't know if they've gone as far as the second one or not. As soon as I saw us come up on monitor, I beat it out of the network and we ran."

Kane blew out a breath. "Lucky the security sim was up, or we'd never have known. They could have picked you off at their leisure."

"They might have gotten Hellhound and Germain anyway," I said tightly. I wrapped my arms around my body as the shivering stepped up a notch.

A faint sound caught my ear and I flung my head up. The sound swelled into a distant rumble, and I muttered, "Oh, please, oh, please," under my breath. Kane and I stood motionless as the engine noise grew louder and then softened as if its rider was idling at low speed. A few seconds later, two headlights appeared, and Kane and I both let out an audible breath.

Germain and Hellhound cut their engines and swung off their bikes. I resisted the urge to run over and hug both of them. They walked over, and I hugged them both anyway.

"Any pursuit?" Kane demanded, and Germain shook his head.

"No sign."

"Good. Let's move the bikes out of sight behind the RV," Kane said, his voice deep with relief. "I don't want them in plain view, but we need to be mobile just in case."

We relocated the motorcycles and trooped into the RV. I looked around at the strained, tired faces.

"Food," I said decisively, and they laughed as I started to scrounge in the cupboards.

A few minutes later, we all crammed onto the dinette benches with our meals. I appreciated the tight fit while I basked in Kane's body heat beside me, my shivering gradually dissipating.

"Now what?" I asked as we finished eating.

"Damage control," Kane said decisively. "Arnie, things are getting too hot around here for civilians. It's time for you to pull out. You can head back to Calgary tomorrow morning."

Hellhound straightened in indignation. "What the hell? What about Aydan? She's a civilian, too."

Kane sighed. "Yes, but she's the only one who can do what we need done. Believe me, if I had any choice at all, she'd be far, far away from here."

"Well, I ain't goin' back and leavin' ya short-handed out here. Ya got somebody to take my place?"

"No." Kane scrubbed his hands tiredly over his face.

"But it's too dangerous to send you in blind, and I can't tell you what you need to know."

"Wouldn't be the first time I went into danger blind, Cap," Arnie said quietly.

Kane's face looked old as he met Arnie's gaze. "I know."

I suppressed a shudder at the ghosts behind their eyes. I knew they'd both seen combat in Yugoslavia. I'd done a bit of reading about the Medak Pocket firefight.

Germain broke the short silence. "We could still use him at base camp. It'd be a little safer than active surveillance."

"I can do that," Hellhound said immediately.

Kane hesitated. I knew he'd want to keep his old friend as far from danger as possible, but it was clear he needed the manpower.

"We'll see what happens in the morning," he said finally. "Our surveillance plans may be completely out the window if they've expanded their perimeter. We don't even know if Aydan can get close enough now. Dammit."

He turned to me. "Did you get a chance to check anything else?"

His eyes flicked almost imperceptibly in Arnie's direction, and I responded carefully. "Yes, I checked. Nothing new tonight."

"Did you get any idea of where the cameras were placed?"

"Where's the site plan?" I asked.

Germain dragged it out and spread it over the table again. We all hunched over it.

"It was pretty hard to identify trees in the dark," I said slowly. "But I was surprised at what I could see. They must have had the apertures cranked wide open. Or maybe it was night vision. What would that look like?"

Hellhound shrugged and handed me the binoculars. "See for yourself."

I poked my head out the door of the RV and peered through the lenses. "Yup, that's definitely what they're using."

"Crap," Germain said. "I was hoping we could still go back and scope things out while it was dark."

I shook my head. "We were wearing black clothes in the dark, and we showed up no problem on the monitor."

Kane's head snapped up. "Were you identifiable?"

"Um..." I thought back, trying to remember the quick glimpse I'd had before I fled. "No. We were both wearing our helmets."

"What about the bikes?" Kane demanded. "Would they have gotten license numbers?"

"I didn't see the bikes in the view."

"Small mercies."

"Yeah." I bent over the plans. "Okay. There's definitely a camera here." I pinpointed the location that had shown the gatehouse. "And here." I added a dot for the view of our stopping place beside the highway.

I jerked up as a thought hit me. "Shit! I bet they saw Hellhound and me earlier. It was daylight, and we had our helmets off then."

Kane hissed forcefully through his teeth. "Dammit! Where exactly did you stop? Is there any chance they could have missed seeing you?"

"We stopped right beside the road," I said slowly. "The camera angle might not have caught us. We parked the bikes in about the same place, and we just went down the side of the ditch a few feet. We weren't over by the fence line where Carl and I were tonight."

Luckily. I suppressed a shudder when I thought about how I'd tried to convince Arnie to take that walk in the woods. That would have been bad. I glanced at Arnie and read the same thought on his face. Dumb civilians. Real spies would never have gotten distracted like that.

"No point in worrying about it," Kane said grimly. "Too late now."

I dragged my attention back to the map. "There's probably another camera here." I marked the first surveillance clearing. "I'm not positive it was the same clearing, but there was that funny-looking twisted tree on the one side, so I think it was."

"What funny-looking twisted tree?" Germain demanded.

I shook my head and grinned at him. "City boy."

"All right, country girl. Tell us where the rest of the cameras are," he challenged.

I grimaced. "I'm not that good. There were at least four other cameras out in the woods. Maybe more. I ran as soon as I saw us come up on the monitors. No funny-looking trees in any of the views. But at least one of them is on the guards' route. I saw a guard and dog walking underneath."

Kane traced an arc on the drawing, connecting the dots I'd drawn. "Okay, let's suppose for the sake of argument that they've created a roughly circular perimeter."

He lightly marked in the completion of the circle. We stared glumly at the result. The building site nestled in one quadrant of the circle. If the cameras followed the line Kane had drawn, we wouldn't be able to get close enough to come within range of the network.

"Damn."

"I second the motion," I agreed. Then I paused and leaned forward, looking at the map again. "Hold on."

"What?" Kane snapped.

"I don't know much about security camera systems. If you were going to install them, would you generally create a perimeter that you'd monitor thoroughly, and then not bother with much inside the perimeter?"

"Generally, yes," Kane agreed.

"I wonder what the creek looks like when it comes through here." I traced the line of the creek on the site map where it intersected Kane's rough circle. "Because this is high land. Remember how the valley dropped off when we came around the corner of the driveway on Saturday?"

"Right," Kane said slowly. "So it might be in a deep cut."

"That's what I'm thinking. I wonder if they've got a camera trained on the cut. Is there any way to detect the cameras?"

"Not without physical surveillance," Germain said.

"Shit." I leaned over the map again and traced a second circle around the building site, intersecting our old surveillance spot by the road and the dot that I'd marked the previous day where I'd accessed the network the first time.

"What's that?" Hellhound asked.

"My usable range. Roughly. I need to be in this vicinity in order to... do what I need to do." I marked the tiny sliver where the arc intersected the creek. "I might be able to get access from here."

"But it's inside the camera perimeter. Theoretically," Germain objected. "If they did actually create a circular perimeter."

I sighed. "Yeah."

CHAPTER 30

I woke the next morning to the quiet rumble of voices from the main part of the RV. The bedroom was bright, and I rolled rapidly out of bed when I realized it was nine A.M. I threw on jeans and a T-shirt and emerged blinking into the sunny dining area.

Germain, Hellhound, and Terry Wheeler sat at the table, drinking coffee and conversing in low tones. Wheeler wore the navy-blue security uniform of Harchman's guards, and his blond good looks reminded me uncomfortably of the man in the sim.

Germain glanced up as I entered. "Good morning, Sleeping Beauty," he kidded me.

"God, I can't remember the last time I slept until nine o'clock," I groaned. "I feel like shit. I don't know how you guys deal with the irregular hours. Hi, Terry, nice to see you again," I added, stifling a yawn.

"Hi, Aydan, good to see you, too. The hours take some getting used to," Wheeler agreed sympathetically.

I glanced around. "Where's Kane?"

Germain and Hellhound exchanged a look.

"What?" I demanded.

"He's scouting the new camera perimeter over at

Harchman's," Germain said reluctantly, while Hellhound glowered. Germain held up a restraining hand at the sight of my expression. "I tried to convince him to let me do it, but he said he wanted to have at least one team member Harchman couldn't identify, just in case. And yes, that's a good strategy," he added, forestalling my protest.

"How long has he been gone?"

"Only an hour. He's already checked in once. His next check-in will be at 9:30."

I swallowed my fear and made my voice level. "Okay. I'm going to take a shower, if nobody needs the bathroom for a while."

"Go ahead."

I shut myself into the tiny room and awkwardly washed my hair in the inadequate shower. By the time I came out, Kane was sitting at the table holding a steaming mug. Everyone looked much happier. The tension released from my shoulders, too, and I beamed at them in relief.

"Good news," Kane greeted me. "It looks like there's a gap in their perimeter right at the creek, as you'd guessed."

"Excellent," I agreed. "Now the question is whether it gives me a usable access point or not."

He nodded. "That's our next step. Wheeler, what can you tell us about the security detail?"

Wheeler frowned. "I'm not getting as much information as I'd hoped. I haven't overheard anything unusual between the men who are staffed through the security company. I think they're all just ordinary rent-a-cops. There's another group of security personnel that spends most of their time around the building site. They're not staffed through the security company, so they must be on directly on Harchman's payroll. I've tried to gather some information there, but no luck yet. They don't mingle."

"Have you seen a young, blue-eyed blond man anywhere?" I interrupted. "I'm not sure if he's a prisoner or not."

"I'd need more information," Wheeler responded. "There are a few men who fit that description."

Kane pushed the laptop across the table. "You know where to start."

I sighed and carried it over to the counter to begin entering parameters, dividing my attention between the database and the continuing briefing.

"Did the analysts get anything from the bugs yet?" Wheeler asked.

"No, nothing yet," Kane replied. "Can you drop a few more?"

"I'll try," Wheeler said. "I get turned back by Harchman's guards if I try to approach the house, but my contact in housekeeping might be able to sneak me in. Which reminds me, she gave me some more information about Harchman's wellness spa."

"Yes, Webb dug into that, too," Kane said. "Apparently it's remarkably profitable. He's reporting almost a million in revenue after only the second quarter. It's definitely suspicious. There isn't that kind of money in the spa business."

Wheeler grinned. "There is in this one."

Kane leaned forward, his eyes lighting with predatory fire. "It's not a spa, is it? Give."

"Oh, it's a spa all right." Wheeler's grin broadened. "No advertising, very exclusive, strictly word-of-mouth. You have to know somebody to get in, and Harchman charges astronomical fees."

"For what?" I demanded. "A stay in the guest house and some nice food? So what? Who'd pay big bucks for that?"

"A man who's having his erectile dysfunction cured." Wheeler grinned at our dumbfounded faces. "Harchman is promoting a new hypnosis cure. One hundred percent guaranteed. His clients will pretty much pay whatever he asks. Clients can bring their wives or girlfriends if they want, but the rumour is that he offers extremely skilled, uh... therapists."

I sank back against the counter, my jaw dropping. "Holy shit. That slimy bastard. What a brilliant scheme. All completely untraceable, and nobody's going to blab. That explains -"

Speaking of blabbing. I caught Kane's tiny headshake and closed my mouth before I blurted anything out in front of Hellhound. Hellhound's keen gaze darted between our faces, his brow furrowed. I knew that look. Give him the tiniest clue, and he'd figure the whole thing out in no time.

"Nice cover," Kane agreed grudgingly. "Hides his true activities, and makes a bundle at the same time. But you haven't heard rumours of any other kind of activity? Say, dead bodies being removed in the dark of night?"

Wheeler sobered. "No. Nothing."

"All right," Kane said. "Aydan, when can you be ready to go?"

I considered for a moment. "I can be physically ready to go out the door in about ten minutes. I just need some breakfast. But if there's no particular rush, I'd like to talk to Spider first and get his take on some of the n..." I remembered Hellhound's presence in the nick of time and bit off what I'd been going to say.

"That's a good idea," Kane said. "Go ahead and eat, and

then call Webb."

I started assembling my breakfast, and Germain and Hellhound propped themselves against the counter to finish their coffee. I gratefully slid into the vacated dinette bench and chowed down on my toast and peanut butter.

"What is it with you and peanut butter?" Germain teased me.

I shrugged and grinned at him. "It satisfies three of the four basic food groups: sugar, salt, fat, and booze. Add a beer, and you're looking at a nutritionally complete meal."

The ring of the phone interrupted the general laughter that followed, and Germain picked up. The smile slid off his face as he listened.

"Damn."

We all sobered, listening to his end of the conversation.

"Okay. Thanks."

He hung up, his face grim. "Richard Willis is dead. He died of a heart attack on Thursday afternoon. Webb dug into his background, and found out he was a computer programmer. No apparent ties to Fuzzy Bunny, no criminal record, no known associates with any suspicious past whatsoever. He lived with his mother. He worked for a software development company. The software company has no known ties to Fuzzy Bunny. The owners are clean. So far, he just looks like an innocent civilian."

Germain blew out a long breath. "And the IDs came through on the two torturers. They were definitely associated with Fuzzy Bunny."

My toast turned into a cold lump in my stomach, and I laid the remainder of the slice back on my plate.

"Dammit!" Kane put his coffee mug down on the table with unnecessary force.

"Do they really believe a young guy like that died of a heart attack?" I asked.

Germain scowled, lifting a shoulder. "What choice do they have? That's all the autopsy will show."

I didn't really want to know, but I had to ask. "What about the other captive?"

Germain turned to the laptop. "Webb did a search for all other men under fifty who died of a heart attack on Wednesday and Thursday. One was a petroleum consultant who was a member of the Calgary scuba club. His name was Arthur Ketchum. Webb sent a photo." He put the laptop on the table in front of me. "Look familiar?"

I sighed as heavy sadness rolled through me. "Yes. Probably. The hair colour and the build is right. I wouldn't be able to identify the face. But if he was a petroleum consultant, he was probably at the party, and the tattoo pretty much tells the story."

"Dammit," Kane said tiredly.

I pushed my plate away and sank my face into my hands. Two innocent men dead.

"Well, that's it, then," Kane broke the short silence. "We've lost our physical surveillance points, and we've lost our chance to find out anything from the questioning of the captives. Aydan, Hellhound, thank you for what you've done. You can both go home. Wheeler, we'll keep you undercover. Go get some sleep so you're ready for your next shift. Looks like we're in for the long haul here."

He leaned his head against the wall behind him, lines of fatigue scoring his face. "Germain and I will set up base camp at the old location and carry on with the investigation. Our next step is to find out if there was a common thread between the captives. Then maybe we can figure out what this was all about."

He blew out a breath. "And once again, Fuzzy Bunny slips through our fingers."

"They just killed two men," I protested.

"Leaving absolutely no evidence," Kane replied grimly. "The only person who can place the captives at Harchman's is you. We can't reveal your identity, and we especially can't reveal how you were able to identify the captives."

"So there's nothing you can do."

Kane's voice was hard. "For now." He rubbed his forehead wearily. "We'll find a way. Once we get more information on the captives, we'll have more to go on. I wish I knew what questions Fuzzy Bunny asked them."

I sat up slowly. "Maybe I can help with that."

"How?"

"I need to talk to Spider," I told him.

"Do it," he said. He turned to Hellhound. "You might as well head out. Thanks again."

Hellhound levered himself away from the counter reluctantly. "Okay, Cap," he growled. "Stay safe. All a' ya." He put his coffee cup in the sink and clumped out of the RV, followed by Wheeler.

As his Harley roared to life outside, I picked up the phone and dialled.

CHAPTER 31

Spider answered immediately. I greeted him, feeling a pang of sympathy at the exhaustion in his voice.

"Sorry to bother you, Spider," I said. "Do you have a minute to talk to me about the network?"

"Sure." There was a short pause, and he spoke again on the tail end of a yawn. "What do you want to know?"

"A couple of things about how the sim files work. Did anyone tell you that we'd discovered a real-time sim of the security room?"

"Yes."

"Okay, so if it's running, it shouldn't matter if anyone goes in or out of it, should it? I mean, in terms of making obvious changes to the date-time stamp or anything?"

"No, the date-time stamp would always be current, because it's always live. But don't forget, it's a data record that can be played back. Anyone using the sim would appear in the data record."

"Unless they were invisible."

I heard the smile in his voice. "Right."

"Okay. Next question. If I open data records or files in the network and just look around in them, would anybody be able to tell I'd been in them?"

"Files, you can look at, as long as you don't make any changes. The only way you'd get caught would be if you had the file open when somebody else tried to access it. Then they'd get a message that the file was in use, until you closed the file."

"So as long as I was quick about it, it should be pretty hard to detect," I surmised.

"Yes." Spider hummed thoughtfully on the line for a few seconds. "Sim data records, though, if you enter the sim, you're updating the file. Even if you're invisible, the timestamp would be updated because your presence would be recorded as part of the sim."

"Crap. So is there a way for me to view a sim data record from within the network, without actually entering the sim record that I'm viewing?"

There was a puzzled silence. "Say what?"

"I need to look at the sim data records from when the captives were being tortured." My voice didn't seem to be working right, and I cleared my tight throat before I continued. "I don't need to go into the sim, I just need to view it. The same as when you played back the sim data record from our network tests at Sirius. But I need to do it from inside the network, because I don't have any way of accessing it externally the way you did at Sirius."

"Oh." He thought for a minute. "That could be tricky. I think it might work if you created a sim of a workstation and played back the sim through your sim. I'll test it here first and see if it works."

"Don't try this at home, kids," I joked, and was rewarded with a faint chuckle.

"Exactly. I'll call you back as soon as I can. It should take me less than an hour."

"Okay, thanks." I hung up the phone and turned to two expectant faces. "He doesn't know. He's going to test it and call me back."

Kane got up to pour himself another cup of coffee. "At least that will give you time to finish your breakfast."

I regarded my cold toast without enthusiasm. "Kind of lost my appetite."

"Eat." The command came in ragged unison from both men, and I raised my hands in surrender.

"Jeez, Mom and Dad. All right, already." I slid back onto the bench and slowly finished my breakfast. Then I brewed a cup of herbal tea, deep in thought.

I'd need to access all the data records that had been created within the last couple of days. Maybe I could find some document files to snoop into as well, but that could take a very long time. Maybe there was a way for me to copy files from the network so I could look at them externally. I'd have to ask Spider.

I sighed and sipped my tea, realizing as I did that Kane and Germain were both watching me intently.

"What?" I asked.

"You had that look. The one you always get right before you figure something out," Germain said.

"I have an idea, but I can't see how it might work," I admitted. "I'm trying to figure out a way to steal some files. I'm wondering if I can get Harchman's guest list. Or anything else that might help."

"Too dangerous," Kane objected.

"Actually, it would be less dangerous than opening them from within the network," I countered. "I think, anyway. I'll ask Spider when he calls back. But I can't think of a way to do it, so it's probably pointless anyway."

Right on cue, the phone rang. When I picked up, Spider's voice was triumphant. "It worked."

"Excellent."

"But..." I heard the jubilation fade. "It worked for me because I understand how network hardware and software works, so I could easily create a workstation sim. I don't know if you'd be able to do it. And I don't have any way to send you the sim file."

"Which brings me to my next question. What about transferring files?" I asked. "Is there any way I can pull files out and transfer them to another system outside of their network?"

"No. As long as you're inside the network, you can create a sim to do anything. But as soon as you leave the network, you're back inside your own head. Short of memorizing the contents of the file, you can't bring any data with you. You need a physical network connection to do that."

"So somebody like Hellhound could do that. He's got a photographic memory."

"Yes..." he said cautiously. "But Hellhound doesn't have the security clearance to do it. And anyway, it wouldn't be much use. You'd know the contents of the file, in your head, but you still couldn't transfer the file to another system."

I sighed. "Okay. I was hoping I'd missed some obvious solution."

"No. Sorry."

"All right. Thanks. At least we know the sim within a sim works."

"For me." His voice was strained. "Aydan, I don't know if you should try it."

"Well, there's only one way to find out. I spent some time as a network administrator, back in the dark ages.

Maybe I still remember enough to get by. The user interfaces have changed so much that I don't know how to use them anymore, but I think the underlying structure is still basically the same, isn't it?"

"Yes... but... Aydan, can I talk to Kane for a minute?"

"Sure. Thanks for the info."

I passed the phone over to Kane and slouched on the bench. Dredging up my ancient computer knowledge, I tried to figure out how the simulation might work. My brain tied itself in a knot while I contemplated sims inside sims, and I made fists in my hair. I really had no idea. I'd just have to try it and hope for the best.

Kane disconnected and gave me a level look. "No."

"What?" I floundered up out of my abstraction, wondering if I'd spoken that last part out loud.

"No," he repeated. "If you're not absolutely positive you can do this, then it's not an option."

"Spider said it worked."

"Webb said it worked *for him*."

"Did he just rat me out?"

"Yes."

I sighed. "It could work for me. You know I used to be a network administrator."

"The operative words are 'used to be'," he said severely.

"Okay, how about this," I proposed. "What if I go in and try to create my workstation sim. If I can't create it at all, then nothing's lost. If I can create it, I could test it with one file, just for a second. Worst case scenario, it updates the data record. It would only be that one record, and I'd only be in it for a couple of seconds. And if it actually works, the best-case scenario gives you exactly the answers you need."

He scowled, and I knew I'd won. The cost/benefit

analysis really didn't leave him much choice.

"All right," he said reluctantly. "When can you be ready to go?"

"Just let me put my leathers on."

CHAPTER 32

We pushed through dense thickets of diamond willow, and I blessed my protective leather clothing as the twigs raked at me. The small creek trickled feebly beside us.

Kane held up a hand, and I waited while he scanned the way before we resumed our slow progress. In a few yards, he dropped to a crouch to thread his way through the beginning of a steep cutbank. I followed, and after a few more minutes of stealthy travel, he straightened with a barely audible sigh.

"We're inside the security perimeter," he whispered. "Try it now."

I obediently sank to the ground and concentrated, but to no avail. I shook my head, and he shrugged resignation and jerked his head to indicate that we should continue. I followed him again while he made his way further west.

I tried to ignore an unpleasant sensation of déjà vu. This is how he'd gotten captured last time, babysitting me. If they caught him this time...

My foot sank up to the ankle in the muck of the stream bed. I pulled it loose with a sucking sound and shook my boot vigorously to dislodge the clinging mud.

I yanked my mind away from my worries and focused on deflecting the twigs that threatened to poke my eyes out.

Mosquitoes swarmed enthusiastically. I shook my hair loose from its ponytail and let it fall around my shoulders to ward them off. Ahead, Kane smeared one of the little blood-suckers across the back of his unprotected neck.

He sidestepped onto solid ground and surveyed the surroundings cautiously before nodding at me again.

I sat, and was surprised when I actually stepped into the network. I took a few deep breaths to slow my pounding heart and began my check for active sims, wondering what creative fantasies I might discover this time. Now that I knew the truth behind the porn simulations, I wasn't sure whether having to spy on them was worse or better.

The security sim was active but unoccupied. I slipped in and surveyed the displays, but I was afraid to alter the camera views, and urgency prodded me on.

In another sim, Harchman was entertaining himself with my construct again. Apparently the cute blonde hadn't held his interest for long. I let out an inaudible sigh of irritation and floated down the virtual corridor.

The happy couple had apparently checked out, and I allowed myself a smile at the thought that Harchman had added a little bit of joy to the world, however unintentionally.

When I approached the blond man's room, my pulse raced a little faster as I wondered yet again about the true nature of his sim.

I peeked in and doubled over the stab of icy horror in my gut, clamping both invisible hands over my mouth to smother my reaction. In an instant, I was rocketing through sim-space to stand in front of the portal.

When I stepped through, I struggled against the pain and the hard hand clamped against my mouth. When I managed to control my frantic whimpering a few moments later, Kane released his grip, staring down at me.

"What?" he snapped.

"Another prisoner! They've got another prisoner! They're torturing him..." I gasped a couple of wheezing breaths. "We have to stop them!"

"Aydan, calm down. Breathe," he commanded.

"But..."

"Stay focused. This might be our only chance to get back in the network, and we can't waste it."

I clutched his hand, trying to control the shrill voice that issued from my throat. "John, we can't leave him!"

"Aydan." He gripped my shoulders, his big warm hands radiating strength into me. "Stop. Focus on the mission."

I fought to bring my breathing under control again, knowing he was right. The best way to save the blond man was to do what we came for. "Okay. I'm okay," I gasped. "Sorry."

"It's all right. Tell me what you saw."

I avoided thinking about what I'd just seen and concentrated on the information Kane needed to know. "There wasn't anybody in the sim with him at the moment. Whoever is torturing him is..." I swallowed hard, reaching for composure. "...obviously more sophisticated that the guys who worked you over. They held him at least twelve hours before they started. It looks like they're planning to make it last this time."

I overcame my revulsion with difficulty and squeezed my eyes shut to consult the horrible memory. "I didn't see any injuries that looked potentially fatal. Yet."

Kane nodded grimly. "That's closer to what I expected. They'll work on him for a while and then leave him to think it over. Repeat that for a while to wear him down with pain and fatigue and hopelessness. Sounds like they've got some professionals at work this time. What else?"

I did a bit more deep breathing. "That's all... so far. I didn't see anything else. I guess... I'd better go back in and see if I can play back the sims to find out what questions they're asking. And look at some files. Sorry I freaked out."

Kane squeezed my hand. "Aydan, you've got nothing to apologize for. You're amazing."

"Thanks," I mumbled, and stepped back into the virtual network's white void before I could blush at the compliment.

As I slipped through the wall into an unoccupied sim room and began to think through the process, the flaw in my logic suddenly became glaringly obvious.

I'd be creating a whole new sim data record. Shit, shit, shit!

I hadn't thought of it until just now. Spider was obviously even more exhausted than I'd realized, because he normally would have caught something like this right away.

I hovered indecisively while my heart practiced layups in my chest. Kane needed this information. I could just go ahead, quickly check the sims, and then delete my own data record once I was done. I was pretty sure Kane would absolutely forbid it if he knew what I was planning. But he wasn't here.

I took a deep breath and started building my sim.

Vibrating with tension, I scrolled through the directory of sim data records and selected the most recent. Without giving myself a chance to reconsider, I opened the record and closed it immediately.

Now I was afraid to look at the directory again.

Fingers crossed, I forced my gaze to the simulated screen. A breath of relief seeped out when I located the unchanged timestamp. Thank God. Now I could get on with it.

I quickly began reviewing the sim data records, beginning the day after the party. The first several featured Harchman and me in various poses, and I closed them as soon as I identified them. God, I was going to need a bottle of brain bleach after this.

I raised a cynical eyebrow at the spate of porn sims starring various unattractive middle-aged men with the Barbie-doll-like 'therapists'. Apparently not too many of the clients brought their wives.

At last, I discovered a record of the first captive. At the beginning of the sim, I saw the middle-aged man whom I'd tentatively identified earlier. Arthur Ketchum. I swallowed a large lump in my throat, and steeled myself for what I knew was coming.

After fast-forwarding through the first few minutes, I paused the playback with trembling hands and turned away, breathing carefully. In. Out. Slow like ocean waves.

When I'd regained some composure, I turned back to the sim and blanked out the video display. The audio alone wasn't much better.

I forced myself to listen to the entire record, making sure I didn't miss any of the torturers' questions. The audio track ended with the sound of a gunshot. One healthy middle-aged man dead of an apparent heart attack. I wished I hadn't known his name. Somehow it made it worse. I bowed my head and fought for control.

No time. I shook myself and moved on to the rest of the data. I hurriedly closed the next record at the sight of Kane hanging from the ceiling. I didn't need to see that again.

I waded rapidly through more porn to find the data

record for Richard Willis. The torturer was the man I'd seen monitoring the security sim the previous night, and the footage was short and brutal. By the time the sound of the gunshot signalled the end of the record, my eyes were closed while I gulped down nausea.

More porn. Then, at last, the handsome young blond man tied to the bed. I immediately flicked the virtual video display off. I would listen; it had to be done. But I couldn't watch.

The audio was very different than the other two records. Other than the torturer's questions, the only sounds were grunts of pain. None of the screaming and helpless crying I'd heard from the others. No abject pleas for mercy. In a way, it was worse. When the recording ended at last, my arms were wrapped tightly around my body while I rocked compulsively.

I forced myself to uncurl and move on to the few remaining records. They all starred Harchman and me, so I closed them as quickly as possible.

I blew out a long, trembling breath and closed down the sim. Time to go hunting for files and delete my own sim record.

I drifted through the wall and visualized a map that would lead me to the storage vault for the sim records. I zipped to my destination and sighed with relief as I made the record vanish.

Then I searched out the data files. I'd work my way backward from the most recently used ones. Fortunately, there didn't seem to be too many of them. I opened the first one and was beginning to read when agony ripped through my skull.

CHAPTER 33

Raw screams wrenched from my throat while my body convulsed, racked with excruciating pain. I thrashed wildly, trying to escape the torture. The world spun and flashed with razor-edged colours. I coiled down into a keening ball.

As the brutal pain began to recede, terror trickled in to take its place. Something had gone disastrously wrong. I forced one eye open, but the stab of light made me cry out and clutch my head again. A few sobbing breaths later, the din in my ears subsided enough for me to hear an urgent voice.

"Ma'am! Ma'am! It's okay, you're safe. It's okay. Ma'am, please calm down."

I squinted up at a clean-cut, uniformed young man leaning over me. I tried to speak, but only a wordless moan came out.

"Ma'am, don't be afraid. It's over. You're safe."

My throbbing brain lurched into gear again. This was one of Harchman's security guards. Shit!

On the upside, he didn't seem to be accusing me of trespassing. Yet. Then again, they'd been nice to Kane when they first captured him, too.

Kane!

I struggled to sit up and blinked hard to clear my eyes. The young security guard hovered in front of me. "Ma'am, are you all right? What happened?"

I spotted Kane standing motionless a couple of yards away, his hands in the air. Another guard held a gun on him, and a dog growled softly inches from his leg.

As I met Kane's eyes, he glared at me and spat. "You fucking dumb cunt!"

The shock of the vulgar words coming from his lips made me recoil as if he'd slapped me.

As I gaped at him, he continued, his face twisted into an ugly expression. "That'll teach you a lesson, cunt. Next time you'll suck my cock when I tell you."

"Shut up, you!" the guard rapped out, and the dog lunged at Kane, snapping at his leg. Kane froze, and the dog subsided onto its haunches again, growling.

Pain still hammered my head, and I didn't have much difficulty summoning up some tears while I struggled to process what was happening. Kane obviously had some kind of plan. His deliberate choice of those words told me he wanted me to be angry. I just didn't know why. I didn't know what the hell he needed me to do, and I was afraid to guess without more information.

"You..." My voice was trembling anyway, so I went with it. "You hurt me! You..." I turned to the young security guard as I sobbed. "Don't let him hurt me..." I buried my face in my hands, thinking furiously. Maybe Kane could take out the other guard if we could separate them. The dog made it too dangerous, though. And we were far from the buildings, so these would be well-meaning staff from the security company. I was sure Kane wouldn't use deadly force against innocent men. Dammit.

The guard laid a hand on my shoulder, and I flinched away from him with a whimper. He jerked his chin at the other guard. "Take him up. We'll follow later."

I heard movement, and then a soft exclamation. I glanced up as the other guard picked up my wristwatch. "Ma'am, is this your watch?"

When my gaze slid over to Kane, his eyes were bleak, and I realized he must have yanked the watch off my wrist, trying to ditch it. Goddammit. We just couldn't catch a break.

"Th-thanks," I quavered. I was afraid to deny that it was mine. With our luck, they'd carry it up to the house and hand it over to Harchman directly, and then all would be lost. I reached out a trembling hand, and the young guard helpfully strapped the watch back on my wrist.

"Move." The other guard prodded Kane ahead of him, and I curled into a shivering ball as they left. Maybe I could stall, and then convince my guard to let me go.

I wept quietly into my hands for a while longer, trying to decide on a course of action.

"Ma'am." The young guard laid a gentle hand on my shoulder. "You're safe now. I won't let anything happen to you."

The irony made me choke. He seemed like a nice kid. Little did he know his good intentions were about to deliver me to torture and death.

"What happened?" he pressed softly.

"I can't... I can't talk about it," I sniffled.

Stall, stall.

"Come up to the house. It'll be okay. You're safe now." He took my arm and helped me to my feet.

I exaggerated my trembling. A bit. Any more and I'd fall down. "I... I can't. Please, I just want to go home. Please let me go home."

"We'll get you home. Come with me, and we'll take you home."

Shit. I wasn't going to be able to convince him to let me blunder off alone down the creek. Maybe I should just run for it.

Yeah, right.

I wasn't exaggerating the trembling that much. There was no way I was going to outrun a fit, healthy male half my age through the mud and bushes in the creek bottom. A despairing whimper escaped me as he led me toward the house.

When we arrived, I hung back in the large foyer. "Is... Is there someplace I can wash? I feel so... dirty."

My guard guided me sympathetically to the powder room I'd used at the party, and I slipped inside. No window. No means of escape here. I collapsed onto the toilet with a hopeless sigh and sank my head into my shaking hands.

Harchman was sure to recognize me. Assuming he saw me at all. Maybe both Kane and I would be diverted directly to torture. I shuddered and tried to focus. Pointless to worry about that.

I took a deep breath and tried to figure out Kane's plan. He was clearly trying to make it look as though we were antagonistic toward each other. As I thought it through, I realized he was trying to protect me.

They'd already caught him once. We'd attended the party together. I would automatically be suspect. And he knew Harchman found me attractive. Maybe he was trying to set up an escape route for me. Drive a wedge between us, let me suck up to Harchman. That seemed plausible. I'd try, anyway. If I got the chance.

That meant I'd better be looking good when or if Harchman saw me. I approached the mirror with trepidation. The 'tears and snot' look usually isn't a good one for me.

Apparently fake tears weren't as bad as the real thing. I carefully rinsed my face with cool water and patted it dry. Thankful yet again for my trusty waist pouch, I pulled out my folding hairbrush and brushed the leaves and spruce needles out of my hair. I tugged the tank top lower and leaned over to shove my boobs into a more favourable position. Then I slicked on some lip gloss and tried a pout.

Here goes nothing. I stepped out of the powder room, going for hot but vulnerable.

CHAPTER 34

The guard led me directly into an ostentatious office, and I hesitated at the sight of Harchman seated behind a huge, ornately carved wooden desk. Kane stood across the room, still guarded. The dog stared menacingly at him, utterly focused.

"Lawrence?" I said softly, letting my voice quaver a bit.

"Aydan, my dear!" He stood hastily and came around the desk to take both my hands in his. "What a pleasant surprise!" His eyes roamed avidly over my snug leather and exposed cleavage.

My young guard stepped forward. "This is the woman he attacked." He shot Kane a contemptuous glare.

Harchman's forehead wrinkled. "But... they're married. She's his wife."

There was a pregnant silence while I gathered my courage. Then I stepped closer to Harchman and pulled our clasped hands up against my chest. "Oh, Lawrence. I'm so ashamed."

I cast my eyes down, feeling his hands burrow in. "I... I lied to you. I'm not really married to him..."

"Shut up, bitch!" Kane grated.

"You shut up," the guard snapped, and the dog growled

again.

I gazed down into Harchman's eyes imploringly. "He tricked me. He's a spy..."

"Aydan..." Kane's voice was tight.

I wheeled around on him. "Stop calling me that! That's not my name! And you should have been nice to me when you had the chance. Instead of lying and hurting me... You pervert! You always hurt me!" I let my voice tremble again as I turned back to Harchman.

"Lawrence, I'm so sorry. My real name is Arlene, not Aydan. I met *him*..." I indicated Kane with a flounce of my shoulders, "In a bar. And he promised we'd be rich, if I did what he said."

Harchman was frowning. "You said he was a spy."

"He said we just had to come to this party and I should be nice to you. But then..."

I looked down again and leaned closer, letting my voice get huskier. "Then I met you, and I really *liked* you. And I found out he was trying to steal the software for your new drilling program. And when I told him I didn't want to, he forced me..."

I leaned close and whispered in his ear. "He forced me to do the most *perverted* things, you can't imagine. And he *hurt* me..." I snuggled closer and Harchman's arms slid around me. So far, so good. Lucky I'd seen enough of Harchman's fantasy life to know just where to focus.

"He lied to me," I whispered. "He was so mean to me. He made me suck his cock, over and over, and all the time I was just thinking of you..."

Harchman's arms tightened around me. "You're dismissed," he addressed the guards. "Take him away," he added, and I looked up in time to see Kane's back as the two guards marched him through the door. An involuntary sob escaped me when I realized it was probably the last time I'd see him alive.

With an effort, I composed myself and concentrated. My responsibility was to get the network key out of Harchman's grasp. If it was within my power, I'd make Kane's sacrifice count. At least Harchman seemed to think I was upset about tricking him, not about Kane's fate.

I turned back to Harchman. "Oh, Lawrence. Please forgive me." I sank to my knees in front of him, deliberately positioning my face in front of his crotch as I gazed up at him. I suppressed a shudder of pure revulsion. "What can I do to make you forgive me?"

His eyes glazed as he ran his hands through my hair. I let him pull my face closer to his pants before I suddenly withdrew.

"Wait." I scrambled to my feet and backed away a step. "How do I know you won't just use me, too? Just because I like you doesn't mean you won't hurt me." I hid my face in my hands. "Oh, I just want a nice man to make love to me."

He stepped close and put his arms around me again. "Arlene, my dear, I won't hurt you. I promise."

"He promised, too," I quavered. "I was nice to him, I did everything he said, and I mean *everything*..."

His sweaty palms slithered greasily across the leather of my jacket. "Arlene, darling, how can I prove I won't hurt you?"

I peeked at him between my fingers. "*He* always promised to treat me nicely, but he never did. *He* promised to take me out to a nice restaurant and treat me like a lady, but he lied and lied..."

"I'll take you out to a nice restaurant," Harchman

promised eagerly. "I'll take you to the nicest restaurant in Calgary."

"Really?" I gazed at him worshipfully. Then I let suspicion cross my face. "When?"

"Now!" He took my hand and towed me toward the desk. I did my best not to shudder in his clammy grasp while he punched a button and picked up the phone.

"Bring the car around," he ordered, and hung up. He slipped an arm around my waist and ushered me to the front door. As we stepped out, a stretch limo pulled up, and the uniformed driver strode smartly around to open the door. Harchman helped me into the back seat of the limo, letting his hand slide over my ass, and took his place close beside me.

"Oh, Lawrence," I breathed as the car pulled away. "I've never ridden in a limo before. How exciting to have your own car and driver!"

He laid his hand on my thigh. "He's not just a driver. He's a bodyguard, too," he said proudly.

Yeah. I'd caught a glimpse of the driver's shoulder holster as he'd closed the car door for us. He was a big guy, too. Great. Now I had to escape from both Harchman and his minion. I hoped my plan would work.

I snuggled closer. "Lawrence, if we're going to a fancy restaurant, I want to look nice for you. Can we stop at my house so I can change my clothes?"

His hand slid farther up my thigh, and his fingertips brushed across my crotch. "I like the way you look now."

I grabbed the offending hand and clasped it in both of my own as I leaned closer to whisper in his ear. "But I have something really *special.* It's red leather, and it's scented like cherries. And the warmer it gets..." I brushed my lips across his ear, "...the better it smells."

He gulped. "All right," he said hoarsely. He leaned forward and spoke to the driver through an intercom. "We're going to make a stop before we go to the restaurant." He gave me a questioning glance, and I supplied the address of the house that I'd recently sold.

The transaction had closed in June, and I'd discovered a spare set of keys a couple of weeks ago. I'd put them on my key ring, planning to drop them off to the new owners the next time I was in Calgary.

Please let this work.

I spent the rest of the drive trying to squirm away from Harchman's moist hands as unobtrusively as possible. When we pulled up in front of the house, I hid a sigh of relief.

The driver opened the car door, and Harchman got out with me. I turned to him. "I'll just be a minute. Why don't you wait in the car?"

"No," he purred. "I want to see your special outfit. In private."

Shit.

He followed me up the driveway to the front door. At least I was reasonably certain the new owners wouldn't be home. I knew they both worked, and it was the middle of the day.

At the front door, I fumbled with my keys, dropping them. As I knelt to pick them up, I reached for my waist pouch. "Oh, that's my phone! Lawrence, would you open the door?" I handed him the key and pulled out my phone. "I'm just going to turn it off."

I fumbled at the tiny button with trembling hands and surreptitiously turned it on instead. Kane and I had missed our check-in time. By now, Germain would be on high alert.

They'd tracked me through my smartphone before. I hoped they could do it this time, too. I prayed Harchman wouldn't recognize my ploy, but he seemed oblivious.

The door swung open, and I swallowed a sigh of relief. People are so trusting. I couldn't believe they hadn't changed the locks yet.

The alarm system triggered its warning tone, and Harchman turned to me. I stepped inside and used my knuckle to punch in the master code. The system didn't disarm.

Shit!

I quickly punched in one of the secondary codes. The happy sound of the acceptance chime made my knees weak. They'd updated the master code, but they hadn't purged the secondary codes from the system. Fools. Thank God for fools.

I took my keys back from Harchman and walked him around the corner into the living room. I pressed him down onto their sofa, leaning over him to show as much of my boobs as possible. "Wait here," I breathed. "I'll be right down."

He reached for me, but I pulled away. "Hurry," he said huskily.

I didn't need any encouragement. I resisted the urge to go up the stairs two at a time, and closed myself into the master bedroom. When I'd replaced that door a few months ago, I'd installed a privacy lock. I breathed fervent thanks as I locked it carefully, using the tail of my tank top to cover my fingers. My fingerprints would still be all over the house, but I didn't want my prints on top of the current owners' prints when they discovered the break-in.

I crossed immediately to the window, opened it, and

removed the screen, still covering my fingers.

If I hadn't been so scared, I would have laughed. Same old, same old. This was an exact replay of what I'd done in March.

I stepped out onto the roof segment of the bay window below and slid over the edge on my stomach. I managed to catch the eavestrough with both hands as I went over, and it creaked ominously but actually held my weight this time. I'd done a good job on that repair.

I swung wildly for a couple of seconds before dropping the last foot or so as lightly as possible to land on the deck below.

Heart hammering, I tiptoed rapidly across the deck and hopped over the railing onto the shed roof. From there, it was an easy step onto the top of the fence, and down into the neighbours' heavily treed back yard.

I stared wildly around, praying nobody had seen me. A black-leather-clad figure sneaking out a window in this quiet neighbourhood would be sure to draw some 911 calls.

I scuttled across the neighbour's yard and hauled myself over their fence and into the community park. Then I ran like hell.

CHAPTER 35

My biking boots weren't exactly designed for sprinting. I dodged off the asphalt path onto the grass to quiet the pounding of my footsteps and reduce the impact on my complaining feet and knees.

Realizing that a fleeing black-leather-clad figure was probably even more suspicious than a walking one, I slowed, gasping for air, and pulled off my hot jacket. The sun beat down on my sweaty shoulders, and I lifted sticky hair off the back of my neck.

I couldn't believe I'd actually gotten away, but I was still far from safe. As soon as Harchman realized I was gone, he'd be after me with the car. And with the armed driver.

As I approached the street, the distinctive sound of a transit bus labouring uphill made me break into a run again. The bus was just pulling away from its stop as I pelted alongside it. The driver mercifully stopped.

"Thanks," I gasped as I scrounged in my waist pouch for change. I dropped the fare into the box and wobbled into the nearest seat to slump against the side of the bus while I sucked air. Sweat streamed from every pore, and the leather pants felt as hot and sticky as a plastic bag. But I'd done it. I'd escaped.

As the urgency faded, reaction rushed in to take its place. I trembled helplessly and fought back tears. Kane was surely dead by now. Or suffering horribly. I wasn't sure which was worse. Our last words to each other were an ugly memory. I struggled to control my uneven breathing. I would *not* cry in public.

I stumbled off the bus at a busy downtown stop, trying to hide myself in the small group of other passengers as we disembarked. My numbed mind dragged itself into action again. Stay focused. Call Spider. Find a pay phone.

I tottered toward the nearest building, but trailed to a halt when I realized I might as well use my cellphone. I'd turned it on anyway. Using it wouldn't make a difference.

Even as I pulled it out, my brain served up a sluggish reminder. A land line was more secure.

I was turning witlessly back in the direction of the building when iron-hard arms grabbed me from behind and jerked me into a gap between the buildings.

I was sucking in a frantic breath to scream when the grip suddenly released. I spun around and came face to face with Kane himself.

The shock was so profound that the air left me in a tiny squeak, and my knees wobbled, nearly dropping me to the pavement. In an instant, his arms were around me again, holding me up.

My strength came back in a rush. I launched myself at him, crushing him in my arms. He staggered back against the side of the building, and I pulled him into a fierce kiss as I pinned him against the wall.

I ran unbelieving hands over his living, breathing, uninjured body while I devoured his lips. His arms tightened around me, and he returned the kiss hungrily. His hands slid down my back, hard and demanding, pulling me against him. Relief blazed into hot lust as I opened my lips to his tongue. His hands slid lower, and I moaned with sheer need under his ravenous mouth.

Suddenly his hands were on my shoulders, pushing me away.

"Aydan," he gasped. "This can't happen."

I panted desperately as he held me at arms' length. "Why the hell not?"

"It's too dangerous. You're distracting me. Driving me crazy. Tight leather. Those black panties..." He swallowed audibly and drew a ragged breath. "If I don't concentrate on this mission, more people could die. You could die. I can't take the risk."

"But..."

"Aydan, I can't. I'm sorry."

I stood silently, getting myself under control. "John, I could die anyway," I said finally. "We both could have died this afternoon. I'd rather live while I can. I've spent my entire life doing the safe thing."

"And it's my job to make sure you keep doing the safe thing," he said quietly.

I blew out a long breath. "Duty."

"Yes."

I sighed again, trying to slow my heartbeat and breathing. I squelched frustration and hurt and anger, rolled them into a ball, and stuffed them down as deep as they would go while I stared at the ground.

"Okay." I looked up at him. "You can let go of me now. I won't try to molest you again."

"Aydan..."

"It's okay." I stepped back and stuck out my hand. "I'm

really glad you're still alive. Friends?"

I might have imagined the spasm of pain in his eyes. He smiled, and his face was composed as he took my outstretched hand in a gentle grip. "I'm really glad you're alive, too. Friends."

He released my hand and reached into his pocket for his phone. He punched a speed dial button. "Got her. Pick us up."

CHAPTER 36

"How did you get away?" I demanded. "How did you get *here*?"

"First I need to know you're all right."

"Yeah, I'm fine," I said impatiently. "It was just pawing and groping. Jeez, why did you grab me like that? You scared the shit out of me."

"I'm sorry I scared you. I didn't know if you were being followed, and I wanted to get you out of plain view." He frowned down at me. "You aren't being followed, are you?"

"No. I'm almost positive nobody's following me." A battered blue Suburban pulled over at the curb in front of our hiding place. I smiled. "Except the good guys."

We stepped across the sidewalk, and Kane opened the passenger door. "Aydan, this is Mark Richardson. He'll take you down to our rendezvous point."

He addressed the driver. "Sorry, I'd take her myself, but I'm on my bike, and I don't have a spare helmet."

"No problem."

I hauled my shaking self into the passenger seat. The brown-haired, blue-eyed driver gave me a quick handshake and a smile. A fleeting dimple appeared in his cheek, incongruous with the thin scar that slashed across his cheekbone. "Good to have you aboard," he said.

He pulled out into traffic as I sagged into the seat with a long sigh. "I am so glad to be aboard."

As we drove south on Macleod Trail, I recovered enough to sit up straight again. "Where are we going?"

"The big-box mall down by 22x."

My stomach growled, and I glanced at my watch. Two o'clock. God, I was starving. My entire body trembled with hollow weakness. "Can we stop at Wendy's?"

His dimple reappeared. "Webb warned me I'd better feed you as soon as I picked you up."

He swung into the drive-through, and a few minutes later, I was gobbling my favourite salad, barely breathing so I could stuff it in as quickly as possible.

By the time we arrived at the mall, I'd finished the salad and started my chocolate ice cream. Richardson headed for the south end of the mall, and I pointed with the spoon. "Over there. That's the RV."

He nodded and parked beside it. Kane pulled up and dismounted from his bike on the other side. As I got out of the truck, the RV door swung open, and Germain stepped out, his face creased in a grin. He gave me a quick one-armed hug. "Glad to have you back."

I returned his grin. "Glad to be back."

Kane joined us, scanning the parking lot. "Let's go inside." He lifted a hand to Richardson. "Thanks for the safe delivery."

"You're welcome." Richardson waved out the window. "Nice to meet you, Aydan. Take care."

"Thanks. You, too."

We trooped up the steps, and I slid into the dinette bench. Kane wedged himself in beside me, and Germain sat across from us in his usual spot. I felt as though I'd been doing this for weeks, not days.

"So what happened?" I demanded as soon as we were settled.

"First, you. Harchman didn't try to harm you in any way?"

"No. Other than the severe nausea caused by his proximity," I joked.

"You didn't hurt him, did you?" Kane regarded me seriously.

"No, of course not." I met Kane's dubious gaze and realized he was thinking of my run-in with the campground neighbours.

"I wouldn't hurt anybody unless they were threatening me," I explained. "And I wouldn't have taken on both him and his big bodyguard anyway, unless I had absolutely no other options. I just tricked him and ran away. Why the tender concern?"

"Because we're almost certain now that he's not connected to any of Fuzzy Bunny's activities on his property."

"What?" I stared at him open-mouthed. "Two innocent people dead? Not to mention the three bodies that you left behind? Sickos torturing people in the sim? And he doesn't know? How could he miss the sim records? They're all there, right in the network."

Kane shrugged. "I know it sounds crazy, but I really don't think he knows. Because he called the police, not the torturers. After the guards marched me out, they held me in the security office until the RCMP arrived."

"What?" I squeezed my eyes shut and tugged a couple of handfuls of hair, trying to get my brain to encompass the new information. "So all this time, we've been thinking Harchman is the evil mastermind, and he's completely clueless?"

I thought about it a little longer. "Well, that explains a lot."

"But what happened to you in the network?" Kane asked. "All of a sudden you started screaming and thrashing around. Did you leave the portal too fast?"

I stared at him in puzzlement. "No. I was just sitting there reading, and the next thing I knew I was on the ground. I thought something had happened at your end."

"No."

I rubbed the frown lines out of my forehead. "So the signal was broken somehow. Maybe a blip in the transmission?"

"I don't know. We were right at the limit of the transmission range, so maybe." He ran his hand over his face. "It couldn't have been worse timing, though. Those guards were there in seconds. I barely had time to get the watch off your wrist."

He looked disgusted. "For all the good it did. Nice acting job, by the way," he added. "I'm sorry about the offensive language."

"It's okay. It was a smart way to tell me what you wanted me to do."

"It was the only thing I could think of," Kane admitted. "What happened to you? How did you get Harchman out the door so fast?"

I felt my lips curl back involuntarily. "Suffice it to say I convinced him we needed to go to Calgary right away," I said. "He was... motivated."

There was a short pause, during which Kane eyed me

expressionlessly, but he apparently decided to let it go. "How did you escape?" he asked.

"I still had keys to my old place. I told him I needed to change my clothes, and got him to take me there. Lucky for me, the new owners hadn't changed the locks, and one of my old security codes still worked. I left him sitting in the living room and went out the bedroom window the same as I did in March."

Kane leaned back in the bench and laughed. "You're kidding."

"Old habits die hard."

Germain eyed our grins, his eyes crinkling. "Share the joke," he demanded.

"That's right, you didn't get involved until later. Long story," Kane told him. "The short version is that the first day I met Aydan, she escaped a gunman, jumped out of a moving vehicle, hurdled over the Suburban even though she'd been shot in the leg, mowed down Webb..."

"I heard about that part from Webb," Germain interrupted.

"Jumped out of a third-story window, beat the crap out of Hellhound, and was all set to beat the crap out of me, too," Kane finished.

"It wasn't like that," I protested. "He's exaggerating. I didn't hurdle over the Suburban, I just kind of rolled off the hood. The bullet wound was barely a scratch, and I didn't jump three storeys, I just got out on the third storey and dropped down to the second. And I didn't beat the crap out of Hellhound. I just... got away from him."

"Leaving him incapacitated," Kane chuckled.

"Only for a minute or two."

Germain laughed. "I always knew you were a dangerous

woman. So you went out the same window today. From three storeys up."

"Yeah."

"I knew it," Germain joked. "All this time, you've been a spy. That bookkeeping business is just a cover. Admit it."

"I'm just a civilian," I said.

A faint line appeared between his brows as his sharp eyes darted from Kane's suddenly serious face to mine. "Okay," he said.

Kane shifted in his seat and changed the subject. "I saw you and Harchman leaving in the limo. I told the police the unclassified parts of the story and then called Webb and headed for Calgary as fast as I could. Webb got a fix on your cellphone. He said you'd turned it on at your old place."

"Yeah, I was hoping you'd be looking for it."

"I caught up with the signal about halfway to downtown. Richardson was converging on it from the other side of town. It took me a few blocks to figure out you were on the bus. Then I had to figure out a way to get to you. Lucky you got off where you did."

I shook my head. "All that fear and effort for nothing. Harchman was never a threat at all. Shit. I wondered why he was so easy to manipulate. I couldn't imagine getting away with that with any of the real Fuzzy Bunny guys."

"You wouldn't want to count on it," Kane agreed.

I sighed and slouched into the corner. "So where does that leave us?"

"That depends. What did you find in the network?"

I hesitated. "Well, I went through the sim records."

Kane's brows snapped together suspiciously. "But..."

I gave him an innocent look, and he frowned at me. "I know there's a but," he said. "Spit it out."

I sighed. "I had to make an executive decision. Spider and I missed a critical flaw in our logic."

"Which was...?" Kane prodded.

"I was able to create the sim within the sim so I could look at the records without updating their timestamps. But..." I glanced at his face, and addressed the tabletop instead. "The problem is, the process of creating a sim creates a new data record. So I had to leave it running while I viewed the existing records, and then I went in and deleted the record afterward."

"So you essentially advertised there was an invisible someone using the network."

His voice was utterly flat, and the small hairs stood up instinctively on the back of my neck.

"It was a calculated risk. The only way anybody would notice would be if they happened to look at the data directory at exactly the time I was in there viewing the sim. That was a pretty short window of opportunity."

I looked up to meet his eyes. "It seemed like the right thing to do at the time."

"No," Kane said dangerously. "The right thing to do would have been for you to *follow orders*, and not take unnecessary risks. Get out of the network immediately and report the flaw in the plan. Revise the plan if necessary. Or scrap it entirely."

My temper rose in response to his inflection, and I squashed it with all my might. I matched his flat tone. "I didn't realize our conversation constituted an *order*. And it's a little late to second-guess me now. It's done. I got the information. Do you want it or not?"

Oops. That came out a little more aggressively than I'd intended.

Kane fixed me with a hard stare. I was in no mood to appreciate intimidation tactics. I felt my chin jerk down in instant rage.

Germain cleared his throat. "What did you find out?" he asked.

I reluctantly broke eye contact with Kane and turned to Germain. "They asked Arthur Ketchum the same questions as they asked Kane. Who he was working for, how he got access to the network, where he'd hidden the key. I don't know why they thought Ketchum was their intruder. I guess we'll never know."

"Were those the only questions they were asking?" Kane inquired.

When I turned back to him, he had his expressionless cop face in place, cool and detached. I tried to decide if that was good or bad as I answered.

"That's all they asked Ketchum. It turned out Richard Willis had a connection after all."

Kane and Germain both jerked forward. "What?" Kane snapped.

"He ran a little computer business on the side, and Harchman had hired him to program the bimbos for the sims. When there was a breach in the network, he was their logical suspect because he'd been working with their systems. And he had a guilty conscience because he had been secretly sharing the porn videos from the sims on the internet. He didn't know anything about the brainwave-driven network, though. Or if he did, he died hiding the fact. But I doubt it. He would have told them anything..." I swallowed the sickening memory.

Kane sat back slowly. "I'll pass that on to Webb and get him to look into Willis's side business. What about the third captive?"

Germain stiffened. "What third captive?"

I crossed my arms over my chest and sat back in the seat to hide my shudder. "There's another captive. In there right now, being tortured." I turned to Kane. "We have to get him out. We can't just sit here."

"We'll get him," Kane said firmly. "As soon as you're finished telling us what you found, I'll call Stemp."

I gulped a breath of relief and sat up straighter. "This prisoner is different. I think he might be a spy or something."

Kane and Germain exchanged a hard glance, and a muscle jumped in Kane's jaw. "What makes you say that?"

"The others cried and screamed and begged. He said nothing. Nothing, no matter what..." A vision of the price he'd paid for his silence made my throat close up, and I sat in silence for a moment. When I could trust my voice again, I continued.

"And they were asking him different questions. Something about an arms deal. It sounded like some weapons had gone missing in a shipment and they suspected he'd had something to do with it."

"You need to find him in the database as soon as possible," Kane said. "Anything else?"

"Yes. I also discovered some interesting documents after I'd finished with the sims. I was just starting to read them when I got kicked out."

"What was in the documents?"

"I'd barely gotten started, but it looked like some financial records. There were names and amounts. I'm wondering if it's Fuzzy Bunny's payroll records. So to speak."

Kane raised a thoughtful eyebrow. "Wouldn't that be nice."

"We have to do something," I burst out. "Call Stemp. We have to shut them down."

He nodded and reached for his phone.

CHAPTER 37

I sat tensely while Kane talked. He finished his report, and the rhythm of the dialogue changed while he answered Stemp's questions. I noticed he didn't accord Stemp the 'Sir' he had given General Briggs. I wondered absently if it was just a military rank thing.

As the conversation progressed, Kane's responses became terse. His already massive shoulders seemed to swell, and his clear grey eyes darkened to iron.

At last, the plastic case of the cellphone emitted a small crackle as his forearm muscles bunched, and he spoke in a hard voice. "No, I can't agree. We can gain valuable intel by questioning their current prisoner ourselves, and Aydan has already ascertained that there are useful documents in the network. If we move in now, we can save a life and seize the documents-"

Pause.

"...No, not yet," he growled. "...no, she wasn't absolutely sure."

Pause.

"He already tried, with no success..." His scowl darkened. "That will take too much time."

The phone creaked another protest under his grip. "Yes,

understood," he ground out. A flush climbed his neck, and a sharp snap signalled the surrender of the plastic under his fist. "Yes. *Sir.*"

Kane pressed the disconnect button, his face rigid. He turned away to place the phone on the counter, and Germain and I exchanged a glance as we silently watched the rise and fall of his shoulders while he took a deep breath. When he turned back to us again, his face was impassive, his posture deceptively relaxed. Only the frosty grey of his eyes betrayed his emotions.

"That didn't sound like it went well," I ventured.

"It's not the way I'd handle it," Kane said evenly, "But we have our orders. You need to identify the prisoner and the torturer, and anybody else you saw in the network. You should get started on the database right away. Webb will try to hack into Harchman's network to retrieve the documents you discovered."

"But..." I crushed my urge to yell and pound the table. "Spider already tried to get into the network. He couldn't." I kept my tone calm and reasonable. "And there's no telling how long it will take me to find these people in the database, if I can find them at all."

Calm and reason fled despite my best efforts. "Goddammit, Stemp hasn't got a fucking clue what's happening to that poor guy! What the hell is his problem? Who the hell does he think he is, playing God..."

I snapped my mouth shut at Germain's touch on my arm. He glanced at the rippling muscles in Kane's jaw before turning to me. "Aydan, let it go. Let's just do the best we can here."

"Stemp won't let us do the best we can! How long is he going to wait? We already know Spider can't get into the network!"

I fell silent as a thought hit me. "But I can," I added.

"No, you can't," Kane said flatly.

I eyed him. "You know I can." When he said nothing, I went on. "You have orders not to take down the operation, right?"

"Right." His face gave away nothing.

"I have orders to find out who those people are, right?"

"Right."

"Do we have specific orders not to go back into the network?"

"No," Kane said reluctantly. "But Aydan, I do have specific orders to safeguard you with my life. And even if I didn't, I wouldn't put you back into danger. It's not an option."

I lunged to my feet, unable to sit still any longer. "John, dammit, two innocent men are dead because of me. You were tortured because of me. This is all my fault." I faced him, resisting the urge to stand on my tiptoes to meet him eye-to-eye. "I can stop this whole fucking mess. Let me do it!"

He frowned. "Aydan, none of this is your fault. Those things happened because those people are criminals, not because of anything you did."

"They never would have known there was a network breach if I'd figured out how to be invisible sooner. I should have thought it through before we went in the first time. This is all my fault."

"You didn't have time to think it through," he argued. "If it's anybody's fault, it's Stemp's. Don't beat yourself up over what you can't change."

It was a cheap shot, but I was desperate. I knew which

button to push. I looked him square in the eye. "Look who's talking."

We locked eyes for a few seconds, and then he sighed and ran a hand over his face. "We can't risk going back to that access point."

"Why not?" I demanded.

"Because they'll have realized there's a gap in their camera perimeter now," he explained patiently. "The guards will have reported where they found us. We can't go back."

"Shit."

We sat in silence for a while. "We really need to see what's in those documents," I said at last. "If it's a roll call of Fuzzy Bunny's associates, it could give Stemp everything he needs to shut the whole operation down."

"Yes, but I think we're out of luck," Kane said. "We have no other potential access points left. We can't get you close enough to the network. And even if we did, it's too risky if you're going to get kicked out of the network randomly." He gave me a wry twist of his lips. "You attract too much attention when that happens."

"Couldn't you just sit on me and keep a hand over my mouth or something?"

He blew out a frustrated breath. "Aydan, I could barely get the watch off your wrist. I had to kneel on your arm."

"Oh." I examined my left arm. "I wondered what those bruises were from."

"Short of tying you up and gagging you, there's no way. And even then, I wouldn't count on it."

"Hmph." I crossed my arms and sank my chin on my chest while I slouched in the corner of the dinette bench, thinking. There had to be a way to get inside the perimeter again.

I sat up slowly. "I have an idea."

Germain's eyes crinkled. "I could smell the smoke."

Kane leaned back to watch me cautiously. "What?"

"If Harchman isn't a threat, I could call him. Tell him it was a big misunderstanding. I could tell him..." I thought for a second. "I could tell him you escaped from the police and called me at the house and threatened me, and I panicked and ran away." I grimaced. "I'm pretty sure he'll give me another chance."

"Another chance to do what, exactly?" Kane asked slowly.

"I could tell him I'm afraid to go home. Ask him to let me stay at the guest house. That would get me inside the perimeter..."

"Absolutely not," Kane said.

"But..."

"Aydan, just because Harchman likely isn't working with Fuzzy Bunny, that doesn't make it safe. They're still there, and we don't know who's involved. You'd have to dodge both unknown enemies, and Harchman. I would hesitate to put a trained agent into a situation like that. It's just too dangerous for you."

"Okay, but pretend for a minute that I am a trained agent," I argued. "Would that change anything?"

I realized I'd let my mouth get me in trouble again when I met intent gazes from both men. "I'm not," I added hastily. "But if I was... Is it a bad plan altogether, or just a bad plan for me?"

"This is a pointless discussion," Kane said expressionlessly. "It's a bad plan for you, and it's not going to happen."

I subsided before I could dig myself in any deeper. I

kicked my heel lightly against the bench while I thought. "Okay, what about this, then," I said slowly.

"What if... we found some pretext to go onto the grounds. Furnace inspection, gas company, carpet cleaning, I don't know, whatever. Nobody has seen Carl before. He could drive a service vehicle in and leave it parked in the lot while he pretended to do whatever he was there for. If it was a truck or van, I could hide in the back and browse through the network to my heart's content from the parking lot. Nobody would be any the wiser."

Germain frowned. "Unless you got kicked out of the network again. Then it would be hard to explain why I had a screaming woman locked in my truck. And you'd be identified instantly."

I sighed. "So tie me up and gag me."

"Aydan," Kane said gently. "That's insane. You're claustrophobic."

"I'd go into the network right away. I wouldn't even know I was tied up."

"And you wouldn't know if you were discovered, either. It would be totally irresponsible for us to put you in that situation with nobody to guard you."

"So guard me. You can hide in the truck, too, with the signalling device."

The two men exchanged a look. "That could work," Germain said reluctantly.

Kane scrubbed his knuckles through his hair. "Maybe," he growled. "I don't like it. But I haven't liked anything about this mission yet. All right. Let's see if we can come up with something that will work."

Some discussion and several phone calls later, we had a plan. Kane leaned back in the dinette bench. "All right.

Let's head to the pickup point. Germain, you can drive the RV back to our original base camp, and I'll follow in the gas company van. Once we're settled at the base camp, we can go ahead with the next phase."

Germain nodded. "Let's load up your bike."

When we arrived at the pickup point, Kane unbuckled his seatbelt. "Aydan, you'll ride with me."

It wasn't a request. I nodded and followed him out of the RV. I waved to Germain as he drove away, and Kane and I got into the van.

He spoke as we cleared the city limits. "Aydan, what was that, back in the RV?"

"What do you mean?"

"First of all, why did you deliberately create that record when you knew it was dangerous? After I'd warned you to be careful? And secondly, why were you so..." he paused, obviously searching for the right word, "Challenging? When I called you on it?"

I tensed defensively, but his voice was even. If he was still angry, he was hiding it well.

I struggled for a reasonable tone. "I didn't mean to undermine your authority. I honestly thought it was the right thing to do at the time. There wasn't significantly more risk than if I'd had files open and locked. You were okay with that risk when we discussed it up front."

"It's not about my authority. The point is, we discussed the plan up front. If you deviate from our plans without telling me, I can't protect you. When the team isn't fully informed, that's when team members die. For no good reason."

His voice was grim, and I realized I'd reawakened his old ghosts long before I took that cheap shot in the RV.

"I'm sorry," I told him sincerely. "I warned Stemp I wouldn't be any damn good at this spy stuff. I told him I didn't want to be put in a position where I could endanger you."

His face softened. "Aydan, I know you're doing your best. And it's not my own life I'm worried about. I'm just trying to keep you and the rest of the team safe."

I sighed. "I know."

"So why did you get in my face?" he asked mildly

I grimaced. "Sorry. It wasn't anything to do with you."

"What was it, then?"

"Apparently, I have some faulty wiring in my psyche somewhere. The instant I feel that somebody's threatening me, I get furious. Usually far out of proportion to the threat."

"But I didn't threaten you."

"You sounded threatening. I was on edge to start with. It was enough."

He glanced over. "That's why you were ready to take on those two men in the campground."

"Yeah." I sighed. "When I lose my temper like that, I'm ready to take on anybody." I shrugged. "It's saved my butt a couple of times. Most guys back down when they realize I'm serious."

He gave me a crooked grin. "You do look kind of... feral... when you get that angry. No offense."

I laughed. "None taken. I'll admit I haven't tried too hard to overcome that particular personality trait." I sobered. "It'll probably get me killed someday."

"Probably," he agreed.

"Thanks."

"Just saying."

When we reached our destination, Germain turned off at the base camp while Kane and I drove on to retrieve the Honda from its hiding place. Kane parked the van near the creek and held out a restraining hand when I reached for the door handle.

"Not so fast," he said. "We don't know if we're walking into an ambush here. I'm coming with you."

I suppressed a sigh. It was nice to be protected, but my ravelled nerves were begging for some silence and solitude. I said nothing and slid out of the van.

As we strode toward the creek, Kane glanced over. "Are you feeling comfortable riding yet?"

"Yeah, I'm okay. It just took a little getting used to. It's good to be back in the saddle."

"Good." He hesitated. "Aydan... I just want you to know how much I appreciate all you've done. You're a great partner. A trained agent couldn't do better." He gave the last sentence a meaningful intonation, which I chose to ignore.

"Thanks." I left it at that.

I felt him watching me. "Don't you ever let your guard down?"

I shrugged. "Do you?"

"Mmm." He gave me a crooked smile and we walked the rest of the way in silence.

Back at the camp, I went straight into the RV and began scrolling data. When a bowl of chili appeared at my elbow, I rubbed my tired eyes and gave Kane a grateful smile.

"Thanks." I slouched back in the bench seat with a sigh and started spooning in chili.

He slid in across from me. "How's it going?"

"Really damn slow. I'm only looking for the blond prisoner, but he doesn't have any distinguishing marks at all, so it's taking forever to look through all the possibilities. I've restricted the search to people who live in Calgary and surrounding area, but there are still tons of young blue-eyed blond guys. I'm so tired, I don't know if I'd even recognize him if I found him anyway."

He grimaced. "Welcome to the glamour of spy work."

"This is a huge waste of time! I don't see why we're doing this at all!" I rolled my aching shoulders, trying to ease the tension. "That poor guy is suffering..." I gulped as a spoonful of chili made a concerted effort to come up at the memory. A couple of hard swallows later, I continued, "... and he's running out of time. Can't we go over there tonight?"

Kane eyed me with sympathy. "I know how hard it is to wait, but the gas company made the appointment for eight o'clock tomorrow morning. We can't afford to blow our cover by rushing in."

"Why didn't you get them to pretend they found a gas leak so we could go in right away?" I demanded.

"Aydan, how would the gas company know there's a leak?" Kane asked patiently. "It's a private estate miles out of town. They wouldn't be just passing through to notice something like that. I'm sorry, I feel the same as you, but that's just the way this work goes sometimes."

Some time later, sounds from outside made me jerk my

head up. I peeked cautiously out the window and relaxed when I identified their source. Rationalizing that it was time for a break anyway, I hovered a safe distance away from the window so I could enjoy the show outside without getting caught.

Kane and Germain were both stripped down to shorts, sparring in the mellow light of the evening sun. I gawked unabashedly, appreciating their obvious skill almost as much as their sweat-sheened muscles. Kane might be off-limits, but I could still enjoy the view. And Germain was definitely easy on the eyes, too. At least I'd get some compensation for this rotten job.

By the time I surfaced from the database a second time, the shadows had accumulated in the corners of the RV and the windows were dark squares. Kane and Germain had come in to escape the mosquitoes, and they looked up from their quiet card game as I straightened slowly, groaning.

"Still no luck?" Germain asked.

"No. I finished looking through the locals hours ago, and now I'm looking at guys from all of western Canada. I still haven't found him."

"Let it go, then," Kane advised. "You're probably too tired now anyway. Get some sleep. Germain and I will cover the watches tonight."

"I'll take a watch," I protested. "You guys need rest, too."

After a short argument, Kane conceded, and I drew the last watch. I might as well have stayed up all night. I tossed and turned, and it was a relief when I finally left the bed to spell off Germain.

My shift dragged on interminably, and by the time the men awoke in the morning, butterflies were performing tight-formation aerobatics in my stomach. I knew our plan was sound, in theory. But I wasn't looking forward to the execution of it.

CHAPTER 38

"All right," Kane summarized as I finished my breakfast. "We'll have exactly two hours if all goes well. If anything goes wrong, we'll signal an abort and regroup at base camp. Aydan will go in to view active sims and read documents only." He gave me a severe look, and I nodded, suitably chastened.

Germain looked at his watch. "Time to go. Let's do it."

I balanced awkwardly inside the cardboard box as the van slowed and cornered. We stopped, and I heard the murmur of voices at the gatehouse. I breathed a quiet sigh of relief when forward motion resumed.

I hunkered down in my box while the van wound around several curves. Then movement halted and the engine stopped. I heard Germain get out of the driver's seat. A few seconds later, the rear doors clicked open.

"All clear," he muttered. I heard him pick up his toolbox, and then the back doors slammed. His cheery whistle receded from the van, and Kane and I uncurled from our boxes, stretching.

"Are you all right?" Kane inquired, indicating the box I'd just vacated.

I pushed the box aside. "Yeah, I'm fine. I knew I could get out of the box any time, so it didn't bother me. If I'd been trapped in there, it would've been a whole different story."

Kane eyed me dubiously in the dimness.

"Are you sure about this?"

I lay down on the floor before I could change my mind. "Let's just do it."

He knelt at my feet and gently tied my ankles together. I breathed slowly and deeply, staying calm. I tensed when he took my hands in his, and he clasped them between his palms.

"Aydan, this is stupid," he said softly. "You don't have to do this. You're shaking like a leaf."

"Just do it," I ground out.

He reluctantly reached for the tie. As it snugged around my wrists, I squeaked, "Stop!"

His knife was instantly in his hand, reaching to cut the tie, but I pulled my wrists away. "No, it's okay." I took a deep breath. "I can do this. Just... just... if you could reach into the front pocket of my waist pouch and give me my folding knife to hold. That would help."

He unzipped the pocket and placed the sturdy knife in my hand. I clutched it like a lifeline and took another deep breath. "Okay, I'm going in."

I concentrated and stepped into the white void of the network, where I swung my invisible arms wildly, trying to shake off the claustrophobia. After a few deep breaths, I calmed down enough to think rationally. I was safe. Kane would protect me. He would cut me loose at the first sign of trouble. And I had my knife. Just in case. I breathed some more before heading for the file repository.

I located and opened the file that had caught my attention the previous day. Sure enough, it contained a list of names and dollar amounts. Damn, I could use Hellhound's photographic memory now. I tried to memorize the names, but they wouldn't stay in my head.

I blew out an irritated breath. An idea struck me, and I read off the first few names, repeating them to myself while I closed the file and stepped carefully out the portal.

I tried to jerk my hands over my aching head, but they wouldn't move. I hissed wordlessly through clenched teeth until the pain receded enough for me to open my eyes. Kane held my bound wrists as he stared down at me in concern.

"It's okay," I whispered. "Got some names for you. They won't stay in my brain. Have to write them down."

He quickly let go of my hands and extracted a notebook and pen from the clutter in the back of the van. "Shoot."

I recited the names, and then ducked back into the network for the next batch.

I struggled against the heavy weight. Pain drilled through my eye sockets while I fought to escape. Inarticulate cries strangled in my throat. When I finally pried my eyes open, Kane lay half on top of me, pinning my arms with his weight while he held my head in an iron grip, his hand pressed over my mouth.

I blinked painfully, and his grip loosened.

"Jesus, Aydan, you have to stop now! You were trying to batter your brains out on the floor. And you're getting louder every time."

"Rella Industries," I croaked. "Sumner, Brian;

Telemetrix Solutions; Tatum, Gerald; Verge Systems; Wexner, Ralph; Williams, Alex."

He scribbled down the names while I panted and tried not to whimper. I pawed at my head with my bound hands, trying to rub away the pain. Kane laid aside the notebook to lift my head and shoulders into his lap. His strong, warm hands firmly massaged my temples and the back of my head and neck. I couldn't suppress a pathetic moan as my muscles relaxed.

"How much time have we got left?" I whispered.

He cradled my head in one large hand while he checked his watch. "An hour and a quarter."

"Good. That was only the first file. I've got a long way to go."

"Take a break," he urged. "It's getting worse every time you come out. Even with you tied up and me holding you down, you're still shaking the whole van. And that's just your normal exit. I don't know what would happen if you actually got kicked out of the network."

"It's only bad because I'm going in and out so often. I hope I won't have to come out so frequently once I get into the rest of the files," I reassured him. "That list was just too good to pass up."

"All right," he agreed doubtfully. "But I'm going to shut this down if it gets any worse. You could be damaging your brain doing this, for all we know. And you'll definitely damage your brain if you keep banging your head against the floor. Try to stop doing that."

"Good advice," I agreed wryly. "Thanks for that."

He blew out a frustrated breath. "You know what I meant."

"Yeah." I sighed. "I'm going back in."

I stepped into the void again. Back in the file repository, I discovered that the files tended to be grouped in clumps around specific dates. I skimmed through the most recent ones first. My excitement built as I read. Fuzzy Bunny ran a tight ship, indeed. And a well-documented one. I froze as an idea hit me.

Dropping the current records, I went back in time to the previous cluster of records, around March. My mouth fell open at the records of their secret tests of the brainwave-driven network. Coldness crawled down my backbone when I read the detailed information about me. Thank God, the file that contained my information still said 'Deceased'.

I eyed the other clusters of files, dating back sporadically several years. My pulse raced. This was gold. My God, if Kane had this information...

A new thought struck me. Who else had this information? They had to be sharing files internally, if the Silverside operation was documented on these servers. Where else was it stored?

I hovered in the file repository while my brain grudgingly unearthed my outdated computer knowledge. Did they have backups? How were they synchronizing data?

Without conscious thought, I burrowed into the operating systems, watching services running and snooping on automated tasks. I caught my breath when I ran across the synchronization routine. It was scheduled to run every night at one A.M., but it could be manually activated as well.

I stretched my insubstantial body down the virtual data tunnels used by the synch routine. The data was being synchronized at six other sites. I snapped back into myself, trembling with excitement. At least six other servers. And I could get to them all.

Triumph filled me when I realized I could give Spider the IP addresses. His über-geek skills would let him pinpoint the locations of the data centres. This could deal a deadly blow to Fuzzy Bunny.

I was about to step back out the portal and deliver the good news to Kane when a newly-created file caught my eye. It had appeared in the system within the last several minutes, and it was still being edited by the user.

I surveyed it cautiously. Maybe I could overcome the file locking and peek at a read-only copy. Ever so carefully, I opened the file.

Panic drove through me.

My heart tried to pound its way out of my chest as I dove back into the services and destroyed the synchronization routine. There was a chance nobody would notice until the next morning when they discovered that it hadn't run. Unless they tried a manual synch...

Adrenaline burned my veins as I flew back to the sim rooms, hoping against desperate hope that I was wrong. My heart stopped when I peeked into an occupied room.

Somebody whimpered, "No, no, no," as I jerked to a halt outside the portal to carefully step through.

It sounded a lot like me.

CHAPTER 39

Back into my pain-wracked body. Terror intensified the agony. I fought impotently against the crushing weight. Screams and curses choked behind my clenched teeth. I failed utterly to control the impulse to beat my raging headache against the nearest hard surface.

I gradually became conscious of Kane sprawling completely on top of me. His legs pinned mine to the floor while his elbows dug into my shoulders, his hands clenched around my head and bruising my lips. Involuntary tears streamed into my hair from under my screwed-shut eyelids.

I tasted blood. My eyes wouldn't open fully despite my best efforts. Kane's weight suddenly lifted, accompanied by a cacophony of noise. Barely in control, I jerked into a ball, gulping air. I realized I was still sobbing, "No, no," like a broken record.

Hands on my shoulders, and an urgent male voice. "Ma'am, it's okay. You're safe now."

Oh, no. Not again.

I let out a wail of despair and let the sobs rack my body as I squinted between my eyelashes, adrenaline pumping while I tried to figure out what was happening.

A uniformed security guard knelt beside me. I heard scuffling and a couple of heavy thuds from outside the rear doors, and then Germain spoke.

"You might not want to rough him up too much. Cops might wonder."

An angry male voice responded. "So there was a struggle when we apprehended him. So what." There was another thud and a grunt that sounded like Kane. "We caught this asshole yesterday and he must've gotten away from the police. Did you see what he did to that poor woman?"

"No." Germain's broad shoulders blocked the light as he looked in the open door. "My God!"

He stepped up into the van and pushed the guard away. "I have first aid training. Let me look at her. And cut her loose, for God's sake." He gently lifted the tear-matted hair away from my face.

"Ma'am, are you all right?" he asked. "Can you speak?"

I opened my eyes and let one eyelid drop in a wink while I sobbed and trembled. The corner of Germain's mouth quirked in an almost imperceptible response.

"I think she's okay," Germain called. "Just hysterical. And it looks like she might have had a nosebleed."

"Maybe." The voice outside the door registered satisfaction. "But maybe it's his blood. She bit him pretty good."

Oops. I was going to owe Kane for that one. Assuming we got out of this in one piece.

"Police are on the way," continued the disembodied voice.

"Good," Germain said. He sat cross-legged on the floor beside me and took my hand. "I don't know anything about being a security guard, but I can sit with her until she's calmer," he said to the guard. "I'll let you do your job and watch that lowlife outside."

"Thanks." The guard stepped out of the van and more scuffling ensued, but it didn't sound as though Kane was being seriously injured.

I quickly stuffed my knife back into my waist pouch as Germain leaned close and whispered, "What happened? Did you get kicked out of the network again?"

"No. Carl, listen, you have to get out of here ASAP and go to Plan B."

He frowned down at me. "That's only to be implemented if you're captured."

"I'm staying. Tell Stemp I'm captured. Please!" I bit off my explanation as the young guard stepped into the van again.

"We can bring her out now," the guard said. "We've brought a car around, and we'll take her up to the house where we can take better care of her until the ambulance arrives."

Germain nodded, still frowning at me. "Okay. I'll help you."

I struggled theatrically to sit up. "I... I'm okay, I think," I stammered as pathetically as I could manage. "I don't need an ambulance. I was just... so scared..."

"That's okay. Just take it slowly," the young guard comforted as he and Germain helped me to my feet. I leaned heavily on them and tottered out into the sunlight.

I sank down to sit at the end of the van. "I just... need a minute," I breathed, and slumped against Germain while I surveyed the situation. Kane was spread-eagled face down on the asphalt, but the only visible damage was the bite mark on his hand. That didn't look too serious. At least I hadn't taken a chunk out.

I drew in a trembling breath. If we were very, very lucky, the police might arrive before the guards decided to take Kane up to the house. I was intensely aware of the passage of time. I wasn't faking my unsteady breathing and shaking body. I needed Germain to get out of there, fast. And I desperately needed to get into the network again.

I stood carefully, and the two men ushered me to the waiting car. I sank into the seat and turned to Germain. "Thank you for all your help. I'm sorry if I made you late for your next appointment. He just... he just dragged me in there..." I faked another sob.

"Ma'am, it's no trouble at all. I hope you'll be okay." He straightened. "I have to get going, I'm late," he said to the guard. "Here's my card, in case the police need to talk to me."

The guard thanked him and took the proffered card. I breathed a silent sigh of relief when Germain's van disappeared down the driveway. One safe. Two to go.

CHAPTER 40

As the car wound up the driveway toward the house, I turned to the young guard. "Please... please don't bring him up to the house. I... don't think I can stand to be in the same room with him."

"We'll keep him down there," he reassured me. "But you need to stay and talk to the police this time."

"I'm sorry," I sniffled. "It was such a stupid mistake, but I was so... so scared, I just wanted to get away. And then he found me again..."

I shuddered and wrapped my arms around my body, trying to look pitiful. Tricky when I was as tall as the guard himself.

"It's okay," he soothed. "You're safe now."

I shrank into the seat and made myself as small as possible. At the house, I turned to him imploringly. "May I use the powder room again, please? I need to wash." I gave him the big brown eyes and let my voice quaver a bit, and he ushered me solicitously to the door.

"Take as long as you need," he said gently.

Perfect. I closed myself into the room and sat immediately on the toilet. In an instant, I was inside the network.

I shot into the operating system and checked the synch routine. Still dead. Thank God. I flew back to the sim rooms.

I slowed as I approached, afraid to look inside. I took a deep breath and prepared myself as best I could. Relief washed over me at the sight of the burly, tattooed figure still seated in the chair.

Fear rushed in to take its place when I drifted through the wall and saw the blood spattered on the floor. His back was to me, and I darted frantically overhead to see his face.

My stomach tried to turn inside out, and I clamped an invisible hand over my mouth. Hellhound sat tied to the chair, motionless, staring straight ahead. Other than a shallow gash on his forehead, he was completely uninjured. Except for his hands.

My guts wrenched again, and I gulped back bile. I could only imagine the horror of a musician threatened with the loss of his hands. The other torturers had been callously brutal, but this focused destruction was the work of the same sadistic and merciless monster who'd tortured the blond man. One who had taken the time to discover his victim's most devastating fear.

The sight of Arnie's broken, mangled fingers burned into my brain. The ends of the severed tendons protruded obscenely from their surgically precise incisions. Those hands would never play the guitar again. Nor even perform the simplest task. I swallowed hard once more, barely able to deal with the desecration.

Thank God, thank God, it was only a sim. So far.

I drifted silently behind him and threw my voice close to his ear, barely whispering. "Arnie, don't respond. It's Aydan. This isn't real. Your hands aren't hurt in real life.

It's not real, I promise."

His body jerked, but his knotted shoulders eased a fraction, and I knew he'd heard and understood.

I had to relieve his obvious agony, but I couldn't think how. I wanted to touch him, but that would reveal more about the sim than I dared.

I whispered again. "I'm going to take away your pain now. In five seconds, it will go away. You'll still look injured, but it won't hurt. Don't say anything."

"Five, four, three, two, one," I counted softly. He made a harsh sound as his shoulders slumped. Then he straightened into silent immobility again.

"We're going to get you out. Just try..." I gulped. "Just try to hang on. It's not real. It's not real, I promise. I have to go. I'll be back as soon as I can."

I seeped through the wall again and stepped carefully through the portal.

I fell to my knees in front of the toilet, sobbing and vomiting. Spasms racked my body while I clutched the toilet seat. My stomach heaved again and again until there was nothing left inside me.

The door rattled under a barrage of knocks, and the young guard's urgent voice shouted, "Ma'am, are you okay? Ma'am?"

"I'm okay." My voice felt like broken glass in my throat. I swallowed another dry heave. "Just sick to my stomach. I'll be okay in a minute."

"Do you want me to come in?"

"No. Thanks." I slumped to the floor, still embracing the toilet bowl. I forced myself into yoga belly breathing. In. Out. Slow and steady.

Desperate compulsion drove me to my feet. I lurched to

the sink and regarded my bone-white face. My tears had tracked through the smears of Kane's blood, and the effect was unflattering to say the least. Jesus, pull it together. No time to be a wimp.

Another knock sounded at the door. "Ma'am, the police are here. A female officer is coming in."

The lock sprang, and a uniformed woman stepped through the door. She took one look at me clinging to the sink, and stepped hurriedly to my side.

"Sit." She guided me firmly back and sat me on the toilet, pushing my head down between my knees.

"Just breathe." She rubbed my back slowly and soothingly. "It's all right. You're safe now."

I couldn't suppress the despairing laugh that came out sounding like a sob. If only.

No time for that.

I pushed myself up with my hands on my knees. "The man from the parking lot. Is he..."

"We have him in custody," she assured me.

"Thank God." I slumped in relief. Kane was safe. One to go.

"I promise he won't hurt you again," she said. "Can you tell me what happened?"

"Could you please close the door?" I asked.

"Of course." She got up and swung the door shut.

I sighed. This was going to get complicated. And I didn't have time to spare.

I straightened up and looked her in the eye. "I need to tell you something in strictest confidence."

"You can tell me anything at all," she soothed.

"The man from the parking lot. His name is John Kane. He's an undercover police officer. He spoke with some of your officers yesterday. He's my partner. It's essential that everyone here thinks that he attacked me."

Her face hardened with suspicion. Shit, I knew this was going to get complicated.

"Please go and talk to him. He can give you more information, and refer you up his chain of command if necessary," I pleaded.

"You're serious?" she demanded.

"Deadly serious. We are in the middle of a time-critical operation. I need you to pretend to arrest him and take him away. He'll be able to take over our operation externally. I need to stay here. Talk to him. Please!" I gazed at her imploringly.

"But..." She studied me. "You're in no shape..."

"Please! Hurry! Don't let anyone hear you talking to him," I begged.

"This is the weirdest... Okay," she said. "You stay here until I get back. And I mean that. I will charge you with resisting arrest if you don't."

"Okay. Thank you. Hurry!" I urged.

She stepped reluctantly out the door and closed it behind her.

Unable to sit still, I went to the sink and washed my face. Then I sat down on the toilet again and vibrated with nerves. My mind raced, turning over panicky ideas. Time was slipping away. As I looked at my watch for the umpteenth time, an appalling thought drove through my brain.

What if they had tortured the secret of the watch out of Hellhound?

I snatched it off and began to root through the contents of my waist pouch.

Several minutes later, there was a tap at the door.

"Ma'am, may I come in?" A female voice. Finally.

"Yes."

The female police officer slipped through the door and closed it again behind her. She frowned down at me. "We've verified your story. I passed your message on to your partner. He says you need to come with us, too. He was adamant."

"He's missing a critical piece of information. I have to stay here. And I need him on the outside." I rummaged in my waist pouch and extracted a pen and a scrap of paper. "Please tell him I'm staying, no negotiation. And get him out of here immediately. Cuff him and drag him out if necessary. And please give him this."

I scribbled on the paper. 'Op blown. Hellhound captured. Go to Plan B. Bring Spider ASAP.'

I knew they wouldn't implement Plan B just to retrieve Arnie. But they'd sure as hell implement it if I was still in here with the network key.

CHAPTER 41

I glanced blindly at my watch again, wondering how long it would take for the reinforcements to show up. The policewoman had left, presumably taking Kane with her. He should be safely off the premises by now.

I ducked compulsively into the network again, checking the dead synch routine. I breathed a sigh of relief when I found it just the way I'd left it. A quick check into the sims revealed that Hellhound was still alone, and I resisted the impulse to go to him again. I couldn't help him any more than I had already, and I didn't dare spend any additional time in the network without knowing what was happening to my physical body.

Back through the portal. I thrashed as silently as possible on the bathroom floor. I'd taken the precaution of lying down this time, and at least I didn't throw up again.

I staggered to my feet and dabbed the involuntary tears from my eyes. I needed to find out where Arnie was being held. I ran my brush through my hair and stepped out into the hallway.

Maria was waiting outside along with the young guard. Her expression crumbled with sympathy when she saw me. "You poor thing!" she exclaimed. "What a horrible experience. Would you like to lie down in the guest house for a while?"

I was surprised she was being cordial after catching me with her husband, but clearly I'd misjudged her. And the guest house was exactly where I wanted to be. That was where Kane had been held. Maybe Arnie was there, too.

"Thank you," I quavered. "That would be wonderful."

Maria and the young guard ushered me slowly down to the guest house. "She just needs to lie down for a while," Maria assured the doorman. He nodded and held the door, concern written on his face.

They guided me into one of the guest rooms, and I recognized the man I'd seen in the security sim as he stood outside one of the other rooms. That had to be where Hellhound was. It was the only guarded room.

Inside the luxurious chamber, Maria dismissed the young guard. "Go ahead and lie down," she encouraged kindly.

I lowered myself to the bed, and she smoothed my hair away from my face and spread a blanket over me. I closed my eyes, feigning exhaustion and watching through the crack in my lashes.

"Just rest," she whispered as she vanished.

Vanished?

Oh, *shit*!

I slipped my hand under the pillow, concentrating on making it insubstantial. My hand slipped through the bed like mist.

She'd put me into a sim.

Heart hammering, I created a construct of myself to occupy the bed and whisked invisibly through the wall of the sim. I stepped out the portal and back into my physical body, bracing for the pain.

It didn't come.

I breathed a slow sigh when I realized she must have attached one of the re-engineered fobs to me when she brushed my hair back. Nice to avoid the pain.

Sudden adrenaline jolted through me when I realized I'd just made two deadly errors.

One was trusting Maria. Obviously.

The other was leaving the sim. With nobody else present in the sim to maintain it with their expectations, my construct had vanished at the same time I left.

I peered frantically through my lashes and realized Maria had left the physical room. I leaped to my feet and peeked out the door in time to see her vanish into the guarded room across the hall. I flung myself back onto the bed, and back into the sim.

Please God, don't let them notice I'd been gone.

Maria tapped on the simulated door and came in. "Just before you rest, there's something I need to show you," she said as she took my arm and pulled me to my feet.

"Can't I just rest for a minute?" I begged. "I'm exhausted."

"Soon," she promised as she towed me out into the hallway. When we approached the other guest room, I looked into the guard's wooden face and brushed against him. I'd imagined my arm insubstantial, and as I'd expected, it went right through him.

A construct. Good.

I knew what I'd see when she opened the door, but the sight of Arnie's maimed hands made me gag again anyway.

Maria remained expressionless.

"Oh, my God!" I choked. "What have you done to this

poor man?" Hellhound's eyes widened as his head snapped around.

"Don't pretend you don't know him," Maria said. She pressed a button on the computer in the corner, and the screen lit up to show footage of Arnie and me cuddled together at the side of the road. Maria's lips twisted into a sardonic smile while she watched us fondling each other.

"Now," she said as she pointed a small snub-nosed revolver at my head. "One of you is going to tell me what I want to know. Move."

She herded me to a chair and I sat with a sense of inevitability while she bound my arms and legs to it. Hellhound hadn't spoken, but his eyes were anguished as he watched.

Maria leaned casually on my shoulder. "Your lover here has been very unhelpful. He hasn't said a single word."

I shuddered at what it had cost him to remain silent, and she smiled again. "So I think I'll kill two birds with one stone. So to speak. Since he's so resistant to my persuasion, we'll see how you do." She turned a malevolent smile on Arnie. "And he can watch."

"No," Arnie croaked.

Her smile turned predatory. "He speaks," she cooed. "How nice." She stepped closer to him. "What would you like to tell me?"

Hellhound's tense shoulders squared. "Let her go, and I'll tell ya what ya wanna know. But ya harm one hair on her head, and I'll never tell ya."

"Oh, you'll tell me anyway," she said silkily.

"This ain't my first dance, lady," Hellhound rasped. "Let her go free, and ya get your information. Otherwise, nothin'. It's the only deal you're gonna get."

Maria picked up a butterfly knife from the table and expertly one-handed it open in a blur of movement. She stepped around behind me, and I resisted the urge to twist around in my seat to keep her in sight.

She ran her fingers through my hair and pulled it back into a ponytail. "Not a hair on her head, you say?"

"Not if ya want what I know."

A sudden movement behind me, and my head jerked. Maria held up the rope of my severed hair tauntingly between us. "Oops." She flung the bundle of hair on the floor.

Hellhound's shoulders turned to stone, his face shutting down except for the rippling muscles in his jaw. He stared straight ahead, and I shuddered again.

"She's not so attractive now, is she?" Maria inquired. "She's going to be a lot less attractive when I'm done. Is there anything you want to tell me?"

Enough was enough. I filled a construct in my place in the chair as I flitted invisibly up to the ceiling. I threw my voice down to Arnie's ear. "It's not real," I whispered. "Remember, it's not real."

The construct screamed as the knife began its work.

Time crept by while the construct that looked like me sobbed and begged hysterically between gut-wrenching screams. Blood slicked the floor and Maria's hands.

Arnie's tormented eyes burned across the room while I whispered denial in his ear. He hadn't moved or spoken. His rigid muscles vibrated finely, like steel cables stretched past their limit.

Finally, Maria snapped the knife shut and glared at Arnie. "You're a heartless bastard. Fine. Maybe you think this isn't real. Here's another option."

She drew her revolver and pointed it at the construct's hanging head. "If I kill her here, she'll die in real life. An unexplained heart attack. So sad." She cocked the hammer. "Say goodbye."

Hellhound's impassive expression changed to horror, and I knew he'd suddenly made the connection with the earlier captives' heart attacks. My mind raced furiously. If she killed me in the sim, she'd expect me to be dead in real life. When she went to retrieve my body, she'd find me alive. Maybe I could overpower her?

"No!" Hellhound's hoarse voice interrupted my thoughts. He gazed at the mutilated construct. "It ain't worth it, darlin'," he grated. "I'm sorry."

"Arnie, don't!" The construct and I spoke simultaneously, one in his ear and the other across the room.

"It's in her watch," he said roughly. "Don't kill her."

"Thank you." Maria smiled. And pulled the trigger.

"NO!" Hellhound's raw-throated bellow almost drowned out the sound of the shot. The construct's ravaged body went limp. I sprang for the portal.

I popped into my body painlessly and muttered a three-word prayer as I fumbled the watch off my wrist. Maria had to leave the network, exit Hellhound's room, and walk across to mine. I had seconds to spare.

I yanked the watch free and pried off the backing as footsteps sounded in the hallway. I had barely enough time to drop the eviscerated watch beside me on the bed and resume my position. Maria came briskly into the room while I held my breath and watched through my lashes.

She froze at the sight of the open wristwatch. "Goddammit!" She wheeled and dashed out of the room. I heard her shout in the hallway. "Someone's here! Search everything! Go, go!"

I heard running feet, followed by silence.

I rolled off the bed and peeked shakily out the door. The hallway was abandoned, and I dashed across the open space into Hellhound's room. I locked the door from the inside and shoved a dresser in front of it. Where the hell was Plan B? What if they weren't coming?

I shook myself. It didn't matter. One way or another, we had to get out. Our cover was completely destroyed.

I approached Arnie's chair carefully. I didn't quite know how to handle this. I knew first-hand how difficult it was to deal with the disorientation in the first few minutes after leaving such a horrible sim. Worse still, he didn't even know it was a sim. And I couldn't explain.

I braced myself and pulled the tiny electronic device off the back of his neck. His eyes snapped open, unfocused. He glanced at me, and then turned to stare straight ahead again. I took his face in my hands and looked into his haunted eyes.

"Arnie," I said softly. "It's over. This is real. It's okay."

He didn't respond, and I stroked his face and kissed him. "This is real. I need you to wake up and be with me now. We're not safe yet. We need to get away."

He slowly pulled away from my grasp and looked down at his undamaged hands, his face like iron. His fingers moved, and his shoulders bunched and then released. When he looked up at me, his face was still hard, his eyes remote.

"If it's really you, why'm I still tied up?"

"I'm sorry, I'll cut you loose. I was afraid you'd freak out." I pulled out my knife and freed his legs. When the blade approached his hand, he stiffened almost imperceptibly, and I moved slowly and carefully to cut the tie. Then I reversed the knife and placed the handle gently in his free hand. I wouldn't make him suffer that fear again.

He cut the remaining tie and stood slowly, still expressionless. Then he suddenly grabbed my wrist, spinning me around and wrenching my arm up behind me. The razor edge of the knife pressed hard against my throat. I froze.

"Arnie, please don't kill me. This is real life. If you kill me now, I'll die for real."

I hoped my hammering pulse wouldn't cut my own throat against the blade. Why the hell did I keep my knives so sharp?

"You're already dead. I saw ya die."

"No! It was all a lie. It was all in your head."

"Prove it. Tell me somethin' nobody would know but you."

I panted shallowly, up on my tiptoes to ease the pain in my shoulder. "You have a cat. His name is John Lee Hooker. You feed him IAMS. His dish is by the fridge. You keep the cat food in the cupboard under the sink."

He yanked my arm, making me cry out. "Ya fuckin'... sick... bitch!" His voice was a savage snarl as the knife pressed harder. "I oughta slit your fuckin' throat just for that alone!"

"No, no, Arnie!" I gasped wildly. "I'm sorry..." Cold fear pierced my heart. "Arnie, did something happen to Hooker?"

"You tell me." I could feel the strain vibrating through his muscles.

A small sob of pain and desperation escaped me. I tried again.

"Back in March, you wrote a song for me. You sang it at Blue Eddy's and embarrassed the hell out of me. Our first night together, we went out for sushi. You promised me seven orgasms. But you lied. It was more than that..."

His grip relaxed and the pressure of the knife eased. I sank gratefully down from my tiptoes.

"I didn't lie," he said softly. "I said, 'or more'."

"You and your photographic memory," I teased weakly. "And a couple of nights ago, you gave me the most amazing moustache ride. And you promised I had something to look forward to. I still want to collect on that, you know."

He dropped the knife and pulled me into a hard embrace. "Aydan. I'm sorry, darlin'," he whispered roughly, his face buried in my hair.

"It's okay. It's okay." I clung to him, loving the feel of his hands on me.

He pulled away to look at me. "How're ya still alive? Those other guys, the prisoners. They died."

"Yes. They died. This was different."

"Because of that thing you're carryin'?"

"Kind of. I can't explain. Arnie... what happened to Hooker?"

He swallowed. "I dunno. These assholes were layin' for me at my place. I dunno what they did to him..."

"Maybe he was hiding." I grasped at straws. "Maybe he got scared and hid."

Arnie's face twisted. "Hooker? That'd never happen. Ya know how friendly he was."

"Is," I said firmly. "If you didn't see him, he's probably okay. Cats can tell when people are dangerous. They know enough to stay away."

He passed a hand over his face. "We don't have time for this. Ya said we gotta get out. Where the hell are we?"

"Harchman's guest house." At long last, I heard the

welcome sound of a helicopter through the open window. "And the cavalry just arrived. Forget what I said about escaping. I need to go into the n... trance. Right now."

I threw myself on the bed. "Don't let anybody wake me until Kane or Germain tells you everything's secure."

"But..." Consternation filled his face. "Where's your watch? I don't have the signallin' thing. How can I wake ya up if I need to?"

I scooped up the knife from the floor and tossed it on the bed beside me. "Poke me. And stand back."

I flung myself into the network toward the operating system. If I was Fuzzy Bunny, I'd push my data to the backup sites and destroy all the local files the instant I realized I was under attack.

I shot through the virtual system, slamming ports shut and deflecting network messages as I went. Please, please...

Sure enough, someone was trying to activate the synch routine. I killed it again. I kicked the user out of the system, and locked down all user and administrator accesses.

Another automated routine sprang up, and I crushed it. I wove a solid ball of protection around the operating system and files, blocking all traffic. Nothing in, nothing out.

I hovered in the centre, extending feelers in all directions, searching for activity. For an unmeasurable time, I hung in the darkened void, watching and waiting.

CHAPTER 42

I clenched into a rigid ball of misery, my throat seared raw. Pain hammered my head and body while jagged colours spun around me. I realized I was still screaming, and I clamped my lips together. Gentle hands massaged my head. I gasped a shaky breath and slowly relaxed my rigid muscles. My eyes remained obstinately closed, tears streaming.

I groaned and tried to rub my eyes, but my arms wouldn't move. My eyes flew open blindly as I let out a frantic cry and started to struggle.

"Let her go." Kane's voice, but he didn't sound angry.

The grip on my arms released immediately. "Sorry, darlin'."

I turned my blurry gaze toward the sound and blinked until Hellhound swam into focus. "Sorry," he repeated. "We were just tryin' to keep ya from hurtin' yourself."

I relaxed when I realized what had happened. "Is everything secure?" I gasped.

"Yes." Kane's voice again, and I swivelled my pounding head to focus on him.

"Is Spider here?" I demanded.

"Not yet. He should be here in about half an hour."

"Shit! I need to go back in..."

Kane laid gentle fingers across my lips. "No, it's secure."

"But..."

"We pulled the plug. Completely."

"Oh. That explains..." I indicated the bed beneath me, its covers churned into wrinkled piles from my convulsive struggles.

"Yes." Kane frowned. "We didn't have a choice. We couldn't wake you. I have the signalling device, but you're not wearing your watch. How..." he trailed off, glancing at Hellhound.

"I had reason to believe the watch might be compromised," I said. "I relocated the technology."

"Where is it?" Kane demanded.

"Um... let's just say that if you were planning to signal me, you'd have to get really friendly."

"...oh. We'll have to relocate it again, then. Soon."

"That would be my preference." I struggled into a semblance of sitting position.

Arnie held my hand, looking pale and shaken. "Jesus Christ, Aydan, what was that?" he muttered.

I winced. "That was the worst-case scenario."

"It's worse than ya said."

"I told you I didn't have the necessary frame of reference."

"Jesus."

I squeezed his hand. "Don't worry, I'm okay." He probably hadn't needed to see that so soon after all the torture in the sim.

Germain poked his head in the door and addressed Kane. "Need you out here. We're still trying to sort out the prisoners." He regarded me with concern. "Are you okay?"

"Fine."

"I'll be there in a minute," Kane told him, and Germain nodded and withdrew.

I dragged myself to the edge of the bed and swung my feet onto the floor. My head swam.

When I opened my eyes, I was lying on the bed again. Kane frowned down at me. "Keep her there," he told Hellhound. "Sit on her if necessary."

"Ya got it."

Kane left, and I moved over. "Lie down," I told Arnie. "You look like hell."

"I don't dare, darlin'. Don't think I'd ever get up." He sat on the bed and leaned back against the headboard, stretching his legs out.

I reached to take his hand again. I held it and stroked his lean, strong fingers over and over, memorizing their wholeness.

When I woke, I was alone in the bed.

I jerked upright with a panicky gasp.

"Aydan, it's all right." Kane's soothing voice came from the chair in the corner.

"Where's Arnie?" My heart pounded wildly.

"He left about two seconds ago," Kane reassured me.

My hand flew to the still-warm spot on the bed. "Thank God." I collapsed back on the bed, recovering. "I thought for a second I'd dreamed it. I was afraid he was still in the sim. How long was I out?"

"Only about ten minutes. What happened here?" His voice developed an edge, and I could tell he was struggling to control it. "What the hell were you thinking, staying behind? When I specifically told you not to? Risking your life. Risking national security..." He snapped his mouth shut and skewered me with a look.

I didn't have the strength to summon up any defensive anger. I stared up at the ceiling and massaged my temples. "I was *protecting* national security," I said tiredly. "And you. You're welcome."

After a short silence, he spoke again, his voice even. "I'm sorry. What happened?"

My head throbbed slowly, and I sighed and spoke with my eyes closed. "We're in a lot more trouble than we knew. Or than I knew, anyway. Maybe you already knew."

Tension sprang into his voice. "How so?"

"This network was connected to six other sites. They were synchronizing data. There are complete records of their ops, going back several years."

"You're right, if there are six other sites, that's more trouble than I knew about, too," Kane said cautiously. "But why would you risk staying? You could have just come out of the network and left with Germain. Or with the police."

I hauled myself upright, scowling. "No, I couldn't."

"Why not? Because of Hellhound?"

"No. Well, yes, that was part of it, of course." I rubbed my aching head. "I told you they were synching data with six other sites. That I know of, anyway."

"Yes."

"It's an automated routine that runs once a day, but it can be run manually as well. And there's a failsafe, kind of a dead-man's switch. If an alert is triggered in the network, the synch automatically starts up and pushes data out. But it's a two-way street. The other sites can also pull data."

"And you discovered this, how?"

"Poking around in the network."

"I thought you said your computer skills were ancient."

"They are. If I had to go in through the standard

administrator interface, I'd be completely lost. But the guts of the system really haven't changed much. Once I'm inside, I just expect to be able to find what I'm looking for, and there it is."

"That's handy," Kane said sceptically.

"Yeah." I shot him a hard look, but he had his cop face on.

"Just as I was getting ready to leave the network, a new file appeared," I continued. "The user was still editing it. I peeked in. It contained a full data record of you, Hellhound, and me."

I heard the hiss as he drew in a breath through clenched teeth. "What do you mean by full data record?"

"I mean details about your cover as an energy consultant, about your work with INSET, about your ...other... work, your home, your office, your chain of command, Briggs and Stemp. Details about Arnie, and his home address. The fact that I'm still alive and suspected of being able to access the network by unknown means. All kinds of stuff. As far as I read. As I said, it was still being edited."

I met his eyes squarely. "I couldn't take a chance on letting that out to Fuzzy Bunny's entire organization. I had to disable the synch and block incoming requests. I had to make sure they didn't restart the routine. And I had to make sure you brought in the big guns to pick up everybody here, because I didn't know who the user was. But I didn't get a chance to tell you. The only way to make all of that happen was to stay."

A muscle rippled in his jaw as he processed that. "Thank you," he said quietly. "I should have known you'd have a good reason. I'm sorry for doubting you."

"It's okay. But I really need Spider the instant he gets here. While the system was up, we had a fabulous opportunity. I could sneak through the virtual data tunnels and get the IPs for the other sites. But the longer the system's down, the greater the chance that the other sites will realize something's wrong and lock us out."

Kane was dialling before I finished speaking. "Webb. Where are you? Good, the sooner the better. It's even more urgent than I originally thought."

He hung up. "Ten minutes, give or take." He hesitated. "You might want to relocate that key. We'll need to be able to signal you."

"Right." I rolled off the bed with a groan. "This could take a minute."

"Call me if you need help."

We eyed each other for a beat. Despite my still-pounding head, I couldn't hold back a wicked grin. "Really?"

A faint flush crept up his face. "That didn't come out quite the way I meant it."

"It's okay." I trudged for the bathroom.

CHAPTER 43

I carefully unwrapped the key from the scrap of plastic I'd used to protect it. The plastic buckled, and the miniscule circuitry bounced and skittered across the counter. My heart in my mouth, I slapped and batted at the tiny dot like a demented cat, trying to pin it down before it escaped completely. When I finally cornered it, I leaned heavily against the counter for a second, recovering from the panic.

Using the tweezers from my waist pouch, I held my breath and shakily tucked the circuitry back into my wristwatch before pressing on the backing again with a sigh of relief. As I emerged from the bathroom, Spider came in, gaping at the opulent decor.

"Wow," he breathed. "I didn't know people actually lived like this."

"This is just the guest house," I told him. "Wait'll you see the real house. Speaking of which." I grabbed his arm and hustled him toward the door. "You can gawk later. We've got to get back into this network ASAP."

I glanced over at Kane. "Are we clear to go up to the main house?"

"Yes. Everything's secure," he assured me. "I'll come with you, though, just in case."

"Thanks. I'll feel better knowing you've got our backs. I'm not sure how long we'll need to be in the network."

I briefed Spider while we walked up to the main house, observing the activity on the grounds with half my attention.

One helicopter sat in the middle of the cul-de-sac, another down by the lake. Armed men moved here and there over the entire property. As we entered the house, I caught a glimpse of rows of prisoners seated in the enormous dining room. I wondered absently how many of them were actually on Fuzzy Bunny's payroll, and how long it would take to sort them all out.

We wove our way through the labyrinth to the server room. Its door stood open, and two armed men straightened to attention at the sight of Kane.

He nodded to them. "I'll take over in here. Guard the door. Nobody comes through without my say-so."

The men took up positions on either side of the door in the hallway, and Kane swung the door shut. He regarded Spider and me. "So?"

I turned to Spider uncertainly. "I have no idea what I've really done. I locked everything down solid from inside, and it was still all dark and quiet when these guys pulled the plug and kicked me out. But I don't know what'll happen when we power it up again. And I can't go in until it's powered up."

"It's okay," he reassured me. "First things first. We'll physically disconnect it from the outside world so it can't transmit or receive any data. Then I'll power it up and shrink the broadcast range down to the size of this room. After that, you can work from the inside, and I'll work from the outside. We'll get it sorted out."

I sighed. "Thank God you're here. Let me know when

you need me."

He approached the consoles cautiously, and methodically traced the cables between servers and external connections. After several minutes of careful study, he disconnected some of the cables and sat down. The whirring of fans and beeping of electronic equipment ensued.

He typed rapidly for several minutes, utterly focused. Then the tempo of his typing picked up. The keystrokes got heavier as he leaned forward, his shoulders tensing. I shot an alarmed glance over to Kane's frowning face.

Spider punched in several key combinations with unnecessary force before throwing himself back in the chair, churning his hands in his hair. "I can't crack it. I'm locked out!"

"Shit! My fault! I locked it down!" I dropped to the floor where I stood, and lunged into the network's void. I rocketed along the virtual corridors, hyper-alert for any activity. What if someone was able to access the network interface and overcome my security?

To my relief, everything was still dark, and I hurried to the user access area. I was afraid to attempt anything else, so I quickly created and enabled an administrator ID for Spider and backed out of the network again.

I wrapped my arms over my head in an attempt to ward off the crushing pain, and croaked out the ID and password as soon as I could speak. Then I panted and rocked miserably until I was reasonably certain my brain wouldn't explode.

Kane sat down on the floor beside me and began to massage my head and neck. I flinched when his fingertips dug into the knotted muscles, and he stopped. "I'm sorry," he said contritely. "I thought this helped."

"It does," I groaned. "Don't stop."

He began again with gentle hands and I slumped forward, letting him gradually work out the pain and tension.

By the time I was able to look up, Spider was engrossed again, his posture telegraphing confidence. I sighed and rolled my shoulders. "Thanks."

"You're welcome."

Spider looked up from his work. "I'm ready for you in the network now."

I bit back the self-pitying whine that tried to escape. Something must have shown in my face, because he grimaced. "I'm so sorry. If there was another way..."

"I know. It's okay." I cracked my neck. "What do you need me to do, exactly?"

"Just go in and gradually undo whatever you did. I'll watch from here, and we can message back and forth so you don't have to come out again until we're done."

"Thank God for that." I ran my hands over my face, procrastinating, and then sighed. "Screw it."

I lay down on the floor. After all the kicking and screaming I'd done recently, dignity was nothing but a distant memory anyway. I stepped into the network and got started.

It took a lot longer to unravel the layers of protection than it had taken to create them. At long last, I spoke to Spider through the network interface. "Okay, that's the last of it. I think."

His voice came back reassuringly. "That looks fine from here. Now I have to hook up the external connections again. I need you to watch, and block absolutely everything, incoming and outgoing. Then I'll sort through it."

"Okay." I braced myself, trembling with nerves. I had a

feeling this was going to be like playing squash against dozens of opponents simultaneously. Or maybe like a video game.

I'd always sucked at video games.

I sighed and tried to let go of that unproductive thought.

True to my mental image, a barrage of squash balls hurtled at me seconds later. There was no way I could possibly respond quickly enough to block each of them. I did the only thing I could think of. I stretched my virtual body into an enormous net and took the beating.

Approximately an eternity later, Spider spoke again. "Okay. Let go now."

I collapsed to the virtual floor and lay still. There was no reason for me to feel so exhausted and battered. This was a sim. I should be able to feel pain-free and full of energy.

I tried.

I failed.

"Good," Spider's voice roused me. "Try the tunnels now."

I crept to my virtual hands and knees. The sim wavered around me. Hooker the cat padded toward me, his yellow eyes alight with intelligence, tail waving like a question mark. "Mow?" he inquired.

I shook my head vigorously and he vanished. Blood spattered the floor. I willed it away, forcing myself to concentrate. My brain dragged itself though a vat of viscous fluid. I reached into the vat and scooped it out, holding the rubbery organ in my hand.

Whoa, bad trip.

I shook myself again and the sim firmed around me. Stay focused. Just one more thing to do.

I couldn't summon up enough energy or concentration to

go down the tunnels simultaneously, so I selected one at random.

The slow attenuation of my virtual body smothered higher thought. I quested blindly through the tunnel like a mole on downers until my virtual nose thudded into a solid wall.

Trapped.

Enclosed in the tunnel as it shrank around me...

My panicked shriek echoed in the void as I snapped back.

"Aydan!" Spider's frantic voice boomed through the sim.

"I'm okay," I gasped. "Just a dead end on one of the tunnels."

I hyperventilated for a few seconds, trembling with the adrenaline pulsing through me. Well, that was one way to regain focus. The sim's detail was razor-sharp around me now.

I chose the next tunnel and went down it more easily. This one was open all the way, and I quickly made notes of the IP addresses as I passed through. Snapping back to the sim, I pushed the IPs to Spider, and headed for the next tunnel.

By the time I entered the last tunnel, I could barely hold the virtual image. The walls were ghostly while I pushed my leaden consciousness forward. The thump on my virtual nose at the end of the blocked tunnel was almost a relief. I was done. I slithered lethargically back into the sim and lay in a formless puddle.

Hellish nightmares swirled around me while I cowered in the void. I knew these things lived in my subconscious. I knew they were constructs of my own exhausted brain as I lost the ability to guide my conscious thought. I curled into a ball. The monsters fed greedily on my fearful cries.

A blip in the sim and a small stab of pain.

Kane.

Signalling me.

The portal was so far away.

I crept toward it, but the cage closed around me. Heavy bars contracted, crushing me. The last of my intellect fled as screams and blood spewed from my throat.

CHAPTER 44

I was still screaming. My flayed throat burned, and I clenched my teeth and panted silently instead. Agony raged through my head and body while dizzying colours swooped and spun.

The deafening noise in the background resolved itself into Kane's insistent voice, calling my name. Pain reverberated in my head, the pounding synchronized to my racing heartbeat. My eyes wouldn't open.

I didn't care.

Maybe he'd just go away.

He didn't.

Finally, I flailed one arm out blindly and croaked, "Stop."

His voice continued, urging and cajoling. Irritation flooded me. I summoned up the energy to open one eye. "Goddammit..."

"She's swearing. Thank God."

My eye tracked sluggishly to the source of the sound and slowly focused on Spider's frightened face hovering over me.

I groaned. "Somebody please... kill me."

I managed to pry open my other eye at the sound of Kane's relieved chuckle. "No such luck," he said.

I moaned when his hands found the red-hot knots in my

head and shoulders. For a long time, I lay inertly while he rubbed away the pain.

At last, I made an effort to sit up. The room turned slowly around me. I blinked muzzily at the two Kanes who were regarding me with concern. When I squeezed my eyes shut and reopened them, the twins were gone, and the single remaining Kane was frowning.

"What happened? Why were you screaming inside the sim? Why didn't you come out?"

I groaned. Too many questions.

"Aydan? What happened?"

"Too tired. Couldn't get out," I mumbled.

"Can you stand?"

I started to shake my head but desisted when the room spun vigorously. "Don't think so," I whispered. Sweat sprang out all over me as my stomach lurched. I closed my eyes to banish the vertigo.

"Webb, get the door."

The dizziness intensified as Kane picked me up without apparent effort and carried me out.

"Put me down," I murmured, my eyes still closed. "You'll hurt yourself."

He chuckled. "I don't think so. What do you weigh, anyway?"

"One-sixty."

"You're joking."

"No."

"Well, that's it. I can't carry you, then." His steady stride never faltered, and his voice betrayed no hint of effort.

"Just tell me if you're going to drop me."

"I'm dropping you now." My eyes flew open as he laid me gently on a sofa. "Kidding," he added.

"Funny," I muttered. I clutched my head with both hands as it attempted to float away. My impossibly heavy arms shook with the effort.

"What happened?" Hellhound's rasp was full of alarm.

"We couldn't wake her. We had to trigger the worst-case scenario again."

"Shit!" Arnie knelt beside the sofa, stroking his hand over my clammy forehead. He eyed my tremors with suspicion. "Aydan, when did ya eat last?"

"Um..."

"Seven o'clock this morning," Kane supplied.

"Shit! It's damn near four! And ya been makin' her do that trance thing? Ya know what that does to her!"

"Aydan, I'm sorry," Kane began, but he was interrupted by Germain's voice.

"Kane, we need you again."

"Go," Hellhound told him. He stroked my hair back from my face. "I'll find ya somethin', darlin'. I'll be right back."

"Thanks," I mumbled to empty air. I felt horridly vulnerable lying on the sofa, but it was all I could do to hold my eyes open. I hoped everything was truly as secure as Kane said.

Several minutes later, Arnie was back, carrying some oranges. "No juice, but these oughta do," he said. He sat on the floor beside the couch and peeled one of the oranges. As he fed it to me section by section, the dizziness and nausea gradually abated.

By the time I'd eaten the second orange, I felt strong enough to drag myself into sitting position. Hellhound hoisted himself up and sprawled beside me on the couch, laying his head against the back of the sofa and closing his eyes.

Deep grooves of pain and fatigue lined his face, and my heart squeezed with sympathy. His experiences in the sim alone would have been enough to bring most men to their knees. I knew he was grieving Hooker as well. I took his hand and stroked it, offering what little comfort I could.

His eyes opened, and he smiled at me. "Sure glad you're okay, darlin'."

"I'm glad you're okay, too." I leaned my head against his shoulder.

When I opened my eyes again, Kane was standing in front of us. He gazed down at me in concern. "Are you all right?"

I dragged myself up from my slumped position against Hellhound's shoulder. "Yeah. Arnie found me some food. I'm fine."

"Good." He frowned. "You know, you should get your blood sugar checked."

"I have. There's nothing wrong with me, I just have an ultra-fast metabolism. I'm fine most of the time, but when I have to really exert myself on an empty stomach, and especially if there's a lot of adrenaline in my system, I just run out of steam."

"All right," he said doubtfully. "Can you walk now?"

"Yeah, I should be fine." I stood up shakily and stretched. "All better."

Kane turned his gaze to Hellhound, taking in his strained, exhausted face. "What about you?"

"I'm good."

Kane reached a hand down, and they clasped each other's forearms as Kane pulled Arnie to his feet.

"We need to debrief back at the RV, and then you can

both head back to the city," Kane told us.

We followed him wordlessly out to the gas company van. Kane ushered me into the passenger seat while Hellhound climbed into the back.

"There's blood back here," he observed as he sat.

"Oh!" I turned to Kane. "I meant to tell you I'm sorry. How's your hand?"

He briefly surveyed the purpled bite mark. "Fine."

"Ya bit him?" Hellhound demanded.

"It was an accident."

"Kinky." Hellhound winked with a shade of his old ribald humour.

Kane glanced at him in the rear-view mirror. "What happened? How did you end up at Harchman's?"

Hellhound's expression darkened. "I made a coupla stops after I left base camp yesterday mornin'. Got back to my place a little after noon. I knew somethin' was wrong when Hooker didn't meet me at the door." He paused, and I knew he was composing himself.

"Coupla assholes hidin' inside my place," he continued levelly. "I got a coupla hits in, but they nailed me with a Taser an' shot me up with some shit. Knocked me out. Didn't know where the hell I was when I woke up, an' then that fuckin' bitch showed up with her goddamn knife. Dunno how long she worked on me. Long time, off an' on. Askin' where the key was, an' who I was workin' for. The key, that's the thing you're carryin'?"

I nodded, and he continued. "I didn't tell her dick-all. Dunno what I woulda done if ya hadn't told me about the mind thing earlier, though. It felt... real."

He went silent again.

"But then she dragged Aydan in. That was some ugly

shit," he added quietly. "An' I cracked. Sorry, Cap." He turned to me. "I thought ya were gonna die. I didn't know what else to do."

"It doesn't matter," I assured him. "I'm pretty sure we contained it. And you didn't tell them anything they didn't already know. Except for where the... um... technology was. And I'd moved it from there anyway."

He rubbed his hand over his face, looking old and tired. "Sorry."

"You've got nothing to be sorry for," Kane told him firmly. "Aydan and I both understand what you went through. Nobody could have done better."

"Thanks," Arnie said simply.

"What I want to know is why they came after you in the first place," Kane said.

"I can answer that," I told him. "They caught Arnie and me on camera at the road. You could see the plates on both the bikes in one of the views. They must have had access to the registries database, so they'd have gotten Arnie's name and home address. They'd also have been able to trace the Honda back to the dealership and find out that it was rented by Kane Consulting. And your cover was already blown. They would have jumped on anything to do with Kane Consulting."

"So we're all up shit creek," Hellhound said gloomily.

"No. I locked everything down," I told him. "I'm absolutely positive that information didn't go outside of the people who were at Harchman's."

I turned to Kane. "As long as you picked up everybody at Harchman's, we should be okay."

He nodded slowly. "It was a clean strike. We had everybody rounded up at the building site in a matter of minutes. The outlying guards took a little longer, but there wouldn't be any way that the information could have been communicated to them."

"So you're safe," I comforted Arnie. "We're all safe. Or at least as safe as we're likely to get, anyway."

Kane drove up to the RV, and we got out of the van. "Hellhound, why don't you go for a walk," Kane suggested. "I need to debrief with Aydan."

"Feed her first," Arnie grunted as he turned away.

We stepped into the RV, and Kane eyed me inquiringly. "What do you want to eat?"

"I'm really not hungry. I'll just snack." I reached into my backpack and pulled out an apple. I still felt a little queasy, and I couldn't face the thought of more canned chili or stew.

"All right." Kane wedged himself onto the bench of the dinette while I ran myself a glass of water. When I slid in opposite him, he pulled his notebook closer and fixed me with a steady gaze. "Tell me everything. Start to finish."

I blew out a long breath while I organized my thoughts. "After I finished giving you those names, I discovered groupings of files. I found records of their operation in March, and that's when I realized they were synching with other sites. I could trace the tunnels to six of them."

I sighed with irritation. "By the time I got in again with Spider, only two were still active. Piss me off."

"Don't knock it," Kane assured me. "If we can identify two sites, that's a tremendous accomplishment. And it's valuable just to know of the existence of the others."

"I guess. Oh!" I exclaimed as another thought hit me. "Did you get the prisoner out?"

"Yes. He was uninjured. Physically, anyway. No wonder

you couldn't find him when you searched the local database. He's an agent from the States who was undercover with Fuzzy Bunny, trying to track that arms deal. Stemp is going to come out of this looking like a hero for retrieving him."

I snorted. "Yeah. Mr. Wait-A-Little-Longer. He'd have been in deep shit if that agent had died."

"Probably not," Kane said seriously. "Undercover work is always dangerous, and that agent knew what he was getting into. I don't always agree with Stemp's approach, but he gets results. By waiting, he got the whole package, all nicely wrapped up."

I sipped some water, trying to soothe my abraded throat. "Yeah. At the expense of other people's suffering."

Kane didn't respond, and after another sip of water, I went on with my narrative. "Anyway, by the time I finished snooping around in the network, this other file had appeared with all our information in it, and I realized how screwed we'd be if that got sent out. And that's when I realized they had Hellhound, too. So I killed the synch routine and went back out of the network to warn you."

I eyed him quizzically as I crunched my apple. "How did we get busted?"

"Remember how I said you were rocking the whole van? One of the guards noticed. Harchman has some good people there. Usually those rent-a-cops are completely oblivious." Kane looked disgusted. "Wouldn't you know, we get the one that's on the ball. He made Germain open up the van."

"Just as I came out of the network kicking and screaming," I completed his sentence.

"And biting."

I winced. "Sorry."

"It's all right. So you were coming out to tell me what

was going on, but you couldn't because we were discovered."

"Yeah. So I told Germain to get out of there and go to Plan B. And I tried to convince the guard to hold you down at the parking lot. I was hoping the police would arrive and take you away before you got dragged up to the house and identified."

"Aydan," Kane said, sounding frustrated. "I'm supposed to be protecting you. Not the other way around."

"You've been protecting me since March," I told him. "Payback's a bitch."

Kane threw up his hands. "Since March, I've failed to protect you from being abducted, tortured, drugged, or manhandled by perverts. And as a special bonus, I've forced you to undergo intense pain on a regular basis and withheld food from you until you collapsed. With friends like me, you don't need enemies."

"Yeah, but it's been such fun."

He snorted. "What happened after you went up to the house?"

"The guard took me up to the house, and I hid in the bathroom and got into the network again. I checked to make sure the synch was still dead, and I went in to make sure Arnie knew it was a sim."

"You told him it was a sim?" Kane's voice was ominously expressionless, and I hastened to reassure him.

"No, no. I just reminded him that it was in his head, that it wasn't real." I swallowed hard. "Don't blame Arnie for telling them about the watch. You didn't see what they did. And he thinks they've killed Hooker, too." My voice wavered a bit, and I sipped some more water.

A spasm crossed Kane's face. "I wouldn't blame him. I don't know anybody who's as tough as Arnie. If he cracked, there's nobody in the world who wouldn't have."

I took a deep breath. "By the time I left Arnie the first time, I was... pretty shaken up. That's when the policewoman arrived. I'm sorry I couldn't give you a more detailed message. I was afraid to tell her anything."

"It's all right. I know now that you couldn't have done anything else."

"Thanks." I gave him a quick smile, relieved he agreed with me this time. "After I was sure you were gone, I went out of the bathroom and Maria was there. She was very kind, and she offered to let me lie down in the guest house. When I got there, I realized she'd dropped me into a sim. She's in deep with Fuzzy Bunny. She was the one who tortured Arnie. And probably the agent, it looked like the same kind of work. And me."

Kane sat forward, his face creasing with concern, and I held up a reassuring hand. "A construct of me. That's why I didn't die when she shot me inside the sim. Arnie was trying to save me by telling her about the watch. He had figured out how the other captives died, so he thought I would die, too."

"Well. He thought I was dead," I amended. "The construct took a bullet to the head, and I had to get out of the sim fast because I knew Maria would come straight to my body to get the watch. So I pried open the watch to make it look like somebody had beaten her to it, and she fell for it. You and the team arrived shortly afterward."

"How did you recover fast enough to deal with the watch?"

"Maria slapped a fob on me. It got me out painlessly. Which reminds me." I peeled it off the back of my neck and handed it to him. "Too bad it only seems to work for specific sims, not for general network access. I would have been happy to skip all the kicking and screaming."

"I wish you could have." Kane rubbed his hands over his face and stood up. "I have to get back to Harchman's. Now that I know how deeply Maria was involved, I'll want to question her personally. And I need to check in with Webb. Can you and Hellhound take the Honda back to Calgary? You can pick up your car, and drop him off at home. And you can go home, too."

"Sure, no problem." I got up, too. "I'll just get changed. Oh." I took off my watch and handed it to him. "You'd better take this." I picked up my backpack and headed for the bathroom.

Kane stopped me with an outstretched hand. "Thank you. For all you've done. I'll likely be in touch again soon with more questions."

"Okay. You know how to find me."

CHAPTER 45

By the time I stepped out of the RV in my leathers, Kane was gone and Hellhound was slouched in the folding chair with his eyes closed.

He jerked upright at the sound of the door. "Ya ready to ride, darlin'?"

I nodded, and he gave me a grin that did nothing to hide the bleakness in his eyes. "Seems to me, ya said once that the only way you'd double on a bike was if ya were drivin'. Ya wanna arm-wrestle for it?"

"Not a chance. I know I wouldn't win, and I wouldn't be safe to double us anyway. You can drive."

"Good. 'Cause I'm hatin' to hafta ride a Honda. 'Specially this pathetic little 750. If I hadta ride on the P-pad, too, my dick'd prob'ly just shrivel up an' fall off."

I laughed. "Can't have that. Let's go, macho man." I stopped. "Wait, what about your helmet?"

"It's back at home." He picked up Germain's full-face helmet and put it on. "This ain't as cool as my brain bucket, but at least it hides my face so nobody'll recognize me on this piece a' shit."

I laughed. "You're such a snob."

He chuckled and swung onto the seat, and I climbed on

behind him. I hooked my boot heels over the passenger pegs and groaned. "We might have to stop halfway there so I can stretch my legs. Why the hell do they think all passengers are five-foot-nothing?"

Hellhound reached back to run a hand down my leg. "Love those long legs of yours."

I wrapped my arms around him. "Let's get out of here."

We arrived at the bike dealership just in time to return the motorcycle before they closed for the day. I dismounted stiffly and limped around for a few minutes, trying to get my knees working while the dealer filled out the paperwork. When everything was duly signed, I gratefully sank into the driver's seat of my Saturn.

Arnie climbed cautiously into the passenger seat. "This ain't bad," he said. "Usually I can barely get into these little tin cans."

"Watch your mouth," I admonished. "Don't talk that way in front of my car. And besides, it's plastic, not tin."

He chuckled. "No offense. This is a fine car, darlin'."

I patted its dash. "Yeah, it is."

As I put the key in the ignition, Hellhound's stomach let out a horrendous growl. I turned to him, counting back hours. "Jesus, Arnie, when did you eat last?"

"Yesterday breakfast," he admitted. "But I don't need food the way you do," he added quickly at my look of horror.

"Yes, you do. Where do you want to go for supper? No argument," I added as he opened his mouth to protest.

He gave me a half-smile and leaned his head back, his eyes closing. "I don't care. Surprise me, darlin'."

By the time I pulled out into traffic, he was fast asleep.

I debated as I drove, and decided on a restaurant as close to his place as possible to prolong the drive. He'd been starving and in agony for a day and a half. At least he'd get nearly half an hour of sleep in the car.

I pulled into the parking lot and spoke his name quietly. He started violently, fists clenching.

"It's okay," I soothed. "We're at the restaurant, that's all."

He blew out a breath. "Shit, did I fall asleep?"

"Yeah. You needed it."

"Yeah." He rubbed a hand wearily over his face. Then he glanced up at the restaurant sign and turned to me with a slow smile. "Is this a hint, darlin'?"

"Maybe." I grinned back at him.

We got out of the car and went into the tiny sushi restaurant we'd visited in the spring. As before, the sushi chef greeted him warmly, and we took our usual seats, our backs to the wall.

We ate a leisurely meal, and I was glad to see some colour return to his face. We didn't talk much, but the silence was comfortable. As we sipped tea after the food, I reached for his hand.

"Do you want some company tonight?" I studied his face, trying to read him. "It's okay if you just want to be alone, though."

His fingers tightened on mine. "I'd like some company, darlin'," he said quietly. "Might feel kinda empty at my place tonight."

I squeezed his hand in sympathy. "Maybe he's hiding."

He said nothing, and we left the restaurant in silence.

When we arrived at his door, Arnie squared his shoulders as he pushed his key into the lock. His foot went automatically to the crack of the door as it swung open, but no furry face appeared. I put my arms around him, feeling his pain as if it was my own.

We were about to step into the apartment when a lock clicked behind us. We swung around, tensing reflexively.

A wizened face with birdlike black eyes regarded us through the crack of the neighbouring door.

"Arnold! Good heavens, young man, what have you done to yourself?" demanded a high, cracked voice. "You look like something the cat dragged in."

I winced inwardly at the unfortunate choice of words, but Arnie gave a tired smile. "Hi, Miz Lacey. I just got in a bit of a scrap. Nothin' to worry about."

"Didn't I warn you that you'd come to grief some day? All the music and drinking and fast women." The door didn't open any further, but the sharp black eyes raked him through the narrow gap. "Well?"

"Well, what, Miz Lacey?"

"Where are your manners, young man? Aren't you going to introduce us?"

"Miz Lacey," Hellhound said patiently. "I'd like you to meet Aydan Kelly. Aydan, this is Miz Emma Lacey."

"It's nice to meet you," I said.

"It's a pleasure to meet you, too," she replied. The eyes rose a couple of inches as she drew herself up proudly. "I'm a retired schoolteacher. I'll be eighty-nine years old in September. Arnold drives me to my appointments and takes me out to buy groceries. And I look after John Lee while Arnold is away."

A spasm of pain crossed Arnie's face, but his voice was even as he said, "It was nice talkin' to ya, Miz Lacey. We gotta be goin' now."

"Not so fast," she snapped. "I have something of yours. I'll give it back if you promise not to be so careless with it in the future."

Hellhound looked puzzled. "Sorry, Miz Lacey, what've ya got?"

"This." The door swung open, and a large, furry body darted into the hallway, bumping up against Arnie's legs and purring like a tractor.

Hellhound fell to his knees and scooped Hooker up. The big cat squirmed up his chest and wrapped both front paws around Arnie's neck while the purring redoubled.

My knees let go, too. I threw my arms around both of them and buried my face in Arnie's shoulder. It took a few moments for me to regain my composure. Finally, we both stood, and I furtively wiped my eyes.

"Thanks, Miz Lacey," Hellhound said gruffly, his face hidden in Hooker's long fur. "Where'd ya find him?"

"Wandering the halls," she replied tartly, but her face was soft as she watched the reunion. "You should be more careful about leaving your door open."

"Yes, ma'am," Hellhound agreed. "I will. Thanks again."

"You're welcome, Arnold." The door clicked closed, and we stood for a moment in the hallway, listening to the purring.

Arnie turned toward his own apartment like a sleepwalker. I followed him inside and locked the door behind us.

"Do you want me to make some coffee?" I headed for the kitchen to give him a minute.

"No, thanks, darlin'. But I could sure use a beer. Grab one for yourself, too, if ya want."

I took my time getting the beer. By the time I returned

to the living room, Hellhound's face was split by an enormous grin. He muttered fond abuse into the twitching ears while he roughly massaged the big cat's scruff. Hooker tucked his scarred nose into Arnie's beard and rumbled with purrs.

"He musta slipped out the door when those two dirtbags came in," Arnie said. He ran his hand tenderly over the long fur. "Goddammit, ya big dumb-ass hairball, ya scared the shit outta me."

I set the beer down beside Arnie's favourite chair and curled up on the sofa opposite. As Arnie sat down, Hooker apparently decided he'd been sufficiently welcomed. He jumped down, wove through my ankles once as I petted him, and then padded into the kitchen. His demanding meows informed us that his dish was empty.

Arnie chuckled as he got up again, and I heard the tinkle of dry cat food hitting the dish. Water ran as the water dish was refilled, too, and then Arnie rejoined me in the living room.

He collapsed into his chair with a sigh that sounded like it came from his toes, and took a deep swallow of his beer. Then he reached down beside his chair for his guitar. I drank some beer, too, watching him while he held the guitar.

His hands caressed it like a lover, and I smiled. He always referred to the guitar as "she". He'd once told me she was the most faithful relationship of his life, and I had no difficulty believing it.

He glanced up and returned my smile. "Don't feel much like singin' the blues tonight, darlin'."

He bowed his head over the instrument and his fingers danced over the strings. An intricate classical piece made me catch my breath. I surreptitiously dabbed my eyes again at the sight of his beautiful, uninjured hands.

I sat spellbound, my beer forgotten while he finished the piece and began another, utterly absorbed in his music.

My beer was warm and Hooker was asleep on the sofa beside me by the time Arnie looked up as if waking from a dream. He smiled. "Ya ain't drinkin' your beer."

"Neither are you."

He laughed and raised the bottle in a toast. I matched it, and we each chugged back the rest of our respective bottles. Hellhound lay back in his chair and let out a thunderous belch.

"Oh, yeah?" I demanded, and let fly with one of my own. I joined in his laughter, giddy with euphoria.

I sobered. "You should probably check the place over and make sure nothing's missing."

He shrugged. "Nah. I don't give a shit. I got the only two things I care about, right here." He caressed the guitar again, and nodded toward Hooker. "Well." He paused. "Three things." He gave me a slight bow from his seated position. "Sorry, darlin'."

"It's okay." I chuckled. "I'm honoured to be included in such illustrious company."

"Ya should be." He played a blues riff on the guitar and looked up with a wicked grin. When he started to play again, I recognized the lead-in. His raspy voice teased my ears as he began to sing. "I want a long-legged red-head woman, oh, but she won't treat me right..."

I got up from the sofa, and he laid aside the guitar. I slid into his lap and whispered against his ear.

"She's going to treat you so right tonight."

CHAPTER 46

I woke in the morning to a heavy weight on my chest. Arnie mumbled and made a sleepy grab for me as I lifted his arm and slid out of the bed.

"Back in a flash," I whispered, and headed for the bathroom, smiling at the memory of the night. Even in his sleep-deprived state, he'd still been amazing.

By the time I returned, Hellhound was reclining against the headboard, sheets thrown back. I stopped in the doorway to appreciate the view. He might not have a handsome face, but his newly muscular body was all that he'd promised.

"Like what ya see, darlin'?" he growled in his rough morning voice.

"Oh, yeah," I breathed. "Like what you see?" I stretched and tossed back my hair, running my hands down my body.

His growl got deeper. "Come on over here, an' I'll show ya how much I like it."

I prowled toward him, pointedly eyeing an outstanding portion of his anatomy. "I can see how much you like it."

"Come a little closer."

When I neared the bed, he suddenly lunged and grabbed me around the waist, pulling me on top of him. I squealed and pretended to struggle, rubbing against him.

His eyes got hotter as he rolled over and pinned me to the bed. "Now I got ya right where I want ya."

His lips traced my collarbone, then drifted down to my breast. As his tongue teased me, I arched against him, opening my legs to beg for his body. One of his hands glided down to begin a leisurely exploration. The hot, sweet tension began to coil up inside me.

He moved up to kiss me again, just the right amount of tongue while his hand continued its magic.

I moaned and reached for the tantalizing hardness pressing against my thigh. He caught my hand gently.

"I wanna pace myself, darlin'. Lemme do a little somethin' for ya first."

Those fabulous fingers did their work, and every muscle in my body tightened as my breath came faster.

"Ya got such a hot body," he growled in my ear, his raspy voice caressing my eardrum while his hands caressed my body. "D'ya like this?"

I gave myself up to his touch. "Oh, yeah... Oh, Hellhound... Oh... *baby*...!"

He chuckled. His hands moved knowingly. "D'ya like this?"

I gasped wordlessly, teetering on the edge.

Through half-closed lashes, I saw him watching me with dilated eyes. His adept fingers never faltered. My breath came faster, rising moans on each exhalation.

"D'ya like this?" he growled as he did something truly exquisite.

The dam burst, and I bucked against him in helpless, mindless ecstasy. As the spasms slowly subsided, he propped himself above me and leaned down to kiss me slowly.

"D'ya like this?" he whispered as he slid hard inside me. The world contracted to pure sensation and the sound of my own cries as he rocked into that perfect rhythm again.

The sun was blazing through the cracks in the blinds by the time I opened my eyes again and flopped over limply. I propped myself shakily up on one elbow and twisted around.

"What?" Arnie croaked, his face still half-buried in the pillow.

"I've got a condom wrapper stuck to my butt." I held it up as he laughed.

He plucked it out of my fingers and tossed it down beside the bed. "I'll pick 'em up later." He rolled over and pulled me on top of him. "You're gonna break me with the cost of condoms alone, darlin'."

I leaned down and kissed him. "Hey, a love machine like you, I figured you'd get them for a bulk discount or something."

"I think you're overestimatin' me," he laughed.

I did some exploration of my own. "No. Definitely not overestimating you."

He groaned, beginning to move to the lazy rhythm of my stroking. "Keep doin' that, an' we're never gonna get outta this bed."

"Sounds good to me. But I won't keep doing that if you don't want me to," I teased. I trailed my lips down his chest, then lower. "What if I do this instead?"

His body tensed under me. "Jesus, darlin'," he gasped. "If ya do that, it'll be over in seconds."

"I told you I was going to treat you right. Let me do a little something for you."

A long, steamy, shared shower and another emptied wrapper later, I kissed him goodbye at the door.

"See ya later?" he asked.

"Hope so. Maybe sooner than later."

"That'd be good," he agreed.

I looked into his heavy eyes. "Go back to bed."

"Yeah," he sighed. The door swung closed between our sated grins.

I floated down the hallway and out to my car, fell into the driver's seat, and smiled all the way home.

CHAPTER 47

Back at my desk after supper, I surveyed my workload with chagrin. I'd planned my schedule based on a five-day work week. I'd lost three workdays and two weekends. And I'd taken on Spider's website clients.

I spent the rest of the evening trying to catch up. After a week of strung-up nerves, my bookkeeping tasks seemed soothing but unreal. A sense of morbid anticipation hung over me, and I twitched at the slightest creak of the house. In bed alone that night, I slept restlessly and woke twice, screaming.

In the morning, I dragged myself out of bed, rubbing scratchy eyes. I pushed my head under the shower before stumbling into the kitchen for breakfast, only to find the last few slices of my bread had gone mouldy. I cooked some oatmeal instead and slogged to my desk.

At lunch time, a brief survey of my fridge convinced me it would be a good idea to eat in town before going to do the books at Up & Coming. I changed my clothes and was heading out the door when my cellphone rang. I checked the call display.

"Hi, Spider."

"Hi, Aydan." His voice still sounded tired. "Do you have

time to come by the office later?"

"Sure, any time after two-thirty. I'm seeing a client at one."

"Will three o'clock work?"

"Fine. See you then. Bye."

I hung up, wondering what our meeting would be about. Maybe they had more information about the operation at Harchman's, although I didn't think they'd share it with me. The less I knew, the better. Or maybe they needed some more information from me. I shrugged and went out the door.

I was smiling when I left Up & Coming after a session of off-colour banter with Lola. The previous evening's sense of foreboding had vanished, and tired as I was, buoyant optimism filled me. I had escaped Fuzzy Bunny unscathed, and my stint as an unwilling spy was over. The summer stretched ahead of me, ripe with the promise of happy time spent drinking ice-cold beer, tinkering with my cars and working in my garden. I could go back to enjoying my new home, my delightful new clients, and my safe, peaceful life.

When I arrived at Kane's office, Spider looked up from his desk with a haggard expression. His stubble had resolved itself into a patchy beard. He did look older, but I thought it had more to do with his eyes than with the growth on his chin.

"Spider, are you okay?" I asked. "You look exhausted."

"I'm... not great," he admitted slowly. "I..."

Kane walked in, and Spider clammed up. My 'uh-oh' detector registered red alert. As far as I knew, Spider and Kane had no secrets between them.

"Hi, Aydan," Kane greeted me pleasantly. "Oh." He reached into his pocket. "Here's your watch. Minus a certain piece of technology." He turned to Spider. "What's up?"

"Let's go into the meeting room," Spider said tensely.

Kane and I exchanged glances. Good, I wasn't the only one who thought something was out of the ordinary. We followed Spider down the hall and took our places at the table.

"Did you get all the prisoners sorted out at Harchman's?" I asked.

"Yes. There weren't as many of Fuzzy Bunny's people as we'd originally thought," Kane responded. "We did some pretty intense questioning, and Webb's been dividing his time working on the network there as well as digging for information on the prisoners." He shot an appreciative look at Spider, and Spider returned a jerky smile.

"It turned out Maria was the mastermind," Kane continued. "She'd been playing Harchman for years. She set him up with enough business to keep herself valuable to him, so they stayed married. And she was able to carry on her own business dealings with Fuzzy Bunny under the cover of his activities. She had a few of her trusted associates planted in the regular rotation of guards and staff at the house. Harchman never had a clue."

"What about the two guys that kidnapped Hellhound?" I asked.

"We got both of them. They were among the group we picked up at the house."

I relaxed back in my chair. "Clean sweep. Sweet."

"Looks like it." He returned my smile.

A movement at the door made us both jerk our heads up. I froze at the sight of two men wearing shoulder holsters. Kane was already on his feet and reaching for his gun when Stemp appeared behind them.

Stemp moved into the room to sit at the table, his reptilian face impassive. The two men took up positions standing at opposite walls of the meeting room.

"What's going on?" Kane asked evenly.

"Sit." Stemp gestured to the chairs.

Kane moved warily to the seat beside me. I could tell he was looking for a position that wouldn't place his back to either of the armed men. I caught his eye, and he gave me an almost imperceptible lift of his eyebrow as we faced Stemp.

"Webb has some fascinating information," Stemp informed us expressionlessly. "Webb, go ahead."

Spider cleared his throat. His eyes flickered to me, and then to the tabletop as he spoke. "Aydan, we've discovered something... unusual in the network out at Harchman's."

Oh God. My heart sped up.

"Unusual, how?" I was pleased that my voice came out sounding calm and level.

Spider glanced at Stemp, then down at the table again. "We can't access any of the files. Everything is heavily encrypted. They're using an encryption system called Blowfish."

"Okay..." I tensed. Now I was definitely waiting for the other shoe to drop.

"It's completely secure. There's no known way to crack the encryption without knowing the code phrase that was used to encrypt it."

"Okay..."

"Aydan, you could read all the files."

"Well, yeah." I shrugged. "I had the network key."

"The network key doesn't crack encryption," Spider said. "You're doing that."

"But you said this Blowfish couldn't be cracked."

"It can't."

I shook my head impatiently. "What are you trying to say?"

"What he's trying to say," Stemp said smoothly, "Is that you've just become the world's most dangerous weapon."

CHAPTER 48

"What?" I stared at him. "How... how do you figure that?"

"There is no known way to crack Blowfish," Stemp repeated patiently. "Everyone in the world knows that. It's used for virtually all clandestine communications. But we've just discovered that what everyone in the world knows... is wrong. *You* can crack it. In real-time. You can read encrypted documents as easily as if they were plain text. Do you have any idea what that means from a security standpoint?"

I glanced from Spider's drawn face to Kane's growing frown. "I'm going to take a wild-ass guess and say it would be disastrous in the wrong hands."

"Yes." Stemp leaned back in his chair. "Which is why we now have to take drastic steps to safeguard you. You are our ultimate secret weapon. With your skills, we can crack almost every scrap of digital data in the world."

Kane shifted suddenly beside me. I glanced over at him, and fear swept over me at his expression. I mentally replayed what Stemp had just said. My mouth went dry. "Define... drastic."

Stemp crossed his arms and tilted his chair back a

fraction on its back legs. "You will go directly from here to a secured underground facility. We will notify the appropriate authorities that you have died, and we will dispose of your home, business, and other assets. You will be given a new identity, and the proceeds from the disposal of your assets will, of course, be transferred to your new identity. Kane will be your handler."

He gave a short nod, as if satisfied with the utter destruction of my life. "If you have no further questions, we'll leave immediately."

"H...hold on." I couldn't seem to draw enough air into my lungs. "What... underground facility? You mean... literally... underground?"

"Of course," he said, as if addressing a particularly backward child.

Adrenaline spiked through my bloodstream. I made a sudden move to push my chair back and the armed men snapped to alertness, their hands on their weapons.

"Stay calm," Kane murmured.

I gasped a couple of shallow breaths. "You know I can't do this," I implored Kane.

"Is there a problem?" Stemp inquired.

"Yes," Kane said firmly. "Aydan is claustrophobic. You can't expect her to stay underground."

Stemp eyed us both with contempt. "That's ridiculous. Kane, deal with your asset."

Anger started to trickle through my terror. Asset. An object, not a person. No discussion. No rights. My beautiful farm. My cars. My clients. My friends. My entire life to be discarded like a used tissue. On Stemp's whim. Who the hell died and made him God?

I drew a deep breath as the trickle of anger turned into a

torrent. My hands clenched with the urge to rip Stemp's snakelike head off and shit down the hole.

Kane turned to me, and his eyes widened almost imperceptibly. "Stay calm," he repeated warningly.

I turned back to Stemp. "And if I refuse?" I was proud that my voice was dead level.

He fixed me with his expressionless gaze as he leaned forward slightly. "You won't."

"Because...?" I inquired.

"Because it's your duty to do this. And I know you feel strongly about duty."

"Sorry," I said flatly. "You're confusing me with Kane. He's the one that's all about duty. Me? Not so much."

"Nonsense," Stemp said. "You were willing to give up your life to protect national security. Several times. You'll do it again."

"No." My voice was beginning to sound dangerous. "I was willing to die. That's different than giving up my life."

Stemp's emotionless eyes held mine. "Let me put this another way. I also happen to know you're very loyal. You go to great lengths to protect the people you care about. Let's just say that if you refuse, there will be consequences." He looked pointedly at Kane and Spider.

I froze. Pure red rage suffused my soul. "Did I just hear you threaten my team?" My voice vibrated with suppressed violence.

Stemp's impassive face faltered for a split second as he sat back in his chair.

His mask firmly in place again, he waved an airy hand. "Threaten is such an ugly word."

I took a deep breath and held my voice steady. "I'm going to say this in small words so you can understand."

Kane caught my eye and shook his head. I ignored him.

"You will not notify anyone that I'm dead. You will not sell my assets. I will not take on a new identity in an underground facility. I will live where and how I please. I will do business with whomever I please. Whenever I please."

I drew another hissing breath. "And you will not, repeat, *not*, cause any *consequences*," I made vicious air quotes around the word, "...for anyone. And that means anyone that I've ever even said hello to. Clients. Neighbours. Team members. Friends. Friends of friends. Any. Fucking. Person. I. Know. On the contrary, you will protect them to the best of your ability. In return, I will aid you with your encryption issues."

Stemp eyed me expressionlessly. "This is not a negotiation. I know where your friends live. I direct your team. I know you'll do whatever is necessary to protect them all. I hold all the cards."

I jerked forward across the table.

"Yes, I can see you hold all the cards," I ground out. "It's really too bad that while you were busy gloating over your cards, you forgot to look under the poker table. Because I've got a .45 aimed at your nuts."

The armed men made a twitchy grab for their weapons, but since both my hands were clearly visible, they apparently realized that I was speaking metaphorically and stood down, watching me warily.

In my peripheral vision, I could see Spider's mouth hanging open. I focused on Stemp and recognized the flicker of uncertainty in his eyes.

"And you're right," I continued in the same deadly voice. "It's not a negotiation. Before you decided to threaten me, it could have been. Now, I've stated my terms. You will abide by them."

Stemp leaned back, adjusting the knot of his tie. His eyes darted to the armed men, then back to me. When he spoke, his voice was as flat as ever. "What makes you think I'll agree to your terms?"

I locked eyes with him. "Because it's your duty to acquire the world's most dangerous weapon." I spat his own words back. "And I know you feel strongly about duty."

"You have exactly two choices," I continued coldly. "You can agree to my terms, and I will do my best to help you with the decryption. Or you can shoot me. Right here and now." I ignored Spider's gasp. "Because if you don't agree to my terms, that's the only safe thing you can do."

"And why would I do either of those things?" Stemp inquired.

I stood, and the guards clutched their weapons again as I glowered down at Stemp. "Because you can drag me underground and destroy my identity and threaten the people I care about, but you can't make me accurately decrypt files."

I leaned my fists on the table and glared into his face. "I get tense when I feel threatened. That might cause me to accidentally make a critical mistake when I decrypt your files. And you'd never know. Until it was too late."

I shoved my face within inches of his. His bland expression slipped as my voice came out in a menacing hiss. "If you hurt someone I care about, you'll find out exactly how dangerous I am."

I gave that a second to sink in while I glared at him from close range. Then I sat in the chair again and leaned it onto its back legs. I spread my hands and gave him a poisonous smile.

"Your choice. Abide by my terms, and reap the benefits.
Or don't. Delude yourself that I'm under your control, and
find out later how much damage I can do. Or kill me where I
sit. Either way, you'll lose the most valuable weapon you'll
ever have access to."

I felt my face twist into a snarl. "Do your *duty*," I spat.

CHAPTER 49

There was a prolonged silence. Nobody moved or spoke as my eyes burned into Stemp's.

Finally, Stemp dropped his gaze. "How do I know you won't sabotage the decryption even if we do agree to your terms?"

I felt my lip curl. "You wouldn't have even had to ask that question if you hadn't threatened me in the first place. But I'll give you my word that I won't sabotage it as long as you abide by my terms. You can ask Kane if he thinks that's sufficient assurance. I'll wait outside so you can discuss it." I stood.

Kane laid his hand on my arm. "Stay here." He turned to Stemp as I sat again. "Aydan's word is sufficient," he said, his voice rock-hard.

Stemp's eyes bored into him. "Fine," Stemp said, without changing expression. He turned to me. "Give me your word."

I gave him a sharp nod. "I will do my absolute best to accurately decrypt your files. If you abide by my terms. To the letter. You have my word."

"I also reserve the right to supply additional security measures to protect you," he added.

"Subject to my approval," I snapped. "I have the final say. On everything. Including who I work with, and how and when and where I work."

"You're just an asset," Stemp protested. "That's unreasonable."

"You forfeited your right to reasonable behaviour. You know my terms. You understand the consequences of breaching them. We're done here."

"Very well." He rose and nodded to the two armed men. He turned to Kane. "As her handler, you have complete responsibility for her performance, and her safety. I expect you understand the magnitude of that task. I hope you'll prove yourself capable of it." He turned and left, trailed by his guards.

I clasped my trembling hands together and took a deep breath.

"Holy... crap!" Spider exploded. "That was the scariest thing I've ever seen!"

"First rule," I snapped. "Don't threaten me."

Kane turned to me gravely. "You realize you've just made a very dangerous enemy."

I snorted. "What's he going to do? Kill me?"

Kane eyed me without speaking.

"He'll be doing me a fucking favour if he does," I snarled. "I'm out of here."

I got up and strode out, hiding my shaking legs as best I could.

Kane caught up to me on the front sidewalk. "Aydan."

"What?" As I turned, I caught sight of Stemp and his men still parked by the curb across the street.

"Aydan, I'm sorry. This shouldn't have happened. I hope you know, I would have stopped it if I'd known what was coming."

I gave him a smile that didn't feel very convincing. "I know you wouldn't willingly put me in this position."

He rocked back as if I'd slapped him. "Aydan, I wouldn't *knowingly* put you in this position. I would have stopped it if I'd known," he repeated.

My eyes slid over to Stemp again. He was watching us intently. Kane was right. I'd made a dangerous enemy. I had no doubt that as soon as Stemp had any alternative at all to using me, I'd die in an unfortunate accident. And I was pretty sure that anyone who was close to me would be destroyed at the same time. Stemp's last words to Kane had been a none-too-subtle threat.

I sighed.

"John, no offense. But no, you wouldn't have stopped it. If you got the command, you'd carry it out. You wouldn't have liked it, but you would have done it. You really are all about duty."

Hurt flashed across his face before his expression closed down. I met his eyes, willing him to understand.

"As soon as you begin to choose which orders you will or won't carry out, you're a threat to Stemp. And, by extension, a threat to national security. And if that happens, your career, and probably your life, is over. You *are* all about duty. You have to be."

He opened his mouth as if to respond, and I steeled myself to do the only thing I could think of to protect him.

I turned on my heel and walked away without another word.

A Request

Thanks for reading!

If you enjoyed this book, I'd really appreciate it if you'd take a moment to review it online. If you've never reviewed a book before, I have a couple of quick videos at http://www.dianehenders.com/reviews that will walk you through the process.

Here are some suggestions for the "star" ratings:

Five stars: Loved the book and can hardly wait for the next one.

Four stars: Liked the book and plan to read the next one.

Three stars: The book was okay. Might read the next one.

Two stars: Didn't like the book. Probably won't read the next one.

One star: Hated the book. Would never read another in the series.

"Star" ratings are a quick way to do a review, but the most helpful reviews are the ones where you write a few sentences about what you liked/disliked about the book.

Thanks for taking the time to do a review!

Want to know what else is roiling around in the cesspit of my mind? Visit my blog and website at http://www.dianehenders.com. Don't forget to leave a comment in the guest book to say hi!

About Me

By profession, I'm a technical writer, computer geek, and ex-interior designer. I'm good at two out of three of these things. I had the sense to quit the one I sucked at.

To deal with my mid-life crisis, I also write adventure novels featuring a middle-aged female protagonist. And I kickbox.

This seemed more productive than indulging in more typical mid-life crisis activities like getting a divorce, buying a Harley Crossbones, and cruising across the country picking up men in sleazy bars. Especially since it's winter most of the months of the year here.

It's much more comfortable to sit at my computer. And hell, Harleys are expensive. Come to think of it, so are beer and gasoline.

Oh, and I still love my husband. There's that. I'll stick with the writing.

Diane Henders

Since You Asked...

People frequently ask if my protagonist, Aydan Kelly, is really me.

Yeah, you got me. These novels are an autobiography of my secret life as a government agent, working with highly-classified computer technology... Oh, wait, what's that? You want the *truth*? Um, you do realize fiction writers get paid to lie, don't you?

...well, shit, that's not nearly as much fun. It's also a long story.

I swore I'd never write fiction. "Too personal," I said. "People read novels and automatically assume the author is talking about him/herself."

Well, apparently I lied about the fiction-writing part. One day, a story sprang into my head and wouldn't leave. The only way to get it out was to write it down. So I did.

But when I wrote that first book, I never intended to show it to anyone, so I created a character that looked like me just to thumb my nose at the stereotype. I've always had a defective sense of humour, and this time it turned around and bit me in the ass.

Because after I'd written the third novel, I realized I actually wanted other people to read my books. And when I went back to change my main character to *not* look like me, my beta readers wouldn't let me. They rose up against me and said, "No! Aydan is a tall woman with long red hair and brown eyes. End of discussion!"

Jeez, no wonder readers get the idea that authors write about themselves. So no, I'm not Aydan Kelly. I just look like her.

Bonus Stuff

Here's an excerpt from **Book 3: Reach For The Spy**

A faint noise woke me. My eyes flew open and I held my breath, listening. Had the sound come from outside the open window? I strained my ears, but heard only the usual quiet of a July night in the country.

A tiny, metallic click from the doorknob made me change the rhythm of my breathing, slow and deep. I let my eyelids droop so I could watch the door through the fringe of my lashes.

Damn that shaft of moonlight. It fell directly across me in the bed, but the doorway itself was in shadow.

The door swung open slowly and silently. A large, dark figure moved toward my bed.

I emitted a small snore followed by a deep sigh and rolled over, letting the bedsheet fall away as I reached under the opposite pillow and clenched my fist around the crowbar. The moonlight emphasized the curves and hollows of my naked body. The intruder froze, staring.

That's right, asshole. Take a good look. It'll be the last thing you ever see. Just come a little closer, now...

He turned away abruptly, and I was instantly in motion. The crowbar hurtled toward his temple in a flat, vicious arc with all my strength behind it.

"Aydan."

At the sound of his whisper, I let out a yelp of dismay. I tried desperately to slow and alter the trajectory of my weapon, but it connected solidly with his head. He fell.

Heart pounding, I floundered toward the huddled form on the floor. As I reached him, he sat up slowly. I flung myself on him from behind, one arm across his massive chest while my other hand clamped over his mouth.

"We're bugged," I breathed urgently in his ear.

His large hand closed around my wrist, and I let him pull my hand away from his mouth.

"I know," he said in normal tones. "I'm jamming them."

I collapsed onto the floor behind him, gasping. "Jesus fucking Christ, John! Don't ever fucking do that! I nearly fucking killed you, for chrissake!" If frequent use of obscenities indicated one's level of intellect, I'd apparently dropped about a hundred IQ points in the last couple of seconds.

"I noticed." He touched his head, and his fingers came away dark in the moonlight.

"Shit!" I started to scramble up, but he grabbed my arm.

"Don't turn on any lights."

"I need to look at that," I argued. "I was going for a home run until the last second. You're bleeding."

"I'll live. It just glanced off."

I blew out an irritated breath and knelt beside him to trace my fingers through his hair, exploring the sticky area near the top of his head. At least there wasn't any squishiness that would indicate a fracture.

I stepped across him into my ensuite bathroom and came out with a clean washcloth. "Here."

He accepted it and pressed it against his head. He glanced up at me, and then looked away quickly. "Aydan... Could you please put some clothes on? This really... distracting."

"Oh!" I glanced down at my white skin, practically glowing in the moonlight. My forty-six-year-old body was in pretty good shape except for the extra ten pounds or so around the middle. I'd never been shy about it. And getting naked with John Kane was near the top of my private list of things to do, but I was pretty sure braining him with a crowbar didn't qualify as foreplay.

Anyway, it didn't matter. Now was not the time. I stepped quickly to the chair in the corner where I kept my clothes laid out for quick access. I pulled on jeans and a sweatshirt before turning back to him.

"Can you stand up?" I asked.

He rose. "I'm fine. We need to talk." He sat on the edge of the bed and I perched beside him.

The moonlight made a dramatic study of his strong, square features. His silvered temples gleamed against his short, dark hair as he turned to eye me piercingly in the pale light.

"How did you find the bugs?" he demanded. "Do you have a scanner?"

"No. I found them the good old-fashioned way. Is Stemp monitoring them?"

"Yes. How did you know you were bugged?"

"I smelled them."

His dark brows snapped together. "What?"

I grinned. "Stemp needs to be more careful choosing his minions. Whoever he sent to install the bugs was a smoker who wore cologne. I smelled him the instant I came in the house. I checked everything over, and when I couldn't find anything missing, I started to look for things that had been added."

Kane nodded slowly. "You're good."

I peered at him in the moonlight. "What the hell are you doing here? Dammit, Stemp is going to notice the bugs are jammed. I didn't want him to know I knew about them."

"He won't know. I got Webb to generate a circular loop to feed the monitor. We have an hour."

"You got Spider involved in this, too? What if you get caught?" I demanded. "It was bad enough when Stemp just thought you were sympathetic toward me. If he finds out about this, you're going to be next on his hit list, right after he whacks me."

He went still, watching me. "What makes you say that?"

"Come on, John. It's not rocket science. Stemp needs me right now, but he doesn't trust me because he can't manipulate me. The instant he's got an alternative, I'm going to get a lead suppository."

I sighed. "In fact, you'll probably be the one to get the order. That's what I'd do if I was Stemp. If you carry out the order to kill me, you keep your job. And live. If you refuse, he passes the order down the food chain to get rid of both of us. And on down the line to get rid of anybody else who isn't willing to follow orders. Get all the housecleaning done at once."

"That's the most paranoid, cynical thing I've ever heard you say."

"Yeah. Tell me I'm wrong."

He blew out a breath. "So that's what you were trying to tell me when you walked away from me last week. You were warning me to keep my distance. To protect me."

"Yeah. And here you are. Shit."

"Will you stop trying to protect everybody else and start looking out for yourself for a change? I'm a big boy. I can take care of myself."

I sighed inwardly. He sure was a big boy. In every sense of the word, from what I'd had the opportunity to observe. Too bad he had to be permanently off-limits if I wanted him to stay alive.

"I know you can take care of yourself," I agreed. "But Stemp was watching us, and I wanted to make sure he didn't see anything that would make him mistrust you. He's your boss, after all. You'll still have to work with him long after I'm gone."

His brows drew together. "What you said last week... About how I'd follow orders no matter what. Do you really believe that? That I'm nothing more than a robot following orders?"

I hesitated, trying to find the right words. "No... But... that's what Stemp needs you to be. And that's the safest thing for you to be right now."

"You really think I'd kill you if he gave me the order." His voice was even, but I could hear the edge of suppressed hurt and anger.

"John..." I sighed and tugged my fingers through my long hair, yanking out the night's tangles. "You're one of our government's top agents. You've spent most of your life in military and law enforcement. That tells me your top priority is doing the right thing for this country. Am I right?"

"Of course." He frowned at me in the shadows. "Where are you going with this?"

"What if it turns out that it's the right thing for you to kill me?"

He jerked back. "That's ridiculous."

"Is it? Think it through. Right now, I'm both incredibly valuable and incredibly dangerous. I can crack any data encryption, and I'm working for our government. Valuable. But I'm a civilian and Stemp doesn't trust me. As soon as he finds another way to break the encryption, I'll stop being valuable, and then all that's left is the danger that our enemies will scoop me up. He can't afford the risk."

"You'd never turn traitor," he said with certainty. "I've seen the sacrifices you've made."

"Thanks for the vote of confidence. But I know what groups like Fuzzy Bunny will do to get what they want. As long as I'm alive, there's the risk that I'll be captured." I looked him square in the eyes. "I'm no hero. I don't have any illusions about how long I'd withstand torture. So killing me might be the right thing for everybody, including me. Would you refuse that order?"

He sat silently, frowning. Finally, he said, "That's what you meant. When you said Stemp would be doing you a favour if he killed you."

"Yeah, something like that." I changed the subject. "So is Stemp actually evil, or is he just an asshole?"

"He's a ruthless bastard," Kane said slowly. "I can't always agree with his methods, but nobody can argue with his results. Since he took over as civilian director two years ago, we've had major improvements in our operations. You shouldn't have threatened him."

"That wasn't a threat. It was a sincere promise. If he does anything to harm anybody I care about, I will utterly destroy him. Or die trying."

He laughed suddenly. "Aydan, you're crazy."

I grinned at him. "You're just discovering that now? What made you come to that conclusion after all this time?"

"Even when you can't possibly win, you fight anyway. Stemp has people and resources you can't even imagine. And you're relying on your nose to sniff out bugs."

I raised a shoulder and gave him a half-smile. "I learned long ago that being willing to fight is sometimes enough to prevent the fight in the first place. Sometimes you win, just because anybody in their right mind would know that you can't possibly win."

He sobered. "Aydan, you can't possibly win this one."

"Ah. Victory will be mine, then. So why are you here? You thought it'd be nice to pop by and get your brains bashed in? You know damn well I keep a crowbar under my pillow. What the hell were you thinking?"

His lips twisted wryly. "Yes, I knew about the crowbar. But I thought you were asleep. No woman would intentionally throw off the sheets and lie there naked if she thought there was an intruder in the house."

"It worked, didn't it?" I smirked at him. "Someday that 'most women' stereotype is going to jump up and bite you. Or crush your skull with a crowbar. You knew I was armed and dangerous, and you still turned your back on me because of your preconceptions."

"I was trying to be a gentleman."

"And it nearly got you killed."

"What if I'd been a murderer or a rapist? What if I hadn't turned my back? Where's your clever strategy then?"

I shrugged. "Tell me you noticed when I reached under the pillow. You didn't, did you? Because you weren't looking at my hand."

He shifted uncomfortably on the bed. "True," he admitted reluctantly.

"So it didn't really matter to me whether you turned away or not," I told him. "Either way, I got a weapon into my hand without you noticing. I might not have won the fight, but at least I had a chance."

"And you'd fight even if you couldn't win."

I patted him on the shoulder. "Now you're getting it. So why are you here? We're wasting our hour."

End of Reach For The Spy, Chapter 1

CPSIA information can be obtained at www.ICGtesting.com
Printed in the USA
LVOW13s1526010714

392546LV00001B/83/P